**Praise for Clarence E. Mulford
and the Hopalong Stories**

"If you liked Louis L'Amour's Hopalong Cassidy
novel—*The Rustlers of West Fork*—you'll *love* these
ones. These are the real things."

—Jackson Cain,
author of *Hellbreak Country*

"The stories teem with wildly exciting events. . . .
They are among the best of their kind."

—*The New York Times*

"The Mulford stories about Cassidy are rousing
adventures, with some of the best action
sequences in early Western fiction."

—Bill Pronzini, editor of *Wild Westerns*

"The Hopalong stories give the reader a grand tour of
the Golden Age of what has become known as
the 'traditional' Western story, of which
Mulford was a master."

—*Roundup Magazine*

Hopalong Cassidy

◆

Bar-20 Days

◆

Clarence E. Mulford

A Tom Doherty Associates Book / New York

HOPALONG CASSIDY AND BAR-20 DAYS

Hopalong Cassidy was originally published in 1910. *Bar-20 Days* was originally published in 1911.

Foreword copyright © 1992 by Tom Doherty Associates, LLC

A Forge Book
Published by Tom Doherty Associates, LLC
175 Fifth Avenue
New York, NY 10010

www.tor-forge.com

Forge® is a registered trademark of Tom Doherty Associates, LLC.

ISBN 978-0-7653-7777-7

Forge books may be purchased for educational, business, or promotional use. For information on bulk purchases, please contact Macmillan Corporate and Premium Sales Department at 1-800-221-7945, extension 5442, or write specialmarkets@macmillan.com.

First Mass Market Edition: August 2014

Printed in the United States of America

0 9 8 7 6 5 4 3 2 1

Contents

Foreword

In June 1991 Bantam published the first of Louis L'Amour's acclaimed Hopalong Cassidy novels, *The Rustlers of West Fork*. Since then, publishers tell me there has been a tremendous ground swell of enthusiasm for Hopalong and his friends. Readers around the country want to know more about these Bar-20 boys—and above all, want more of their books.

Consequently, Forge Books is bringing back the original novels, written by Clarence E. Mulford, the man who created Cassidy and company. It's a good thing too. These are really first-rate books, full of true grit and pulse-pounding action, the kind of books you can't put down.

If you liked Louis L'Amour's Hopalong Cassidy novel—*The Rustlers of West Fork*—you'll *love* these ones. These are no imitations, but the real things.

A lot of western writers—people like Richard S. Wheeler, Earl Murray, Al Dempsey and yours truly—when we get together for a few beers, we sometimes talk about books. We talk about the books that inspired us; the authors who made us love the West and even want to write ourselves. For whatever it's worth, it's a short list.

And for a lot of us, the guy at the top is Clarence Mulford.

Clarence, old hoss, wherever you are, here's a Lone Star beer to you.

—Jackson Cain,
author of *Hellbreak Country*
and *Hangman's Whip*

Hopalong
Cassidy

◆

*Affectionately Dedicated
to My Father*

I

◆

Antonio's Scheme

The raw and mighty West, the greatest stage in all the history of the world for so many deeds of daring which verged on the insane, was seared with grave-lined trails. In many localities the bad-man made history in a terse and business-like way, and also made the first law for the locality—that of the gun.

There were good bad-men and bad bad-men, the killer by necessity and the wanton murderer; and the shifting of these to their proper strata evolved the foundation for the law of to-day. The good bad-man, those in whose souls lived the germs of law and order and justice, gradually became arrayed against the other class, and stood up manfully for their principles, let the odds be what they might; and bitter, indeed, was the struggle, and great the price.

From the gold camps of the Rockies to the shrieking towns of the coast, where wantonness stalked unchecked; from the vast stretches of the cattle ranges to the ever-advancing terminals of the persistent railroads, to the cow towns, boiling and seething in the loosed passions of men who brooked no restraint in their revels, no one section of country ever boasted of such numbers of genuine bad-men of both classes as the great, semi-arid Southwest. Here was one of the worst collections of raw humanity ever broadcast in one locality; it was a word and a shot, a shot and a laugh or a curse.

In this red setting was stuck a town which we will call Eagle, the riffle which caught all the dregs of passing humanity. Unmapped, known only to those who had visited it, reared its flimsy buildings in the face of God and rioted day and night with no thought of reckoning; mad, insane with hellishness unlimited.

Late in the afternoon rode Antonio, "broncho-buster" for the H2, a man of little courage, much avarice, and great capacity for hatred. Crafty, filled with cunning of the coyote kind, shifty-eyed, gloomy, taciturn, and scowling, he was well fitted for the part he had elected to play in the range dispute between his ranch and the Bar-20. He was absolutely without mercy or conscience; indeed, one might aptly say that his conscience, if he had ever known one, had been pulled out by the roots and its place filled with viciousness. Coldblooded in his ferocity, easily angered and quick to commit murder if the risk were small, he embraced within his husk of soul the putrescence of all that was evil.

In Eagle he had friends who were only a shade less evil than himself; but they had what he lacked and because of it were entitled to a forced respect of small weight—they had courage, that spontaneous, initiative, heedless courage which toned the atmosphere of the whole West to a magnificent crimson. Were it not for the reason that they had drifted to his social level they would have spurned his acquaintance and shot him for a buzzard; but, while they secretly held him in great contempt for his cowardice, they admired his criminal cunning, and profited by it. He was too wise to show himself in the true light to his foreman and the outfit, knowing full well that death would be the response, and so lived a lie until he met his friends of the town, when he threw off his cloak and became himself, and where he plotted against the man who treated him fairly.

Riding into the town, he stopped before a saloon and slouched in to the bar, where the proprietor was placing a new stock of liquors on the shelves.

"Where's Benito, an' th' rest?" he asked.

"Back there," replied the other, nodding toward a rear room.

"Who's in there?"

"Benito, Hall, Archer an' Frisco."

"Where's Shaw?"

"Him an' Clausen an' Cavalry went out 'bout ten minutes ago."

"I want to see 'em when they come in," Antonio remarked, headed towards the door, where he listened, and then went in.

In the small room four men were grouped around a table, drinking and talking, and at his entry they looked up and nodded. He nodded in reply and seated himself apart from them, where he soon became wrapped in thought.

Benito arose and went to the door. *"Mescal, pronto,"* he said to the man outside.

"Damned *pronto*, too," growled Antonio. "A man would die of alkali in this place before he's waited on."

The proprietor brought a bottle and filled the glasses, giving Antonio his drink first, and silently withdrew.

The broncho-buster tossed off the fiery stuff and then turned his shifty eyes on the group. "Where's Shaw?"

"Don't know—back soon," replied Benito.

"Why didn't he wait, when he knowed I was comin' in?"

Hall leaned back from the table and replied, keenly watching the inquisitor, "Because he don't give a damn."

"You—!" Antonio shouted, half rising, but the others interfered and he sank back again, content to let it pass. But not so Hall, whose Colt was half drawn.

"I'll kill you some day," he gritted, but before any-thing could come of it Shaw and his companions entered the room and the trouble was quelled.

Soon the group was deep in discussion over the merits of a scheme which Antonio unfolded to them, and the more it was weighed the better it appeared. Finally Shaw leaned back and filled his pipe. "You've got th' brains of th' devil,' 'Tony."

"Eet ees not'ing," replied Antonio.

"Oh, drop that lingo an' talk straight—you ain't on th' H2 now," growled Hall.

"Benito, you know this country like a book," Shaw continued. "Where's a good place for us to work from, or ain't there no choice?"

"Thunder Mesa."

"Well, what of it?"

"On the edge of the desert, high, big. The walls are stone, an' so very smooth. Nobody can get up."

"How can we get up then?"

"There's a trail at one end," replied Antonio, crossing his legs and preparing to roll a cigarette. "It's too steep for cayuses, an' too narrow; but we can crawl up. An' once up, all hell can't follow as long as our cartridges hold out."

"Water?" inquired Frisco.

"At th' bottom of th' trail, an' th' spring is on top," Antonio replied. "Not much, but enough."

"Can you work yore end all right?" asked Shaw.

"Yes," laughed the other. "I am 'that fool, Antonio,' on th' ranch. But they're th' fools. We can steal them blind an' if they find it out—well," here he shrugged his shoulders, "th' Bar-20 can take th' blame. I'll fix that, all right. This trouble about th' line is just what I've been waitin' for, an' I'll help it along. If we can get 'em fightin' we'll run off with th' bone *we* want. That'll be easy."

"But can you get 'em fightin'?" asked Cavalry, so called

because he had spent several years in that branch of the Government service, and deserted because of the discipline.

Antonio laughed and ordered more *mescal* and for some time took no part in the discussion which went on about him. He was dreaming of success and plenty and a ranch of his own which he would start in Old Mexico, in a place far removed from the border, and where no questions would be asked. He would be a rich man, according to the standards of that locality, and what he said would be law among the peons. He liked to day-dream, for everything came out just as he wished; there was no discordant note. He was so certain of success, so conceited as not to ask himself if any of the Bar-20 or H2 outfits were not his equal or superior in intelligence. It was only a matter of time, he told himself, for he could easily get the two ranches embroiled in a range war, and once embroiled, his plan would succeed and he would be safe.

"What do you want for your share, 'Tony?" suddenly asked Shaw.

"Half."

"What! *Half?*"

"*Si.*"

"You're loco!" cried the other. "Do you reckon we're going to buck up agin th' biggest an' hardest fightin' outfit in this country an' take all sorts of chances for a measly half, to be divided up among seven of us!" He brought his fist down on the table with a resounding thump. "You an' yore game can go to hell first!" he shouted.

"I like a hog, all right," sneered Clausen, angrily.

"I thought it out an' I got to look after th' worst an' most important part of it, an' take three chances to you fellers' one," replied Antonio, frowning. "I said half, an' it goes."

"Run all th' ends, an' keep it all," exclaimed Hall. "An', by God, we've got a hand in it, now. If you try to hog it we'll drop a word where it'll do th' most good, an' don't you forget it, neither."

"Antonio is right," asserted Benito, excitedly. "It's risky for him."

"Keep yore yaller mouth shut," growled Cavalry. "Who gave you any say in this?"

"Half," said Antonio, shrugging his shoulders.

"Look here, you," cried Shaw, who was, in reality, the leader of the crowd, inasmuch as he controlled all the others with the exception of Benito and Antonio, and these at times by the judicious use of flattery. "We'll admit that you've got a right to th' biggest share, but not to no half. You have a chance to get away, because you can watch 'em, but how about us, out there on th' edge of hell? If they come for us we won't know nothing about it till we're surrounded. Now we want to play square with you, and we'll give you twice as much as any one of th' rest of us. That'll make nine shares an' give you two of 'em. What more do you want, when you've got to have us to run th' game at all?"

Antonio laughed ironically. "Yes. I'm where I can watch, an' get killed first. You can hold th' mesa for a month. I ain't as easy as I look. It's my game, not yourn; an' if you don't like what I ask, stay out."

"We will!" cried Hall, arising, followed by the others. His hand rested on the butt of his revolver and trouble seemed imminent. Benito wavered and then slid nearer to Antonio. "You can run yore game all by yore lonesome, as *long* as you *can*!" Hall shouted. "I know a feller what knows Cassidy, an' I'll spoil yore little play right now. You'll look nice at th' end of a rope, won't you? It's this: share like Shaw said or get out of here, and look out for trouble aplenty to-morrow morning. I've put up with yore gall an' swallered yore insultin' actions just as long as I'm going to, and I've got a powerful notion to fix you right here and now!"

"No fightin', you fools!" cried the proprietor, grabbing his Colt and running to the door of the room. "It's up to you fellers to stick together!"

"I'll be damned if I'll stand—" began Frisco.

"They want too much," interrupted Antonio, angrily, keeping close watch over Hall.

"We want a fair share, an' that's all!" retorted Shaw. "Sit down, all of you. We can wrastle this out without no gunplay."

"You-all been yappin' like a set of fools," said the proprietor. "I've heard every word you-all said. If you got a mite of sense you'll be some tender how you shout about it. It's shore risky enough without tellin' everybody this side of sun-up."

"I mean just what I said," asserted Hall. "It's Shaw's offer, or nothin'. We ain't playing fool."

"Here! Here!" cried Shaw, pushing Hall into a seat. "If you two have got anything to settle, wait till some other time."

"That's more like it," growled the proprietor, shuffling back to the bar.

"Good Lord, 'Tony," cried Shaw in a low voice. "That's fair enough; we've got a right to something, ain't we? Don't let a good thing fall through just because you want th' whole earth. Better have a little than none."

"Well, gimme a third, then."

"I'll give you a slug in th' eye, you hog!" promised Hall, starting to rise again, but Shaw held him back. "Sit down, you fool!" he ordered, angrily. Then he turned to Antonio. "Third don't go; take my offer or leave it."

"Gimme a fourth; that's fair enough."

Shaw thought for a moment and then looked up. "Well, that's more like it. What do you say, fellers?"

"No!" cried Hall. "Two-ninths, or nothin'!"

"A fourth is two-eighths, only a little more," Shaw replied.

"Well, all right," muttered Hall, sullenly.

"That's very good," laughed Benito, glad that things were clearing.

The others gave their consent to the division and Shaw smiled. "Well, that's more like it. Now we'll go into this thing an' sift it out. Keep mum about it—there's twenty men in town that would want to join us if they knowed."

"I'm goin' to be boss; what I say goes," spoke up Antonio. "It's my game an' I'm takin' th' most risky end."

"You ain't got sand enough to be boss of anything," sneered Hall. "Yore sand is chalk."

"You'll say too much someday," retorted Antonio, glaring.

"Oh, not to *you*, I reckon," rejoined Hall, easily.

"Shut up, both of you!" snapped Shaw. "You can be boss, 'Tony," he said, winking at Hall. "You've got more brains for a thing like this than any of us. I don't see how you can figger it out like you do."

Antonio laughed but he remembered one thing, and swore to take payment if the plan leaked out; the proprietor had confessed hearing every word, which was not at all to his liking. If Quinn should tell, well, Quinn would die; he would see to that, he and Benito.

II

◆

Mary Meeker Rides North

Mary Meeker, daughter of the H2 owner and foreman, found pleasure in riding on little tours of investigation. She had given the southern portions her attention first and found, after the newness had worn off, that she did not care for the level, sandy stretches of half-desert land which lay so flat for miles. The prospect was always the same, always uninteresting and wearying and hot. Now she determined upon a step which she had wished to take for a long time, and her father's request that she should not take it grew less and less of a deterrent factor. He had given so much thought and worry to that mysterious valley, that she at last gave rein to her curiosity and made ready to see for herself. It was green and hilly, like the rugged Montana she had quitted to come down to the desert. There were hills of respectable size, for these she saw daily from the ranch house door, and she loved hills; anything would be better than the limitless sand.

She had known little of restraint; her corner of the world had been filled entirely by men and she had absorbed much of their better traits. Self-reliant as a cowgirl should be, expert with either Colt or Winchester, and at home in the saddle, she feared nothing the desert might hold, except thirst. She was not only expert with weapons, but she did not fear to use them against men, as she had proved on one occasion in wild Montana. So she would ride to the hills which called her so insistently and examine the valley.

One bright morning just before the roundup began she went to the corral and looked at her horse, a cross between Kentucky stock and cow-pony and having in a great degree the speed of the first and the hardiness of the last, and sighed to think that she could not ride it for days to come. Teuton was crippled and she must choose some other animal. She had overheard Doc Riley tell Ed Joyce that the piebald in the smaller corral was well broken, and this was the horse she would take. The truth of the matter was that the piebald was crafty and permitted the saddle to be fixed and himself ridden for varying periods of time before showing what he thought of such things. Doc, unprepared for the piebald's sudden change in demeanor, had taken a tumble, which made him anxious to have his wounded conceit soothed by seeing Ed Joyce receive the same treatment.

Mary found no trouble in mounting and riding the animal and she was glad that she had overheard Doc, for now she had two horses which were thoroughly reliable, although, of course, Teuton was the only really good horse on the range. She rode out of the corral and headed for the White Horse Hills, scarcely twelve miles away. What if her father had warned her not to ride near the lawless punchers who rode the northern range? They were only men and she was sure that to a woman they would prove to be gentlemen.

The southern boundary of the Bar-20 ran along the top of the hills and from them east to the river, and it was being patrolled by three Bar-20 punchers, Hopalong, Johnny, and Red, all on the lookout for straying cattle of both ranches. Neither Hopalong nor Red had ever seen Mary Meeker, but Johnny had upon the occasion of his scout over the H2 range, and he had felt eminently qualified to describe her. He had finished his eulogistic monologue by asserting that as soon as his more unfortunate friends saw her they would lose sleep and sigh often, which prophecy was received in various ways and called forth widely differing comment. Red had snorted outright and Pete swore to learn that a woman was on the range; for Pete had been married, and his wife preferred another man. Hopalong, remembering a former experience of his own, smiled in knowing cynicism when told that he again would fall under the feminine spell.

Red was near the river and Johnny half-way to the hills when Hopalong began the ascent of Long Hill, wondering why it was that Meeker had made no attempt to cross the boundary in force and bring on a crisis; and from Meeker his mind turned to the daughter.

"So there's a woman down here now," he muttered, riding down into an arroyo and up the other bank. "This country is gettin' as bad as Kansas, damned if it ain't. First thing we know it'll be nursin' bottles an' school houses, an' hell loose all th' time instead of once in a while."

He heard hoofbeats and glanced up quickly, alert and ready for trouble, for who would be riding where he was but some H2 puncher?

"What th'—!" he exclaimed under his breath, for riding towards him at an angle was Mary Meeker; and Johnny was wrong in his description of her, but, he thought, the Kid had done as well as his limited vocabulary would allow. She *was* pretty, pretty as—she was more than pretty!

She had seen him at the same time and flashed a quick glance which embraced everything; and she was surprised, for he was not only passably good-looking, barring the red hair, but very different from the men her father had told her made up the outfit of the Bar-20. He removed his sombrero instantly and drew up to let her pass, a smile on his face. Yes, he thought, Johnny had wronged her, for no other woman could have such jet-black hair crowning such a face.

"By God!" he whispered, and went no farther, for that was the summing up of his whole opinion of her.

"He *is* a gentleman," she thought triumphantly, for he had proved that she was right in her surmise regarding the men of the northern ranch. She spurred to pass him and then her piebald took part in the proceedings. The prick of the spur awakened in him a sudden desire to assert his rights, and he promptly pitched to make up for his hitherto gentle behavior. So taken up with what the last minute had brought forth she was unprepared for the vicious bucking and when she opened her eyes her head was propped against Hopalong's knee and her face dripping with the contents of his canteen. "Damn yore ugly skin!" he was saying to the piebald, which stood quietly a short distance away, evidently enjoying the result of his activity. "Just you wait! I'll show you what's due to come yore way purty soon!" He turned again to the woman and saw that her eyes were closed as before. "By God, yore—yore beautiful!"

She moved slightly and color came into her cheeks with a sudden rush and he watched her anxiously. Soon she moved again and then, opening her eyes, struggled to gain her feet. He helped her up and held her until she drew away from him.

"What was it?" she asked.

"That ugly cayuse went an' pitched when you wasn't lookin' for it," he told her. "Are you hurt much?"

"No, just dizzy. I don't want to make you trouble," she replied.

"You ain't makin' me any trouble, not a bit," he assured her earnestly. "But I'd like to make some trouble for that ornery cayuse of yourn. Let me tone him down some."

"No; it was my fault. I should'a been lookin—I never rode him before."

"Well, you've got to take my cayuse to get home on," he said. "He's bad, but he's a regular angel when stacked up agin that bronc. I'll ride the festive piebald, an' we can trade when you get home." Under his breath he said: "Oh, just wait till I get on you, pinto! I'll give you what you need, all right!"

"Thank you, but I can ride him now that I know just what he is," she said, her eyes flashing with determination. "I've never let a bronc get th' best of me in th' long run, an' I ain't goin' to begin now. I came up here to look at th' hills an' th' valley, an' I'm not going back home till I've done it."

"That's the way to talk!" he cried in admiration. "I'll

get him for you," he finished, swinging into his saddle. He loosened the lariat at the saddle horn while he rode towards the animal, which showed sudden renewed interest in the proceedings, but it tarried too long. Just as it wheeled and leaped forward the rope settled and the next thing it knew was that the sky had somehow slid under its stomach, for it had been thrown over backward and flat on its back. When it had struggled to its feet it found Hopalong astride it, spurring vigorously on the side farthest from Mary, and for five minutes the air was greatly disturbed. At the end of that time he dismounted and led a penitent pony to its mistress, who vaulted lightly into the saddle and waited for her companion to mount. When he had joined her they rode up the hill together side by side.

Johnny wished to smoke and felt for his tobacco pouch, which he found to be empty. He rode on for a short distance, angry with himself for his neglect, and then remembered that Hopalong had a plentiful supply. He could overtake the man on the hill much quicker than he could Red, who had said that he was going to ride south along the river to see if Jumping Bear Creek was dry. If it were, Meeker could be expected to become active in his aggression. Johnny wheeled and cantered back along the boundary trail, alertly watching for trespassing cattle.

It was not long before he came within sight of the thicket which stood a little east of the base of Long Hill, and he nearly fell from the saddle in astonishment, for his friend was on the ground, holding a woman's head on his knee! Johnny didn't care to intrude, and cautiously withdrew to the shelter of the small chaparral, where he waited impatiently. Wishing to stretch his legs, he dismounted and picketed his horse and walked around the thicket until satisfied that he was out of sight of his friend.

Suddenly he fancied that he heard something suspicious and he crept back around the thicket, keeping close to its base. When he turned the corner he saw the head of a man on the other side of the chaparral which lay a little southwest of his position. It was Antonio, and he was intently watching the two on the slope of the hill, and entirely unaware that he was being watched in turn.

Johnny carefully drew his Colt and covered Antonio who he hated instinctively. He had seen the shifty-eyed broncho-buster on more than one occasion and never without struggling with himself to keep from shooting. Now his finger pressed gently against the trigger of the weapon and he wished for a passable excuse to send the other into eternity; but Antonio gave him no cause, only watching eagerly and intently, his face set in such an expression of malignancy as to cause Johnny's finger to tremble.

Johnny arose slightly until he could see Hopalong and his companion and he smothered an exclamation. "Gosh A'mighty!" he whispered, again watching Antonio. "That's Meeker's gal or I'm a liar! Th' son-of-a-gun, keeping quiet about it all this time. An' no wonder Antonio's on th' trail!"

It was not long before Johnny looked again for Hopalong and saw him riding up the hill with his companion. Then he crept forward, watching Antonio closely, his Colt ready for instant use. Antonio slowly drew down until he was lost to sight of the Bar-20 puncher, who ran slightly forward and gained the side of the other thicket, where he again crept forward, and around the chaparral. When he next caught sight of the broncho-buster the latter was walking towards his horse and his back was turned to Johnny.

"Hey, you!" called the Bar-20 puncher, arising and starting after the other.

Antonio wheeled, leaped to one side and half drew his revolver, but he was covered and he let the weapon slide back into the holster.

"What are you doing?"

Antonio's reply was a scowl and his inquisitor continued without waiting for words from the other.

"Never mind that, I saw what you was doing," Johnny said. "An' I shore knew what you wanted to do, because I came near doing it to you. Now it ain't a whole lot healthy for you to go snooping around this line like you was, for I'll plug you on suspicion next time. Get on that cayuse of yourn an' hit th' trail south—go on, make tracks!"

Antonio mounted and slowly wheeled. "You hab drop, now," he said significantly. "Nex' time, *quien sabe*?"

Johnny dropped his Colt into the holster and removed his hand from the butt. "You're a liar!" he shouted, savagely. "I ain't got th' drop. It's an even break, an' what are you going to do about it?"

Antonio shrugged his shoulders and rode on without replying, quite content to let things stand as they were. He had learned something which he might be able to use to advantage later on and he had strained the situation just a little more.

"Huh! Next time!" snorted Johnny in contempt as he turned to go back to his horse. "It'll allus be 'next' time' with him, 'less he gets a good pot shot at me, which he won't. He ain't got sand enough to put up a square fight. Now for Red; he'll shore be riding this way purty soon, an' that'll never do. Hoppy won't want anybody foolin' around th' hills for a while, lucky devil."

More than an hour had passed before he met Red and he forthwith told him that he had caught Antonio scouting on foot along the line.

"I ain't none surprised, Kid," Red replied, frowning. "You've seen how th' H2 cows are being driven north agin us an' that means we'll be tolerable busy purty soon. Th' Jumping Bear is dry as tinder, an' it won't be long before Meeker'll be driving to get in th' valley."

"Well, I'm some glad of that," Johnny replied, frankly. "It's been peaceful too blamed long down here. Come on, we'll ride east an' see if we can find any cows to turn. Hey! Look there!" he cried, spurring forward.

III

♦

The Roundup

The Texan sky seemed a huge mirror upon which were reflected the white fleecy clouds sailing northward; the warm spring air was full of that magnetism which calls forth from their earthy beds the gramma grass and the flowers; the scant vegetation had taken on new dress and traces of green now showed against the more sombre-colored stems; while in the distance, rippling in glistening patches where, disturbed by the wind, the river sparkled like a tinsel ribbon flung carelessly on the grays and greens of the plain. Birds winged their joyous way and filled the air with song; and far overhead a battalion of tardy geese flew, arrowlike, towards the cool lakes of the north, their faint honking pathetic and continuous. Skulking in the coulees or speeding across the skyline of some distant rise occasionally could be seen a coyote or gray wolf. The cattle, less gregarious than they had been in the colder months, made tentative sorties from the lessening herd, and began to stray off in search of the tender green grass which pushed up recklessly from the closely cropped, withered tufts. Rattlesnakes slid out and uncoiled their sinuous lengths in the warm sunlight, and copperheads raised their burnished armor from their winter retreats. All nature had felt the magic touch of the warm winds, and life in its multitudinous forms was discernible on all sides. The gaunt tragedy of a hard winter for that southern range had added its chilling share to the horrors of the past and now the cattle took heart and lost their weakness in the sunlight, hungry but contented.

The winter had indeed been hard, one to be remembered for years to come, and many cattle had died because of it; many skeletons, stripped clean by coyotes and wolves, dotted the arroyos and coulees. The cold weather had broken suddenly, and several days of rain, followed by sleet, had drenched the cattle thoroughly. Then from out of the north came one of those unusual rages of nature, locally known as a "Norther," freezing pitilessly; and the cattle, weakened by cold and starvation, had dumbly succumbed to this last blow. Their backs were covered with an icy shroud, and the deadly cold gripped their vitals with a power not to be resisted. A glittering sheet formed over the grasses as far as eye could see, and the cattle, unlike the horses, not knowing enough to stamp through it, nosed in vain at the sustenance beneath, until weakness compelled them to lie down in the driving snow, and once down, they never arose. The storm had raged for the greater part of a week, and then suddenly one morning the sun shown down on a velvety plain, blinding in its whiteness; and when spring had sent the snow mantle roaring through the arroyos and water courses in a turmoil of yellow water and driftwood, and when the range riders rode forth to read the losses on the plain, the remaining cattle were staggering weakly in search of food. Skeletons in the coulees told the story of the hopeless fight, how the unfortunate cattle had drifted before the wind to what shelter they could find and how, huddled together for warmth, they had died one by one. The valley along Conroy Creek had provided a rough shelter with its scattered groves and these had stopped the cattle drift, so much dreaded by cowmen.

It had grieved Buck Peters and his men to the heart to see so many cattle swept away in one storm, but they had done all that courage and brains could do to save them. So now, when the plain was green again and the warm air made riding a joy, they were to hold the calf roundup. When Buck left his blanket after the first night spent in the roundup camp and rode off to the horse herd, he smiled from suppressed elation, and was glad that he was alive.

Peaceful as the scene appeared there was trouble brewing, and it was in expectation of this that Buck had begun the roundup earlier than usual. The unreasoning stubbornness of one man, and the cunning machinations of a natural rogue, threatened to bring about, from what should have been only a misunderstanding, as pretty a range war as the Southwest had seen. Those immediately involved were only a few when compared to the number which might eventually be brought into the strife, but if this had been pointed out to Jim Meeker he would have replied that he "didn't give a damn."

Jim Meeker was a Montana man who thought to carry out on the H2 range, of which he was foreman, the same system of things which had served where he had come from. This meant trouble right away, for the Bar-20, already short in range, would not stand idly by and see him encroach upon their land for grass and water, more especially when he broke a solemn compact as to range rights which had been made by the former owners of the H2 with the Bar-20. It meant not only the forcible use of Bar-20 range, but also a great hardship upon the herds for which Buck Peters was responsible.

Meeker's obstinacy was covertly prodded by Antonio

for his own personal gains, but this the Bar-20 foreman did not know; if he had known it there might have been much trouble averted.

Buck Peters was probably the only man of all of them who realized just what such a war would mean, to what an extent rustling would flourish while the cowmen fought. His best efforts had been used to avert trouble, so far successfully; but that he would continue to do so was doubtful. He had an outfit which, while meaning to obey him in all things and to turn from any overt act of war, was not of the kind to stand much forcing or personal abuse; their nervous systems were constructed on the hair-trigger plan, and their very loyalty might set the range ablaze with war. However, on this most perfect of mornings Meeker's persistent aggression did not bother him, he was free from worry for the time.

Just north of Big Coulee, in which was a goodly sized water hole, a group of blanket-swathed figures lay about a fire near the chuck wagon, while the sleepy cook prepared breakfast for his own outfit, and for the eight men which the foreman of the C80 and the Double Arrow had insisted upon Buck taking. The sun had not yet risen, but the morning glow showed gray over the plain, and it would not be long before the increasing daylight broke suddenly. The cook fires crackled and blazed steadily, the iron pots hissing under their dancing and noisy lids, while the coffee pots bubbled and sent up an aromatic steam, and the odor of freshly baked biscuits swept forth as the cook uncovered a pan. A pile of tin plates was stacked on the tail-board of the wagon while a large sheet-iron pail contained tin cups. The figures, feet to the fire, looked like huge, grotesque cocoons, for the men had rolled themselves in their blankets, their heads resting on their saddles, and in many cases folded sombreros next to the leather made softer pillows.

Back of the chuck wagon the eastern sky grew rapidly brighter, and suddenly daylight in all its power dissipated the grayish light of the moment before. As the rim of the golden sun arose above the low sand hills to the east the foreman rode into camp. Some distance behind him Harry Jones and two other C80 men drove up the horse herd and enclosed it in a flimsy corral quickly extemporized from lariats; flimsy it was, but it sufficed for cow-ponies that had learned the lesson of the rope.

"All ready, Buck," called Harry before his words were literally true.

With assumed ferocity but real vociferation Buck uttered a shout and watched the effect. The cocoons became animated, stirred and rapidly unrolled, with the exception of one, and the sleepers leaped to their feet and folded the blankets. The exception stirred, subsided, stirred again and then was quiet. Buck and Red stepped forward while the others looked on grinning to see the fun, grasped the free end of the blanket and suddenly straightened up, their hands going high above their heads. Johnny Nelson, squawking, rolled over and over and, with a yell of surprise, sat bolt upright and felt for his gun.

"Huh!" he snorted. "Reckon yo're smart, don't you!"

"Purty near a shore 'nuf pin-wheel, Kid," laughed Red.

"Don't you care, Johnny; you can finish it tonight," consoled Frenchy McAllister, now one of Buck's outfit.

"Breakfast, Kid, breakfast!" sang out Hopalong as he finished drying his face.

The breakfast was speedily out of the way, and pipes were started for a short smoke as the punchers walked over to the horse herd to make their selections. By exercising patience, profanity, and perseverance they roped their horses and began to saddle up. Ed Porter, of the

C80, and Skinny Thompson, Bar-20, cast their ropes with a sweeping, preliminary whirl over their heads, but the others used only a quick flit and twist of the wrist. A few mildly exciting struggles for the mastery took place between riders and mounts, for some cow-ponies are not always ready to accept their proper places in the scheme of things.

"Slab-sided jumpin' jack!" yelled Rich Finn, a Double Arrow puncher, as he fought his horse. "Allus raisin' th' devil afore I'm all awake!"

"Lemme hold her head, Rich," jeered Billy Williams.

"Her laigs, Billy, not her head," corrected Lanky Smith, the Bar-20 rope expert, whose own horse had just become sensible.

"Don't hurt him, bronc; we need him," cautioned Red.

"Come on, fellers; gettin' late," called Buck.

Away they went, tearing across the plain, Buck in the lead. After some time had passed the foreman raised his arm and Pete Wilson stopped and filled his pipe anew, the west-end man of the cordon. Again Buck's arm went up and Skinny Thompson dropped out, and so on until the last man had been placed and the line completed. At a signal from Buck the whole line rode forward, gradually converging on a central point and driving the scattered cattle before it.

Hopalong, on the east end of the line, sharing with Billy the posts of honor, was now kept busy dashing here and there, wheeling, stopping, and maneuvering as certain strong-minded cattle, preferring the freedom of the range they had just quitted, tried to break through the cordon. All but branded steers and cows without calves had their labors in vain, although the escape of these often set examples for ambitious cows with calves. Here was where reckless and expert riding saved the day, for the cow-ponies, trained in the art of punching cows, entered into the game with zest and executed quick turns which more than once threatened a catastrophe to themselves and riders. Range cattle can run away from their domesticated kin, covering the ground with an awkward gait that is deceiving; but the ponies can run faster and turn as quickly.

Hopalong, determined to turn back one stubborn mother cow, pushed too hard, and she wheeled to attack him. Again the nimble pony had reasons to move quickly and Hopalong swore as he felt the horns touch his leg.

"On th' prod, hey! Well, stay on it!" he shouted, well knowing that she would. "Pig-headed old fool—*all right*, Johnny; I'm comin'!" and he raced away to turn a handful of cows which were proving too much for his friend. *"Ki-yi-yeow-eow-eow-eow-eow!"* he yelled, imitating the coyote howl.

The cook had moved his wagon as soon as breakfast was over and journeyed southeast with the cavvieyh; and as the cordon neared its objectives the punchers could see his camp about half a mile from the level pasture where the herd would be held for the cutting-out and branding. Cookie regarded himself as the most important unit of the roundup and acted accordingly, and he was not far wrong.

"Hey, Hoppy!" called Johnny through the dust of the herd, "there's Cookie. I was 'most scared he'd get lost."

"Can't you think of anythin' else but grub?" asked Billy Jordan from the rear.

"Can you tell me anything better to think of?"

There were from three to four hundred cattle in the herd when it neared the stopping point, and dust arose in low-hanging clouds above it. Its pattern of differing shades of brown, with yellow and black and white relieving it, constantly shifted like a kaleidoscope as the cattle changed positions; and the rattle of horns on horns and the muffled bellowing could be heard for some distance.

Gradually the cordon surrounded the herd and, when the destination was reached, the punchers rode before the front ranks of cattle and stopped them. There was a sudden tremor, a compactness in the herd, and the cattle in the rear crowded forward against those before; another tremor, and the herd was quiet. Cowpunchers took their places around it, and kept the cattle from breaking out and back to the range, while every second man, told off by the foreman, raced at top speed towards the camp, there to eat a hasty dinner and get a fresh horse from his *remuda*, as his string of from five to seven horses was called. Then he galloped back to the herd and relieved his nearest neighbor. When all had reassembled at the herd the work of cutting-out began.

Lanky Smith, Panhandle Lukins, and two more Bar-20 men rode some distance east of the herd, there to take care of the cow-and-calf cut as it grew by the cutting-out. Hopalong, Red, Johnny, and three others were assigned to the task of getting the mother cows and their calves out of the main herd and into the new one, while the other punchers held the herd and took care of the stray herd when they should be needed. Each of the cutters-out rode after some calf, and the victim, led by its mother, worked its way after her into the very heart of the mass; and in getting the pair out again care must be taken not to unduly excite the other cattle. Wiry, happy, and conceited cow-ponies unerringly and patiently followed mother and calf into the press, nipping the pursued when too slow and gradually forcing them to the outer edge of the herd; and when the mother tried to lead its offspring back into the herd to repeat the performance, she was in almost every case cleverly blocked and driven out on the plain where the other punchers took charge of her and added her to the cow-and-calf cut.

Johnny jammed his sombrero on his head with reckless strength and swore luridly as he wheeled to go back into the herd.

"What's th' matter, Kid?" laughingly asked Skinny as he turned his charges over to another man.

"None of yore damned business!" blazed Johnny. Under his breath he made a resolve. "If I get you two out here again I'll keep you here if I have to shoot you!"

"Are they slippery, Johnny?" jibed Red, whose guess was correct. Johnny refused to heed such asinine remarks and stood on his dignity.

As the cow-and-calf herd grew in size and the main herd dwindled, more punchers were shifted to hold it; and it was not long before the main herd was comprised entirely of cattle without calves, when it was driven off to freedom after being examined for other brands. As soon as the second herd became of any size it was not necessary to drive the cows and the calves to it when they were driven out of the first herd, as they made straight for it. The main herd, driven away, broke up as it would, while the guarded cows stood idly beside their resting offspring awaiting further indignities.

The drive had covered so much ground and taken so much time that approaching darkness warned Buck not to attempt the branding until the morrow, and he divided his force into three shifts. Two of these hastened to the camp, gulped down their supper, and rolling into their blankets, were soon sound asleep. The horse herd was driven off to where the grazing was better, and night soon fell over the plain.

The cook's fires gleamed through the darkness and piles of biscuits were heaped on the tail-board of the wagon, while pots of beef and coffee simmered over the fires, handy for the guards as they rode in during the night to awaken brother punchers, who would take their places while they slept. Soon the cocoons were quiet in the grotesque shadows caused by the fires and a deep silence reigned over the camp. Occasionally some puncher would awaken long enough to look at the sky to see if the weather had changed, and satisfied, return to sleep.

Over the plain sleepy cowboys rode slowly around the herd, glad to be relieved by some other member of the outfit, who always sang as he approached the cattle to reassure them and save a possible stampede. For cattle, if suddenly disturbed at night by anything, even the waving of a slicker in the hands of some careless rider, or a wind-blown paper, will rise in a body—all up at once, frightened and nervous. The sky was clear and the stars bright and when the moon rose it flooded the plain with a silvery light and made fairy patterns in the shadows.

Snatches of song floated down the gentle wind as the riders slowly circled the herd, for the human voice, no matter how discordant, was quieting. A low and plaintive "Don't let this par-ting grieve y-o-u" passed from hearing around the resting cows, soon to be followed by "When-n in thy dream-ing, nights like t-h-e-s-e shall come a-gain—" as another watcher made the circuit. The serene cows, trusting in the prowess and vigilance of these low-voiced centaurs to protect them from danger, dozed and chewed their cuds in peace and quiet, while the natural noises of the night relieved the silence in unobtruding harmony.

Far out on the plain a solitary rider watched the herd from cover and swore because it was guarded so closely. He glanced aloft to see if there was any hope of a storm and finding that there was not, muttered savagely and rode away. It was Antonio, wishing that he could start a stampede and so undo the work of the day and inflict heavy losses on the Bar-20. He did not dare to start a grass fire for at the first flicker of a light he would be charged by one or more of the night riders and if caught, death would be his reward.

While the third shift rode and sang the eastern sky became a dome of light reflected from below and the sunrise, majestic in all its fiery splendor, heralded the birth of another perfect day.

Through the early morning hours the branding continued, and the bleating of cattle told of the hot stamping irons indelibly burning the sign of the Bar-20 on the tender hides of calves. Mother cows fought and plunged and called in reply to the terrified bawling of their offspring, and sympathetically licked the burns when the frightened calves had been allowed to join them. Cowboys were deftly roping calves by their hind legs and dragging them to the fires of the branding men. Two men would hold a calf, one doubling the foreleg back on itself at the knee and the other, planting one booted foot against the calf's under hind leg close to its body, pulled back on the other leg while his companion, who held the foreleg, rested on the animal's head. The third man, drawing the hot iron from the fire, raised and held it suspended for a second over the calf's flank, and then there was an odor and a puff of smoke; and the calf was branded with a mark which neither water nor age would wipe out.

Pete Wilson came riding up dragging a calf at the end of his rope, and turned the captive over to Billy Williams and his two helpers, none of them paying any attention to the cow which followed a short distance behind him. Lanky seized the unfortunate calf and leaned over to secure the belly hold, when someone shouted a warning and he dropped the struggling animal and leaped back and to one side as the mother charged past. Wheeling to return the attack, the cow suddenly flopped over and struck the earth with a thud as Buck's rope went home. He dragged her away and then releasing her, chased her back into the herd.

"*Hi!* Get that little devil!" shouted Billy to Hopalong, pointing to the fleeing calf.

"Why didn't you watch for her," demanded the indignant Lanky of Pete. "Do you think this is a ten-pin alley!"

Hopalong came riding up with the calf, which swiftly became recorded property.

"Bar-20; tally one," sang out the monotonous voice of the tally man. "Why didn't you grab her when she went by, Lanky?" he asked, putting a new point on his pencil.

"Hope th' next one leads yore way!" retorted Lanky, grinning.

"Won't. I ain't abusin' th' kids."

"Bar-20; tally one," droned a voice at the next fire.

All was noise, laughter, dust, and a seeming confusion, but every man knew his work thoroughly and was doing it in a methodical way, and the confusion was confined to the victims and their mothers.

When the herd had been branded and allowed to return to the plain, the outfit moved on into a new territory and the work was repeated until the whole range, with the exception of the valley, had been covered. When the valley was worked it required more time in comparison with the amount of ground covered than had been heretofore spent on any part of the range; for the cattle were far more numerous, and it was no unusual thing to have a herd of great size before the roundup place had been reached. This heavy increase in the numbers of the cattle to be herded made a corresponding increase in the time and labor required for the cutting-out and branding. Five days were required in working the eastern and central parts of the valley and it took three more days to clean up around the White Horse Hills, where the ground was rougher and the riding harder. And at every cutting-out there was a large stray-herd made up of H2 and Three Triangle cattle. The H2 had been formerly the Three Triangle. Buck had been earnest in his instructions regarding the strays, for now was the opportunity to rid his range of Meeker's cattle without especial significance; once over the line it would be a comparatively easy matter to keep them there.

For taking care of this extra herd and also because Buck courted scrutiny during the branding, the foreman accepted the services of three H2 men. This addition to his forces made the work move somewhat more rapidly and when, at the end of each day's cutting-out, the stray herd was complete, it was driven south across the boundary line by Meeker's men. When the last stray-herd started south Buck rode over to the H2 punchers and told them to tell their foreman to let him know when he could assist in the southern roundup and thus return the favor.

As the Bar-20 outfit and the C80 and Double Arrow men rode north towards the ranch house they were met by Lucas, foreman of the C80, who joined them near Medicine Bend.

"Well, got it all over, hey?" he cried as he rode up.

"Yep; bigger job than I thought, too. It gets bigger every year an' that blizzard didn't make much difference in th' work, neither," Buck replied. "I'll help you out when you get ready to drive."

"No you won't; you can help me an' Bartlett more by keeping all yore men watchin' that line," quickly responded Lucas. "We'll work together, me an' Bartlett, an' we'll have all th' men we want. You just show that man Meeker that range grabbin' ain't healthy down here—that's all we want. Did he send you any help in th' valley?"

"Yes, three men," Buck replied. "But we'll break even on that when he works along the boundary."

"Have any trouble with 'em?"

"Not a bit."

"I sent Wood Wright down to Eagle th' other day, an' he says the town is shore there'll be a big range war," remarked Lucas. "He said there's lots of excitement down there an' they act like they wish th' trouble would hurry up an' happen. We've got to watch that town, all right."

"If there's a war th' rustlers'll flock from all over," interposed Rich Finn.

"Huh!" snorted Hopalong. "They'll flock out again if we get a chance to look for 'em. An' that town'll shore get into trouble if it don't live plumb easy. You know what happened th' last time rustlin' got to be th' style, don't you?"

"Well," replied Lucas, "I've fixed it with Cowan to get news to me an' Bartlett if anything sudden comes up. If you need us just let him know an' we'll be with you in two shakes."

"That's good, but I don't reckon I'll need any help, leastwise not for a long time," Buck responded. "But I tell you what you might do, when you can; make up a vigilance committee from yore outfits an' ride range for rustlers. We can take care of all that comes on us, but we won't have no time to bother about th' rest of th' range. An' if you do that it'll shut 'em out of our north range."

"We'll do it," Lucas promised. "Bartlett is going to watch th' trails north to see if he can catch anybody runnin' cattle to th' railroad construction camps. Every suspicious looking stranger is going to be held up an' asked questions; an' if we find any runnin' irons, you know what that means."

"I reckon we can handle th' situation, all right, no matter how hard it gets," laughed the Bar-20 foreman.

"Well, I'll be leavin' you now," Lucas remarked as they reached the Bar-20 bunk house. "We begin to round up next week, an' there's lots to be done by then. Say, can I use yore chuck wagon? Mine is shore done for."

"Why, of course," replied Buck heartily. "Take it now, if you want, or any time you send for it."

"Much obliged; come on, fellers," Lucas cried to his men. "We're going home."

IV

♦

In West Arroyo

Hopalong was heading for Lookout Peak, the highest of the White Horse Hills, by way of West Arroyo, which he entered half an hour after he had forded the creek, and was half way to the line when, rounding a sharp turn, he saw Mary Meeker ahead of him. She was off her horse picking flowers when she heard him and she stood erect, smiling.

"Why, I didn't think I'd see you," she said. "I've been picking flowers—see them? Ain't they pretty?" she asked, holding them out for his inspection.

"They shore are," he replied, not looking at the flowers at all, but into her big, brown eyes. "An' they're some lucky, too," he asserted grinning.

She lowered her head, burying her face in the blossoms and then picked a few petals and let them fall one by one from her fingers. "You didn't look at them at all," she chided.

"Oh, yes, I did," he laughed. "But I see flowers all th' time, and not much of you."

"That's nice—they are so pretty. I just love them."

"Yes. I reckon they are," he said doubtfully.

She looked up at him, her eyes laughing and her white teeth glistening between their red frames. "Why don't you scold me?" she asked.

"Scold you! What for?"

"Why, for being on yore ranch, for being across th' line an' in th' valley."

"Good Lord! Why, there ain't no lines for you! You can go anywhere."

"In th' valley?" she asked, again hiding her face in the flowers.

"Why, of course. What ever made you think you can't?"

"I'm one of th' H2," she responded. "Paw says I run it. But I'm awful glad you won't care."

"Well, as far as riding where you please is concerned, you run this ranch, too."

"There's a pretty flower," she said, looking at the top of the bank. "That purple one; see it?" she asked, pointing.

"Yes. I'll get it for you," he replied, leaping from the saddle and half way up the bank before she knew it. He slid down again and handed the blossom to her. "There."

"Thank you."

"See any more you wants?"

"No; this is enough. Thank you for getting it for me."

"Oh, that was nothing," he laughed, awkwardly. "That was shore easy."

"I'm gong to give it to you for not scolding me about being over th' line," she said, holding it out to him.

"No; not for that," he said slowly. "Can't you think of some other reason?"

"Don't you want it?"

"Want it!" he exclaimed, eagerly. "Shore I want it. But not for what you said."

"Will you wear it because we're friends?"

"Now yo're talking!"

She looked up and laughed, her cheeks dimpling, and then pinned it to his shirt. It was nice to have a flower pinned on one's shirt by a pretty girl.

"There," she laughed, stepping back to look at it.

"You've pinned it up so high I can't see it. Why not put it lower down?"

She changed it while he grinned at how his scheming had born fruit. He was a hog, he knew that, but he did not care.

"Oh, I reckon *I'm* all right!" he exulted. "Shore you don't see no more you want?"

"Yes; an' I must go now," she replied, going towards her horse. "I'll be late with th' dinner if I don't hurry."

"What! Do you cook for that hungry outfit?"

"No, not for them—just for Paw an' me."

"When are you comin' up again for more flowers?"

"I don't know. You see, I'm going to make cookies some day this week, but I don't know just when. Do you like cookies, an' cake?"

"You bet I do! Why?"

"I'll bring some with me th' next time. Paw says they're th' best he ever ate."

"Bet I'll say so, too," he replied, stepping forward to help her into the saddle, but she sprang into it before he reached her side, and he vaulted on his own horse and joined her.

She suddenly turned and looked him straight in the eyes. "Tell me, honest, has yore ranch any right to keep our cows south of that line?"

"Yes, we have. Our boundaries are fixed. We gave th' Three Triangle about eighty square miles of range so our valley would be free from all cows but our own. That's all th' land between th' line an' th' Jumping Bear, an' it was a big price, too. They never drove a cow over on us."

She looked disappointed and toyed with her quirt.

"Why don't you want to let Paw use th' valley?"

"It ain't big enough for our own cows, an' we can't share it. As it is, we'll have to drive ten thousand on leased range next year to give our grass a rest."

"Well—" she stopped and he waited to hear what she would say, and then asked her when she would be up again.

"I don't know! I don't know!" she cried.

"Why, what's the matter?"

"Nothing. I'm foolish—that's all," she replied, smiling, and trying to forget the picture which arose in her mind, a picture of desperate fighting along the line; of her father—and him.

"You scared me then," he said.

"Did I? Why, it wasn't anything."

"Are you shore?"

"Please don't ask me any questions," she requested.

"Will you be up here again soon?"

"If th' baking turns out all right."

"Hang the baking! Come anyway."

"I'll try; but I'm afraid," she faltered.

"Of what?" he demanded, sitting up very straight.

"Why, that I can't," she replied, hurriedly. "You see, it's far coming up here."

"That's easy. I'll meet you west of the hills."

"No, no! I'll come up here."

"Look here," he said, slowly and kindly. "If yo're afraid of bein' seen with me, don't you try it. I want to see you a whole lot, but I don't want you to have no trouble with yore father about it. I can wait till everything is all right if you want me to."

She turned and faced him, her cheeks red. "No, it ain't that, exactly. Don't ask me any more. Don't talk about it. I'll come, all right, just as soon as I can."

They were on the line now and she held out her hand.
"Good-bye."

"Good-bye for now. Try to come up an' see me as soon
as you can. If yo're worryin' because Antonio don't like
me, stop it. I've been in too many tight places to get piped
out where there's elbow room."

"I asked you not to say nothing more about it," she
chided. "I'll come when I can. Good-bye."

"Good-bye," he replied, his sombrero under his arm.
He watched her until she became lost to sight and then,
suspicious, wheeled, and saw Johnny sitting quietly on his
horse several hundred yards away. He called his friend to
him by one wide sweep of his arm and Johnny spurred
forward.

"Follow me, Johnny," he cried, dashing towards the
arroyo. "Take th' other side an' look for Antonio. I'll take
this side. Edge off; yo're too close. Three hundred yards
is about right."

They raced away at top speed, reckless and grim,
Johnny not knowing just what it was all about; but the
name Antonio needed no sauce to whet his appetite since
the day he had caught him watching his friend on the hill,
and he scanned the plain eagerly. When they reached the
other end of the arroyo Hopalong called to him: "Sweep
east an' back to th' line on a circle. If you catch him, shoot
off yo're colt an' hold him for *me*. I'm going west."

When they saw each other again it was on the line,
and neither had seen any traces of Antonio, to Johnny's
vexation and Hopalong's great satisfaction.

"What's up, Hoppy?" shouted Johnny.

"I reckoned that Antonio might a' followed her so he
could tell tales to Meeker," Hopalong called.

Johnny swept up recklessly, jauntily, a swagger almost
in the very actions of his horse, which seemed to have
caught the spirit of its rider.

"Caught you that time," he laughed—and Johnny, when in a teasing mood, could weave into his laughter an affectionate note which found swift pardon for any words he might utter. "You an' her shore make a good—" and then he saw the flower on his friend's shirt and for the moment was rendered speechless by surprise. But in him the faculty of speech was well developed and he recovered quickly. "Sufferin' coyotes! Would you look at that! What's comin' to us down here, anyway? Are you loco? Do you mean to let th' rest of th' outfit see *that*?"

"Calamity is comin' to th' misguided mavericks that get funny about it!" retorted Hopalong. "I wear what I feels like, an' don't you forget it, neither."

" 'In thy d-a-r-k eyes splendor, where th' l-o-v-e light longs to dwel-l,' " Johnny hummed, grinning. Then his hand went out. "Good luck, Hoppy! Th' best of luck!" he cried. "She's a dandy, all right, but she ain't too good for you."

"Much obliged," Hopalong replied, shaking hands. "But suppose you tell me what all th' good luck is for. To hear you talk anybody'd think all a feller had to do was to ride with a woman to be married to her."

"Well, then take off that wart of a flower an' come on," Johnny responded.

"What? Not to save yo're spotted soul! An' that ain't no wart of a flower, neither."

Johnny burst out laughing, a laugh from the soul of him, welling up in infectious spontancity, triumphant and hearty. "Oh, oh! You bit that time! Anybody'd think about right in yo're case, as far as *wantin'* to be married is concerned. Why, yo're hittin' th' lovely trail to matrimony as hard as you can."

In spite of himself Hopalong had to laugh at the jibing of his friend, the Kid. He thumped him heartily across the shoulders to show how he felt about it and Johnny's breath was interfered with at a critical moment.

"Oh, just wait till th' crowd sees that blossom! Just wait," Johnny coughed.

"You keep mum about what you saw, d'y' hear?"

"Shore; but it'll be on my mind all th' time, an' I talk in my sleep when anything's on my mind."

"Then that's why I never heard you talk in yo're sleep."

"Aw, g'wan! But they'll see th' flower, won't they?"

"Shore they will; but as long as they don't know how it got there they can't say much."

"They can't, hey!" Johnny exclaimed. "That's a new one on me. It's usually what they don't know about that they talks of most. What they don't know they can guess in this case, all right. Most of 'em are good on readin' signs, an' that's plain as th' devil."

"But don't you tell 'em!" Hopalong warned.

"No. I won't tell 'em, honest," Johnny replied. He could convey the information in a negative way and he grinned hopefully at the fun there would be.

"I mean it, Kid," Hopalong responded, reading the grin. "I don't care about myself; they can joke all they wants with me. But it ain't nowise right to drag her into it, savvy? She don't want to be talked about like that."

"Yo're right; they won't find out nothin' from me," and Johnny saw his fun slip from him. "I'm goin' east; comin' along?"

"No; th' other way. So long."

"Hey!" cried Johnny anxiously, drawing rein, "Frenchy said Buck was going to put some of us up in Number Five so Frenchy an' his four could ride th' line. Did Buck say anything to you about it?"

Line house Number Five was too far from the zone of excitement, if fighting should break out along the line, to please Johnny.

"He was stringin' you, Kid," Hopalong laughed. "He won't take any of th' old outfit away from here."

"Oh, I knowed that; but I thought I'd ask, that's all," and Johnny cantered away, whistling happily.

Hopalong looked after him and smiled, for Johnny had laughed and fought and teased himself into the heart of every man of the outfit: "He's shore a good Kid; an' how he likes a fight!"

V

♦

Hopalong Asserts Himself

Paralleling West Arroyo and two miles east of it was another arroyo, through which Hopalong was riding the day following his meeting with Mary. Coming to a place where he could look over the bank he saw a herd of H2 and Three Triangle cows grazing not far away, and Antonio was in charge of them. Hopalong did not know how long they had been in the valley, nor how they had crossed the line, but their presence was enough. It angered him, for here was open and, it appeared, authorized defiance. Not content to let his herds run as they wished, Meeker was actually sending them into the valley under guard, presumably to find out what would be done about it. The H2 foreman would find that out very soon.

Antonio looked around and wheeled sharply to face the danger, his listlessness gone in a flash. He was not there because of any orders from Meeker, but for reasons of his own. So when the Bar-20 puncher raised his arm and swept it towards the line he sat in sullen indifference, alert and crafty.

"You've got gall!" cried Hopalong. "Who told you to herd up here!"

Antonio frowned but did not reply.

"Yo're three miles too far north," continued Hopalong, riding slowly forward until their stirrups almost touched.

Antonio shrugged his shoulders.

"I ain't warbling for my health!" cried Hopalong. "You start them cows south right away."

"I can't."

Hopalong stared. "You can't! Well, I reckon you can, an' will."

"I can't. Boss won't let me."

"Oh, he won't! Well, I feel sorry for yore boss but yo're going to push 'em just th' same."

Antonio again shrugged his shoulders and lifted his hands in a gesture of helplessness.

"How long you been here, an' how'd you get in?"

"'N'our. By de *rio*."

"Oh, yore foreman's goin' to raise hell, ain't he!" Hopalong snorted. "He's going to pasture on us whether we like it or not, is he? He's a land thief, that's what he is!"

"De boss ees all right!" asserted Antonio, heatedly.

"If he is he's lop-sided, but he'll be *left* if he banks on this play going through without a smash-up. You chase them cows home an' keep 'em there. If I find you flittin' around th' ends of th' line or herdin' on this side of it I'll give you something to nurse—an' you'll be lucky if you can nurse it. Come on, get a-going!"

Antonio waved his arm excitedly and was about to expostulate, but Hopalong cut him short by hitting him across the face with his quirt: "Damn you!" he cried, angrily. "Shut yore mouth! Get them cows going! I've a mind to stop you right now. Come on, get a move on!"

Antonio's face grew livid and he tried to back away,

swearing. Stung to action by the blow, he jerked at his gun, but found Hopalong's Colt pushing against his neck.

"Drop that gun!" the Bar-20 puncher ordered, his eyes flashing. "Don't you know better'n that? We've put up with yore crowd as long as we're going to, an' th' next thing will be a slaughter if that foreman of yourn don't get some sense, an' get it sudden. Don't talk back! Just start them cows!"

Antonio could do nothing but obey. His triumph at the success of his effort was torn with rabid hatred for the man who had struck him; but he could not fight with the Colt at his neck, and so sullenly obeyed. As they neared the line Hopalong ceased his personal remarks and, smiling grimly, turned to another topic.

"I let you off easy; but no more. Th' next herd we find in our valley will go sudden an' hard. If anybody is guardin' it they'll never know what hit 'em." He paused for a moment and then continued, cold contempt in his voice: "I reckon you had to obey orders, but you won't do it again if you know what's good for you. If yore boss, as you calls him, don't like what I've done, you tell him I said to drive th' next herd hisself. If he ain't man enough to bring 'em in hisself, tell him that Cassidy says to quit orderin' his men to take risks he's a-scared of."

"He ees brafe; he ain't 'fraid," Antonio rejoined. "He weel keel you ef I tell heem what you say."

"Tell him jus' th' same. I'll be riding th' line mostly, an' if he wants to hunt me up an' talk about it he can find me any time."

Antonio shrugged his shoulders and rode south, filled with elation at his success in stirring up hostility between the two ranches, but his heart seethed with murder for the blow. He would carry a message to Meeker that would call for harsh measures, and the war would be on.

As Antonio departed Lanky Smith rode into sight and cantered forward to meet his friend.

"What's up?" he asked.

"I don't know, yet," replied Hopalong. "He could be lying, I don't know what to think," and he related the matter to his companion.

"Lord, but you sent a stiff message to Meeker!" Lanky exclaimed. "You keep yore eyes plumb open from now on. Meeker'll be wild, an' Antonio won't forget that blow."

"Was anybody on th' east end this morning?"

"Shore; me an' Pete," Lanky replied, frowning. "He couldn't get a cow across without us seein' him—he lied."

"Well, it makes no difference how he got across; he was there, an' that's all I care about."

"There's one of his outfit now," Lanky said.

Hopalong looked around and saw an H2 puncher riding slowly past them, about two hundred yards to the south.

"Who is he?" Lanky asked.

"Doc Riley. Meeker got him an' Curley out of a bad scrape up north an' took them both to punch for him. I hear he is some bad with th' Colt. Sort of reckons he's a whole war-party in breech-cloths an' war-paint just 'cause he's got his man."

"He's gettin' close to th' line," Lanky remarked.

"Yes, because we've been turnin' their cows."

"Reckon he won't stop us none to speak of."

Doc had stopped and was watching them and while he looked a cow blundered out of the brush and started to cross the line. Hopalong spurred forward to stop it, followed by Lanky, and Doc rode to intercept them.

"G'wan back, you bone-yard!" Hopalong shouted, firing his Colt in front of the animal, which now turned and ran back.

Doc slid to a stand, his Colt out. "What do you think you're doing with that cow?"

"None of yore business!" Hopalong retorted.

Doc backed away so he could watch Lanky, his hand leaping up, and Hopalong fired. Doc dropped the weapon and grabbed at his right arm, cursing wildly.

Hopalong rode closer. "Next time you gets any curious about what I'm doing, you better write. You're a fine specimen to pull a gun on me, you are!"

"You'll stop turnin' our cows, or you'll get a pass to hell!" retorted Doc. "We won't stand for it no more, an' when th' boys hears about this, you'll have all you can take care of."

"I ain't got nothing to do but ride th' line an' answer questions like I did yourn," Hopalong rejoined. "I will have lots of time to take care of any little trouble that blows up from yore way. But *Meeker's* th' man I want to see. Tell him to take a herd across this line, will you?"

"You'll see him!" snapped Doc, wheeling and riding off.

"Things are movin' so fast you better send for Buck," Lanky suggested. "Hell'll be poppin' down here purty soon."

"I'll tell him what's going on, but there ain't no use of bringing him down here till we has to," Hopalong replied. "We can handle 'em. But I reckon Johnny had better go up an' tell him."

"Johnny ought to be riding this way purty quick; he's coming from th' hills."

"We'll meet him an' get him off."

They met Johnny and when he had learned of his mission he protested against being sent away from the line when things were getting crowded. "I don't want to miss th' fun!" he exclaimed. "Send Red, or Lanky."

"Red's too handy with th' Winchester; we might need him," Hopalong replied, smiling.

"Then you go, Lanky," Johnny suggested. "I'm better'n you with th' Colt."

"You're better'n nothing!' retorted Lanky. "You do what you're told, an' quick. Nothing will happen while you're gone, anyhow."

"Then why don't you want to go?"

"I don't want th' ride," Lanky replied. "It's too fur."

"Huh!" snorted Johnny. "Too bad about you an' th' ride! Poor old man, scared of sixty miles. I'll toss up with you."

"One of you has got to ride to Red an' tell him. He mustn't get caught unexpected," Hopalong remarked.

"What do you call?" asked Johnny, flipping a coin and catching it when it came down.

"All right, that's fair enough. Heads," Lanky replied.

"Whoop! It's tails!" cried Johnny, wheeling. "I'm going for Red," and he was gone before Lanky had time to object.

"Blasted Kid!" Lanky snorted. "How'd I know it was tails?"

"That's yore lookout," laughed Hopalong. "You ought to know him by this time. It's yore own fault."

"I'll tan his hide one of these fine days," Lanky promised. "He's too fresh," and he galloped off to cover the thirty miles between him and the bunk house in the least possible time so as to return as soon as he could.

VI

♦

Meeker Is Told

When Antonio had covered half of the distance between the line and the H2 bunk house he was hailed from a chaparral and saw Benito ride into view. He told his satellite what had occurred in the valley, gave him a message for Shaw, who was now on the mesa, and cantered on to tell Meeker his version of the morning's happenings.

The H2 foreman was standing by the corral when his broncho-buster rode up, and he stared. "Where'd you get that welt on th' face?" he demanded.

Antonio told him, with many exclamations and angry gestures, that he had ridden through the valley to see if there were any H2 cows grazing on it, that he had found a small herd and was about to return to his own range when he was held up and struck by Hopalong, who accused him of having driven the cattle across the line. When he had denied this he had been called a liar and threatened with death if he was ever again caught on that side of the line.

"By God!" cried the foreman. "That's purty high-handed! I'll give 'em something to beller about when I finds out just what I want to do!"

"IIc say, 'Tell that boss of yourn to no send you, send heemself nex' time.' He say he weel keel you on sight. I say he can't. He laugh, *so*!" laughing in a bloodcurdling manner. "He say he keel nex' man an' cows that cross line. He ees *uno* devil!"

"He will, hey!" Meeker exclaimed, thoroughly angered. "We'll give him all th' chance he wants when we get things fixed. 'Tony, what did you do about getting those two men you spoke of? You went down to Eagle, didn't you?"

"*Si, si,*" assured Antonio. "They come, *pronto*. They can keel heem. They come to-day; *quien sabe?*"

"I'll do my own killin'—but here comes Doc," Meeker replied. "Looks mad, too. Mebby they was going to kill him an' he objected. Hullo, Doc; what's th' matter?"

"That Cassidy damn near blowed my arm off," Doc replied. "Caught him turnin' back one of our cows an' told him not to. When I backed off so I could keep one eye on his friend he up an' plugs me through my gun arm."

"I see; they owns th' earth!" Meeker roared. "Shootin' up my men 'cause they stick up for me! Come in th' house an' get that arm fixed. We can talk in there," he said, glancing at Antonio. "They cut 'Tony across th' face with a quirt 'cause he was ridin' in their valley!"

"Let's get th' gang together an' wipe 'em off th' earth," Doc suggested, following Meeker towards the house.

Mary looked up when they entered: "What's th' matter, Dad? Why, are you hurt, Doc?"

"Don't ask questions, girl," Meeker ordered. "Get us some hot water an' some clean cloth. Sit down, Doc; we'll fix it in no time."

"We better clean 'em up to-morrow," Doc remarked.

"No; there ain't no use of losin' men fighting if there's any other way. You know there's a good strong line house on th' top of Lookout Peak, don't you?"

"Shore; reg'lar fort. They calls it Number Three."

Mary had returned and was tearing a bandage, listening intently to what was being said.

"What's th' matter with getting in that some day soon an' holdin' it for good?" asked the foreman. "It overlooks a lot of range, an' once we're in it it'll cost 'em a lot of lives to get it back—if they can get it back."

"You're right!" cried Doc, eagerly. "Let me an' Curley get in there to-night an' hold her for you. We can do it."

"You can't do that. Somebody sleeps in it nights. Nope, we've got to work some scheme to get it in th' daylight. They are bound to have it guarded, an' we've got to coax him out somehow. I don't know how, but I will before many hours pass. Hullo, who's this?" he asked, seeing two strangers approach the house.

"The new punchers," grunted Doc.

"Hey, you," cried Meeker through the open door. "You go down to th' corral an' wait for me."

"Sure thing."

"What's th' matter, Dad?" asked Mary. "How did Doc get shot?"

Meeker looked up angrily, but his face softened.

"There's a whole lot th' matter, Mary. That Bar-20 shore is gettin' hot-headed. Cassidy hit 'Tony across th' face with a quirt an' shot Doc. 'Tony was riding through that valley, an' Doc told Cassidy not to drive back a cow of ourn."

She flushed. "There must 'a been more'n that, Dad. He wouldn't 'a shot for that. I know it."

"You know it!" cried Meeker, astonished. "How do you know it?"

"He ain't that kind. I know he ain't."

"I asked how you knew it!"

She looked down and then faced him. "Because I know him, because he ain't that kind. What did you say to him, Doc?"

Meeker's face was a study and Doc flushed, for she was looking him squarely in the eyes.

"What did you say to him?" she repeated. "Did you make a gun-play?"

"Well, by God!" shouted Meeker, leaping to his feet. "You know him, hey! 'He ain't that kind!' How long have you known him, an' where'd you meet him?"

"This is no time to talk of that," she replied, her spirit aroused. "Ask Doc what he did an' said to get shot. Look at him; he lied when he told you about it."

"I told him to quit driving our cows back," Doc cried. "Of course I had my hand on my gun when I said it. I'd been a fool if I hadn't, wouldn't I?"

"That ain't all," she remarked. "Did you try to use it?"

Meeker was staring first at one and then at the other, not knowing just what to say. Doc looked at him and his mind was made up.

"What'd you do, Doc?" he asked.

"I said: 'What are you doing with that cow?' an' he said it wasn't none of my business. I got mad then an' jerked my gun loose, but he got me first. I wasn't going to shoot. I was only getting ready for him if he tried to."

"How did he know you wasn't going to shoot?" Meeker demanded. "Reckon I can't blame him for that. He must be quick on th' draw."

"Quickest I ever saw. He had his gun out to shoot in front of a cow. At th' time I thought he was going to kill it. That's what made me get in so quick. He slid it back in th' holster an' faced me. I told you what happened then."

"Well, we've got to show them fellers they can't fool with us an' get away with it," Meeker replied. "An' I've got to have th' use of that crick somehow. I'll think of some way to square things."

"Wait, I'll go with you," Doc remarked, following the other towards the door.

"You go in th' bunk house an' wait for me.

"Wonder how much 'Tony didn't tell," mused the foreman, as he went towards the corral. "But I've got to notice plays like that or they'll think I'm scared of 'em. I'll go up an' have it out, an' when I get ready I'll show them swaggerin' bucks what's what."

When he returned he saw Antonio leaning against his

shack, for he was not tolerated by the rest of the outfit and so lived alone. He looked at his foreman and leered knowingly, and then went inside the building, where he laughed silently. "That's a joke, all right! Meeker hiring two of my friends to watch his cows an' do his spying! We'll skin this range before we're through."

Meeker frowned when he caught his broncho-buster's look and he growled: "You never did look good, an' that welt shore makes you look more like th' devil than ever." He glanced at the house and the frown deepened. "So you know Cassidy! That's a *nice* thing to tell me! I'll just go up an' see that coyote, right now," and he went for his horse, muttering and scowling.

Antonio knew of a herd of cows and calves which had not been included in the H2 roundup, and which were fattening on an outlying range. There was also a large herd of Bar-20 cattle growing larger every day on the western range far outside the boundaries. Benito was scouting, Shaw and the others were nearly ready for work on the mesa. Added to this was the constantly growing hostility along the line, and this would blaze before he and Benito had finished their work. Everything considered he was very much pleased and even his personal vengeance was provided for. Doc had more cause for animosity against Hopalong than he had, and if the Bar-20 puncher should be killed some day when Doc rode the northern range, Doc would be blamed for it. But Meeker had not acted as he should have done when two of his men had been hurt on the same day, and that must be remedied. The faster things moved towards fighting the less chance there would be of the plot becoming known.

Antonio was the broncho-buster of the H2 because he was a positive genius at the work, and he was a good, all-around cowman; but he was cruel to a degree with both horses and cattle. Because of his fitness Meeker had

overlooked his undesirable qualities, which he had in
plenty. He was entirely too fond of liquor and gambling,
was uncertain in his hours, and used his time as he saw
fit when not engaged in breaking horses. A natural liar,
vindictive and with a temper dry as tinder, he was shunned
by the other members of the outfit. This filled his heart
with hatred for them and for Meeker, who did not interfere. He swore many times that he would square up everything some day, and the day was getting closer.

In appearance he was about medium height, but his
sloping shoulders and lax carriage gave his arms the appearance of being abnormally long. His face was sharp
and narrow, while his thin, wiry body seemed almost devoid of flesh. Like most cowboys he was a poor walker
and his toes turned in. Such was Antonio, who longed
to gamble with Fortune in a dangerous game for stakes
which to him were large, and who had already suggested
to Meeker that the line house on Lookout Peak was the
key to the situation. It was the germ, which grew slowly
in the foreman's brain and became more feasible and insistent day by day, and it accounted for his fits of abstraction; it would not do to fail if the attempt were made.

VII

◆

Hopalong Meets Meeker

When Meeker was within a mile of the line he met
Curley, told him what had occurred and that he
was going to find Hopalong. Curley smiled and replied
that he had seen that person less than ten minutes ago
and that he was riding towards the peak, and alone.

"We'll go after him," Meeker replied. "You come because I want to face him in force so he won't start no gun-play an' make me kill him. That'd set hell to pop."

Hopalong espied Johnny far to the east and he smiled as he remembered the celerity with which that individual had departed after glancing at the coin.

"There ain't no flies on th' Kid, all right," he laughed, riding slowly so Johnny could join him. He saw Curley riding south and looked over the rough plain for other H2 punchers. Some time later as he passed a chaparral he glanced back to see what had become of his friend, but found that he had disappeared. When he wheeled to watch for him he saw Meeker and Curley coming towards him and he shook his holster to be sure his Colt was not jammed in it too tightly.

"Well, here's where th' orchestry tunes up, all right," he muttered grimly. "Licked Antonio, plugged Doc, an' sent word to Meeker to come up if he wasn't scared. He's come, an' now I'll have to lick two more. If they push me I'll shoot to kill!"

The H2 foreman rode ahead of his companion and stopped when fifty yards from the alert line-rider. Pushing his sombrero back on his head, he lost no time in skirmishing. "Did you chase my broncho-buster out of yore valley, cut his face with yore quirt, an' shoot Doc? Did you send word to me that you'd kill me if I showed myself?"

"Was you ever an auctioneer," calmly asked Hopalong, "or a book agent?"

"What's that got to do with it?" Meeker demanded. "You heard what I said."

"I don't know nothing about yore broncho-buster, taking one thing at a time, which is proper."

"What! You didn't drive him out, or cut him?"

"No; why?" asked Hopalong, chuckling.

"He says you did—an' somebody quirted him."

"He's loco—he wasn't in th' valley," Hopalong replied.

"Think he could get in that valley? Him, or any other man we didn't want in?"

"You're devilish funny!" retorted Meeker, riding slowly forward, followed by his companion, who began to edge away from his foreman. "Since you are so exact, did you chase him off yore range an' push him over th' line at th' point of yore gun?"

"You've got me. Better not come too close—my cayuse don't like gettin' crowded."

"That's all right," Meeker retorted, not heeding the warning. "Do you mean to tell me you don't know? Yore name's Cassidy, ain't it?" he asked, angrily, his determination to avoid fighting rapidly becoming lost.

"That's my own, shore 'nuf name," Hopalong answered, and then: "Do you mean Antonio, the one I caught stealing our range?"

"Yes!" snapped Meeker, stopping again.

"Why didn't you say so, then, 'stead of calling him yore broncho-buster?" Hopalong demanded. "How do I know who yore broncho-buster is? I don't know what every land pirate does in this country."

"Then you shot Doc—do you know who I mean this time?" sarcastically asked the H2 foreman.

"Oh, shore. He didn't get his gun out quick enough when he went after it, did he? Any more I can tell you before I begins to say things, too?"

Meeker, angered greatly by Hopalong's contemptuous inflection and the reckless assertiveness of his every word and look, began to ride to describe a circle around the Bar-20 puncher, Curley going the other way.

"You said you'd kill me when you saw me, didn't you, you—"

Hopalong was backing away so as to keep both men in front of him, alert, eager, and waiting for the signal to begin his two-handed shooting. "I ain't a whole lot deaf—I can hear you from where you are. You better stop, for I've ridden out of tighter holes than this, an' you'll shore get a pass to hell if you crowd me too much!"

Adown th' road, an' gun in hand,
Comes Whiskey Bill, mad Whiskey Bill—

This fragment of song floated out of a chaparral about twenty yards behind Hopalong, who grinned pleasantly when he heard it. Now he knew where Johnny was, and now he had the whip hand without touching his guns; while the youngster was not in sight he was all the more dangerous, since he presented no target. Johnny knew this and was greatly pleased thereby, and he was more than pleased by the way Hopalong had been talking.

The effect of the singing was instant and marked on Meeker and his companion, for they not only stopped suddenly and swore, but began to back away, glancing around in an endeavor to locate the joker in the deck. This they failed to do because Johnny was far too wise to advertise his exact whereabouts. Meeker looked at Curley and Curley looked at Meeker, both uneasy and angry.

"As I was sayin' before th' concert began," Hopalong remarked, laughing shortly, "it's a pass to hell if you crowd me too much. Now, Meeker, you'll listen to me an' I'll tell you what I didn't have time to say before: I told an Antonio that th' next herd of yourn to cross th' line should be brought in by you, 'less you was scared to run th' risks yore men had to take. He said you'd kill me for that message, an' I told him you knew where you could find me. Now about Doc: When a man pulls a gun on me he wants to be quicker than *he* was or he'll shore get hurt. I could 'a killed him just as easy as to plug his gun arm, an' just as easy as I could 'a plugged both of you if you pulled on me. You came up here looking for my scalp an' if you still wants it I'll go away from th' song bird in the chaparral an' give you th' chance. I'd ruther let things stay as they are, though if you wants, I'll take both you an' Curley, half-mile run together, with Colts."

"No, I didn't come up here after your scalp, but I got mad after I found you. How long is this going to last? I won't stand for it much longer, nohow."

"You'll have to see Buck. I'm obeying orders, which are to hold th' line again you, which I'll do."

"H'm!" replied Meeker, and then: "Do you know my girl?"

Hopalong thought quickly. "Why, I've seen her ridin' around some. But why?"

"She says she knows you," persisted Meeker, frowning.

The frown gave Hopalong his cue, but he hardly knew what to say, not knowing what she had said about it.

"Hey, you!" he suddenly cried to Curley. "Keep yore hand from that gun!"

"I didn't—"

"You're lying! Any more of that an' I'll gimlet you!"

"What in hell are you doing, Curley?" demanded Meeker, the girl question out of his mind instantly. He had been looking closely at Hopalong and didn't know that Curley was innocent of any attempt to use his Colt.

"I tell—"

"Get out of here! I've wasted too much time already. Go home, where that gun won't worry you. You, too, Meeker! Bring an imitation bad-man up here an' sayin' you didn't want my scalp! Flit!"

"I'll go when I'm damn good and ready!" retorted Meeker, angry again. "You're too blasted bossy, you are!" he added, riding towards the man who had shot Doc.

A-looking for some place to land—

floated out of the chaparral and he stiffened in the saddle and stopped.

"Come on, Curley! We can't lick pot-shooters. An' let that gun alone!"

"Damn it! I tell you I wasn't going for my gun!" Curley yelled.

"Get out of here!" blazed Hopalong, riding forward.

They rode away slowly, consulting in low voices. Then the foreman turned and looked back. "You better be careful how you shoot my punchers! They ain't all like Doc."

"Then you're lucky," Hopalong retorted. "You keep yore cows on yore side an' we won't hurt none of yore outfit."

When they had gone Hopalong wheeled to look for Johnny and saw him crawling out of a chaparral, dragging a rifle after him. He capered about, waving the rifle and laughing with joy and Hopalong had to laugh with him. When they were rid of the surplus of the merriment Johnny patted the rifle. "Reckon they was shore up against a marked deck that time! Did you see 'em stiffen when I warbled? Acted like they had roped a puma an' didn't know what to do with it. Gee, it was funny!"

"You're all right, Kid," laughed Hopalong. "It was yore best play—you couldn't 'a done better."

"Shore," replied Johnny. "I had my sights glued to Curley's shirt pocket, an' he'd been plumb disgusted if he'd tried to do what you said he did. I couldn't 'a missed him with a club at that range. I nearly died when you pushed Meeker's girl question up that blind canyon. It was a peach of a throw, all right. Bet he ain't remembered yet that he didn't get no answer to it. We're going to have some blamed fine times down here before everything is settled, ain't we?"

"I reckon so, Kid. I'm going to leave you now an' look around by West Arroyo. You hang around th' line."

"All right—so long."

"Can you catch yore cayuse?"

"Shore I can; he's hobbled," came the reply from behind a spur of the chaparral. *"Stand still, you hen! All right, Hoppy."*

Johnny cantered away and, feeling happy, began singing:

> *Adown th' road, an' gun in hand,*
> *Comes Whiskey Bill, mad Whiskey Bill;*
> *A-looking for some place to land*
> *Comes Whiskey Bill.*
> *An' everybody'd like to be*
> *Ten miles away behind a tree*
> *When on his joyous, achin' spree*
> *Starts Whiskey Bill.*
>
> *Th' times have changed since you made love,*
> *Oh, Whiskey Bill, oh, Whiskey Bill;*
> *Th' happy sun grinned up above*
> *At Whiskey Bill.*
> *An' down th' middle of th' street*
> *Th' sheriff comes on toe-in feet,*
> *A-wishing for one fretful peek*
> *At Whiskey Bill.*
>
> *Th' cows go grazin o'er th' lea—*
> *Pore Whiskey Bill, pore Whiskey Bill,*
> *An' aching thoughts pour in on me*
> *Of Whiskey Bill.*
> *Th' sheriff up an' found his stride,*
> *Bill's soul went shootin' down th' slide—*
> *How are things on th' Great Divide,*
> *Oh, Whiskey Bill?*

VIII

♦

On the Edge of the Desert

Thunder Mesa was surrounded by almost impenetrable chaparrals, impenetrable to horse and rider except along certain alleys, but not too dense for a man on foot. These stretched away on all sides as far as the eye could see and made the desolate prospect all the more forbidding. It rose a sheer hundred feet into the air, its sides smooth rock and affording no footing except a narrow, precarious ledge which slanted up the face of the southern end, too broken and narrow to permit of a horse ascending, but passable to a man.

The top of the mesa was about eight acres in extent and was rocky and uneven, cut by several half-filled fissures which did not show on the walls. Uninviting as the top might be considered it had one feature which was uncommon, for the cataclysm of nature which had caused this mass of rock to tower above the plain had given to it a spring which bubbled out of a crack in the rock and into a basin cut by itself; from there it flowed down the wall and into a shallow depression to the rock below, where it made a small water hole before flowing through the chaparrals, where it sank into the sand and became lost half a mile from its source.

At the point where the slanting ledge met the top of the mesa was a hut built of stones and adobe, its rear wall being part of a projecting wall of rock. Narrow, deep loopholes had been made in the other walls and a rough door, massive and tight fitting, closed the small doorway. The roof, laid across cedar poles which ran from wall to wall, was thick and flat and had a generous layer of adobe to repel the rays of the scorching sun. Placed as it was the hut overlooked the trail leading to it from the plain, and should it be defended by determined men, assault by that path would be foolhardy.

On the plain around the mesa extended a belt of sparse grass, some hundreds of feet wide at the narrowest point and nearly a mile at the widest, over which numerous rocks and boulders and clumps of chaparral lay scattered. On this pasture were about three score cattle, most of them being yearlings, but all bearing the brand HQQ and a diagonal ear cut. These were being watched by a careless cowboy, although it was belittling their scanty intelligence to suppose that they would leave the water and grass, poor as the latter was, to stray off onto the surrounding desert.

At the base of the east wall of the mesa was a rough corral of cedar poles set on end, held together by rawhide strips, which, put on green, tightened with the strength of steel cables when dried by the sun. In its shadow another man watched the cattle while he worked in a desultory way at repairing a saddle. Within the corral a man was bending over a cow while two others held it down. Its feet were tied and it was panting, wild-eyed and frightened. The man above it stepped to a glowing fire a few paces away and took from it a hot iron, with which he carefully traced over the small brand already borne by the animal. With a final flourish he stepped back, regarding the work with approval, and thrust the iron into the sand. Taking a knife from his pocket he trimmed the V notch in its ear to the same slanting cut seen on the cattle outside on the pasture. He tossed the bit of cartilage from him, stepping back and nodding to his companions, who loosened the ropes and leaped back, allowing the animal to escape.

Shaw, who had altered the H2 brand, turned to one of the others and laughed heartily. "Good job, eh Manuel? Th' H2 won't know their cow now!"

Manuel grinned. *"Si, si;* eet ees!" he cried. He was cook for the gang, a bosom friend of Benito and Antonio. In his claw-like fingers he held a husk cigarette, without which he was seldom seen. He spoke very little but watched always, his eyes usually turned eastward. He seemed to be almost as much afraid of the east as Cavalry was of the west, where the desert lay. He ridiculed Cavalry's terror of the desert and explained why the east was to be feared the more, for the eastern danger rode horses and could come to them.

"Hope 'Tony fixes up that line war purty soon, eh, Cavalry?" remarked Shaw, suddenly turning to the third man in the group.

Cavalry was staring moodily towards the desert and did not hear him.

"Cavalry! Get that desert off yore mind! Do you want to go loco? Who's going to take th' next drive an' bring back th' flour, you or Clausen?"

"It's Clausen's turn next."

Manuel slouched away and began to climb the slanting path up the mesa. Shaw watched him reflectively and laughed. "There he goes again. Beats th' devil how scared he is, spending most of his time on th' lookout. Why, he's blamed near as scared of them punchers as you are of that skillet out yonder."

"We ain't got no kick, have we?" retorted Cavalry. "Ain't he looking out for us at th' same time?"

"I don't know about that," Shaw replied, frowning. "I ain't got no love for Manuel. If he saw 'em coming an' could get away he'd sneak off without saying a word. It'd give him a chance to get away while we held 'em."

"We'll see him go, then; there's only one way down."

"Oh, the' devil with him!" Shaw exclaimed. "What do you think of th' chances of startin' that range war?"

"From what Antonio says it looks good."

"Yes. But he'll get caught some day, or night, an' pay for it with his life."

Cavalry shrugged his shoulders. "I reckon so. I'd ruther they'd get him out there than to follow him here. If he goes, I hope it's sudden, so he won't have time to squeal."

"He's a malignant devil, an' he hates that H2 outfit like blazes," replied Shaw. "An' now he's got a pizen grudge agin' th' Bar-20. He might let his hate get th' upper hand an' start in to square things; if he does that he'll over-reach, an' get killed."

"I reckon so; but he's clever as th' devil hisself."

"Well, if he gets too big-headed out here Hall will take care of him, all right," Shaw laughed.

"I don't like them saddled us with," Cavalry remarked. "There's Manuel an' Benito. One of 'em is here all th' time an 'close to you, too, if you remember. Then he's going to put two or three on th' range; why?"

"Suspects we'll steal some of his share, I reckon. An' if he gets in trouble with us they'll be on his side. Oh, he's no fool."

"If he 'tends to business an' forgets his grudges it'll be a good thing for us. That Bar-20 has got an awful number of cows. An' there's th' H2, an' th' other two up north."

"We've tackled th' hardest job first—th' Bar-20," replied Shaw, laughing. "I used to know some fellers what said that outfit couldn't be licked. They died trying to prove themselves liars."

"Wonder how much money 'Tony totes around on him?" asked Cavalry.

"Not much; he's too wise. He's cached it somewhere. Was you reckonin' on takin' it away from him at th' end?"

"No, no. I just wondered what he did with it."

The man at the gate looked up. "Here comes 'Tony."

Shaw and his companion rode forward to meet him.

"What's up?" cried Shaw.

"I have started th' war," Antonio replied, a cruel smile playing over his sharp face. "They'll be fightin' purty soon."

"That's good," responded Shaw. "Tell us about it."

Antonio, with many gestures and much conceit, told of the trick he had played on Hopalong, and he took care to lose no credit in the telling. He passed lightly over the trouble between Doc and the Bar-20 puncher, but intimated that he had caused it. He finished by saying: "You send to th' same place tomorrow an' Benito'll have some cows for you. They'll soon give us our chance, an' it'll be easy then."

"Mebby it will be easy," replied Shaw, "but that rests with you. You've got to play yore cards plumb cautious. You've done fine so far, but if you ain't careful you'll go to hell in a hurry an' take us with you. You can't fool 'em all th' time, someday they'll get suspicious an' swap ideas. An' when they do that it means fight for us."

Antonio smiled and thought how easy it might be, if the outfits grew suspicious and he learned of it in time, to discover tracks and other things and tell Meeker he was sure there was organized rustling and that all tracks pointed to Thunder Mesa. He could ride across the border before any of his partners had time to confess and implicate him. But he assured Shaw that he would be careful, adding: "No, I won't make no mistakes. I hate 'em all too much to grow careless."

"That's just where you'll miss fire," the other rejoined. "You'll pamper your grouch till you forget everything else. You better be satisfied to get square by taking their cows."

"Don't worry about that."

"All right. Here's yore money for th' last herd," he said digging down into his pocket and handing Antonio some gold coins. "You know how to get more?"

Antonio took the money, considered a moment and then pocketed it, laughing. "Good! But I mus' go back now.

I won't be out here again very soon; it's too risky. Send me my share by Benito," he called over his shoulder as he started off.

The two rustlers watched him and Cavalry shook his head slowly. "I'm plumb scairt he'll bungle it. If he does we'll get caught like rats in a trap."

"If we're up there we can hold off a thousand," Shaw replied, looking up the wall.

"Here comes Hall," announced the man at the gate.

The newcomer swept up and leaped from his hot and tired horse. "I found them other ranches are keeping their men ridin' over th' range an' along th' trails—I near got caught once," he reported. "We'll have to be careful how we drives to th' construction camps."

"They'll get tired watchin' after a while," replied the leader. "'Tony was just here."

"I don't care if he's in hell," retorted Hall. "He'll peach on us to save his mangy skin, one of these days."

"We've got to chance it."

"Where's Frisco?"

"Down to Eagle for grub to tide us over for a few days."

"Huh!" exclaimed Hall. "Everything considered we're goin' to fight like th' devil out here someday. Down to Eagle!"

"We can fight!" retorted Shaw. "An' if we has to run for it, there's th' desert."

"I'd ruther die right here fighting than on that desert," remarked Cavalry, shuddering. "When I go I want to go quick, an' not be tortured for 'most a week." He had an insistent and strong horror of that gray void of sand and alkali so near at hand and so far across. He was nervous and superstitious, and it seemed always to be calling him. Many nights he had awakened in a cold sweat because he had dreamed it had him, and often it was all he could do to resist going out to it.

Shaw laughed gratingly. "You don't like it, do you?"

Hall smiled and walked towards the slanting trail.

"Why, it ain't bad," he called over his shoulder.

"It's an earthly hell!" Cavalry exclaimed. He glanced up the mesa wall. "We can hold that till we starve, or run out of cartridges—then what?"

"You're a calamity howler!" snapped Shaw. "That desert has wore a saddle sore on yore nerves somethin' awful. Don't think about it so much! It can't come to you, an' you ain't going to it," he laughed, trying to wipe out the suggestion of fear that had been awakened in him by the thought of the desert as a place of refuge. He had found a wanderer, denuded of clothes, sweating blood and hopelessly mad one day when he and Cavalry had ridden towards the desert; and the sight of the unfortunate's dying agonies had remained with him ever since. "We ain't going to die out here—they won't look for us where they don't think there's any grass or water."

Fragments of Manuel's song floated down to them as they strode towards the trail, and reassured that all would be well, their momentary depression was banished by the courage of their hearts.

The desert lay beyond, quiet; ominous by its very silence and inertia; a ghastly, malevolent aspect in its every hollow; patient, illimitable, scorching; fascinating in its horrible calm, sinister, forbidding, hellish. It had waited through centuries—and was still waiting, like the gigantic web of the Spider of Thirst.

IX

♦

On the Peak

Hopalong Cassidy had the most striking personality of all the men in his outfit; humorous, courageous to the point of foolishness, eager for fight or frolic, nonchalant when one would expect him to be quite otherwise, curious, loyal to a fault, and the best man with a Colt in the Southwest, he was a paradox, and a puzzle even to his most intimate friends. With him life was a humorous recurrence of sensations, a huge pleasant joke instinctively tolerated, but not worth the price cowards pay to keep it. He had come onto the range when a boy and since that time he had laughingly carried his life in his open hand, and although there had been many attempts to snatch it he still carried it there, and just as recklessly.

Quick in decisions and quick to suspect evil designs against him and his ranch, he was different from his foreman, whose temperament was more optimistic. When Buck had made him foreman of the line riders he had no fear that Meeker or his men would take many tricks, for his faith in Hopalong's wits and ability was absolute. He had such faith that he attended to what he had to do about the ranch house and did not appear on the line until he had decided to call on Meeker and put the question before him once and for all. If the H2 foreman did not admit the agreement and promise to abide by it then he would be told to look for trouble.

While Buck rode towards Lookout Peak, Hopalong dismounted at the line house perched on its top and found Red Connors seated on the rough bench by the door. Red, human firebrand both in hair and temper, was

Hopalong's loyal chum—in the eyes of the other neither could do wrong. Red was cleaning his rifle, the pride of his heart, a wicked-shooting Winchester which used the Government cartridge containing seventy grains of powder and five hundred grains of lead. With his rifle he was as expert as his friend was with the Colt, and up to six hundred yards, its limit with accuracy, he could do about what he wished with it.

"Hullo, you," said Red, pleasantly. "You looks peevish."

"An' you look foolish. What you doing?"

"Minding my business."

"Hard work?" sweetly asked Hopalong, carelessly seating himself on the small wooden box which lay close to his friend.

"Hey, you!" cried Red, leaping up and hauling him away. "You bust them sights an' you'll be sorry! Ain't you got no sense?"

"Sights? What are you going to do with 'em?"

"Wear 'em 'round my neck for a charm! What'd you reckon I'd do with 'em!"

"Didn't know. I didn't think you'd put 'em on that thing," Hopalong replied, looking with contempt at his friend's rifle. "Honest, you ain't a-goin' to put 'em on that lead ranch, are you? Yo're like th' Indians—want a lot of shots to waste without re-loadin'."

"I ain't wasting no shots, an' I'm going to put sights on that lead ranch, too. These old ones are too coarse," Red replied, carefully placing the box out of danger. "Now you can sit down."

"Thanks; please can I smoke?"

Red grunted, pushed down the lever of the rifle, and began to re-assemble the parts, his friend watching the operation. When Red tried to slip the barrel into its socket Hopalong laughed and told him to first draw out the magazine, if he wanted to have any success.

The line foreman took a cartridge from the pile on the bench and compared it with one which he took from his belt, a huge, 45-caliber Sharps special, shooting five hundred and fifty grains of lead with one hundred and twenty grains of powder out of a shell over three inches long; a cartridge which shot with terrific force and for a great distance, the weight of the large ball assuring accuracy at long ranges. Besides this four-inch cartridge the Government ammunition appeared dwarfed.

"When are you going to wean yoreself from popping these musket caps, Red?" he asked, tossing the smaller cartridge away and putting his own back in his belt.

"Well, you've got gall!" snorted Red, going out for his cartridge. Returning with it he went back to work on his gun, his friend laughing at his clumsy fingers.

"Yore fingers are all thumbs, an' sore at that."

"Never mind my fingers. Have you seen Johnny around?"

"Yes; he was watching one of them new H2 punchers. He'll go off th' handle one of these days. He reminds me a whole lot of a bull-pup chained with a corral-ful of cats."

Red laughed and nodded. "Where's Lanky?"

"Johnny said he was at Number Four fixin' that saddle again. He ain't done nothin' for th' last month but fix it. Purty soon there won't be none of it left to fix."

"There certainly won't!"

"His saddle an' yore gun make a good pair."

"Let up about the gun. You can't say nothin' more about it without repeatin' yoreself."

"It's a sawed-off carbine. I'd ruther have a Spencer any day."

"You remind me a whole lot of a feller I once knowed," Red retorted.

"That so?" asked Hopalong suspiciously. "Was he so nice?"

"No; he was a fool," Red responded, going into the house.

"Then that's where you got it, for they say it's catching."

Red stuck his head out of the door. "On second thought you remind me of another feller."

"You must'a knowed some good people."

"An' he was a liar."

"Hullo, Hop Wah!" came from the edge of the hilltop and Hopalong wheeled to see Skinny Thompson approaching.

"What you doing?" Skinny asked, using his stock question for beginning a conversation.

"Painting white spots on pink elephants!"

"Where's Red?"

"In th' shack, rubbin' 'em off again."

"Johnny chased that Antonio off'n th' ranch," Skinny offered, grinning.

"Good for him!" cried Hopalong.

"Johnny's all right—here comes Buck," Red said, coming out of the house. "Johnny's with him, too. Hullo, Kid!"

"Hullo, Brick-top!" retorted Johnny, who did not like his nickname. No one treated him as anything but a boy and he resented it at times.

"Did he chase you far?" Hopalong queried.

"I'd like to see anybody chase me!"

Buck smiled. "How are things down here?"

Hopalong related what had occurred and the foreman nodded. "I'm going down to see Meeker—he's th' only man who can tell me what we're to look for. I don't want to keep so many men down here. Frenchy has got all he can handle, an' I want somebody up in Two. So long."

"Let me an' Red go with you, Buck," cried Hopalong.

"Me, too!" exclaimed Johnny, excitedly.

"You stay home, an' don't worry about me," replied the foreman, riding off.

"I don't like to see him go alone," Hopalong muttered.

"He may get a raw deal down there. But if he does we'll wipe 'em off'n th' earth."

"Mamma! Look there!" softly cried Johnny, staring towards the other side of the plateau, where Mary Meeker rode past. Red and Skinny were astonished and Johnny and Hopalong pretended to be; but all removed their sombreros while she remained in sight. Johnny was watching Hopalong's face, but when Red glanced around he was staring over the Hill.

"Gosh, ain't she a ripper!" he exclaimed softly.

"She is," admitted Skinny. "She shore is."

Hopalong rubbed his nose reflectively and turned to Red. "Did you ever notice how pretty a freckle is?"

Red stared, and his friend continued: "Take a purty girl an' stick a freckle on her nose an' it sort of takes yore breath."

Red grinned. "I ain't never took a purty girl an' stuck a freckle on her nose, so I can't say."

Hopalong flushed at the laughter and Skinny cried, joyously: "She's got two of us already! Meeker's got us licked if he'll let her show herself once in a while. Oh, these young fellers! Nothing can rope 'em so quick as a female, an' th' purtier she is th' quicker she can do it."

A warning light came into Hopalong's eyes. "Nobody in this outfit'll go back on Buck for all th' purty women in th' world!"

"Good boy!" thought Johnny.

"We've got to watch th' Kid, just th' same," laughed Skinny.

"I'll knock yore head off!" cried Johnny. "You're sore 'cause you know you ain't got no chance with women while me an' Hoppy are around!"

Red looked critically at Hopalong and snickered. "If we've got to look like him to catch th' women, thank God we don't want 'em!"

"Is that so!" retorted Hopalong.

"Say," drawled Skinny. "Wouldn't th' Kid look nice hobbled with matrimony? That is, after he grows up."

"You go to th' devil!"

"Gee, Kid, you look bloodthirsty," laughed Red.

"You go to," Johnny retorted, swinging into the saddle. "I'm going along th' line to see what's loose."

"I'll lick you when I see you again!" shouted Red, grinning.

Johnny turned and twirled his fingers at his red-haired friend. "Yah, you ain't man enough!"

"Johnny's gettin' more hungry for a fight every day," Hopalong remarked. "He's itching for one."

"So was you a few years back, an' you ain't changed none," replied Red. "You used to ride around looking for fights."

"To hear you talk, anybody'd think you was a Angel of Peace," Hopalong retorted.

"One's as bad as th' other, so shut up," Skinny remarked, going into the house for a drink.

X

Buck Visits Meeker

As Buck rode south he went over the boundary trouble in all its phases, and the more he thought about it the firmer his resolution grew to hold the line at any cost. He had gone to great expense and labor to improve the water supply in the valley and he saw no reason why the H2 could not do the same; and to him an agreement was an agreement, and ran with the land. What Meeker thought about it was not the question—the point at issue was whether or not the H2 could take the line and use the valley, and if they could they were welcome to it.

But while there was any possibility for a peaceable settlement it would be foolish to start fighting, for one range war had spread to alarming proportions and had been costly to life and property. Then there was the certainty that once war had begun, rustling would develop. But, be the consequences what they might, he would fight to the last to hold that which was rightfully his. He was not going to Meeker to beg a compromise, or to beg him to let the valley alone; he was riding to tell the H2 foreman what he could expect if he forced matters.

When he rode past the H2 corrals he was curiously regarded by a group of punchers who lounged near them, and he went straight up to them without heeding their frowns.

"Is Meeker here?"

"No, he ain't here," replied Curley, who was regarded by his companions as being something of a humorist.

"Where is he?"

"Since you asks, I reckon he's in th' bunk house," Curley replied. "Where he ought to be," he added, pointedly, while his companions grinned.

"That's wise," responded Buck. "He ought to stay there more often. I hope his cows will take after him. Much obliged for th' information," he finished, riding on.

"His cows an' his punchers'll do as they wants," asserted Curley, frowning.

"Excuse me. I reckoned *he* was boss around here," Buck apologized, a grim smile playing about his lips. "But you better change that 'will' to 'won't' when you mean th' valley."

"I mean *will*!" Curley retorted, leaping to his feet. "An' what's more, I ain't through with that game laig puncher of yourn, neither."

Buck laughed and rode forward again. "You have my sympathy, then," he called over his shoulder.

Buck stopped before the bunk house and called out, and in response to his hail Jim Meeker came and stood in the door.

The H2 foreman believed he was right, and he was too obstinate to admit that there was any side but his which should be considered. He wanted water and better grass, and both were close at hand. Where he had been raised there had been no boundaries, for it had been free grass and water, and he would not and could not see that it was any different on his new range. He had made no agreement, and if one had been made it did not concern him; it concerned only those who had made it. He did not buy the ranch from the old owners, but from a syndicate, and there had been nothing said about lines or restrictions. When he made any agreements he lived up to them, but he did not propose to observe those made by others.

"How'dy, Meeker," said Buck, nodding.

'How'dy, Peters; come in?"

"I reckon it ain't worth while. I won't stay long," Buck replied. "I came down to tell you that some of yore cows are crossing our line. They're gettin' worse every day."

"That so?" asked Meeker, carelessly.

"Yes."

"Um; well, what's th' reason they shouldn't? An' what is that 'line,' that we shouldn't go over it?"

"Dawson, th' old foreman of th' Three Triangle, told you all about that," Buck replied, his whole mind given to the task of reading what sort of a man he had to deal with. "It's our boundary; an' yourn."

"Yes? But I don't recognize no boundary. What have they got to do with me?"

"It has this much, whether you recognize it or not: It marks th' north limit of yore grazin'. *We* don't cross it."

"Huh! You don't have to, while you've got that crick."

"We won't have th' crick, nor th' grass, either, if you drive yore cows on us. That valley is our best grazing, an' it ain't in th' agreement that you can eat it all off."

"What agreement?"

"I didn't come down here to tell you what you know," Buck replied, slowly. "I came to tell you to keep yore men an' yore cows on yore own side, that's whatever."

"How do you know my cows are over there?"

"How do I know th' sun is shining?"

"What do you want me to do?" Meeker asked, leaning against the house and grinning.

"Hold yore herds where they belong. Of course some are shore to stray over, but strays don't count—I ain't talkin' about them."

"Well, I've punched a lot of cows in my day," replied Meeker, "an' over a lot of range, but I never seen no boundary lines afore. An' nobody ever told me to keep on one range, if they knowed me. I've run up against a wire fence or two in th' last few years, but they didn't last long when I hit 'em."

"If you want to know what a boundary line looks like I can show you. There's a plain trail along it where my men have rode for years."

"So you say; but I've got to have water."

"You've got it; twenty miles of river. An' if you'll put down a well or two th' Jumping Bear won't go dry.'

"I don't know nothing about wells," Meeker replied. "Natural water's good enough for me without fooling with wet holes in th' ground."

"No; but, by God, yo're willin' enough to use them what *I* put down! Do you think I spent good time an' money just to supply *you* with water? Why don't you get yore own, 'stead of hoggin' mine!"

"There's water enough, an' it ain't yourn, neither."

"It's mine till somebody takes it away from me, an' you can gamble on that."

"Oh, I reckon you'll share it."

"I reckon I won't!" Buck retorted. "Look here; my men have held that range for many years against all kinds of propositions an' we didn't get pushed into th' discard once; an' they'll go right on holding it. Hell has busted loose down here purty often during that time, but we've allus roped an' branded it; an' we hain't forgot how!"

"Well, I don't want no trouble, but I've got to use that water, an' my men are some hard to handle."

"You'll find mine worse to handle before you gets through," Buck rejoined.

"They're restless now, an' once they start, all hell can't stop 'em." Meeker started to reply, but Buck gave him no chance. "Do you know why I haven't driven you back by force? It wasn't because I figgered on what *you'd* do. It was on account of th' rustling that'll blossom on this range just as soon as we get too busy to watch things. That's why, but if yo're willing to take a chance with cow thieves, I am."

"I'm willing. I've got to have water on my northwest corner," Meeker replied. "An' I'm going to have it! If my cows get on yore private reservation, it's up to you to drive 'em off; but I wouldn't be none hasty doing it if I was you. You see, my men are plumb touchy."

"That's final, is it?"

"I ain't never swallered nothing I ever said."

"All right. I can draw on forty men to fill up gaps, an' I'll do it before I let any range jumper cheat me out of what's mine. When you buck that line, come ready for trouble."

"Yore line'll burn you before I'm through," retorted Meeker, angrily.

Meeker laughed, stretched, and slipped his thumbs in the armholes of his vest, watching the Bar-20 foreman ride away. Then he frowned and snapped his fingers angrily. "We'll keep you busy on yore 'line' when I get ready to play th' cards I'm looking for!" he exclaimed. "Th' gall of him! Telling me I can't pasture where I wants! By God, I'll be told I'm using his sunlight an' breathing his air!"

He stepped forward. "Curley! Chick! Dan!"

A moment later the three men stood before him.

"What is it, Jim?" asked Curley.

"You fellers drive north to-morrow. Pick up th' stragglers an' herd 'em close to that infernal line. Don't drive 'em over till I tell you, but don't let none stray south again; savy? If they want to stray north it's none of our business."

"Good!"

"Fine!"

"That's th' way to talk!"

"Don't start nothing, but if trouble comes yore way take care of yoreselves," Meeker remarked. "I'm telling you to herd up on our north range, that's all."

"Shore; we'll do it!" laughed Curley.

"Is that house on th' peak guarded?" Meeker asked.

"Somebody's there most of th' time," replied Dan Morgan.

"Yes; it's their bunk house now," explained Chick.

"All right; don't forget to-morrow."

XI

♦

Three Is a Crowd

When Buck reached the line on his return Hopalong was the first man he met and his orders were to the point: "Hold this line till hell freezes, drive all H2 cows across it, an' don't start a fight; but be shore to finish any that zephyrs up. Keep yore eyes open."

Hopalong grinned and replied that he would hold the line that long and then skate on the ice, that any cow found trying to cross would get indignant, and that he and trouble were old friends. Buck laughed and rode on.

"Red Eagle, old cayuse!" said the line rider, slapping the animal resoundingly. "We're shore ready!" And Red Eagle, to show how ready he was to resent such stinging familiarities, pitched viciously and bit at his rider's leg.

"Hit her up, old devil!" yelled Hopalong, grabbing his sombrero and applying the spurs. Red Eagle settled back to earth and then shot forward at top speed along the line trail, bucking as often as he could.

It was not long before Hopalong saw a small herd of H2 cows on Bar-20 land and he rode off to head them. When he got in front of the herd he wheeled and dashed straight at it, yelling and firing his Colt, the horse squealing and pitching at every jump.

"Ki-yi, yeow-eow-eow-eow!" he yelled, and the herd, terror-stricken, wheeled and dashed towards their ranch. He followed to the line and saw them meet and terrorize another herd, and he gleefully allowed that it would be a "shore 'nuf stampede."

"Look at 'em go, old Skyrocket," he laughed. The horse began to pitch again but he soon convinced it that play time had passed.

"You old, ugly wart of a cayuse!" he cried, fighting it viciously as it reared and plunged a bit. "Don't you know I can lick four like you an' not touch leather! There, that's better. If you bite me again I'll kick yore corrugations in! But we made 'em hit th' high trail, didn't we, old hinge-back?"

He looked up and stiffened, feeling so foolish that he hardly knew enough to tear off his sombrero, for before him, sitting quietly in her saddle and looking clean through him, was Mary Meeker, a contemptuous firmness about her lips.

"Good-afternoon, Miss Meeker," he said, wondering how much she had seen and heard.

"I'll not spoil yore fun," she icily replied, riding away.

He stared after her until she had ridden around a chaparral and out of his sight, and he slammed his sombrero on the ground and swore.

"Damn th' luck!"

Then he spurred to overtake her and when he saw her again she was talking to Antonio, who was all smiles.

Hopalong muttered, savagely, "I'll spill him all over hisself some day, th' squint-eyed mud-image! Th' devil with him, if he don't like my company he can amble."

He swept up to them, his hair stirred by the breeze and his right hand resting on the butt of his Colt. Antonio was talking when he arrived, but he had no regard for him and interrupted without loss of time.

"Miss Meeker," he began, backing his horse so he could watch Antonio. "I shore hope you ain't mad. Are you?"

She looked at him coldly, and her companion muttered something and found Hopalong's eyes looking into his soul.

"Speak up if you've got anything to say, which you ain't," Hopalong commanded and then turned to the woman. "I'm shore sorry you heard me. I didn't think you was anywhere around."

"Which accounts for you terrorizing our cows an' calves," she retorted. "An' for trying to start a stampede."

Antonio stiffened at this, but did nothing because Hopalong was watching him.

"You ought to be ashamed of yoreself!" she cried, her eyes flashing and deep color surging into her cheeks. "You had no right to treat them calves that way, or to start a stampede!"

"I didn't try to start no stampede, honest," he replied, fascinated by the color playing across her face.

"You did!" she insisted, vehemently. "You may think it's funny to scare calves, but it ain't!"

"I was in a hurry," he replied, apologetically. "I shore didn't think nothing about th' calves. They was over on us an' I had to drive 'em back before I went on."

"You have no right to drive 'em back," she retorted. "They have every right to graze where the grass is good an' where they can get water. They can't live without water."

"They shore can't," he replied in swift accord, as if the needs of cattle had never before crossed his mind. "But they can get it at th' river."

"You have no right to drive 'em away from it!"

"I ain't going to argue none with you, Miss," he responded. "My orders are to drive 'em back, which I'll do."

"Do you mean to tell me that you'll keep them from water?" she demanded, her eyes flashing again.

"It ain't my fault that yore men don't hold 'em closer to th' river," he replied. "There's water a-plenty there. Yore father's keeping 'em on a dry range."

"Don't say anything about my father," she angrily retorted. "He knows his business better'n you can tell it to him."

"I'm sorry if I've gone an' said anything to make you mad," he earnestly replied. "I just wanted to show you that I'm only obeying orders. I don't want to argue with you."

"I didn't come here to argue," she quickly retorted. "I don't want you to drive our calves so hard, that's all."

"I'll be plumb tender with 'em," he assured her, grinning. "An' I didn't try to scare that other herd, honest."

"I saw you trying to scare them just before you saw me."

"Oh!" he exclaimed, chuckling as he recalled his fight with Red Eagle. "That was all th' fault of this ornery cayuse. He got th' idea into his fool head that he could throw me, so me an' him had it out right there."

She had been watching his face while he spoke and she remembered that he had fought with his horse, and believed that he was telling the truth. Then suddenly, the humorous side struck her and brought a smile to her face. "I'm sorry I didn't understand," she replied in a low voice.

"Then you ain't mad no more?" he asked eagerly.

"No; not a bit."

"I'm glad of that," he laughed, leaning forward. "You had me plumb scared to death."

"I didn't know I could scare a puncher so easy, 'specially you," she replied, flushing. "But where's yore sombrero?"

"Back where I threw it," he grinned.

"Where you threw it?"

"Shore. I got sore when you rode away, an' didn't care much what happened," he replied, coolly. Then he transfixed Antonio with his keen eyes. "If yo're so anxious to get that gun out, say so or do it," he said, slowly. "That's th' second time."

Mary watched them breathlessly, but Hopalong didn't intend to have any fighting in her presence.

"You let it alone before I take it away from you," he said. "An' I reckon you better pull out—you ain't needed around here. Go on, flit!"

Antonio glanced at Mary for orders and she nodded her head. "I don't need you; go."

Hopalong watched him depart and turned to his companion. "What's eating him, anyhow?"

"I don't know. I never saw him act that way before."

"H'm. I reckon I know; but he don't want to act that way again," he said, decisively.

"All men are funny," she replied. "Th' idea of being scared by me when you ain't afraid of a man like him."

"That's a different kind of a scare, an' I never felt like that before. It made me want to kill somebody. I don't want you to get mad at me. I like you too much. You won't will you?"

She smiled. "No."

"Never? No matter what happens?"

"Do you care?"

"Do I care! You know I do. Look at me, Mary!"

"No; don't come any nearer. I must go—good-bye."

"Don't go; let's ride around for a while."

"But 'Tony may tell Dad; an' if he does Dad'll come up here an' make trouble. No, I must go."

"Tell 'Tony I want to see him," he replied. "If he says anything I'll make him pay for it; an' he won't do it again."

"You mustn't do that! It would make things all th' worse."

"Will you come up again to-morrow?"

She laughed. "That'll be too soon, won't it?"

"Not by a blamed sight."

"Well, I don't know. Good-bye."

"Good-bye," he said, holding out his hand.

She gave him her hand and then tried to push him away. "No, no! No, I say! I won't come any more if you do that!"

Despite her struggles he drew her to him and kissed her again and again.

"I hate you! I hate you!" she cried, her face the color of fire. "What made you do it! You've spoiled everything, an' I'll never see you again! I hate you!" and she wheeled and galloped away.

He spurred in pursuit and when he had overtaken her he grasped her horse by the bridle and stopped her. "Mary! Don't be mad—I love you!"

"Will you let me go?" she demanded, her face crimson.

"Not till you say yo're not mad."

"Please let me go," she replied, looking in his eyes. "I'm not mad at you; but you mustn't do that again. Won't you let me go before someone sees us?"

He released her and she impulsively put her hand on his arm. "Look out—an' watch 'Tony," and she was gone.

"Yo're th' best girl ever rode a cayuse," he muttered, joyously. " 'Look out—an' watch 'Tony,' " he cried. "What do I care about him? I can clean out th' whole gang now. Just let 'em start something."

When he neared the place where his sombrero lay he saw Johnny in the act of picking it up, and Johnny might take a notion to make a race out of it before giving it up. "Hey, you!" Hopalong cried, dashing forward, "gimme that cover!"

"Come an' get it; I don't want it," Johnny retorted. "What made you lose it?"

"Fighting."

"Fighting! Fighting who?"

"Just fighting, Kid."

"Ah, come on an' tell me," begged Johnny. Then, like a shot: "Was it Antonio?"

"Nope."

"Who was it?"

"None of yore business," laughed Hopalong, delighted to be able to tease him.

"All right!" Johnny cried. "You wait; th' boys will be glad to learn about you an' her!"

Hopalong's hand shot out and gripped his friend's shoulder. "Don't you say a word about it, do you hear?"

"Shore. I was only fooling," replied Johnny. "Think I tell them kind of things!"

"I was too quick, Kid. I know yo're a thoroughbred. An' now I'll tell you who I was fighting. It was Red Eagle. He got a fit of pitching, an' I had to take it out of him."

"I might 'a knowed it," responded Johnny, eyeing the tracks in the sand. "But I reckoned you might 'a had a run-in with Antonio. I was saving him for myself."

"Why do you hate him so much?"

"Never mind that now. I'll tell you after I get him."

"Have you seen Buck since he came back?"

"No; why?"

Hopalong told him what the foreman had said and his friend grinned. "The good old days are coming back again, Hoppy!" he exulted.

"Shoo, fly! Shoo, fly," laughed Hopalong.

"Where are you going now?" asked Johnny.

"Where I please."

"Shore. I knowed that. That's where you want to go," grinned Johnny. "But where do you want to go?"

"Where I can't go now."

"Ah, shut up! Come on. I'll go with you."

"Well, I'm going east to tell th' fellers what Buck said."

"Go ahead. I'm with you," Johnny said, wheeling.

"I didn't ask you to come.'

"I didn't ask you to go," retorted Johnny. "Here," he said, holding out a cigar and putting another in his mouth. "Have a smoke; they're all right."

"Where the devil did you get 'em?"

"Up in Number Five."

"In Number Five!"

"Shore. Frenchy, th' son-o'-a-gun, had three of 'em hid over th' windy," Johnny explained. "I hooked 'em."

"So I reckoned; did you take 'em all?"

"Was you going up?"

"No; but did you?"

"Well, I looked good, but I didn't see none to leave."

"You wait till he finds it out," Hopalong warned.

"He won't do nothing," assured Johnny, easily. "Anyhow,

yo're as guilty as me. He ain't got no right to cache cigars when we can't get to town for any. Besides, he's afraid of me."

"Scared of you! Oh, Lord, that's good!"

"Quit fooling an' get started," Johnny said, kicking his friend's horse.

"You behave, or I'll get that Antonio to lick you good," threatened Hopalong as he quieted Skyrocket.

"Let's get a-going!"

They cantered eastward, driving back Meeker's cows whenever they were found too close to the line or over it, and it was not long before they made out Lanky riding towards them. He had not yet seen them and Johnny eagerly proposed that they prepare an ambush and scare him.

"He don't scare, you fool," replied Hopalong. "A joke is a joke, but there ain't no use getting shot at when you can't shoot back. No use getting killed for a lark."

"He might shoot, mightn't he," Johnny laughed. "I didn't think about that."

Lanky looked around, waved his hand and soon joined them. "I see yo're taking care of th' Kid, Hopalong. Hullo, Kid."

"Go to blazes!" snorted Johnny.

"Has he been a good boy, Hoppy?"

"No more'n usual. He's looking for Antonio."

"*Again?*" asked Lanky, grinning. "Ain't you found him yet?"

"Ah, go on. I'll find him when I want him," Johnny retorted.

When Lanky had heard Buck's orders he frowned.

"We'll hold it all right. Wait for Billy, he'll be along purty soon. I left him chasing some cows."

"Got yore saddle so it'll stay together for more'n ten minutes at a time?" asked Johnny.

"I bought Billy's old one," Lanky replied. "Got anything to say about it?"

Billy Williams, pessimist by nature and choice, rode up and joined them and, laughing and joking, they rode towards the Peak, to see if Buck had any further orders. But they had not gone far before Hopalong stopped and thought. "You go on. I'll stay out here an' watch things."

"I'm with you, Hoppy," Johnny offered. "You fellers go on; me an' Hopalong'll take care of th' line out here."

"All right," replied Lanky. "So long."

A few minutes later Johnny turned in his saddle. "Hey, Billy!" he shouted.

"What?"

"Has Lanky paid you for that saddle yet?"

"Shore; why?"

"Oh, nothing. But yo're lucky."

Billy turned and said something to Lanky and they cantered on their way.

"Hey, Hoppy; don't you tell Frenchy about them cigars," Johnny suddenly remarked some time later.

XII

♦

Hobble Burns and Sleepers

The western part of the Bar-20 ranch was poor range and but few cattle were to be found on it until Big Coulee had been reached. This portion of the ranch fed quite a large number of cattle, many of which were outlaws, but because of the heavy work demanded on the more fertile southern and eastern sections it was the custom with Buck to pay little attention to the Big Coulee herds; if a man rode up there once in a while he was satisfied. This time it was Skinny who was to look over the condition of affairs around Number Two, which was not far from Big Coulee.

Detouring here and there he took his own time and followed the general direction of the western line, and about four hours after he had quitted the Peak he passed line house Number Two and shortly afterward stopped on the rim of the coulee, a brush-grown depression of a score of acres in extent, in which was a pond covering half an acre and fed by springs on the bottom, its outlet being a deep gorge cut in the soft stone. Half a mile from the pond the small stream disappeared in the sand and was lost.

He rode through the coulee without seeing a single cow and an exploration lasting over an hour resulted no better. Beyond a bear track or two among the berry bushes he saw no signs of animal life. This did not disturb him because he took it for granted that the herds had wandered back to where the grass was better. Stopping at the line house to eat, he mounted and rode towards the hills to report to Hopalong.

Suddenly it struck him that he had seen no cow tracks in the mud around the water hole and he began to hunt for cattle. Using Pete's glasses constantly to sweep the plain for the missing herds, it was not until he had reached a point half-way to the Peak that his search was rewarded by seeing a calf far to the east of him. Watching it until it stood out boldly to his sight he followed an impulse and rode towards it to examine it at close range.

Upon getting near it he saw that it bore the V notch of the H2 cut in its ear, and that it was not branded. He thought it strange that an H2 "sleeper" should be so far from home, without a mother to lead it astray, and he roped it to look more closely at the notch. His opinion was that it had been done very recently, for the cartilage had not yet dried on the edges. Releasing the animal he mounted and started for the line, muttering to himself.

As he swung into the line trail he saw a lame cow limping around a thicket and he spurred forward, roped and threw it, this time giving no thought to the ears, for its brand was that of the Bar-20. He looked at the hocks and found them swollen and inflamed, and his experience told him that it had been done by hobbles. This, to him, explained why the calf was alone, and it gave him the choice of two explanations for the hobbling and the newly cut ear notch on the calf. Either the H2 was sleepering Bar-20 calves for their irons later on, or rustlers were at work. It seemed incredible that any H2 puncher should come that distance to make a few sleepers—but the herd had not been to the water hole! He was greatly wrought up and it was none the more pleasant to be unable to say where the blame lay. There was only one thing to do and that was to scout around and try to find a clue to the perpetrators—and, perhaps, catch the thieves at work. This proved to be unfruitful until he came to North Hill, where he found a cow dead from gunshot. He put spurs to his horse and rode straight for the Peak, which he reached as night fell and as Hopalong, Red, Pete, and Lanky were eating supper and debating the line conditions.

Skinny joined them and listened to the conversation, wordless, nodding or shaking his head at the points made. When he had finished eating he leaned back against his saddle and fumbled for tobacco and pipe, gazing reflectively into the fire, at which he spat. Hopalong turned in time to see the act and, knowing Skinny's peculiarities, asked abruptly: "What's on yore mind, Skinny?"

"Little piece of hell," was the slow reply, and it gained the attention of the others at once. "I saw a H2 sleeper, up just above th' Bend and half way between it an' th' line."

"That so!" exclaimed Hopalong.

"Long way from home—starting in young to ramble," Red laughed. "Lazy trick, that sleepering."

"This here calf had a brand new V—hadn't healed yet," Skinny remarked, lighting his pipe. "An' it didn't—*puff*—have no—*puff*—mother," he added, significantly.

"Huh, weaned, you chump—but that fresh V is shore funny."

"Go on, Skinny," ordered Hopalong, eagerly.

"I found its mother an hour later—hobble-burned an' limping; an' it wasn't no H2 cow, neither; it was one of ourn."

"Rustling!" cried Hopalong.

"Th' H2 is doing it," contradicted Red, quickly.

"They wouldn't take a chance like that," replied Hopalong.

"There ain't no rule for taking chances," Red rejoined. "Some men'll gamble with hell itself—you, for instance, in gun-play."

"What else?" demanded Hopalong of Skinny.

"That Big Coulee herd ain't up there, an' hain't been near th' water hole for so long th' mud's smooth around the edges of th' pond; kin savvy?"

"It's rustlers, by God!" cried Hopalong, looking triumphantly at Red.

"An' I found a dead cow—shot—on th' upper end of North Hill," Skinny added.

"H2!" Red shouted. "They're doing it!"

"Yes, likely; it was an H2 cow," Skinny placidly explained.

"Why in hell can't you tell things in a herd, 'stead of stringin' 'em out like a stiff reata trailing to soften!" Red cried. "Yo're the damndest talker that ever opened a mouth!"

Skinny took the pipe from his mouth and looked at Red.

"I allus get it all out, don't I? What are you kicking about?"

"Yes, you do; like a five thousand herd filtering through a two-foot gate!"

"Mebby th' herd drifted to th' valley," Pete offered.

"Mebby nothing!" Red retorted. "Why, we can't *drive* 'em down here without 'em acting loco about it."

"Cows are shore fool animals," Pete suggested in defence.

"There's more than cows that are fool animals," Red snapped, while Skinny laughed to see Pete get his share.

Sixteen miles to the southeast of the Peak, Meeker sat on a soap box and listened, with the rest of his outfit, to what Curley was saying—"an' when I got down a good ways south I found two young calves bellering for their maws. They was sleepers; an' an hour later I found them same maws bellering for them calves—they was limping a-plenty an' their hocks looked burned—hobble burns."

Meeker mused for a moment and then arose. "You ride that range regular, an' be cautious. Watch towards Eagle. If you catch any sons-of-skunks gamboling reckless, an' they can't explain why they are flitting over our range, shoot off yore gun accidental—there won't be no inquest."

XIII

♦

Hopalong Grows Suspicious

The eastern sky grew brighter and the dim morning light showed a group of men at breakfast on the Peak. They already had been given their orders and as soon as each man finished eating he strode off to where his horse was picketed with the others, mounted, and rode away. Pete had ridden in late the night before and was still sleeping in the house, Hopalong not wishing to awaken him until it was absolutely necessary.

Red Connors, riding back to the house from the horse herd, drew rein for a final word. "I'm going out to watch that unholy drift of Meeker's cows, just this side of th' half-way point. They was purty thick last night when I rode in. I told Johnny to keep on that part of th' line, for I reckon things will get too crowded for one man to handle. Th' two of us can take care of 'em, all right. You knows where you can find us if you need us."

"I don't like that drift, but I'll stay here an' give Pete an hour more sleep," Hopalong replied. "Buck didn't know just when he'd be down again, but I'm looking for him before noon, just th' same."

"Well, me an' Johnny'll stop th' drift. So long," and Red cantered away, whistling softly.

Hopalong kicked out the fire and walked restlessly around the plateau, puzzled by the massing of the H2 cows along the line. The play was obvious enough on its face, for it meant that Meeker, tired of inaction, had decided to force the issue by driving into the valley. But Hopalong, suspicious to a degree, was not satisfied with that solution.

On more than one occasion he had searched past the obvious and found deeper motives, and to this ferment of thought he owed his life many times. He, himself, essentially a schemer and trusting no one but the members of his outfit, accused others of scheming and bent his mind to outwit them. Buck often irritated him greatly, for the foreman, optimistic and believing all men honest until they proved to be otherwise, held that Meeker thought himself to be in the right and so was justified in his attempt to use the valley. Hopalong believed that Meeker was not square, that he knew he had no right to the valley and was trying to steal range; he maintained that the wiser way was to believe all men crooked and put the burden on them of proving otherwise; then he was prepared for anything.

A better cow-man than Buck Peters never lived; he knew the cattle industry thoroughly, was honest, fair, and fearless, maintained an even temper and tried to avoid fighting until the last ditch had been reached. But it was an indisputable fact that Hopalong Cassidy had proved himself to be the best man on the ranch when danger threatened. He grasped situations quickly and clearly and his companions looked to him for suggestions when the sky was clouded by impending conflict. Buck realized that his line-foreman was eminently better qualified to handle the skirmish line than himself, that Hopalong could carry out things which would fall flat if any one else attempted them. Back of Buck's confidence was the pleasing knowledge that no man had ever yet got in the first shot against Hopalong on an "even break," and that when his puncher's gun exploded it was all over; this is why Hopalong could, single-handed, win out in any reasonable situation.

While Hopalong turned the matter over in his mind he thought he saw a figure move among the chaparrals far to the south and he whipped out his glasses, peering long and steadily at the place. Then he put them away and laughed softly. "You can't fool me, by God! I'll let you make yore play—an' if Pete don't kill a few of you I'm a liar. Here are th' shells—pick out th' pea."

Returning to the house he shook Pete. "Hey, get up!"

Pete bounded up, wide awake in an instant. "Yes?"

"Put on yore clothes an' come outside a minute," he ordered, going out.

Pete finished buttoning his vest when he joined his friend, who was pointing south. "Pete, they're playing for this house, an' I can't stay—Red an' Johnny may need me any minute. Down there an H2 rider is watching this house. Meeker is massing his cows along th' line for two reasons; he's trying to draw us away from here so he can get in, an' he's going to push over th' line if he falls down here. You stay in that shack. Don't leave it for a second, understand? Stop anybody that comes up here if you have to kill him. But don't leave this house for nothing, savvy?"

"Go ahead. I savvy."

Hopalong vaulted to his saddle and started away. "I'll get somebody to help you as soon as I can," he called.

"Don't need anybody!" Pete shouted, going inside and barring the door.

Hopalong was elated by the way he had forestalled Meeker, and also because it was Pete who guarded the house. He knew his companions only as a man can know friends with whom he has lived for nearly a score of years. Red was too good a fighter to be cooped up while trouble threatened in the open; Johnny, rash and hot-tempered, could be tempted to leave the house to indulge in personal combat if taunted enough, and he, too, was too good a man in a *mêlée* to remain on the Peak. The man for the house was Pete, for he was accurate enough for that short range, he was unemotional and did not do much thinking for himself when it ran counter to his instructions; he had been told to stay in the house and hold it, and that, Hopalong felt certain, he would do.

"Pete'll hold 'em with one leg in th' air if they happen to be taking a step when he sees 'em," he laughed.

But Pete was to be confronted with a situation so unexpected and of such a nature that for once in his life he was going to forget orders—and small blame to him.

XIV

♦

The Compromise

It was night and on the H2 sickly, yellow lights gleamed from the ranch houses. From the bunk house came occasional bursts of song, the swinging choruses thundering out on the night air, deep-toned and strong. In the foreman's quarters the clatter of dishes was soon stilled and shortly afterward the light in the kitchen could be seen no more. A girl stood in the kitchen door for a moment and then, singing, went inside and the door closed. The strumming of a guitar and much laughter came from Antonio's shack, for now he had Juan and Sanchez to help him pass the time.

Meeker emerged from a corral, glanced above him for signs of the morrow's weather, and then stood and gazed at the shack. Turning abruptly on his heel he strode to the bunk house and smiled grimly as the chorus roared out, for he had determined upon measures which might easily change the merriment to mourning before another day passed. He had made up his mind to remain inactive no longer, but to put things to the test—his outfit and himself against the Bar-20.

He entered the building and slamming the door shut behind him, waited until the chorus was finished. When the last note died away he issued his orders for the next day, orders which pleased his men, who had chafed even more than he under the galling inaction, since they did not thoroughly understand the reasons for it.

"I had them cows herded up north for th' last three days so they'd be ready for us when we wanted 'em," he said, and then leaped at the door and jerked it open, peering about outside. Turning, he beckoned Doc Riley to him and the two stepped outside, closing the door behind them. Great noise broke out within the house as his orders were repeated and commented on. Meeker and Doc moved to the corner of the building and consulted earnestly for several minutes, the foreman gesticulating slowly.

"But Juan said they had a man to guard it," Doc replied.

"Yes; he told me," Meeker responded. "I'm going to fix that before I go to bed—we've got to coax him out on some excuse. Once we get him out of th' house we can cover him, an' th' rest'll be easy. I won't be able to be with you—I'll have to stay outside where I can move around an' look out for th' line trouble, an' where they can see me. But you an' Jack can hold it once you get in. By God, you *must* get in, an' you *must* hold it!"

"We'll do it if it's possible."

"That's th' way to talk. Th' boys seem pleased about it," Meeker laughed, listening to the joy loose in the house.

"Pleased! They're tickled plumb to death. They've got so sore about having to keep their guns quiet that when they cut loose—well, something's due to happen."

"I don't want that if there's any other way," Meeker replied earnestly. "If this thing can be done without wholesale slaughter we've got to do it that way. Remember, Doc, this whole country is backing Peters. He's got thirteen men now, an' he can call on thirty more in two days. Easy is th' way, easy."

"I'll spend th' next hour pounding that into their hot heads," Doc replied. "They're itching for a chance to square up for everything. They're some sore, been so for a couple of days, about that line house being guarded— they get sore plumb easy now, you know."

"Well, good-night, Doc."

"Good-night, Jim."

Meeker went towards his own house and as he neared the kitchen door a deep-throated wolf-hound bayed from the kennels, inciting a clamorous chorus from the others. Meeker shouted and the noise changed to low, deep, rumbling growls which soon became hushed. Chains rattled over wood and the fierce animals returned to their grass beds to snarl at each other. The frightened crickets took up their song again and poured it on the silence of the night.

Meeker opened the door and strode through the kitchen and into the living room, his eyes squinting momentarily because of the light. His daughter was sitting in a rocking chair, sewing industriously, and she looked up, welcoming him. He replied to her and, dexterously tossing his sombrero on a peg in the wall where it caught and hung swinging, walked heavily to the southern window and stood before it, hands clasped behind his back, staring moodily into the star-stabbed darkness. Down the wind came the faint, wailing howl of a wolf, quavering and distant, and the hounds again shattered the peaceful quiet. But he heard neither, so absorbed was he by his thoughts. Mary looked at him for a moment and then took up her work again and resumed sewing, for he had done this before when things had gone wrong, and frequently of late.

He turned suddenly and in response to the movement she looked up, again laying her sewing aside. "What is it?" she asked.

"Trouble, Mary. I want to talk to you."

"I'm always ready to listen, Daddy," she replied. "I wish you wouldn't worry so. That's all you've done since we left Montana."

"I know; but I can't help it," he responded, smiling faintly. "But I don't care much as long as I've got you to talk it over with. Yo're like yore mother that way, Mary; she allus made things easy, somehow. An' she knew more'n most women do about things."

"Yo're my own Daddy," she replied affectionately. "Now tell me all about it."

"Well," he began, sitting on the table, "I'm being cheated out of my rights. I find lines where none exist. I'm hemmed in from water, th' best grazing is held from me, my cows are driven helter-skelter, my pride hurt, an' my men mocked. When I say I must have water I'm told to go to th' river for it, twenty miles from my main range, an' lined with quicksands; an' yet there is water close to me, water enough for double th' number of cows of both ranches! It is good, clean water, unfailing an' over a firm bottom, flowing through thirty miles of th' best grass valley in this whole sun-cursed section. Two hundred miles in any direction won't show another as good. An' yet, I dassn't set my foot in it—I can't drive a cow across that line!"

He paused and then continued: "I'm good an' sick of it all. I ain't going to swaller it no longer, not a day. Peace is all right, but not at th' price I'm paying! I'd ruther die fighting for what's mine than put up with what I have since I came down here."

"What are you going to do?" she asked quietly.

"I'm going to have a force on that line by to-morrow

night!" he said, gradually working himself into a temper.
"*I'm* going to hold them hills, an' th' springs at th' bottom of 'em. *I'm* going to use that valley an' I'll fight until
th' last man goes under!"

"Don't say that, Daddy," she quickly objected. "There
ain't no line worth yore life. What good will it do you
when yo're dead? You can get along without it if it comes
to that. An' what'll happen to me if you get killed?"

"No, girl," he replied. "You've held me back too long.
I should 'a struck in th' beginning, before they got so set.
It would 'a been easier then. I don't like range wars any
more'n anybody, but it's come, an' I've got to hold up my
end—an' my head!"

"But th' agreement?" she queried, fearful for his
safety. She loved her father with all her heart, for he had
been more than a father to her; he had always confided in
her and weighed her judgment; they had been companions since her mother died, which was almost beyond her
memory; and now he would risk his life in a range war,
a vindictive, unmerciful conflict which usually died out
when the last opponent died—and perhaps he was in
the wrong. She knew the fighting ability of that shaggy,
tight-lipped breed of men that mocked Death with derisive, profane words, who jibed whether in *mêlée* or duel
with as light hearts as if engaged in nothing more dangerous than dancing. And she had heard, even in Montana, of the fighting qualities of the outfit that rode range
for the Bar-20. If they must be fought, then let it be for
the right principles and not otherwise. And there was
Hopalong!—she knew in her heart that she loved him,
and feared it and fought it, but it was true; and he was the
active leader of his outfit, the man who was almost the
foreman, and who would be in the thickest of the fighting. She didn't purpose to have him killed if he was in
the right, or in the wrong, either.

"Agreement!" he cried, hotly. "Agreement! I hear that every time I say anything to that crowd, an' now you give it to me! Agreement be damned! Nason never said nothing about any agreement when he told me he had found a ranch for me. He wouldn't 'a dealt me a hand like that, one that'd give me th' worst of it in a show-down! He found out all about everything before he turned over my check to 'em."

"But they say there is one, an' from th' way they act it looks that way."

"I don't believe anything of th' sort! It's just a trick to hog that grass an' water!"

"Hopalong Cassidy told me there was one—he told me all about it. He was a witness."

"Hopalong hell!" he cried, remembering the day that Doc had been shot, and certain hints which Antonio had let fall.

"Father!" she exclaimed, her eyes flashing.

"Oh, don't mind me," he replied. "I don't know what I'm saying half th' time. I'm all mixed up, now-a-days."

"I believe he was telling the truth— he wouldn't lie to me," she remarked, decisively.

He looked at her sharply. "Well, am I to be tied down by something I don't know about? Am I to swallow everything I hear? *I* don't know about no agreement, except what th' Bar-20 tells me. An' if there was one it was made by th' Three Triangle, wasn't it?—an' not by Nason or me? Am I th' Three Triangle? Am I to walk th' line on something I didn't make? *I* didn't make it!—oh, I'm tired arguing about it."

"Well, even if there wasn't no agreement you can't blame them for trying to keep their land, can you?" she asked, idly fingering her sewing. "The land is theirs, ain't it?"

"Did you ever hear of free grass an' free water?"

"I never heard of nothing else till I came down here," she admitted. "But it may be different here."

"Well, it ain't different!" he retorted. "An' if it is it won't stay so. What goes in Montanny will go down here. Anyhow, I don't want their land—all I want is th' use of it, same as they have. But they're hogs, an' want it all."

"They say it ain't big enough for their herds."

"Thirty-five miles long, and five miles wide, in th' valley alone, an' it ain't big enough! Don't talk to me like that! You know better."

"I'm only trying to show it to you in every light," she responded. "Mebby yo're right, an' mebby you ain't; that's what we've got to find out. I don't want to think of you fightin', 'specially if yo're wrong. Suppose yo're killed—an' you might be. Ain't there some other way to get what you want, if yo're determined to go ahead?"

"Yes, I might be killed, but I won't go alone!" he cried savagely. "Fifty years, man an' boy, I've lived on th' range, taking every kick of fortune, riding hard an' fightin' hard when I had to. I ain't no yearling at any game about cows, girl."

"But can't you think of some other way?" she repeated.

"I've got to get that line house on th' hill," he went on, not heeding her question. "Juan told me three days ago, that they've put a guard in it now—but I'll have it by noon to-morrow, for I've been thinking hard since then. An' once in it, they can't take it from me! With that in my hands I can laugh at 'em, for I can drive my cows over th' line close by it, down th' other side of th' hill, an' into th' valley near th' springs. They'll be under my guns in th' line house, an' let anybody try to drive 'em out again! Two men can hold that house—it was built for defense against Indians. Th' top of th' hill is level as a floor an' only two hundred yards to th' edge. Nobody can cross that space under fire an' live."

"If they can't cross it an' live, how can *you* cross it, when th' house is guarded? An' when th' first shot is fired you'll have th' whole outfit down on you from behind like wild fire. Then what'll you do? You can't fight between two fires."

"By God, yo're right! Yo're th' brains of this ranch," his eyes squinting to hide his elation. He paced back and forth, thinking deeply. Five minutes passed, then ten, and he suddenly turned and faced her, to unfold the plan he had worked out the day before. He had been leading up to it and now he knew how to propose it. "I've got it. I've got it! Not a shot, not a single shot!"

"Tell me," she said smiling.

He slowly unfolded it, telling her of the herds waiting to be driven across the line to draw the Bar-20 men from the Peak, and of the part she was to play. She listened quietly, a troubled frown on her face, and when he had finished and asked her what she thought of it she looked at him earnestly and slowly replied: "Do you think that's fair? Do you want *me* to do that?"

"What's unfair about it? They're yore enemies as much as they are mine, ain't they? Ain't everything fair in love an' war, as th' books say?"

"In war, perhaps; but not in love," she replied in a low voice, thinking of the man who wore her flower.

"Now look here!" he cried, leaning forward. "Don't you go an' get soft on any of that crowd! Do you hear?"

"We won't mix love an' war, Daddy," she said, decisively. "You take care of yore end, that's war; an' let me run my part. I'll do what I want to when it comes to falling in love; an' I'll help you to-morrow. I don't want to do it, but I will; you've got to have th' line house, an' without getting between two fires. I'll do it, Daddy."

"Good girl! Yo're just like yore mother—all grit!" he cried, going towards the door. "An' I reckon I won't have to take no hand in *yore* courting," he said, grabbing his sombrero. "Yo're shore able to run yore own."

"But *promise* me you won't interfere," she said, calmly, hiding her triumph.

"It's a go. I'll keep away from th' sparking game," he promised. "I'm going out to see th' boys for a minute," and the door slammed, inciting the clamor of the kennels again, which he again hushed. "Damn 'em!" he muttered, exultantly. "They tried to hog th' range, an' then they want my girl! But they *won't* hog th' range no more, an' I'll put a stop to th' courting when she plays her cards to-morrow, an' without having any hand in it. Lord, I win every trick!" he laughed.

XV

♦

Antonio Meets Friends

Before daylight the next morning Antonio left the ranch and rode south, bearing slightly to the west, so as not to leave his trail in Curley's path. He was to meet some of Shaw's men who would come for more cattle. When a dozen miles southwest of the ranch house he espied them at work on the edge of an arroyo. They had a fire going and were re-branding a calf. Far out on the plain was a dead cow, the calf's mother, shot because they had become angered by its belligerency when it had gone "on th' prod." They had driven cow and calf hard and when they tried to separate the two the mother had charged viciously, narrowly missing one of them, to die by a shot from the man most concerned. Meanwhile the calf had run back over its trail and they had roped it as it was about to plunge over the bank of the arroyo.

"You fools!" yelled Antonio, galloping towards them. "Don't you know better'n to blot on this range! How many times have I told you that Curley rides south!"

"He never gets this far west—we've watched him," retorted Clausen, angrily.

"Is that any reason why he can't!" demanded Antonio. "How do you know what he'll do?"

"Yes!" rejoined Clausen. "An' I reckon he can find that steep-bank hollow with th' rope gate, can't he? Suppose he finds th' herds you holds in it for us—what then?"

"It's a whole lot farther west than here!" retorted Antonio, hotly. "They never go to Little Muddy, an' if they do, that's a chance we've got to take. But you can wait till you get to th' mesa before you change brands, can't you!"

"Aw, close yore pie-sump!" cried Frisco. "Who th' devil is doing this, anyhow? You make more noise than Cheyenne on th' Fourth of July!"

"What right have you fellers got to take chances an' hobble *me* with trouble?"

"Who's been doing all th' sleepering, hey?" sarcastically demanded Dick Archer. "Let Meeker's gang see the God-forsaken bunch of sleepers running on their range an' you'll be hobbled with trouble, all right."

Through laziness, carelessness, or haste calves might not be branded when found with branded cows. Feeling was strong against the use of the "running iron," a straight iron rod about eighteen inches long which was heated and used as a pencil on the calf's hide, and a man caught with one in his possession could expect to be dealt with harshly; it was a very easy task to light a fire and "run" a brand, and the running iron was easily concealed under the saddle flap. But it was not often that a puncher would carry a stamping iron, for it was cumbersome. With a running iron a brand could be changed, or the wrong mark put on unbranded cattle; but the stamping iron would give only one pattern.

When a puncher came across an unbranded calf with its branded mother, and the number which escaped the roundup was often large, he branded it, if he had an iron; if he did not have the iron he might cut the calf's ear to conform to the notch in its mother's ears. When the calf was again seen it might have attained its full growth. In that case there was no branded mother to show to whom it belonged; but its cut ears would tell.

These unbranded, ear-cut calves were known as "sleepers" and, in localities where cattle stealing was being or had been carried on to any extent, such sleepering was regarded with strong suspicion, and more than one man had paid a dear price for doing the work.

The ear mark of the H2 was a V, while the Bar-20 depended entirely on the brand, and part of its punchers' saddle equipment was a stamping iron.

Cowmen held sleepering in strong disfavor because it was an easy matter for a maverick hunter or a rustler to drive off these sleepers and, after altering the ear cut, to brand them with his own or some strange brand; and it was easy to make sleepers.

In the case of rustling the separation of branded calves and mothers was imperative, for should any one see a cow of one brand with a calf of another, it was very probable that a committee of discretionary powers would look into the matter. Hobbling and laming mothers and then driving away the calves were not the only ways of separating them and of weaning the calves, for a shot was often as good a way as any; but as dead cows, if found, were certain to tell the true story, this was not generally employed.

"Yes," laughed Frisco. "What about th' sleepers?"

They were discreetly silent about the cow they had

killed, for they were ashamed of having left such a sign; but they would not stand Antonio's scorn and anger, and that of the other members of the band, and so said nothing about it.

"Where's th' mother of this calf?" demanded Antonio, not heeding the remarks about sleepers.

"Hanged if I know," replied Clausen, easily; "an' hanged if I care—we can leave *one* cow, I reckon."

"Got many for us this time?" asked Archer as they rode west, driving before them the newly branded calf.

"Not many," replied Antonio. "It's risky, with Curley loose. We won't be able to do much till th' fighting starts."

When they reached their destination they came to a deep, steep-walled depression, exit from which was had at only one end where a narrow trail wound up to the plain. Across this trail at its narrowest point was stretched a lariat.

The depression itself was some ten acres in extent and was well covered with grass, while near the southwest corner was a muddy pool providing water for the herd which was now held captive.

Clausen rode down and removed the rope, riding into the basin to hasten the egress of the herd. When the last cow had scrambled out and joined its fellows, Archer and Frisco drove them west, leaving Clausen to say a few final words with Antonio before joining them.

"How's th' range war coming on?"

"Fine!" laughed Antonio. "Meeker's going to attack th' line house on th' Peak, though what good it'll do him is more than I can figure out. I put it in his head because it'll start th' fight. I had to grin when I heard Meeker and Doc planning it last night—they're easy."

"Gee!" laughed Clausen. "It's a stiff play. Who's going to win? Meeker?"

"Meeker's going to get th' licking of his life. I know that Bar-20 gang, every one. I've lived down here for

some time, an' I know what they've done. Don't never
get in a six-shooter argument with that feller Cassidy; an'
if his friend Connors tells you to stop under eight hundred yards, you do it, an' trust to yore tongue, or Colt.
He's th' devil hisself with a Winchester."

"Much obliged—but I ain't so bad that way myself.
Well, I'm going to ooze west. Got any word for Shaw?"

"I'll sent word by Benito—I'll know more about it
tomorrow."

"All right," and Clausen was being jerked over the
scenery by his impatient mount.

Antonio wheeled and rode at a gallop, anxious to be
found on northern range, and eager to learn the result of
his foreman's attack.

"Salem," once a harpooner on a whaling vessel, now
cook for the H2, drove home from Eagle in the chuck
wagon, which contained food supplies for his ranch. He
was in that state hovering between tears and song, which
accounted for the winding trail his wagon wheels left, and
also for him being late. He had tarried in Eagle longer than
he should have, for he was reluctant to quit the society of
his several newly made friends, who so pleasantly allowed
him to "buy" for them. When he realized how the time had
flown and that his outfit would be clamoring for the noon-
day meal, such clamoring being spicy and personal in its
expression, he left the river trail before he should and es-
sayed a shorter way home, chanting a sea song.

> *A pirate bold, on th' Spanish Main—*
> *Set sail, yo-ho, an' away we go—*

"Starboard yore helm, you lubbers!" he shouted when
the horses headed towards Mexico. Then he saw a large
bulk lying on the sand a short distance ahead and he sat
bolt upright.

"There she blows! No, blast me, it's a dead cow!"

He drove closer to it and, stopping the team, staggered over to see what had killed it.

"Damn me, if it ain't shot in th' port eye!" he ejaculated. "If I find the lubber what's sinkin' our cows, I'll send him to Davy Jones' locker!"

He returned to the wagon and steered nor' by nor' east, once more certain of his bearings, for he knew the locality now, and sometime later he saw Curley riding towards him.

"Ahoy!" he yelled. "Ahoy, you wind-jammer!"

"What's eating you? Why are you so late?" demanded Curley, approaching. "You needn't say—I know."

"Foller my wake an' you'll see a dead cow," cried Salem. "Deader'n dead, too! Shot in th' starboard—no, was it starboard? Now, damned if I know—reckon it was in th' port eye, though I didn't see no port light; aye, 'twas in th' port—"

"What in the hell do I care what eye it was!" shouted Curley. "Where is it?"

"Eight knots astern. Shot in th' port eye, an', as I said, deader'n dead. Flew our flag, too."

Curley, believing that the cook had seen what he claimed, wheeled abruptly and galloped away to report it to Meeker.

"Hey! Ain't you going to *see* it?" yelled Salem, and as he received no reply, turned to his team. "Come on, weigh anchor! Think I want to lay out here all night? 'A-sailing out of Salem town—'" he began, and then stopped short and thought. "I *knowed* it!—it *was* th' port eye! Same side th' flag was on!" he exclaimed, triumphantly.

XVI

♦

The Feint

On the boundary line alert and eager punchers rode at a canter to and fro, watching the herds to the south of them, and quick to turn back all that strayed across the line. Just east of the middle point of the boundary Red and Johnny met and compared notes, and both reported the same state of affairs, which was that the cattle came constantly nearer.

Johnny removed his field glasses from his eyes.

"There's punchers with that herd, Red. Three of 'em."

"I reckoned so."

"Wonder what they think they're going to do?"

"We'll know purty soon."

"They're coming this way."

"If you had th' brains of a calf you'd know they wouldn't go south."

"Think they're going to rush us?" Johnny asked, eagerly.

"No; course not!" retorted Red. "They're going to make 'em stand on their heads!"

Johnny began to hum—

> *Joyous Joe got a juniper jag*
> *A-jogging out of Jaytown;*
> *Joyous Joe got a juniper jag—*

"We'll show that prickly pear from Montanny some fine points."

"Now, look here, Kid; don't you let 'em get a cow across th' line. Shoot every one, but keep yore eyes on th' gang."

" 'Joyous Joe got a juniper jag—' Come on, you fools!"

"Wonder where Hopalong is?" Red asked.

"Up on th' Peak, I reckon. *Hey*, Billy!" he yelled. "Here comes Billy, Red."

"I guessed as much when you yelled; if you don't yell away from my ear next time I'll kick yore pants over yore hat. Damned idiot, you!"

"Hullo, Billy," cried Johnny, ignoring Red's remarks. "Just in time for th' pie. Where's Hopalong?"

"In th' hills."

"You get along an' tell him what's doing out here," ordered Red. "Go lively!"

"Reckon I'd better stay an' give you a hand; you'll need it before long," Billy replied.

"You know what Hopalong said, don't you?" blazed Red. "What do you think me an' th' Kid are made of, anyhow? You go on, an' quick!"

"Send Johnny," Billy suggested, hopefully.

"Why, you coyote!" cried Johnny, excitedly. "Th' idea! You go on!"

"Yo're a pair of hogs," grumbled Billy, riding off. "I'll get square, someday. Hope they lick you!"

"Run along, little boy," jeered Johnny. "Oh, gee! Here they come!" he cried as Billy rode behind the chaparral. "Look at 'em!"

"*Let* 'em come!" cried Billy, returning. "We'll lick 'em!"

"Get out of here!" shouted Red, drawing his Winchester from its sheath. "For God's sake, do what yo're told! Want to let Meeker win out?"

"Nope; so long," and Billy galloped away.

"That ain't a herd!" cried Johnny, elated. "That's only a handful. It's a scrawny looking bunch, men an' all. Come on, you coyotes!" he yelled, waving his rifle.

"You chump; this ain't the real play—it's a blind, a

wedge," Red replied. "They're pushing a big one through somewhere else."

"I'm shore glad Billy went, an' not me," Johnny remarked.

"There's Morgan," Red remarked. "I know his riding."

"Bet you won't know it when th' show's over. An' there's Chick, too. He needs a licking. You won't know his riding, neither."

The herd came rapidly forward and the men who were guarding it waved their sombreros and urged it on. Red, knowing that he would be crowded if he waited until the cows were upon him, threw his rifle to his shoulder and began to shoot rapidly, and cow after cow dropped, and the rush was stopped. Before the H2 men could get free from the panic-stricken herd Red and Johnny were within a hundred yards of them and when they looked up it was to see Red covering them, while Johnny, pleased by the reduced range, was dropping more cows.

"Stop!" Red shouted, angrily.

"Huh!" exclaimed Johnny, looking up. "Oh, I thought you was talking to me," he muttered, and then dropped another cow.

"What in hell do you think yo're doing?" yelled Morgan.

"Just practicing," retorted Johnny. He quickly swung his rifle on Chick. "Hands up! No more of that!"

"You've got gall, shooting our cows!" replied Chick.

"Get 'em up, boy!" snapped Johnny, and Chick slowly raised his arms, speaking rapidly.

"What do you take us for!" shouted Ed Joyce, frantic at his helplessness.

"Coyotes," replied Red. "An' since coyotes don't ride, you get off'n them cayuses, *pronto*."

"Like hell!" retorted Ed.

Johnny's rifle cracked and Ed tumbled off his dead horse, and when he arose the air was blue.

"Nex' gent say 'I,' " called Johnny.

"I'll be damned if I'll stand for that!" yelled Morgan, reaching for his gun. The next thing he knew was that the air was full of comets, and that his horse was dead.

Chick sullenly dismounted and stood watching Red, who was now in vastly better spirits, since the H2 rifles were on the horses and too far away from their owners to be of any use. The range was too great for good revolver shooting even if they could get them into action.

"Watch 'em," said Red, firing. Chick's horse, stung to frenzy by the wound, kicked up its heels and bolted, leaving the three punchers stranded ten miles from home.

"Turn around an' hit th' back trail," ordered Red. "No back talk!"

"I'll bust you wide open, someday, you red-headed wart!" threatened Dan, shaking his fist at the grinning line man. "That's a hell of a thing to do, that is."

"Shut up an' go home. Ain't you got enough?" shouted Red.

"Just wait," yelled Ed Joyce.

"That's two with th' waiting habit," laughed Johnny.

"What do—" began Chick, stepping forward.

"Shut up! Who told you to open yore face!" cried Red, savagely. "Get home! G'wan!"

"Walk, you coyotes, walk!" exulted Johnny.

He and his companions watched the three angry punchers stride off towards the H2 and then Red told Johnny to ride west while he, himself, would go east to help his friends if they should need him. They had just begun to separate when Johnny uttered a shout of joy. Antonio had joined the trio of walkers and they were pulling him from his horse. He waved his arms excitedly, but Chick had him covered. Dan and Ed were already on the animal and they quickly pulled Chick up behind them, narrowly watching Antonio all the while. The horse fought for some time and then started south, the riders shouting while Antonio, still waving his arms, plodded homeward on foot.

Great joy filled Johnny's heart as he gloated over Antonio's predicament. "Hoof it, you snake! Kick up th' dust!"

"They can't get in th' game again for some time, till they get cayuses," remarked Red. "That makes four less to deal with."

"He acts like he had all eternity to get nowhere—look at him! Let's go down an' rope him. He's on th' prod now—we can have a lot of fun."

"If I go down there it'll be to plug him good," Red replied. "You hang around out here for a while. I'm goin' west—Pete's in that house alone—so long, Kid."

Johnny grinned a farewell to Antonio and followed instructions while his friend rode towards the Peak to assist Pete, the lonely, who as it happened, would be very glad to see him.

XVII

♦

Pete Is Tricked

Pete Wilson grumbled, for he was tiring of his monotonous vigil, and almost hoped the H2 would take the house because of the excitement incident to its recapture. At first his assignment had pleased, but as hour after hour passed with growing weariness, he chafed more and more and his temper grew constantly shorter.

With the exception of smoking he had exhausted every

means of passing the time; he knew to a certainty how many bushes and large stones were on the plateau, the ranges between him and distant objects, and other things, and now he had to fell back on his pipe.

"Wish some son-of-a-thief would zephyr up an' start something," he muttered. "If I stays in this fly-corral much longer I'll go loco. A couple of years back we wouldn't have waited ten minutes in a case like this—we'd 'a chased that crowd off th' range quick. What's getting into us has got me picking out th' festive pea, all right."

He stopped at the east window and scrutinized the line as far as he could see the dim, dusty, winding trail, hoping that some of the outfit would come into sight. Then he slid the Sharps out of the window and held it on an imaginary enemy, whom he pretended was going to try to take the house. While he thought of caustic remarks, with which to greet such a person, he saw the head of a horse push up into view over the edge of the hill.

Sudden hope surged through him and shocked him to action. He cocked the rifle, the metallic clicks sweet to his ears. Then he saw the rider, and it was—Mary Meeker.

Astonishment and quick suspicion filled his mind and he held the weapon ready to use on her escort, should she have one. Her horse reared and plunged and, deciding that she was alone, and ashamed to be covering a woman, he slid the gun back into the room, leaning it against the wall close at his hand, not losing sight of the rider for a moment.

"Now, what th' devil is she doing up here, anyhow?" he puzzled, and then a grin flickered across his face as the possible solution came to him. "Mebby she wants Hopalong," he muttered, and added quickly, "Purty as blazes, too!" And she did make a pretty picture even to his scoffing and woman-hating mind.

She was having trouble with her mount, due to the spurring it was getting on the side farther from the water. It reared and plunged, bucking sideways, up-and-down and fence-cornered, zigzagging over the ground forward and back, and then began to pitch "stiff-legged." Pete's eyes glowed with the appreciation of a master rider and he was filled with admiration, which soon became enthusiastic, over her saddle-ease and cool mastery. She seemed to be a part of the horse.

"She'd 'a been gone long ago if she was fool enough to sit one of them side saddle contraptions," he mused. "A-straddle is th' only—*Good!* All right! Yo're a stayer!" he exclaimed as she stepped from one stirrup and stood up in the other when the animal reared up on its hind legs.

He glanced out of the other windows of the house and fell to watching her again, his face darkening as he saw that she appeared to be tiring, while her mount grew steadily worse. Then she "touched leather," and again and again. Her foot slipped from the stirrup, but found it again, while she frantically clung to the saddle horn.

"Four-legged devil!" Pete exclaimed. "Wish *I* was on you, you ornery dog! Hey! Don't you bite like that! Keep yore teeth away from that leg or I'll blow yore damned head off!" he cried wrathfully as the animal bit viciously several times at the stirrup leather. "I'll whale th' stuffin' outen you, you wall-eyed claybank! Yo're too bronc for *her* to ride, all right."

Then, during another and more vicious fit of stiff-legged pitching the rider held to the saddle horn with both hands, while her foot, again out of the stirrup, sought for it in vain. She was rapidly losing her grip on the saddle and suddenly she was thrown off, a cry reaching Pete's ears. The victorious animal kicked several times and shook its head vigorously in celebration of its freedom and then buck-jumped across the plateau and out of sight down the hill, Pete strongly tempted to stop its exuberance with a bullet.

Pete glanced at the figure huddled in the dust and then, swearing savagely and fearing the worst, he threw down the bar and jerked open the door and ran as rapidly as his awkward legs would take him to see what he could do for her, his hand still grasping his rifle. As he knelt beside her he remembered that he had been told not to leave the house under any circumstances and he glanced over his shoulder, and just in time to see a chap-covered leg disappear through the doorway. His heart sank as the crash of the bar falling into place told him that he had been unworthy of the trust his best friend had reposed in him. It was plain enough, now, that he had been fooled, to understand it all and to know that as he left the house one or more H2 punchers had sprinted for it from the other side of the plateau.

Red fury filled him in an instant and tearing the revolver from the girl's belt he threw it away and then, grasping her with both hands, he raised her up as though she weighed nothing and threw her over his shoulder, sprinting for the protection of the hillside, which he reached in a few bounds. Throwing her down as he would throw a bag of flour he snarled at her as she arose and brushed her clothes. Years ago in Pete's life a woman had outraged his love and trust and sent him through a very hell of sorrow; and since then he had had no love for the sex—only a bitter, scathing cynicism, which now found its outlet in words. "Yo're a nice one, you are!" he yelled. "You've done yore part! Yo're all alike, every damned one of you—Judas wasn't no man, not by a damned sight! You know a man won't stand by an' see you hurt without trying to help you—an' you play it against him!"

She was about to retort, but smiled instead and went on with her dusting.

"Tickled, hey! Well, you watch an' see what *we* do to coyotes! You'll see what happens to line-thieves down here!"

She looked up quickly and suspected that instead of averting a fight she had precipitated one. Both Hopalong and her father were in as much danger now as if she had taken no part in the trouble.

Pete emptied his revolver into the air as rapidly as he could work the hammer and hurriedly reloaded it, all the time watching his prisoner and the top of the hill. Three quick reports, muffled by distance, replied from Long Hill and he turned to her.

"Now why don't you laugh?" he gritted savagely. He caught sight of her horse grazing calmly further down the hill and his Sharps leaped to his shoulder and crashed. The animal stiffened, erect for a moment, and then sank slowly back on its quivering haunches and dropped.

"*You* won't pitch no more, damn you!" he growled, reloading.

Her eyes snapped with anger and she fought at her holster. "You coward! You coward!" she cried, stamping her foot. "To kill that horse, an' steal my gun—afraid of a woman!" she taunted. "Coward!"

"I'll pull a snake's fangs rather than get bit by one, when I can't shoot 'em!" he retorted, stung by her words. "You'll see how big a coward I am purty soon—an' you'll stay right here an' see it, too!"

"*I* won't run away," she replied, sitting down and tucking her feet under her skirts. "*I'm* not afraid of a coward!"

Another shot rang out just over the top of Stepping Stone Hill and he replied to it. Far to the west a faint report was heard and Pete knew that Skinny was roweling the lathered sides of his straining horse. Yet another sounded flatly from the direction of the dam, the hills multiplying it into a distant fusillade.

"Hear 'em!" he demanded, fierce joy ringing in his voice. "Hear 'em! You've kicked th' dynamite, all right—you'll smell th' smoke of yore little squib clean down to yore ranch house!"

"That's grand—yo're doing it fine," she laughed, strangling the fear which crept slowly through her. "Go on—it's grand!"

"It'll be a whole lot grander when th' boys get here an' find out what's happened," he promised. "There'll be some funerals start out from what's left of yore ranch house purty soon."

"K-i-i-i-e-e-p! Ki-ip ki-ip!" came the hair-raising yell from the top of Stepping Stone Hill, and Pete withheld the rest of his remarks to reply to it in kind. Suddenly Red Connors, his quirt rising and falling, bounded over the top of the hill and shot down the other side at full speed. Close behind him came Billy Williams, who rode as recklessly until his horse stepped into a hole and went down, throwing him forward like a shot out of a catapult. He rolled down the hill some distance before he could check his impetus and then, scrambling to his feet, drew his Colt and put his broken-legged mount out of its misery before hobbling on again.

Red slid to a stand and leaped to the ground, his eyes on the woman, but his first thought was for the house. "What's the matter? Why ain't you in that shack? Didn't Hopalong tell you to hold it?" he demanded. Turning to Mary Meeker he frowned. "What are you doing up here? Don't you know this ain't no place for you today?"

Pete grasped his shoulder and swung him around so sharply that he nearly lost his balance, crying: "Don't talk to her, she's a damned snake!"

Red's hand moved towards his holster and then stopped,

for it was a friend who spoke. "What do you mean, damn you? Who's a snake? What's wrong here, anyhow?"

Billy limped up and stood amazed at the strange scene, for besides the presence of the woman, his friends were quarreling and he had never seen that before. Seeing Mary look at him he flushed and sneaked off his sombrero, ashamed because he had forgotten it.

Pete swiftly related all that had occurred, and ended with another curse flung at his prisoner, who looked him over with a keen, critical glance and then smiled contemptuously.

"That's a fine note!" Red cried, his sombrero also coming off. He looked at Mary and saw no fear in her face, no sign of any weakness, but rather a grimness in the firmness of her lips and a battling light in her eyes, which gained her immunity from his tongue, for he admired grit. "Here, you, stop that cussing! You can't cuss no woman while I'm around!" he cried hotly. "Hopalong'll break you wide open if he hears you. Cussing won't do no good; what we want is thinking, an' fighting!" Catching sight of Billy, who looked self-conscious and a little uncomfortable, he cried: "An' what's th' matter with you?"

Billy jerked his thumb over his shoulder in the direction of the dead horse and Red, following the motion, knew. "By th' Lord, you got off easy! Pete, you watch yore prisoner; keep her out of danger, an' there'll be lots of it purty soon. We'll get th' house for you."

"Send up to Cowan's saloon; he had some dynamite, an' if we can get any we can blow them sneaks off th' face of th' earth," Pete exclaimed, his anger and shame urging him against his better nature. "Go ahead. I'll take th' chances using th' stuff—I lost th' house."

The pathetic note of self-condemnation in his last words stopped Red's reprimand and he said, instead: "We'll talk about that later. But don't you lose no sleep—they can't hold it, dynamite or no dynamite. We'll have it before sundown."

Dynamite! Mary caught her breath and sudden fear gripped her heart. Dynamite! And two men were in the house, Doc Riley and Jack Curtis, men who would not be there if she had not made it possible for them—she was responsible.

"Here comes Skinny!" cried Billy, waving his arm.

"An' here's Hopalong!" joyously cried Pete, elated, for he pinned his faith in his line-foreman's ability to get out of any kind of a hole, no matter how deep and wide. "Now things'll happen! We're going to get busy *now*, all right!"

The two arrived at the same instant and both asked the same question. Then Hopalong saw Mary and he was at her side in a trice.

"Hullo! What are *you* doing up here?" he cried in astonishment.

"I'm a prisoner—of *that*!" she replied, pointing at Pete.

Hopalong wheeled. "What! What have you been doing to her? Why ain't you in th' house, where you belongs?"

Pete told him, briefly, and he turned to the prisoner, a smile of admiration struggling to get through his frown. She looked at him bravely, for now was the crisis, which she had feared, and welcomed.

"By th' Lord!" he cried, softly. "Yo're a thoroughbred, a fighter from start to finish. But you shouldn't come up here to-day; there's no telling, sometimes, where bullets go after they start." Turning, he said, "Pete, you chump, stay on this side of th' hills an' watch th' house. Billy, lay so you can watch th' door. Red, come with me. An' if anybody gets a shot at them range stealers, shoot to kill. Understand? Shoot to kill—it's time."

"Dynamite?" queried Pete, hopefully. "I'll use it. Cowan—"

Hopalong stared. "Dynamite! Dynamite! We ain't fighting 'em that way, even if they are coyotes. You go an' do what I told you."

"Yes, but—"

"Shut up!" snapped Hopalong. "I know how you feel *now*, but you'll think different to-morrow."

"Let's swap th' girl for th' house," suggested Skinny, grinning. "It's a shore cinch," he added, winking at Billy, who laughed.

Hopalong wheeled to retort, caught Skinny's eye closing, and laughed instead. "I reckon that would work all right, Skinny. It'd be a good joke on 'em to take th' house back with th' same card they got it by. But this ain't no time for joking. Pete, you better stay here an' watch th' window on this side; Billy, take the window on th' south side. Skinny can go around west an' Red'll take th' door. They won't be so joyous after they get what's coming their way. This ain't no picnic; shoot to kill. We've been peaceful too blamed long!"

"That's th' way to talk!" cried Pete. "If we'd acted that way from th' very first day they crossed our line we wouldn't be fighting to capture our own line house! You know how to handle 'em all right!"

"Pete, how much water is in there?" Hopalong asked.

"'Bout a hatful—nobody brought me any this morning, th' lazy cusses."

"All right; they won't hold it for long, then. Take yore places as I said, fellers, an' get busy," he replied, and then turned to Mary. "Where's yore father? Is *he* in that house?"

"I don't know—an' I wouldn't tell if I did!"

"Say, yo're a regular hummer! Th' more you talk th' better I like you," he laughed, admiringly. "You've shore stampeded me worse than ever—I'm so loco I can't wait much longer—when are you going to marry me? Of course you know that you've got to someday."

"Indeed I have *not!*" she retorted, her face crimson. "If you wait for me to marry you you will die of old age! An' I'm shore somebody's listening."

"Then *I'll* marry *you*—of course, that's what I meant."

"Indeed you *won't!*"

"Then th' minister will. After this line fighting is over I won't wait. I'll just rope you an' drive you down to Perry's Bend to th' hobbling man, if you won't go any other way. We'll come back a team. I mean what I say," and she knew that he did, and she was glad at heart that he thought none the less of her for the trick she had·played on Pete. He seemed to take everything as a matter of course, and as a matter of course he was going to re-take the house.

"You just *dare* try it! Just *dare!*" she cried, hotly.

"Now you have gone an' done it, for I never take a dare, *never,*" he laughed. "It's us for th' sky pilot, an' then th' same range for life. Yo're shore purty, an' that fighting spunk doubles it. You can begin to practice calling yourself Mrs. Hopalong Cassidy, of th' Bar-20."

Pete fired, swore, and turned his head. "How th' devil can I hit a house with all that fool talk!" and the two, suddenly realizing that Pete had been ordered to remain close by, looked foolish, and both laughed.

"It gets on my nerves," Pete growled, and then: "Here comes Johnny like a greased coyote."

They looked and saw Johnny tearing down Stepping Stone Hill as if he were afraid that the fighting would be over before he could take a hand in it. When he came within hailing distance he stood up in his stirrups, shouting, "What's up?" and then, seeing Pete, understood. Leaping from the saddle he jerked his rifle out of the sheath and ran to him, jeering. "Oh, Pete! Oh you damned fool!"

"Hey, Johnny! How's things east?" Hopalong demanded.

Johnny stopped and hastily recounted how he and Red had driven back the herd, adding: "Her dad is out there now looking at his dead cows—I saw him when I came back from East Arroyo. An' I saw them three punchers ride over that ridge down south; and they shore made good time. Say, how did they get Pete out?" he asked eagerly.

"I'll tell you that later—Pete, you go an' tell Red to come here, an' take his place. We can't swap Mary for th' house, but we can swap her dad! Mary, you better go home—this won't be no place for you in a little while. Where's yore cayuse?" he asked, looking around.

"It's down there—he shot it," she replied, nodding at Pete.

"Shot it? Lord, but he must 'a been mad! Well, you can get square—Pete, where's yore cayuse?"

"How th' devil do I know!" Pete blazed, indignantly. "I wasn't keeping track of no cayuse after they got th' house!"

"It's down there on th' hill—see it?" volunteered Johnny. "Shall I get it?" he asked, grinning at the disgruntled Pete.

"Yes; an' strip th' fixings off her cayuse while yo're about it—lively."

Johnny vaulted into his saddle and loped down the hill, shortly returning with Mary's saddle and bridle in front of him and Pete's horse at the end of his rope. Hopalong quickly removed Pete's saddle and put the other in its place, Pete eloquent in his silence, and Johnny manifestly pleased by the proceedings.

"Now you can ride," Hopalong smiled, helping her into the saddle. "Pete don't care at all—he ain't saying a word," whereat Pete said a word, several of them in fact, under his breath and vowed that he would kill the men in the house to get square.

"I'll send it back as soon as I can," she promised, and then, when Hopalong leaned closer and whispered something to her, she flushed and spurred the animal, leaving him standing in a cloud of dust, a smile on his face.

Johnny, grinning until his face threatened to be ruptured, wheeled on Pete. "Yo're a lucky fool, even if you did go an' lose th' house for us—wish she'd ride *my* cayuse!"

Pete replied in keeping with his feelings now that there was no woman present, and walked away to change places with Red, who soon came up. Then the three mounted and cantered east to find the H2 foreman, Johnny mauling "Whiskey Bill" in his exuberance. Suddenly he turned in his saddle and slapped his thigh: "I'll bet four cents to a tooth brush that she's telling her dad to get scarce. She heard what you said, Hoppy!"

"Right! Come on!" exclaimed Hopalong, spurring into a gallop, his companions racing behind, spurring and quirting to catch him.

"Say, Red, she's a straight flush," Johnny shouted to his companion. "Can't be beat—if she turns Hoppy down I'm next in th' line-up!"

"You don't want no wife—you wants a nurse!" Red retorted.

XVIII

◆

The Line House Re-Captured

After Chick, Dan Morgan, and Ed Joyce had commandeered Antonio's horse and left him on foot they rode as rapidly as they could to the corrals of their ranch, where they saddled fresh mounts and galloped back to try conclusions with the men who had humbled them. They also wished to find their foreman, who they knew was somewhere along the line. Chick rode to the west, Dan to the east, and Ed Joyce straight ahead; intending to search for Meeker and then ride together again.

Meanwhile Antonio, tired of walking, returned to the line and lay in ambush to waylay the first Bar-20 puncher to ride past him, hoping to get a horse and also leave a dead man for the Bar-20 to find and lay the blame on the H2. He knew that his rustler allies had scouts in the chaparrals and were ready to run off a big herd as soon as conditions were propitious, and he was anxious to give them the word to begin.

It chanced, however, that Ed Joyce was the first man to approach Antonio, and he paid dearly for being a party to taking his horse. The dead man would not inflame the Bar-20, but the H2, and the results would be the same in the end. Mounting Ed's horse Antonio galloped north into the valley through West Arroyo so as to leave tracks in the direction of the Bar-20, intending to describe a semi-circle and return to his ranch by way of the river trail, leaving the horse where the trail crossed the Jumping Bear. By going the remainder of the way on foot he would not be seen on the horse of the murdered puncher, which might naturally enough stray in that direction, and so be free from suspicion.

Lanky Smith, wondering why none of his friends had passed him on the line, followed the trail west to see if things were as they should be. He was almost in sight of a point opposite West Arroyo, his view being obstructed by chaparrals, when he heard a faint shot, and spurred forward, his rifle in the hollow of his arm ready for action. It could mean only one thing—one of his friends was shooting H2 cows, and complications might easily follow. When he had turned out of an arroyo which made part of the line for a short distance he saw a body huddled on the sand several hundred feet ahead of him. At that instant Meeker, with Chick and Dan close at his heels, came into view on the other side, saw the body and, drawing their own conclusions, opened a hot fire on the Bar-20 puncher, riding to encircle him. Surprised for an instant, and then filled with rage because they had killed one of his friends, as he thought, he returned their fire and raced at Chick, who was now some distance from his companions. Dan and Meeker wheeled instantly and rode to the aid of their friend, and Lanky's horse dropped from under him. Luckily for him he felt a warning tremor go through the animal and jerked his feet free from the stirrups as it sank down, quickly crawling behind it for protection.

Immediately thereafter Chick lost his hat, then the use of his right arm, followed by being deprived of the services of a very good cow-pony, for Lanky now had a rest for his rifle and while his markmanship was not equal to that of his friend Red, it was good enough for his present needs. Dan Morgan started to shout to his foreman and then swore luridly instead, for Lanky was pleased to drill him at five hundred yards, the bullet tearing a disconcerting hole in Dan's thigh.

Meeker had been most zealously engaged all this time in making his rifle go off at regular intervals, his bullets kicking up the dust, humming viciously about Lanky's head, and thudding into the carcass of the dead horse. Then Lanky swore and shook the blood from his cheek, telling Meeker what he thought about the matter. Settling down again he determined to husk Meeker's body from its immortal soul, when he found his magazine empty. Reaching to his belt for the wherewithal for the husking he discovered the lamentable fact that he had only three cartridges left for the Winchester, and the Colt was more ornamental than useful at that range. To make matters worse both Chick and Dan were now sitting up wasting cartridges in his direction, while Meeker seemed to have an unending supply. Just then the H2 foreman found his mark again and rendered his enemy's arm useless. At that point the clouds of misfortune parted and Hopalong, Red, and Johnny at his heels, whirled into sight from the west, firing with burning zeal.

Meeker's horse went down, pinning its rider under it; Dan Morgan threw up his arms as he sat in the saddle, for his rifle was shattered; Chick, propping up his good arm first, arose from behind his fleshy breastwork and announced that he could not fight, although he certainly wanted to; but Meeker said nothing.

Riding first to Lanky, his friends joked him into a better humor while they attended to his wounds. Then they divided to extend the wound-dressing courtesy. First they tried to kill a man, then to save him; but, of course, they desired mostly to render him incapable of injuring them and as long as this was accomplished it was not necessary to deprive him of life.

Hopalong, being in command, went over to look at the H2 foreman and found him unconscious. Dragging him from under the body of his horse Hopalong felt along the pinned leg and found it was not broken. Pouring a generous amount of whiskey down the unconscious man's throat he managed to revive him and then immediately disarmed him. Meeker complained of pains in his groin, not by words but by actions. His left leg seemed paralyzed and would not obey him. Hopalong called Red, who took the injured man up in front of him, where Hopalong bound his hands to the pommel of the saddle.

Meeker preserved a stolid silence until Lanky joined them and then his rage poured out in a torrent of abuse and accusations for the killing of Ed Joyce. Lanky retorted by asking who Ed Joyce was, and wanted to know whose body he had found just before Meeker had come onto the scene. When he found that they were the same he explained that he had not seen it before Meeker had, which the H2 foreman would not believe. Red captured Dan Morgan's horse and led it up. After Chick and Dan had been helped to mount the Bar-20 men's horses, placed before the saddles and bound there, all started towards Lookout Peak, Lanky riding Dan's horse.

When they had arrived at their destination Meeker suddenly realized what he was to be used for and stormed impotently against it. He heard the intermittent firing around the plateau and knew that Doc and Jack still held the house, and believed they could continue to hold it, since the thick adobe walls were impenetrable to rifle fire.

"Well, Meeker, it's you for th' house," Hopalong remarked after he had sent Red to stop the fire of the others. "You got off damned lucky to-day; th' next time you raise heck along our line we'll pay yore ranch houses a visit an' give you something to think about. We handled you to-day with six of us up north, an' what th' whole crowd can do you can guess. Now walk up there an' tell them range-jumpers to vamoose th' house!"

"They'll shoot me before they sees who I am," Meeker retorted, sullenly. "If yo're so anxious to get 'em out, do it yoreself—I don't want 'em."

By this time the others were coming up and heard Meeker's words, and Hopalong, turning to Skinny and Billy, curtly ordered them to mount. "Take this royal fool up to th' bunk house to Buck. Tell Buck what's took place down here, an' also that we're going to shoot hell out of th' fellers in th' house before he sees us. After that those of us who can ride are going down to th' H2 an' clean up that part of th' game, buildings an' all. Go on, lively! Red, Johnny, Pete; cover th' windows an' fill that shack plumb full of lead. It's clouding up now an' when it gets good an' dark we'll bust in th' door an' end it. Skinny, you come back again, quick, with all th' grub an' cartridges you can carry. Meeker started this, but *I'm* going to finish it an' do it right. There won't be no more line fights down here for a long time to come."

"I reckon I'll have to order 'em out," Meeker growled. "What'll you do to 'em if I do?"

"Send 'em home so quick they won't have any time to say 'good-bye,'" Hopalong rejoined. "We've seen too much of you fellers now. An' after I send 'em home you see that they stays away from that line—we'll shoot on sight if they gets within gunshot of it! You've shore had a gall, pushing us, you an' yore hatful of men an' cows! If it wasn't for th' rustling we'd 'a pushed you into th' discard th' day I found yore man herding on us."

Meeker, holding his side because of the pain there from the fall, limped slowly up the hill, waving his sombrero over his head as he advanced.

"What do you want now?—*Meeker!*" cried a voice from the building. "What's wrong?"

"Everything; come on out—we lose," the foreman cried, shame in his voice.

"Don't you tell us that if you wants us to stay here," came the swift reply. "We're game as long as we last, an' we'll last a long time, too."

"I know it, Doc—" his voice broke "—they've killed Ed an' captured Chick, Dan an' me. I'd say fight it out, an' I'd to th' end, only they'll attack th' ranch house if we do. We're licked, *this time*!"

"First sensible words you've said since you've been on this range," growled Lanky. "You was licked before you began, if you only knowed it. An' you'll get licked *every* time, too!"

"Well, we'll come out an' give up if they'll let us all go, including you," called Doc. "I ain't going to get picked off in th' open while I've got this shack to fight in, not by a blamed sight!"

"It's all right, Doc," Meeker replied. "How's Jack?" he asked, anxiously, not having heard Doc's companion speak.

"Wait an' see," was the reply, and the door opened and the two defenders stepped into sight, bandaged with strips torn from their woollen shirts, the remains of which they did not bother to carry away.

"Who played that gun through th' west window?" asked Doc, angrily.

"Me!" cried Skinny, belligerently. "Why?"

"Muzzle th' talk—you can hold yore pow-wow some other time," interposed Hopalong. "You fellers get off this range, an' do it quick. An' stay off, savvy?"

Meeker, his face flushed by rage and hatred for the men who had so humiliated him, climbed up on Dan's horse and Dan was helped up behind. Then Chick was helped to mount in front of his foreman and they rode down the hill, followed by Doc and Jack. The intention was to let Dan ride to the ranch after they had all got off the Bar-20 range, and send up the cook with spare horses. Just then Doc remembered that he and Jack had left their mounts below when they walked up the hill to take the house, and they went after them.

At this instant Curley was seen galloping up and he soon reported what Salem had seen. Meeker flew into a rage at this and swore that he would never give in to either foe. While Curley was learning of the fighting, Doc and his companion returned on foot, reporting that their horses had strayed, whereupon Meeker got off the horse he rode and told Doc and Chick to ride it home, Curley being despatched for mounts, while the others sat down on the ground and waited.

When Curley returned with the horses he was very much excited, crying that during his absence Salem had seen six men run off a herd of several hundred head toward Eagle and had tried to overtake them in the chuck wagon.

"God A'mighty!" cried Meeker, furiously. "Ain't I got enough, *now*! Rustling, an' on a scale like that! Peters was right after all about th' rustling, damn him. A whole herd! Why didn't they take th' rest, an' th' houses, an' th' whole ranch? An' Salem, th' fool, chasing 'em in th' chuck wagon! Wonder they didn't take him, too."

"I reckon he wished he had his harpoon with him," Chick snorted, the ridiculousness of Salem's action bringing a faint grin to his face, angry and wounded as he was. "He's the locoedest thing that wears pants in this section, or any other!"

"It was a shore fizzle all around," Meeker grumbled. "But I ain't through with that line yet—no, by th' Lord, I ain't got started yet! But this rustling has got to be cleaned up first of all—th' line can wait; an' if we don't pay no attention to th' valley for a while they'll think we've given it up an' get off their guard."

"Shore!" cried Dan, whose fury had been aroused almost to madness by the sting of the bitter defeat, and who itched to kill, whether puncher or rustler it little mattered; he only wanted a vent for his rage.

"We'll parade over that south range like buzzards sighting carrion," Meeker continued, leading the way homeward. "I ain't a-going to get robbed all th' time!"

"Wonder if Smith did shoot Ed?" queried Dan, thoughtfully. "There was quite a spell between th' shot I heard an' us seeing him, an' he acted like he had just seen Ed. But it's tough, all right. Ed was a blamed good feller."

"Who did shoot him, then?" snapped Meeker, savagely. "There's no telling what happened out there before we got there. Here, Curley, you ain't full of holes like us—you ride up there and get him while we go home. He's laying near that S arroyo right close to th' line—th' one we scouted through that time."

"Shore, I'll get him," replied Curley, wheeling. "See you later."

XIX

♦

Antonio Leaves the H2

On the H2 Jim Meeker rolled and muttered in his sleep, which had been more or less fitful because of his aching groin and strained leg. Gazing confusedly about him he sat bold upright, swearing softly at the pain and then, realizing that he was where he should be, grumbled at the kaleidoscopic dreams that had beset him during his few hours of sleep, and glanced out of the window. Hastily dressing he strode to the kitchen door, calling his daughter as he passed her room, and looked out. The bunk house and the corrals were beginning to loom up in the early light and the noise in the cook shack told him that Salem was preparing breakfast for the men. He did not like the looks of the low, huge, black cloud east of him and as he figured that it would not pass over the ranch houses unless the wind shifted sharply he suddenly stared at a corral and then hastened back to his room for the Colt which lay on the floor beside his bunk. He had seen a man flit past the further corral, speed across the open, and disappear behind the corral nearest to the bunk house. This ordinarily would have provoked no further thought, but his men were crazy-headed enough to do anything, but while rustling flourished, and so audaciously, and while a line war was on, it would stand prompt investigation.

Peering again from the door, Colt in hand, Meeker slipped out silently and ran to the corral wall as rapidly as his injuries would allow. When he reached it he leaned close to it and waited, his gun levelled at the corner not ten feet from him. Half a minute later and without a sound a man suddenly turned it, crouching and alertly watching the bunk house and cook shack at his left, and then stopped with a jerk and reached to his thigh as he became aware that he was being watched at such close range. Straightening up and smothering an exclamation he faced the foreman and laughed, but to Meeker's suspicious ears it sounded very much forced and strained.

"No *sabe* Anton?" asked the prowler, smiling innocently and raising his hand from the gun.

Meeker stood silent and motionless, the Colt as steady as a rock, and a heavy frown covered his face as he searched the evil eyes of his broncho-buster, whose smile remained fixed.

"No *sabe Anton*?" somewhat hastily repeated the other, a faint trace of anxiety in his voice, but the smile did not waver, and his eyes did not shift. He began to realize that it was about time for him to leave the H2, for he knew that few things grow so rapidly as suspicion.

Meeker slowly lowered his weapon and swore; he did

not like the prowling any better than he did the smile and the laugh and the treacherous eyes.

"I no savvy why yo're flitting around th' scenery when you should ought to be in bed," he replied, his words ominously low and distant. "I'm curious as to why yo're prowling around so early before breakfast. It ain't a whole lot like you to be out so early before grub time. What dragged you from th' bunk so damned early, anyhow?"

Antonio rolled a cigarette to gain time, being elaborately exacting, and thought quickly for an excuse. Tossing the match in the air and letting the smoke curl slowly from his nostrils he grinned pleasantly. "I no sleep—have bad dreams. I wake up, *uno, dos* times an' teenk someteeng ees wrong. Then I ride to see. Eet ees soon light after that an' I am hungry, so I come back. Eet ees no more, at all."

"Oh, it ain't!" retorted the foreman, still frowning, for he strongly doubted the truth of what he had heard, so strongly that he almost passed the lie. "It's some peculiar how this ranch has been shedding dreams last night, all right. However, since I had some few myself I won't say I had all there was loose. But you listen to me, an' listen good, too. When I want any scouting done before daylight I'll take care of it myself, savvy? An' if yo're any wise you'll cure yoreself of th' habit of being out nights percolating around when you ought to be asleep. You ain't acted none too wide awake lately an' yore string of cayuses has shore been used hard, so I want it stopped, an' stopped *sudden*; hear me? I ain't paying you to work nights an' loaf days an' use up good cayuses riding hell-bent for nothing. You ain't never around no more when I want you, so you get weaned of flitting around in th' night air like a whip-poor-will; you might go an' catch malaria!"

"I no been out bafo'—Juan, he tell you that ees so, *si*."

"Is that so? I sort of reckon he'd tell me anything you want him to if he thought I'd believe it. Henceforth an' hereafter you mind what *I've* just told *you*. You might run up against some rustler what you don't know very well, an' get shot on suspicion," Meeker hazarded, but he found no change in the other's face, although he had hit Antonio hard, and he limped off to the ranch house to get his breakfast, swearing every time he put his sore leg forward, and at the ranch responsible for his condition.

Antonio leaned against the corral wall and smoked, gazing off into space as the foreman left him, for he had much to think about. He smiled cynically and shrugged his shoulders as he shambled to his shack, making up his mind to leave the H2 and join Shaw on the mesa as soon as he could do so, and the sooner the better. Meeker's remark about meeting strange rustlers, thieves he did not know, was very disquieting, and it was possible that things might happen suddenly to the broncho-buster of the H2. Soon emerging from his hut he walked leisurely to the fartherest corral and returned with his saddle and bridle. After holding a whispered consultation with Juan and Sanchez, who both showed great alarm at what he told them, and who called his attention to the fact that he had lost one of the big brass buttons from the sleeve of his coat, the three walked to the cook shack for their breakfast, where, every morning, they fought with Salem.

"Here comes them Lascars again to fill their holds with grub," the cook growled as he espied them. "If I was th' old man I'd maroon them, or make 'em walk th' plank. Here, *you*! Get away from that bench!" he shouted, running out of the shack. "That's *my* grub! If you ain't good enough to eat longside of th' crew, damned if you can eat with th' cook! Some day I'll slit you open, tail to gills, see if I don't! Here's yore grub—take it out on th' deck an' fight for it," and Salem, mounting guard over the bench, waved a huge butcher knife at them and ordered them off. "Bilgy smelling lubbers! I'll run afoul of 'em some morning an' make shark's food out of th' whole lot!"

Meanwhile Meeker, finding his breakfast not yet ready, went to Antonio's shack and glanced in it. The bunk his broncho-buster used was made up, which struck him as peculiar, since it was well known that Antonio never made up his bunk until after supper. As he turned to leave he espied the saddle and saw that the stirrups were streaked with clay. "Now what was he doing over at th' river last night?" he soliloquized. Shrugging his shoulders he wheeled and went to the bunk house, where he stumbled over a box, whacking his shins soundly. His heartfelt and extemporaneous remarks regarding stiff legs and malicious boxes awakened Curley, who sat up and vigorously rubbed his eyes with his rough knuckles. Grunts and profanity came from the other bunks, Dan swearing with exceptional loquacity and fervor at his wounded thigh.

"Somebody'll shore have to lift me out like a baby," he grumbled. "I'll get square for this, all right!"

"Aw, what you cussing about?" demanded Chick, whose arm throbbed with renewed energy when he sat up. "How'd you like to have an arm like mine so you can't use it for grub, hey?"

"You an' yore arm can—"

"What's matter, Jim?" interrupted Curley, dropping his feet to the floor and groping for his trousers. "You got my pants?" he asked Dan, whereupon Dan told him many things, ending with: "In th' name of heaven what do I want with pants on this leg! I can't get my own on, let alone yourn. Mebby Chick has put 'em on his scratched wing!" he added, with great sarcasm, whereupon Curley found them under his bunk and muttered a profane request to be told why they had crawled so far back.

"Yo're a hard luck bunch if yo're as sore as me,"

growled Meeker, kicking the offending box out of doors. "I cuss every time I hobble."

"Oh, I ain't sore, not a bit—I'm feeling fine," exulted Curley, putting one foot into a twisted trouser leg while he hopped recklessly about to keep his balance, Dan watching him enviously. He grabbed Chick's shoulder to steady himself and then arose from the floor to find Chick calling him every name in the language and offering to whip him with one hand if he grabbed the wounded arm again.

"Aw, what's th' matter with you!" he demanded, getting the foot through without further trouble. "I didn't stop to think, you chump!"

"Why didn't you?" snapped Chick, aggressively.

"Curley, yo're a plain, damned nuisance—get outside where you'll have plenty of room to get that other leg in," remarked Dan.

"Not satisfied with keeping us all awake by his cussed snoring an' talking, he goes an' *hops* right on my bad arm!" Chick remarked. "He snores something awful, Jim; like a wagon rumbling over a wooden bridge; an' he whistles every lap."

"You keep away from *me*, you cow!" warned Doc, weighing a Colt in his hand by the muzzle. "I'll shore bend this right around yore face if you don't!"

"Aw, go to th' devil! Yo're a bunch of sore-heads, just a bunch of—" Curley snapped, his words becoming inaudible as he went out to the wash bench, where Meeker followed him, glad to get away from the grunting, swearing crowd inside.

"Curley," the foreman began, leaning against the house to ease his thigh and groin, "Antonio is either going *loco*, or he is up to some devilment, an' I a whole lot favors th' devilment. I thought of telling him to clean out, get off th' range an' stay off, but I reckon I'll let him hang around a while longer to see just what his game is. Of course if he is crooked, it's rustling. I'd like an awful lot to ketch him rustling; it'd wipe out a lot of guessing, an' him at th' same time."

"All three of 'em crooked," Curley replied, refilling the basin. "Every blasted one, an' he's worse than th' others—he's a coyote!"

"Yes, I reckon you ain't far from right," replied Meeker. "Well, anyway, I put in a bad night an' rolled out earlier'n usual. I looked out an' saw somebody sneaking around th' corral, an', gettin' my gun, I went after him hot foot. It was Antonio, an' when I asks for whys an' wherefores, he gives me a fool yarn about having a dream. He woke up an' was plumb scared to death somebody was running off with th' ranch, an', being so all-fired worried about th' safety of th' ranch he's too lazy to work for, he just couldn't sleep, but had to get up an' *saddle his cayuse* an' *ride* around th' corrals to see if it was here. Now, what do you think of that?"

"Huh!" snorted Curley. "He don't care a continental cuss about this ranch or anybody on it, an' never did."

"Which same I endorses; it shore was a sudden change," Meeker replied, glancing at his shack. "I looked in his hut an' saw his bunk hadn't been used since night afore last, so he must 'a had his dreams then. There was yaller clay on his stirrups—he must 'a been scared somebody was going to run off with th' river, too. Now he shore was rampaging all over creation last night—he didn't have no dreams nor no sleep in that bunk last night, nohow. Now, th' question is, where was he, an' what th' devil was he doing? I'd give twenty-five dollars if I knowed for shore."

"That's easy!" snorted Curley, trying to get water out of his ear. "Where'd I 'a been last night if I wasn't broke? Why, down in Eagle having a good time—there's lots of good times in that town if you've got th' price of more than a look-in. Or, mebby, he was off seeing his girl. That's a good way to pass th' evening, too." Then, seeing the frown on Meeker's face he swiftly contradicted himself, realizing that it was no time for jesting. "Why, it looks to me like he might be a little interested in some of th' promiscuous cattle lifting that's going on 'round here. I'll pump him easy so he won't know what I'm driving at."

"Yes, you might do that if yo're shore you won't scare him away, but I want you to pass th' horse corral, anyhow, an' see what horse he rode. See how hard he pushed it riding around th' corrals, an' if there's any yellow clay on its legs. Don't let him see you doing it or he'll get gun-shy an' jump th' country. I'm going up to breakfast—Mary's calling me."

Curley looked up. "Shore I'll do it. It's raining some on th' hills, all right. Look yonder!'

"Yes. I saw it this morning early. It passed to th' northeast of us. I'll be back soon," and the foreman limped away. "Hey, Curley," he called over his shoulder for Antonio's benefit, "take a look at them sore yearlings in th' corral," referring to several calves they had quarantined.

"All right, Jim. They was some better last night. I don't think it's anything that's catching."

"O-o-h!" yawned Jack in the doorway. "Seems like I just turned in—gosh, but I'm sleepy."

"Nothing like cold water for that feeling," laughed Curley. "We stayed up too late last night talking it over. Hullo, Chick; still going to lick me one-handed?"

"You get away from that water, so I can wash one-handed," replied Chick. "But you shouldn't ought to 'a done that. No, Jack—go ahead; but I'm next. Hey, Dan!" he cried, laughing, "shall I bring some water in to you?"

"I won't stay here an' listen to such language as Dan's ripping off," Curley grinned, starting away. "I'm going up to look at them sick yearlings in Number Two corral."

True to his word Curley looked the animals over thoroughly and then dodged into the horse corral, where he quickly examined the horses as he passed them, alert for trouble, for a man on foot takes chances when he goes among cow-ponies in a corral. Not one of the animals forming Antonio's *remuda* appeared to have been ridden and it was not until he espied Pete, Doc's favorite horse, that he found any signs. Pete's hair was roughened and still wet from perspiration, there was a streak of yellow clay along its belly on one side but none on its hoofs, and dried lather still clung to its jaws. Pete made no effort to get away, for he was one of the best trained and most intelligent animals on the ranch, a veteran of many round-ups and drives, and he knew from experience that he would not be called on to do double duty; he had done his trick while the others rested.

"An' you know I ain't a-going to ride you, hey?" Curley muttered. "You've had yore turn, an' you know you won't be called on to-day, you wise old devil. Pete, some people say cayuses ain't got no sense, that they can't reason— they never knowed you, did they? Well, boy, you'll have yore turn grazing with th' rest purty soon."

He returned to the bunk house and spent a few minutes inside and then sauntered easily towards the ranch house, where the foreman met him.

"So there wasn't no clay on his hoofs, hey?" Meeker exclaimed. "Some on his belly, an' none on his hoofs. Hum! I reckon Pete was left by hisself while Antonio wrastled with th' mud. Must 'a thought he was prospecting. Well, he's a liar, an' a sneak; watch him close, an' tell th' rest to do th' same. Mebby we'll get th' chance soon of stretching his neck some bright morning. I'll be down purty soon to tell you fellers where to ride."

Curley returned to the wash bench and cleansed his hands, and because the cold water felt so good, he dipped his face into it again, blowing like a porpoise. As he squilgeed his face to lessen the duty of the overworked towel, he heard a step and looked up quickly. Antonio was leaning against the house and scowling at him, for he had looked through a crack in the corral wall and had seen Pete being examined.

"Eet ees *bueno* thees mornin'," Antonio offered.

"What's good?" Curley retorted, staring because of Antonio's unusual loquacity.

"*Madre de Dios*, de weatha."

"Oh, salubrious," replied Curley, evading a hole in the towel. "Plumb sumptuous an' highfalutin', so to speak. You had a nice night in Eagle, all right. Who-all was down there?"

"Antone not en Eagle—he no leev de rancho," Antonio replied. He hesitated as if to continue and Curley noticed it.

"What's on yore mind, 'Tony? What's eating you? *Pronto*, I'm hungry."

Antonio hesitated again. "What you do een de corral thees mornin'?"

"Oh, I was looking at them yearlings—they were purty bad, but they're gettin' along all right. What do you think about 'em?"

"No; een de *beeg* corral."

"Oh, you do!" snapped Curley. "Well, I remembered you was riding around this morning before sunup so I reckoned I'd look in an' see if you rid my cayuse, which you didn't, an' which is good for you. I ain't a whole lot intending to go moping about on no tired-out bronc, an' don't you forget it, neither. An' seeing as how it ain't none of your damned business what I do or where I go, that's about all for you."

"You no spik true—*Pah*! eet ees a lie!" cried Antonio excitedly, advancing a step, and running into the wash water and a fist, both of which met him in the face. Curley, reaching for his holster and finding that he had forgotten to buckle it on, snatched the Remington from

Antonio's sheath while the fallen man was half dazed. Pointing it at his stomach, he ordered him up and then told him things.

"I reckon you got off easy—th' next time you calls me a liar shoot first, or there'll be one less, shifty-eyed coyote to ride range nights."

Antonio, drenched and seething with fury, his discolored face working with passion and his small, cruel eyes snapping, sprang to the wall and glared at the man who had knocked him down. But for the gun in Curley's hand there would have been the flash of a knife, but the Remington was master of the situation. Knife throwing is a useful art at times, but it has its limitations. Cursing, he backed away and slunk into his shack as Doc Riley stuck his head out of the bunk house doorway, hoping to be entertained.

"Worth while hanging 'round, Curley? Any chance of seeing a scrap?" Doc asked, eyeing the gun in his friend's hand.

"You could 'a seen th' beginning of a scrap a couple of minutes earlier," Curley replied. "I didn't give him a chance to throw. Why, he was out all night on Pete, yore cayuse—rode him hard, too. He said—"

"My Pete! Out all night on Pete!" yelled Doc, taking a quick step towards Antonio's hut, the door of which slammed shut, whereupon Doc shouted out his opinions of Antonio. "Is that right?" he asked, turning to Curley. "Was he out on Pete?"

"He shore was—used him up, too."

"I'll break every bone in his yaller carcass!" Doc shouted, shaking his fist at the hut. "Every time I see him I want to get my gun going, an' it's getting worse all th' time. I'll fill him full of lead pills surer than anything one of these days."

"If you don't I will," replied Curley. "I just don't know why I didn't then because—"

"Four bells—grub pile!" rang out the stentorian voice of Salem, who could shout louder than any man on the ranch, and the conversation came to an abrupt end, to be renewed at the table.

When Antonio heard the cook's shout he opened the door a trifle and then, seeing that the coast was clear, picked up the bundle which contained his belongings, shouldered his saddle, slipped his rifle under his arm, and ran to the corral. Juan and Sanchez had been there before him and he found that they not only had taken four of the best horses, but that they had also picketed two good ones for him, and had driven off the remainder to graze, which would delay pursuit should it be instituted. Saddling the better of the two, he left the other and cantered northwest until hidden from the sight of any one at the ranch, and then galloped for safety.

Meeker, returning to the bunk house, found his men in far better humor than they were in when he left them, although the death and burial of Ed Joyce and the other misfortunes of the day before had quieted them a little. As he entered the room he heard Salem in the cook shack, droning a mournful dirge-like air as he slammed things about.

"Hey, cook!" shouted the foreman, standing in the door of the gallery. "Cook!"

"Aye, aye, sir!"

"You are shore you didn't recognize none of them thieves that ran off our herd yesterday?"

"Nary a one, sir. They was running with all sails set two points off my port bow, which left me astarn of 'em. I was in that water-logged, four-wheeled hunk of a chuck wagon an' I couldn't overhaul 'em, sir, 'though I gave chase. I tried a shot with th' chaser, but I was rolling so hard I couldn't hull 'em. But I'll try again when I'm sober, sir."

"All right, Salem," laughed Meeker. "Curley, you take

yore regular range. Doc, suppose you take th' west, next to Curley? Chick an' Dan will have to stay here till they get well enough to ride, an' I'll need somebody on th' ranch after yesterday, anyhow. Jack, how do you feel? Good! Ride between here an' Eagle. I'm going to go down to that town an' see what I can find out."

"But I can ride, Jim," offered Chick, eagerly. "This arm won't bother me much. Let me stick close to Doc, or one of th' boys. Maybe they might need me, Jim."

"You stay right here, like I said. We'll have to wait till we're all right before we can get down to work in earnest. An' every one of you look out for trouble—shoot first an' talk after." He turned again to the gallery. "Salem, kill a cow an' sun cure th' meat; we might want it in a hurry sometime soon. That'll be one cow they don't get, anyway."

"Who's going to ride north, Jim?" asked Doc.

"Nobody; th' Bar-20 has been so damned anxious to turn our cows an' do our herding for us, an' run th' earth, we'll just let 'em for a while. Not much danger of any rustlers buzzing reckless around *that* neighborhood; they'll earn all they steal if they get away with it."

> *I saw her face grow cold in death,*
> *I saw her—*

came Salem's voice in a new wail. Meeker grabbed a quirt and, leaping to the gallery, threw it. The song stopped short and other words, less tuneful, finished the cook's efforts.

"You never mind what you saw!" shouted the foreman. "If you can't sing anything but graveyard howls, you shut up yore singer!"

XX

◆

What the Dam Told

About the time Meeker caught Antonio prowling around the corral, Hopalong stepped out of the line house on the Peak and saw the approaching storm, which gladdened him, notwithstanding the fact that he and Red would ride through it to the bunk house. The range was fast drying up, the grass was burning under the fierce heat of the sun, and the reservoir, evaporating as rapidly as it was supplied, sent but little water down the creek through the valley. This storm, if it broke over the valley, promised to be almost a flood, and would not only replenish the water supply, but would fortify the range for quite a while against the merciless sun.

After he had sent Meeker and his men on their homeward journey he ordered all but Red to report to Buck at the bunk house, believing that the line fighting was at an end for a while, at least. But to circumvent any contingency to the contrary, he and Red remained to guard the house and discuss the situation. The rest of the line riders were glad to get away for a day, as there was washing and mending to be done, clothes to be changed, and their supply of cartridges and tobacco to be replenished.

After throwing his saddle on his horse he went back to the house to get his "slicker," a yellow water-proof coat, and saw Red gathering up their few belongings.

"Going to rain like th' devil, Red," he said. "We'll get soaked before we reach th' dam, but it'll give th' grass a chance, all right. It's due us, an' we're going to get it."

Red glanced out of the window and saw the onrushing,

low black mass of clouds. "I reckon yes. Going to be some fireworks, too."

Hopalong, slipping into the hideous slicker, followed Red outside and watched him saddle up. "It'll seem good to be in th' house again with all th' boys, an' eat cook's grub once more. I reckon Frenchy an' some of his squad will drift in—Johnny said he was going to ride out that way on his way back an' tell 'em all th' news."

"Yes. Mind yore business, Ginger!" Red added as his horse turned its head and nipped at his arm, half in earnest and half in playful expostulation. Ginger could not accustom himself to the broad, hind cinch which gripped his soft stomach, and he was wont to object to it in his own way. "Yes, it's going to be a shore enough cloudburst!" Red exclaimed, glancing apprehensively at the storm. "Mebby we better take th' hill trail—we won't have no cinch fording at th' Bend if *that* lets loose before we get there. We should 'a gone home with th' crowd last night, 'stead of staying up here. I knowed they wouldn't try it again—it's all yore fault."

"Oh, yo're a regular old woman!" retorted Hopalong. "A wetting will do us good—an' as for th' ford, I feel like having a swim."

The close, humid air stirred and moaned, and fitful gusts bent the sparse grass and rustled across the plateau, picking up dust and sending it eddying along the ground. A sudden current of air whined around the corners of the line house, slamming the door violently and awakening the embers of the fire into a mass of glowing coals, which crackled and gave off flying sparks. Several larger embers burst into flame and tumbled end over end across the ground, and Hopalong, running them down, stamped them out, returning and kicking dust over the fire, actuated by the plainsman's instinct. Red watched him and grinned.

"Of course that cloud-burst won't put the fire out," he remarked, sarcastically, although he would have done the same thing if his friend had not.

"Never go away an' leave a fire lit," Hopalong replied, sententiously, closing the banging door and fastening it shut. A streak of lightning quivered between earth and clouds and the thunder rolled in many reverberations along the cliffs of the valley's edge, to die out on the flat void to the west. Down the wind came the haunting wail of a coyote, sounding so close at hand that Red instinctively reached for his rifle and looked around.

"Take *mine*!" jeered Hopalong, mounting, having in mind the greater range of his weapon. "You'll shore need it if you want to get that feller. Gee, but it's dark!"

It was dark and the air was so charged with electricity that blue points of flame quivered on the ears of their horses.

"We're going to get hell!" shouted Red above the roar of the storm. "Every time I spits I make a streak in th' air—an' ain't it hot!"

One minute it was dark; another, the lightning showed things in a ghastly light, crackling and booming like a huge fireworks exhibition. The two men could feel the hearts of their horses pounding against their sides, and the animals, nervous as cats, kept their ears moving back and forth, the blue sparks ghostly in the darkness.

"Come on, get out of this," shouted Hopalong. "Damn, there goes my hat!" and he shot after it.

For reply Red spurred forward and they rode down the steep hill at a canter, which soon changed to a gallop, then to a dead run. Suddenly there came a roar that shook them and the storm broke in earnest, the rain pouring down in slanting sheets, drenching them to the skin in a minute, for their slickers were no protection against that deluge. Hopalong stripped his off, to see it torn from his grasp and disappear in the darkness like a frightened thing.

"Go, then!" he snapped. "I was roasting in you, anyhow! I won't have no clothes left by th' time I hits th' Bend—which is all th' better for swimming."

Red slackened pace, rode at his friend's side, their stirrups almost touching, for it was safer to canter than to gallop when they could not see ahead of them. The darkness gradually lessened and when they got close to the dam they could see as well as they could on any dull day, except for a distance—the sheets of water forbade that.

"What's that?" Hopalong suddenly demanded, drawing rein and listening. A dull roar came from the dam and he instinctively felt that something was radically wrong.

"Water, of course," Red replied, impatiently. "This is a *storm*," he explained.

Hopalong rode out along the dam, followed by Red, peering ahead. Suddenly he stopped and swore.

"She's *busted*! Look there!"

A turbulent flood poured through a cut ten feet wide and roared down the other side of the embankment, roiled and yellow.

"Good God! She's a goner shore!" cried Red excitedly.

"It shore is—*No*, Red! It's over th' stone work—see where that ripple runs? We can save it if we hustle," Hopalong replied, wheeling. "Come on! Dead cows'll choke it—get a move on!"

When Buck had decided to build the dam he had sent for an engineer to come out and look the valley over and to lay out the lines to be followed. The west end, which would be built against the bluff, would be strong; but Buck was advised to build a core of rubble masonry for a hundred feet east of the centre, where the embankment must run almost straight to avoid a quicksand bottom. This had been done at a great increase over the original estimate of the cost of the dam, but now it more than paid for itself, for Antonio had dug his trench over the rubble core—had he gone down a foot deeper he would have struck it and discovered his mistake.

Hopalong and Red raced along the dam and separated when they struck the plain, soon returning with a cow apiece dragging from their lariats, which they released and pushed into the torrent. Their bodies floated with the stream and both men feared their efforts were in vain. Then Hopalong uttered a shout of joy, for the carcasses, stranding against the top of the masonry core, stopped, the water surging over them. Racing away again they dragged up more cows until the bodies choked the gap, when they brought up armfuls of brush and threw them before the bodies. Then Red espied a shovel, swore furiously at what it told him, and fell to throwing dirt into the breach before the brush. He had to take it from different places so as not to weaken the damn, and an hour elapsed before they stopped work and regarded the results of their efforts with satisfaction.

"Well, she's there yet, and she'll stay, all right. Good thing we didn't take th' hill trail," Hopalong remarked.

"Somebody cut it, all right," Red avowed, looking at the shovel in his hands. "*H2*! Hoppy, see here! This is *their* work!"

"Shore enough H2 on th' handle, but Meeker an' his crowd never did that," Hopalong replied. "I ain't got no love for any of 'em, but they're too square for this sort of a thing. Besides, they want to use this water too much to cheat themselves out of every chance to get it."

"You may be right—but it's damned funny that we find their shovel on th' job," Red rejoined, scowling at the brand burned into the wooden handle.

"What's that yo're treading on?" Hopalong asked, point-ing to a bright object on the ground.

Red stooped and then shouted, holding up the object so his friend could see it. "It's a brass button as big as a half-dollar—bet it belonged to th' snake that used this shovel!"

"Yo're safe. I won't bet you—an' Antonio was th' only one I've seen wearing buttons like that in these parts," Hopalong replied. "I'm going to kill him on sight!" and he meant what he said.

"Same here, th' ornery coyote!" Red gritted.

"Antonio had me guessing, but I'm beginning to see a great big light," Hopalong remarked, taking the button and looking it over. "Yep, it's hissn, all right."

"Well, we've filled her," Red remarked after a final in-spection.

"She'll hold until to-morrow, anyhow, or till we can bring th' chuck wagon full of tools an' rocks down here," Hopalong replied. "We'll make her solid for keeps. You better take th' evidence with you, Red, an' let Buck look 'em over. It's a good thing Buck spent that extra money putting in that stone core! Besides losing th' reservoir we'd have had plenty of dead cows by this time if it wasn't for that."

"An' that Antonio went an' picked out the weakest spot in th' whole thing, or th' spot what would be th' weakest if that wall wasn't there," Red remarked. "He ain't no fool, but a stacked deck can beat a good head time after time."

When they reached the ford they found a driftwood-dotted flood roaring around the bend, three times as wide as it was ordinarily, for the hills made a watershed that gave quick results in such a rain.

"Now Red Eagle, old cayuse, here's where you swim," Hopalong laughed, riding up stream so he would not be

carried past the bottom of the hill trail on the farther
side. Plunging in the two horses swam gallantly across,
landing within a few feet of the point aimed at, and
scrambled up the slippery path, down which poured a
stream of water.

When they reached the half-way point between the
ford and the ranch houses the storm slackened, evolv-
ing into an ordinary rain, which Hopalong remarked
would last all day. Red nodded and then pointed to a
miserable, rain-soaked calf, which moved away at their
approach.

"Do you see that!" he exclaimed. "Our brand, an'
Meeker's ear notch!"

"That explains th' shovel being left on th' dam," quickly
replied Hopalong. "It would be plumb crazy for th' H2 to
make a combination like that ear notch an' our brand,
an' you can gamble they don't know nothing bout it.
Th' gent that left Meeker's shovel *for us to find* did that,
too. You know if any of th' H2 cut th' dam they wouldn't
forget to take th' shovel with 'em, Red. It's Antonio, that's
who it is. He's trying to make a bigger fight along th' line
an' stir things up generally so he can rustle promiscuous.
Well, we'll give all our time to th' rustling end from now
on, if I have got any voice in th' matter. An' I hope to th'
Lord I can get within gun range of that coyote. Why, by
th' A'mighty, I'll go down an' plug him on his own ground
just as soon as I can get away, which will be to-morrow!
That's just what I'll do! I'll stop his plays or know th'
reason why."

"An' I'm with you—you'll take a big chance going
down there alone," Red replied. "*After* Meeker hears what
we've got to say he'll be blamed glad we came."

An hour later they stopped at the ranch house, a squat,
square building, flat of roof, its adobe walls three feet
thick and impenetrable to heat. Stripping saddles and

bridles from their streaming mounts, they drove the animals into a large corral and ran to the bunk house, where laughter greeted their appearance.

"Swimming?" queried Johnny, putting aside his harmonica.

"Hey, you! Get out of here an' lean up against th' corral till you shed some of that water!" yelled Lanky, the wounded, watching the streams from their clothes run over the floor. "We'll be afloat in a minute if you don't get out—we ain't no fishes."

"You shut up," retorted Red. "We'll put you out there to catch what water we missed if you gets funny," he threatened, stripping as rapidly as he could. He hung the saturated garments on pegs in the gallery wall and had Pete rub him down briskly, while Billy did the same for his soaked companion.

Around them were their best friends, all laughing and contented, chaffing and exchanging personal banter with each other, engaged in various occupations, from sewing buttons on shirts to playing cards and mending riding gear. Snatches of songs burst forth at odd intervals, while laughter was continually heard. This was the atmosphere they loved, this repaid them for their hard work, this and the unswerving loyalty, the true, deep affection, and good-natured banter that pricked but left no sting. Here was one of the lures of the range, the perfect fellowship that long acquaintance and the sharing of hard work and ubiquitous danger breeds among the members of a good, square outfit. Not one of them ever counted personal safety before duty to his ranch and his companions, taking his hard life laughingly and without complaint, generous to a fault, truthful and loyal and considerate. There was manhood for you, there was contempt for restricting conventions, for danger; there was a unity of thought and purpose that set the rough-spoken, ready-fighting men of the saddle and rope in a niche by themselves, a niche where fair play, unselfishness, and a rough but sterling honor abides always. Their occupation gave more than it exacted and they loved it and the open, windswept range where they were the dominating living forces.

Buck came in with Frenchy McAllister and Pie Willis and grinned at his crowd of happy "boys," who gave warm welcome. The foreman was not their "boss," their taskmaster, but he was their best friend, and he shared with them the dangers and joys which were their lot, sympathetic in his rough way, kind and trusting.

Hopalong struggling to get his head through a dry shirt, succeeded, and swiftly related to his foreman the occurrences of the morning, pointing to the shovel and button as the total exhibit of his proofs against Antonio. The laughter died out, the banter was hushed, and the atmosphere became that of tense hostility and anger. When he had ceased speaking angry exclamations and threats filled the room, coming from men who always "made good." When Red had told of the H2-Bar-20 calf, an air of finality, of conviction, settled on them; and it behooved Antonio to hunt a new range, for his death would be sudden and merciless if he met any of the Bar-20 outfit, no matter when or where. They never forgot.

After a brief argument they came to the decision that he was connected with the rustling going on around them, and this clenched his fate. Several, from the evidence and from things which they had observed and now understood, were of the opinion that he was the ringleader of the cattle thieves.

"Boys," Buck remarked, "we won't bother about th' line very much for a while. It's been a peaceable sort of a fracas, anyhow, an' I don't expect much further trouble. If H2 cows straggle across an' yo're right handy to 'em an' ain't got nothing pressing to do, drive 'em back; but don't look for 'em particularly. There won't be no more drives against us for a long time. We've got to hunt rustlers from now on, an' hunt hard, or they'll get too numerous to handle very easy. Let th' cows take care of themselves along th' river, Frenchy, an' put your men up near Big Coulee, staying nights in Number Two. Pete an' Billy will go with you. That'll protect th' west, an' there won't be no rustling going on from the river, nohow. Don't waste no time herding—put it all in hunting. Hopalong, you, Johnny, Red, an' Skinny take th' hills country an' make yore headquarters in Number Three an' Four. Lanky will stay up here until he can handle hisself good again. I'll ride promiscuous, but if any of you learn anything you want me to know, leave it with Lanky or th' cook if you can't find me. Just as soon as we have anything to go on, we'll start on th' war path hot foot an' clean things up right an' proper."

"What'll we do if we catches anybody rustling?" asked Johnny, assuming an air of ignorance and curiosity, and ducking quickly as Red swung at him.

"Give 'em ten dollars reward an' let 'em go," Buck grinned.

"Give me ten if I brings Antonio to you?"

"I'll fine you twenty if you waste that much time over him," Buck replied.

"Whoop!" Johnny exulted. "Th' good old times are coming back again! Remember Bye-an'-Bye an' Cactus Springs, Buckskin an' Slippery Trendley? Remember th' good old scraps? Now we'll have something else to do besides chasing cows an' wiping th' rust off our guns!"

Lanky, who took keen delight in teasing the youngster, frowned severely. "Yo're just a fool kid, just a happy idiot!" he snorted, and Johnny looked at him, surprised but grinning. "Yes, you are! I never seen such a bloody-

minded animal in all my born days as you! After all th'
fighting you've gone an' got mixed up in, you still yap for
more! You makes me plumb disgusted, you do!"

"He *is* awful gory," remarked Hopalong soberly. "Just
a animated massacre in pants."

"Regular Comanche," amended Red, frowning. "What
do you think about him, Frenchy?"

"I'd ruther not say it," Frenchy replied. "You ask
Pie—he ain't scared of nothing, massacre *or* Comanche."

Johnny looked around the room and blurted out, "You
all think th' same as me, every one of you, even if you
are a lot of pussy-cats, an' you know it, too!"

"Crazy as a locoed cow!" Red whispered across the
room to Buck, who nodded sorrowfully and went into
the cook shack.

"You wait till I sees Antonio an' you'll find out how
crazy I am!" promised Johnny.

"I shore hopes he spanks you an' sends you home
a-bawling," Lanky snorted. "You needs a good licking,
you young cub!"

"Yah, yah!" jibed Johnny. "Needing an' getting are
two different tunes, grand-pop!"

"You wasn't down here, was you, Frenchy, when Johnny
managed to rope a sleepy gray wolf that was two years
old, an' tried to make a pet out of him?" asked Hopalong,
grinning at his recollection of the affair.

"No!" exclaimed Frenchy in surprise. "Did he do it?"

"Oh, yes, he did it; with a gun, after th' pet had torn
his pants off an' chewed him up real well. He's looking
for another, because he says that was too mean a beast to
have any luck with."

Buck stepped into the room again. "Who wants to go
with me to th' dam in th' wagon?" he asked. "I want to
look at that cut an' fix it for keeps if it needs fixing. All
right! All right! Anybody'd think I asked you to go to a

dance," he laughed. "Pete, you an' Billy an' Pie will be enough."

"Can't we ride alongside?" asked Pie. "Do we have to sit in that thing?"

"You can walk, if you want to. I don't care how you go," Buck replied, stepping into the rain with the three men close behind him. Soon the rattling of the wagon was heard growing fainter on the plain.

The banter and the laughter ran on all the rest of the morning. After dinner Hopalong built a fire in the huge stove and put a ladleful of lead on the coals, while Frenchy and Skinny re-sized and re-capped shells from the boxes on the wall. Hopalong watched the fire and smoked the bullet moulds, while Lanky managed to measure powder and fill the shells after Frenchy and Skinny had finished with them. Hopalong filled the moulds rapidly while Johnny took out the bullets and cooled them by dropping them into cold rain water, being cautioned by Hopalong not to splash any water into the row of moulds. As soon as he found them cool enough, Johnny wiped them dry and passed them on to Red, who crimped them into the charged shells. Soon the piles of cartridges grew to a goodly size, and when the last one had been finished the crowd fell to playing cards until supper was ready. Hopalong, who had kept on running bullets, sorted them, and then dropped them into the boxes made for each size. Finally he stopped and went to the door to look for signs of the morrow's weather.

"Clearing up in th' west an' south—here comes Buck an' th' others," he called over his shoulder. "How was it, Buck?" he shouted, and out of the gathering dusk came the happy reply: "Bully!"

XXI

◆

Hopalong Rides South

The morning broke clear and showed a clean, freshened plain to the men who rode to the line house on the Peak, there to take up their quarters and from there to ride as scouts. Hopalong sent Red to ride along the line for the purpose of seeing how things were in that vicinity and, leaving the others to go where they wished, struck south down the side of the hill, intending to hunt Antonio on his own ground. Tied to his saddle was the shovel and in his pocket he carried the brass button, his evidence for Meeker. As he rode at an easy lope he kept a constant lookout for signs of rustling. Suddenly he leaned forward and tightened his knee grip, the horse responding by breaking into a gallop, while its rider took up his lariat, shaking it into a long loop, his twisting right wrist imparting enough motion to it to keep it clear of the vegetation and rocks.

A distant cow wheeled sharply and watched him for a moment and then, snorting, its head down and its tail up, galloped away at a speed not to be found among domesticated cattle. It was bent upon only one thing—to escape that dreaded, whirling loop of rawhide, so pliant and yet so strong. Hopalong, not as expert as Lanky, who carried a rope nearly sixty feet long and who could place it where he wished, used one longer than the more common lariats.

The cow did its best, but the pony steadily gained, nimbly executing quick turns and jumping gullies, up one side of a hill and down the other, threading its way with precision through the chaparrals and deftly avoiding the holes in its path. Closer and closer together came the pursued and pursuers, and then the long rope shot out and sailed through the air, straight for the animal's hind legs. As it settled, a quick upward jerk of the arm did the rest and there was a snubbing of rope around the saddle horn, a sudden stopping and dropping back on haunches on the part of the pony, and the cow went down heavily. The rider did not wait for the horse to get set, but left the saddle as soon as the rope had been securely snubbed, and ran to the side of his victim.

The cow was absolutely helpless, for the rope was taut, the intelligent pony leaning back and being too well trained to allow the least amount of slack to bow the rawhide closer to the earth. Therefore Hopalong gave no thought to his horse, for while cinches, pommel, and rope held, the small, wiry, wild-eyed bundle of galvanic cussedness would hold the cow despite all its efforts to get up.

"Never saw *that* brand before, an' I've rid all over this country for a good many years, too," he soliloquized. "There sure ain't no HQQ herd down this way, nor no place close enough for a stray. Somebody is shore starting a herd on his own hook; from th' cows on this range, too.

"By th' great horned spoon! I can see Bar-20 in them marks!" he cried, bending closer. "All he had to do was to make a H out of th' Bar, close up th' 2, an' put a tail on th' O! Hum—whoop! There is H2 in it, too! Close th' 2 an' add a Q, an' there you are! I don't mind a hog once in a while, but working both ranches to a common mark is shore too much for me. Stealing from both ranches an' markin' 'em all HQQ!"

He moved up to look at the ears and swore when he saw them. "Damn it! That's all I want to know! Mebby a sheriff wouldn't get busy on th' evidence, but I ain't no sheriff—I'm just a plain cow-punch with good common sense. Meeker's cut is a V in one ear—here I finds a slant like Skinny saw, an' in both ears. If that don't cut under Meeker's notch I'm a liar! All framed up to make a new herd out of our cows. Just let me catch some coyote with a running iron under his saddle flap an' see what happens!"

He quickly slacked the rope and slipped off the noose, running as fast as he could go to his pony, for some cows get "on the prod" very easily, and few cows are afraid of a man on foot; and when a long-horned Texas cow has "its dander up," it is not safe for an unmounted man to take a chance with its horns, unless he is willing to shoot it down. This Hopalong would not do, for he did not want to let the rustlers know that the new brand had been discovered. Vaulting into his saddle he eluded the charge of the indignant cow and loped south, coiling up his rope as he went.

Half an hour after leaving the HQQ cow he saw a horseman ahead of him, threading his way through a chaparral. As Hopalong overtook him the other emerged and stopped, uncertain whether to reach for his gun or not. It was Juan, who had not gone to Mesa overnight, scouting to learn if any new developments had taken place along the boundary. Juan looked at the shovel and then at the puncher, his face expressionless.

Hopalong glanced at the other's cuff, found it was all right, and then forced himself to smile. "Looking for rustlers?" he bantered.

"*Si.*"

"What! There ain't no rustlers loose on this range, is there?" asked Hopalong, surprised.

"*Quien sabe?*"

"Oh, them sleepers were made by yore own, lazy outfit, an' you might as well own up to it," Hopalong grinned, deprecatingly. "You can fool Meeker, all right, he's easy;

but you can't throw dust in my eyes like that. On th' level, now, ain't I right? Didn't you fellers make them sleepers?"

Juan shrugged his shoulders. *"Quien sabe?"*

"That *'Quien sabe'* is th' handiest an' most used pair of words in yore cussed language," replied Hopalong grinning. "Ask one of you fellers something you don't want to tell an' its *'Quien sabe?'* ain't it?"

"Si," laughed Juan.

"I thought so," Hopalong retorted. "You can't tell me that any gang that would cut a dam like they did ourn wouldn't sleeper, an' don't you forget it, neither!"

Juan's face cleared for a moment as he gloated over how Antonio's scheme had worked out, and he laughed. "No can fool you, hey?" Then he pressed his knee tighter against his saddle skirt and a worried look came into his eyes.

Hopalong took no apparent notice of the action, but he saw it, and it sent one word burning through his brain. They were riding at a walk now and Hopalong, not knowing that Juan had left the H2, suggested that they ride to the ranch together. He was watching Juan closely, for it would not be unusual for a man in his position to try to get out of it by shooting. Juan refused to ride south and Hopalong, who was determined to stay with his companion until he found out what he wanted to know, proposed a race to a barranca that cut into the plain several hundred yards ahead. He would let Juan beat him, and all the way, so he could watch the saddle flap, and if this failed he would waste no more time in strategy, but would find out about it quickly. Juan also declined to race, and very hurriedly, for the less his saddle was jolted the better it would be for him. He knew Hopalong's reputation as a revolver fighter and would take no chances.

"That ain't a bad cayuse you got there. I was wondering it it could beat mine, what's purty good itself. Is it very bronc?" he asked, kicking the animal in the ribs, whereupon it reared and pranced. Juan's left hand went to the assistance of his knee, his right grasped the cantle of his saddle, where it was nearer the butt of his Colt, and a look of fear came into his eyes.

Hopalong watched his chance and as the restive animal swung towards him he spurred it viciously, at the same time crying: "Take yore hand from off that flap, you damned cowlifter!"

The command was unnecessary, for a thin, straight rod of iron slipped down and stuck in the sand, having worked loose from its lashings. Juan had put off until tomorrow to heat it and bend a loop in one end for more secure fastening.

At the instant it fell Juan leaned back and dropped over on the far side of his horse, his right leg coming up level with his enemy, and reached for his gun, intending to shoot through the end of the holster and save time. But he went farther than he had intended, not stopping until he struck the earth, his bullet missing Hopalong by only a few inches.

The Bar-20 puncher slipped his Colt back into the sheath and, leaning down, deftly picked up the iron and fastened it to his saddle. Roping Juan's horse he continued on his way to the H2, leaving Juan where he had fallen.

When he arrived at the ranch he turned the horse into the corral and started to ride to the bunk house; but Salem, enjoying a respite from cooking and washing dishes, saw him and started for him on an awkward run, crying: "Where'd you git that hoss? Where'd you clear from, an' who are you?"

"Th' cayuse belongs to Meeker—Juan was riding it. Is anybody around?"

"I'm around, ain't I, you fog-eyed lubber! Where's th' Lascar? Who are you?"

"Well, Duke, I'm from th' Bar-20, an' my name is Hop—"

"Weigh anchor an' 'bout ship! You can't make this port, you wind-jamming pirate!"

"I want to see yore foreman. This is his shovel, an' I—"

"Then where'd you get it, hey? How'd you get his—"

"Hang it!" interrupted Hopalong, losing his patience. "I tell you I want to see Meeker! I want to see him about some—"

"An' where's th' man that rid that hoss?" demanded the cook, belligerently.

"You won't see that thief no more. That's one of th' things I want to—"

"Hooray!" cried Salem. "Was he drowned, or shanghaied?"

"Was he what? What are you talking about, anyhow? Where did you ever learn how to talk Chinese?"

"What! Chinese! You whale-bellied, barnacle-brained bilge pirate, I've got a good notion—"

"Say, is there anybody around here that ain't loco? Are they all as crazy as you?" Hopalong asked.

Salem grabbed up one of the bars of the corral gate and, roaring strange oaths, ran at the stranger, but Hopalong spurred his horse and kept clear of the pole while Salem grew short winded and more profane. Then the puncher thought of Mary and cantered towards the ranch house intending to ask her where he could find her father, thus combining business with pleasure. Salem shook the pole at him and then espied the saddled horse in the corral. He disliked horses as much as they disliked him, so much, in fact, that he said the only reason he did not get out of the country and go back to the sea was because he had to ride a horse to do it. But any way was acceptable under the present exigencies, so he clambered into the saddle after more or less effort and found it not quite roomy enough for one of his growing corpulency. Shouting "Let fall!" he cantered after the invader of his ranch, waving the pole valiantly. He did not see that the ears of his mount were flattened or that its eyes were growing murderous in their expression, and he did not know that the lower end of the pole was pounding lustily against the horse's legs every time he waved the weapon. All he thought about was getting his pleasant duty over with as soon as possible, and he gripped the pole more firmly.

Hopalong looked around curiously to see what the cook was doing to make all that noise, and when he saw he held his sides. "Well, if th' locoed son-of-a-gun ain't after me! Lord! Hey, stranger," he shouted, "if you want him to run fast, take hold of his tail an' pull it three times!"

He was not averse to having a little fun at the tenderfoot's expense and he deferred his visit to the house to circle around the angry cook and shout advice. Instead of laying the reins against his mount's neck to turn it, Salem jerked on them, which the indignant animal instantly resented. It had felt all along that it was being made a fool of and imposed upon, but now it would have a sweet revenge. Leaping forward suddenly it stopped stiff-legged and arched its back several times with all the force it was capable of; but it could have stopped immediately after the first pitch, for Salem, still holding to the pole, executed a more or less graceful parabola and landed in a sitting posture amid much dust.

"*Whoof!* What'd we strike?" he demanded dazedly. Then, catching sight of the cause of his flight, which was at that moment cropping an overlooked tuft of grass as if it were accustomed to upsetting pole-waving cooks, Salem scrambled to his feet and ran at it, getting in one good whack before the indignant and groping pony could move.

"There, blast you!" he yelled. "I'll show you what you get for a trick like that!" Turning, and seeing Hopalong laughing until the tears ran down his face, he roared, "What are you laughing at, damn you?"

A rope sailed out and tightened around Salem's feet and he once more sat down, unable to arise this time, because of Hopalong's horse, which backed slowly, step by step, dragging the captive, who was now absolutely helpless.

"Now I want to talk to you for a few minutes, an' I'm going to," Hopalong remarked. "Will you listen quietly or will you risk losing th' seat of yore pants? You've *got* to listen, anyhow."

"Wha—what—go ahead, only stop th' headway of yore craft! Lay to! I'm on th' rocks!"

Laughing, Hopalong rode closer to him. "Where's Antonio?"

"In hell, I hope, leastwise that's where he ought to be."

"Well, I just sent his friend Juan there—had to; he toted a running iron an'—"

"Did you? Did you?" cried Salem in accents of joy. "Why didn't you say so before! Come in an' splice th' main brace, shipmate! Juan is in Davy Jones' locker, is he? Hey, wait till I get these lashings cast off—yo're a good hand after all. Come in an' have some grog—best stuff this side of Kentucky, where it was made."

"I ain't got time," replied Hopalong, smiling. "Where's that Antonio?"

"Going to send *him* down too? Damn my tops'ls, wish I knowed! He deserted, took shore leave, an' ain't reported since. Yo're clipper-rigged, a regular AB, you are! Spin us th' yarn, matey."

Hopalong told him about the dam and the shooting of Juan and gave him the shovel and button for Meeker, Salem's mouth wide open at the recital. When he had finished the cook grabbed his stirrup and urged him towards the grog, but Hopalong laughingly declined and, looking towards the ranch house, saw Jim Meeker riding like mad in their direction.

"What do you want?" blazed the foreman, drawing rein, his face dark with anger.

"I want to plug Antonio, an' his friend Sanchez," Hopalong replied calmly. "I just caught Juan with a running iron under his saddle flap an' I drilled him for good. Here's th' iron."

"Good for you!" cried Meeker, taking the rod. "They've jumped, all of 'em. I'm looking for 'em myself, an' we're all looking for coyotes toting these irons. I'm glad you got one of 'em!"

"Antonio scuttled their dike—here's th' shovel he did it with," interrupted Salem eagerly. "An' here's th' button off Antonio's jacket. He left it by th' shovel. My mate, here, is cruising to fall in with 'em, an' when he does there'll be—"

"Why, that's *my* shovel!" cried Meeker. "An' that's his button, all right."

Hopalong told him all about the attempt to cut the dam and when he had ceased Meeker swore angrily. "Antonio and his men are on th' rustle, for shore! They're trying to keep th' fighting going on along th' line so we'll be too busy to bother 'em in their stealing. I've been losing cows right an' left—why, they run off a herd of beef right here by th' houses. Salem saw 'em. They killed cows down south an' covered my range with sleepers an' lame mothers. How did you come to guess he had an iron?"

Hopalong told of the HQQ cow he had found and, dismounting, traced the brand in the sand, Meeker bending over eagerly.

"You see this Bar-20?" he asked, pointing it out, and his interested companion interrupted him with a curse.

"Yes, I do; an' do *you* see this H2?" he demanded. "They've merged our brands into one—stealing from both of us!"

"Yes. I figgered that out when I saw th' mark; that's one of th' things I came down to tell you about," Hopalong replied, mounting again. "An' Red an' me found a Bar-20 calf with a V ear notch, too. That proves what th' dam was cut for, don't it?"

"Why didn't I drop that coyote when I caught him skulking th' other morning!" growled Meeker, regretfully. "He had just come back from yore dam then—had yaller mud on his cayuse an' his stirrups. Out all night on a played-out bronc, an' me too thick to guess he was up to some devilment an' shoot him for it! Oh, hell! I thought purty hard of you, Cassidy, but I reckon we all make mistakes. Any man what would stop to think out th' real play when he found that shovel is square."

"Oh, that's all right. I allus did hate Antonio, an' mebby that was why I suspected him, that an' th' button."

Meeker turned to the cook. "Where's Chick an' Dan?" he asked, impatiently. "I ain't seen 'em around."

"Why, Chick rid off down south an' Dan cleared about an hour ago."

"What! With that leg of hissen!"

"Aye, aye, sir; he couldn't leave it behind, you know, sir."

"All right, Cassidy; much obliged. I'll put a stop to th' rustling on *my* range, or know th' reason why. Damn th' day I ever left Montanny!" Meeker swore, riding towards the ranch house.

"Say, I hope you find them Lascars," remarked Salem. "Yo're th' boy that'll give 'em what they needs. Wish you had caught 'em all four instead of only one."

Hopalong smiled. "Then they might 'a got me instead."

"No, no, siree!" exclaimed the cook. "You can lick 'em

all, an' I'll gamble on it, too! But you better come in an'
have a swig o' grog before you weighs anchor, matey. As
I was saying, it's th' best grog west of Kentucky. Come
on in!"

XXII

♦

Lucas Visits the Peak

When Hopalong returned to the line house on the
Peak he saw Johnny and Skinny talking with Lucas, the C80 foreman, and he hailed them.

"Hello, Lucas!" he cried. "What are you doing down
here?"

"Glad to see you, Hopalong," Lucas replied, shaking
hands. "Came down to see Buck, but Lanky, up in th'
bunk house, said he was off somewhere scouting. From
what Lanky said I reckon you fellers had a little joke down
here last week."

"Yes," responded Hopalong, dismounting. "It was a
sort of a joke, except that somebody killed one of Meeker's men. I'll be blamed if I know who done it. Lanky
says he didn't an' he don't have to deny a thing like that
neither. Looks to me like he caught some brand-blotter
dead to rights, like I did a little while ago, an' like he got
th' worst of th' argument."

"What's that about catching somebody dead to rights?"
eagerly asked Johnny.

"Who was it?" asked Skinny.

"Juan. He toted a running iron an' I caught him just
after I looked over a cow with a new brand—"

"Did you get him good?" quickly asked Johnny. "Did
he put up a fight?"

"Yes; an' what was th' brand?" Skinny interposed.

"Here, here!" laughed Hopalong. "I reckon I'll save time if I tell you th' whole story," and he gave a short account of his ride, interrupted often by the inquisitive and insistent Johnny.

"An' who is Salem?" Johnny asked.

"Meeker's cook."

"What did Meeker say about it when you told him?"

"Gimme a chance to talk an' I'll tell you!" and Johnny remained silent for a moment. Finally the story was told and Johnny, asked one more question, grinning broadly: "An' what did Mary say?"

"You say Meeker lost a whole herd?" asked Lucas. "Let me tell you there's more people mixed up in this rustling than we think. But I'll tell you one thing; that herd didn't go north, unless they drove ten miles east or west of our range."

"Well, I reckon it's under one man, all right," Hopalong replied. "If it was a lot of separate fellers running it by themselves there'd 'a been a lot of blunders an' some few of 'em would 'a been shot before Juan went. It's a gang, all right. But why th' devil did they turn loose that H2 rebranded cow, that HQQ that I found? They might 'a knowed it would cause some hot thinking when it was found. That cow is just about going to lick 'em."

"Stray," sententiously remarked Skinny.

"Shore, that's what it was," Lucas endorsed.

"An' do you know what that means?" asked Hopalong, looking from face to face. "It means that they can't be holding their heads very far away. It's three to one that I'm right."

"Mebby they're down in Eagle," suggested Johnny hopefully, for Eagle would be a good, exciting proposition in a fight.

"No, it ain't there," Hopalong replied. "There's too

many people down there. They would all know about it an' want a share in th' profits; but it ain't a whole lot foolish to say that Eagle men are in it."

"Look here!" cried Skinny. "Mebby that HQQ is their road brand—that cow might 'a strayed from their drive. They've got to have some brand on cows they sell, an' they can't have ours on an' get back alive."

"You are right, but not necessarily so about th' road brand," Hopalong rejoined. "But that don't tell us where they are, does it?"

"We've got to hunt HQQ cows on th' drive," Johnny interposed as Skinny was about to speak. "I'll go down to Eagle an' see if I can't get on to a drive. Then I'll trail th' gang all th' way an' back to where they hangs out. That'll tell us where to go, all right."

"You keep out of Eagle—you'd be shot before you reached Quinn's saloon," Hopalong said. "No; it ain't Eagle, not at all. See here, Lucas; have you watched them construction camps along that railroad? There ain't a better market nowhere than them layouts; they don't ask no questions if th' beef is cheap."

"Yes, I've watched th' trails leading to 'em."

"Why, they wouldn't cross yore range!" Hopalong cried. "They'd drive around you an' hit th' camp from above; they ain't fools. Hey! I've got it! They can't go around th' Double Arrow unless they are willing to cross th' Staked Plain, an' you can bet they ain't. That leaves th' west, an' there's a desert out there they wouldn't want to tackle. They drive between th' desert an yore range."

"If they drive to th' camps, yo're right without a doubt," Skinny remarked. "But mebby they are driving south—mebby they're starting a ranch along th' Grande, or across it."

"Well, we'll take th' camps first," Hopalong replied.

"Lucas, can you spare a man to look them camps over? Somebody that can live in 'em a month, if he has to?"

"Shore. Wood Wright is just th' man."

"No, he ain't th' man," contradicted Hopalong quickly. "Anybody that wears chaps, or walks like he does would arouse suspicion in no time, an' get piped out in one night. This man had got to have business up there, like looking for a job. Say! Can you get along without yore cook for a while? If you can't we will!"

"You bet yore life I can!" exulted Lucas. "That's good. He can get a job right where th' meat is used, an' where th' hides will be kicking around. He goes tomorrow!"

"That's th' way; th' sooner th' better," Hopalong responded. "But we won't wait for him. We'll scout around lively down here an' if we don't find anything he may. But for th' Lord's sake, don't let him ride a cayuse into that camp that has brands of this section. Cowan will be glad to lend you his cayuse; he got it up north too far to make them suspicious."

"Yes; I reckon that'll be about the thing."

"Here comes Red," Johnny remarked. "Hey, Red, Hoppy got Juan this morning. Caught him toting a straight iron!"

"Johnny, you get away lively an' tell Frenchy to scout west," Hopalong ordered. "You can stay up in Number Two with them to-night, but come down here again in th' morning. Red, to-morrow at daylight we go west an' comb that country.

"That's th' way," remarked Lucas, mounting. "Get right at it. Have you got any word for Buck? I'll go past th' house an' leave it if you have."

"Yes; tell him what we've talked over. An' you might send yore outfit further west, too," Hopalong responded. "I'll bet a month's pay we end this cow-lifting before two weeks roll by.

"Oh, yes; I near forgot it—Bartlett thinks we-all ought to get together after th' rustling is stopped an' shoot that town of Eagle plumb off th' earth," Lucas said. "It's only a hell hole, anyhow, an' it won't do no harm to wipe it out." He looked around the group. "What do you fellers think about it?" he asked.

"Well, we might, then; we've got too many irons in th' fire now, though," Hopalong replied. "Hey, Johnny! Get a-going! We'll talk about Eagle later."

"I'm forgetting lots of things," laughed Lucas. "We had a little fight up our way th' other day. Caught a feller skinning one of Bartlett's cows, what had strayed over on us. Got him dead to rights, too. He put up a fight while he lasted. Said his name was Hawkins."

"Hawkins!" exclaimed Hopalong. "I've heard that name somewhere."

"Why, that's th' name on th' notice of reward posted in Cowan's," Red supplied. "He's wanted for desertion from th' army, an' for other things. They want him bad up at Roswell, an' they'll pay for him, dead or alive."

"Well, they won't get him; he ain't keeping good enough," Lucas replied. "An' we don't want that kind of money. So long," and he was off.

"So you got Juan," Red remarked. "You ought to have took him alive—we could get it all out of him an' find out where his friends are hanging out."

"He went after his gun, an' he had an iron," Hopalong replied. "I didn't know he had left Meeker, an' I didn't stop to think. He was a brand-blotter."

"What's Meeker going to do about th' line?" Red asked.

"Nothing for a while; he's too worried an' busy look-ing after his sleepers. He ain't so bad, after all."

"Say," remarked Skinny, thoughtfully. "Mebby that gang is over east, like Trendley was. There's lots of water thereabouts, an' good grass, too, in th' Panhandle. Look how close it is to Fort Worth an' th' railroad."

"Too many people over there," Hopalong replied. "An' *they* know all about th' time we killed Trendley an' wiped out his gang. They won't go where they are shore we'll look."

"If I can get sight of one of them I'll find out where they are," Red growled. "I'll put green rawhide around his face if I have to, an' when he savvys what th' sun is going to do to that hide an' him, he'll talk, all right, an' be glad of th' chance."

"To hear you, anybody would think you'd do a thing like that," Hopalong laughed. "I reckon he'd drop at eight hundred, clean an' at th' first shot. But, say, green rawhide wouldn't do a thing to a man's face, would it! When it shrunk he'd know it, all right."

"Crush it to a pulp," Skinny remarked. "But who is going to cook th' supper? I'm starved."

Hopalong awakened suddenly and listened and found Red also awake. Hoofbeats were coming towards the house and Hopalong peered out into the darkness to see who it was, his Colt ready.

"Who's that?" he challenged, sharply, the clicks of his gun ringing clear in the night air.

"Why, me," replied a well-known voice. "Who'd you think it was?"

"Why didn't you stay up in Number Two, like I told you? What's wrong?"

"Nothing," Johnny replied, stripping off his saddle and bridle.

"An' you came all th' way down here in th' dark, just to wake us up?" Hopalong asked, incredulously. "Twenty miles just for that!"

"No. I ain't got here yet—I'm only half way," Johnny

retorted. "Can't you see I'm here? An' I didn't care about you waking up. I wanted to get here, an' here I am."

"In the name of heaven, are you drunk, or crazy?" asked Red. "Of all th' damn fools I ever—"

"Oh, shut up, all of you!" growled Skinny, turning over in his bunk. "Lot of locoed cusses that don't know enough to keep still! Let th' Kid alone, why don't you!" he muttered and was sound asleep again.

"No, I ain't drunk or crazy! Think I was going to stay up there when you two fellers are going off scouting to-morrow? Not by a jugful! I ain't letting nothing get past me, all right?" Johnny rejoined.

"Well, you ain't a-going, anyhow," muttered Hopalong, crawling into his bunk again. "You've got to stay with Skinny—" he did not speak very loud, because he knew it would cause an argument, and he wished to sleep instead of talk.

"What'd you say?" demanded Johnny.

"For God's sake!" marvelled Red. "Can't nobody go an' scratch 'emselves unless th' Kid is on th' ground? Come in here an' get to sleep."

> *Adown th' road, his gun in hand,*
> *Comes Whiskey Bill, mad Whiskey—*

Johnny hummed. "Hey! What you doing?" he yelled, leaping back.

"You heave any more guns on my face an' you'll find out!" roared Skinny, sitting up and throwing Johnny's Colt and belt to the floor. "Fool infant!"

"Tumble in an' shut up!" cried Red. "We want some sleep."

"Yo're a lot of tumble-bugs!" retorted Johnny, indignantly. "How did I know Skinny had his face where I threw my gun! He's so cussed thin I can't hardly see him in daylight, th' chalk mark! Why didn't he say so? Think I can see in th' dark?"

"I don't talk in my sleep!" retorted Skinny, "or go flea-hopping around in th' dark like a—"

"Shut up!" shouted Hopalong, and silence at last ensued.

XXIII

◆

Hopalong and Red Go Scouting

As Hopalong and Red rode down the slope of the Peak the rays of the sun flashed over the hills, giving promise of a very hot day. They were prepared to stay several days, if need be, on the semi-arid plain to the west of them, for it would be combed thoroughly before they returned. On they loped, looking keenly over the plain and occasionally using their field glasses to more closely scrutinize distant objects, searching the barrancas and coulees and threading through mesquite and cactus growths. Hopalong momentarily expected to find signs of what they were looking for, while Red, according to his habit, was consistently contradictory in his words and disproportionately pessimistic.

Moving forward at a swinging lope they began to circle to the west and as they advanced Hopalong became eager and hopeful, while his companion grumbled more and more. In his heart he believed as Hopalong did, but there had to be something to talk about to pass the time more pleasantly; so when they met in some barranca to ride together for a short distance they exchanged pleasantries.

"Yore showing even more than yore usual amount of

pigheaded ignorance to-day," Hopalong grumbled. "Yore blasted, ingrowing disposition has been shedding cussedness at every step. I'll own up to being some curious as to when it's going to peter out."

"As if that's any of yore business," retorted Red. "But I'll just tell you, since you asks; it's going to stop when I get good an' ready, savvy?"

"Yo're awful cheerful at times," sarcastically snorted his companion.

Red's eyes had been roving over the plain and now he raised his glasses and looked steadily ahead.

"What's that out there? Dead cow?" he asked, calmly.

Hopalong put his glasses on it instantly, "Cow?" he asked, witheringly. "No; it's an over-grown lizard! Come on," he cried, spurring forward, Red close behind him.

Riding around it they saw that it bore the brand of the H2, and Hopalong, dismounting, glanced it over quickly and swore.

"Shot in th' head—what did I tell you!"

"You didn't have to get off yore cayuse to see that," retorted Red. "But get on again, an' come along. There's more out here. I'll take th' south end of this—don't get out of hearing."

"Wait! Wonder why they shot it, instead of driving it off after they got it this far?" Hopalong mused.

"Got on th' prod, I reckon, leaving its calf an' being run so hard. I've seen many a one I'd like to have shot. Looks to me like they hang out around that water hole— they drove it that way."

"You can bet yore head they didn't drive it straight to their hangout—they ain't doing nothing like that," Hopalong replied. "They struck south after they thought they had throwed off any pursuit. They drove it almost north, so far; savvy?"

"Well, they've got to have water if they're holding

cows out on this stove," Red rejoined. "An' I just told you where th' water is."

"G'wan! Ten cows would drain that hole in two days!" Hopalong responded. "They've also got to have grass, though mebby you never knew that. An' what about that herd Meeker lost? They wouldn't circle so far to a one-by-nothing water hole like that one is."

"Well, then, where'll they find grass an' water out here?" demanded Red, impatiently. "Th' desert's west, though mebby you never knew that!"

"Red, we've been a pair of fools!" Hopalong cried, slapping his thigh by way of emphasis. "Here we are skating around up here when Thunder Mesa lays south, with plenty of water an' a fair pasture on all sides of it! That's where we'll go."

"Hoppy, once in a great while you do show some intelligence, but we better go up to that water hole first," Red replied. "We can swing south then. We're so close to it now that there ain't nothing to be gained by not taking a look at it. Mebby we'll find a trail, or something."

"Right you are; come on. There ain't no use of us riding separate no more."

Half an hour later Hopalong pointed to one side, to a few half-burned greasewood and mesquite sticks which radiated like the spokes of a wheel.

"Yes, I saw 'em," Red remarked. "They couldn't wait till they got home before they changed th' brand, blamed fools."

"Yes, an' that explains th' HQQ cow I discovered," Hopalong quickly replied. "They got too blamed hasty to blot it an' it got away from 'em."

"Well, it shore beats th' devil how Meeker had to go an' stir up this nest of rattlers," Red grumbled, angrily.

"If these fellers hang out at Thunder Mesa an' drive to th' railroad camps we ought to strike their trail purty close to th' water hole," Hopalong remarked. "It's right in their path."

Red nodded his head. "Yes, we ought to."

An hour later they rode around a chaparral and came within sight of the water hole, which lay a few hundred yards away. As they did so a man rode up out of the depression and started north, unconscious of his danger.

The two men spurred to overtake him, both drawing their rifles and getting ready for action. He turned in his saddle, saw them, and heading westward, quirted and spurred his horse into a dead run, both of his pursuers shouting for him to stop as they followed at top speed. He glanced around again and, seeing that they were slowly but surely gaining, whipped up his rifle and fired at them several times, both replying. He kept bearing more and more to the west and Red rode away at an angle to intercept him. Ten minutes later the fleeing man turned and rode north again, but Red had gained fifty yards over Hopalong and suddenly stopping his horse to permit better shooting, he took quick aim and fired. The pursued man found that his horse was useful only as a breastwork as Red's report died away, and hastily picked himself up and crawled behind it.

"Look out, Red!" warned Hopalong as he flung himself off his horse and led it down into a deep coulee for protection. "That's Dick Archer, an' he can shoot like th' very devil!"

Red, already in a gully, laughed. "An' so can I."

"Hey, I'm going around on th' other side—look out for him," Hopalong called, starting away. "We can't waste no more time up here than we has to."

"All right; go ahead," Red replied, pushing his sombrero over the edge of the gully where the rustler could see it; and he laughed softly when he saw the new hole in it. "He shore can shoot, all right," he muttered. Working down the gully until he came to a clump of greasewood he crawled up the bank and looked out at the man behind the dead horse, who was intently watching the place where he had seen Red's sombrero. "I knowed Eagle was holding cards in this game," Red remarked, smiling grimly. "Wonder how many are in it, anyhow?"

Hearing the crack of a gun he squinted along the sights of his Winchester and waited patiently for a chance to shoot. Then he heard another shot and saw the rustler raise himself to change his position, and Red fired. "I knowed, too, that Hoppy would drive him into range for me, even if he didn't hit him. Wonder what Mr. Dick Archer thinks about *my* shooting about now? Ah!" he cried as the smoke from his second shot drifted away. "Got you again!" he grunted. Then he dropped below the edge of the gully and grinned as he listened to the bullets whining overhead, for the rustler, wounded twice inside of a minute by one man, was greatly incensed thereby and petulantly bombarded the greasewood clump. He knew that he was done for, but that was no reason why he shouldn't do as much damage as he could while he was able.

"Bet he's mad," grinned Red. "An' there goes that Sharps—I could tell Hoppy's gun in a fusillade."

Crawling back up the gully to his first position Red peered out between some gramma grass tufts and again slid his rifle to his shoulder, laughing softly at the regular reports of the Sharps.

A puff of smoke enveloped his head and drifted behind him as he worked the lever of his rifle and, arising, he walked out towards the prostrate man and waved for his friend to join him. As he drew near the rustler struggled up on one elbow, and Red, running forward with his gun raised half-way to his shoulder, cried: "Don't make no gun-play, or I'll blow you apart! Where's th' rest of yore gang?"

"Go to hell!" coughed the other, trying to get his Colt out, for his rifle was empty. He stiffened and fell flat.

Ten minutes later Hopalong and Red were riding southwest along a plain and well beaten trail, both silent and thoughtful. And at the end of an hour they saw the ragged top of Thunder Mesa towering against the horizon. They went forward cautiously now and took advantage of the unevenness of the plain, riding through barrancas and keeping close to chaparrals.

"Well, Red, I reckon we better stop," Hopalong remarked at last, his glasses glued to his eyes. "No use letting them see us."

"Is that smoke up there?" asked Red.

"Yes; an' there's somebody moving around near th' edge."

"I see him now."

"I reckon we know all that's necessary," Hopalong remarked. "That trail is enough, anyhow. Now we've got to get back to th' ranch without letting them fellers see us."

"We can lead th' cayuses till we can get in that barranca back there," Red replied. "We won't stick up so prominent if we do that. After we make it we'll find it easy to keep from being seen if we've any caution."

Hopalong threw himself out of the saddle. "Dismount!" he cried. "That feller up there is coming towards this end. He's their lookout, I bet."

They remained hidden and quiet for an hour while the lookout gazed around the plain, both impatient and angry at the time he gave to his examination. When he turned and disappeared they waited for a few minutes to see if he was coming back, and satisfied that the way was clear, led their horses to the barranca and rode through it until far enough away to be safe from observation.

Darkness caught them before they had covered half of

the distance between the mesa and the ranch, and there being no moon to light the way, they picketed their mounts, had supper, and rolling up in their blankets, spent the night on the open plain.

XXIV

◆

Red's Discomfiture

On their return they separated and Red, coming to an arroyo, rode along its edge for a mile and then turned north. Ten minutes after he had changed his course he espied an indistinct black speck moving among a clump of cottonwoods over half a mile ahead of him, and as he swung his glasses on it a cloud of smoke spurted out. His horse reared, plunged, and then sank to earth where it kicked spasmodically and lay quiet. As the horse died Red, who had dismounted at the first tremor, threw himself down behind it and shoved his rifle across the body, swearing at the range, for at that distance his Winchester was useless. A small handful of sand flew into the air close beside him with a vicious spat, and the bullet hummed away into the brush as a small pebble struck him sharply on the cheek. A few seconds later he heard the faint, flat report.

"It's a clean thousand, an' more," he growled. "Wish I had Hopalong's gun. I'd make that feller jump!"

He looked around to see how close he was to cover and when he glanced again at the cottonwoods they seemed to be free of an enemy. Then a shot came from a point to the north of the trees and thudded into the carcass of the horse. Red suddenly gave way to his accumulated anger which now seethed at a white heat and, scrambling to his feet, ran to the brush behind him. When he gained it he plunged forward to top speed, leaping from cover to cover as he zig-zagged towards the man who had killed Ginger, and who had tried his best to kill him.

He ran on and on, his rifle balanced in his right hand and ready for instant use, his breath coming sharply now. Red was in no way at home out of the saddle. His high-heeled, tight-fitting boots cramped his toes and the sand made running doubly hard. He was not far from the cottonwoods; they lay before him and to his right.

Turning quickly he went north, so as to go around the plot of ground on which he hoped to find his accurate, long-range assailant, and as he came to a break in the hitherto close-growing brush he stopped short and dropped to one knee behind a hillock of sand, the rifle going to his shoulder as part of the movement.

Several hundred yards east of him he saw two men, who were hastily mounting, and running from them was a frightened calf. One of the pair waved an arm towards the place where Ginger lay and as he did so a puff of smoke lazily arose from behind the hillock of sand to the west and he jumped up in his saddle, his left arm falling to his side. Another puff of smoke arose and his companion fought his wounded and frightened horse, and then suddenly grasped his side and groaned. The puffs were rising rapidly behind the hillock and bullets sang sharply about them; the horse of the first man hit leaped forward with a bullet-stung rump. Spurring madly the two rustlers dashed into the brush, lying close along the necks of their mounts, and soon were lost to the sight of the angry marksman.

Red leaped up, mechanically re-filling the magazine of his rifle, and watched them out of sight, helpless either to stop or pursue them. He shook his rifle, almost blind

with rage, crying: "I hope you get to Thunder Mesa before *we* do, an' stay there; or run into Frenchy an' his men
on yore way back! If I could get to Number Two ahead of
you you'd never cross that boundary."

As he returned to his horse his rage cooled and left
him, a quiet, deep animosity taking its place, and he
even smiled with savage elation when he thought how he
had shot at eight hundred yards—they had not escaped
entirely free from punishment and his accuracy had impressed them so much that they had not lingered to have
it out with him, even as they were two to one, mounted,
and armed with long-range rifles. And he could well allow them to escape, for he would find them again at the
mesa, if they managed to cross the line unseen by his
friends, and he could pay the debt there.

He swore when he came to the body of his horse and
anger again took possession of him. Ginger had been
the peer of any animal on the range and, contrary to
custom, he had felt no little affection for it. At cutting
out it had been unequalled and made the work a pleasure to its rider; at stopping when the rope went home
and turning short when on the dead run it had not been
excelled by any horse on the ranch. He had taught it
several tricks, such as coming to him in response to a
whistle, lying down quickly at a slap on the shoulder,
and bucking with whole-hearted zeal and viciousness
when mounted by a stranger. Now he slapped the carcass and removed the saddle and bridle which had so
often displeased it.

"Ginger, old boy," he said, slinging the forty-pound
saddle to his shoulder and turning to begin his long
tramp toward the dam, "I shore hate to hoof it, but I'd do
it with a lot better temper if I knowed you was munching
grass with th' rest of the cavvieyh. You've been a good
old friend, an' I hates to leave you; but if I get any kind of

a chance at th' thief that plugged you I'll square up for you good an' plenty."

To the most zealous for exercise, carrying a forty-pound double-cinch saddle for over five miles across a hot, sandy plain and under a blazing, scorching sun, with the cinches all the time working loose and falling to drag behind and catch in the vegetation, was no pleasant task; and add to that a bridle, full magazine rifle, field glasses, canteen, and a three-pound Colt revolver swinging from a belt heavily weighted with cartridges, and it becomes decidedly irksome, to say the least. Red's temper can be excused when it is remembered that for years his walking had been restricted to getting to his horse, that his footwear was unsuited for walking, that he had been shot at and had lost his best horse. Each mile added greatly to his weariness and temper and by the time he caught sight of Hopalong, who rode recklessly over the range blazing at a panic-stricken coyote, he was near the point of spontaneous combustion.

He heaved the saddle from him, kicked savagely at it as it dropped, for which he was instantly sorry, and straightened his back slowly for fear that any sudden exertion would break it. His rifle exploded, twice, thrice; and Hopalong sat bolt upright and turned, his rifle going instinctively to his shoulder before he saw his friend's waving sombrero.

The coyote-chaser slid the smoking Sharps into its sheath and galloped to meet his friend who, filling the air with sulphurous remarks, now seated himself on the roundly cursed saddle.

Hopalong swept up and stopped, grinning expectantly and, to Red, exasperatingly. "Where's yore cayuse?" he asked. "Why are you toting yore possessions on th' hoof? Are you emigrating?"

Red's reply was a look wonderfully expressive of all

the evils in human nature; it was fairly crowded with murder and torture, and Hopalong held his head on one side while he weighed it.

"Phew!" he exclaimed in wondering awe. "Yo're shore mad! You'd freeze old Geronimo's blood if he saw that look!"

"An' I'll freeze yourn; I'll let it soak into th' sand if you don't change yore front!" blazed Red.

"What's the matter? Where's Ginger?"

A rapid-fire string of expletives replied and then Hopalong began to hear sensible words, which more and more interspersed the profanity, and it was not long before he learned of Red's ride along the arroyo's rim.

"When I turned north," Red continued, wrathfully, "I saw something in them dozen cottonwoods around that come-an'-go spring; an' then what do you think happened?" he cried. Not waiting for any reply he continued hastily: "Why, some murdering squaw's dog went an' squibbed at me at long range! With me on my own ranch, too! An' he killed Ginger first shot. He missed me three straight an' *I* couldn't do nothing at a thousand an' over with this gun."

"Th' damn pirate!" exclaimed Hopalong, hotly.

"I was a whole lot mad by that time, so I jumped back into th' brush an' ran for th' grove, hoping to get square when I got in range. After I'd run about a thousand miles I came to th' edge of th' clearing west of th' trees an' damned if I didn't see two fellers climbing on their cayuses, an' some hasty, too. Reckon they didn't know how many friends I might have behind me. Well, I was some shaky from running like I did, an' they was a good eight hundred away, but I let drive just th' same an' got one in th' arm, th' other somewhere else, an' hit both of their cayuses. I wish I'd 'a filled 'em so full of holes they couldn't hang together, th' thieves!"

"I'd shore like to go after them, Red," Hopalong re-marked. "We could ride west an' get 'em when they pass that water hole if you had a cayuse."

"Oh, we'll get 'em, all right—at th' mesa," Red re-joined. "I'm so tired I wouldn't go now if I could. Walk-ing all th' way down here with that saddle! You get off that cayuse an' let me ride him," he suggested, mopping his face with his sleeve.

"What! Me? *Me* get off an' walk! I reckon not!" re-plied Hopalong, and then his face softened. "You pore, unfortunate cowpunch," he said, sympathetically. "You toss up yore belongings an' climb up here behind me. I'll take you to th' dam, where Johnny has picketed his cay-use. Th' Kid's going in for a swim; said he didn't know how soon he'd get a chance to take a bath. We can rustle his cayuse for a joke—come on."

"Oh, wait a minute, can't you?" Red replied, wearily. "I can't lift my legs high enough to get up there—they're like lead. That trail was hell strung out."

"You should 'a cached yore saddle an' everything but th' gun an' come down light," Hopalong remarked. "Or you could 'a gone to th' line an' waited for somebody to come along. Why didn't you do that?"

"I ain't leaving that saddle nowhere," Red responded. "Besides I was too blamed mad to stop an' think."

"Well, don't wait very long—Johnny may skin out if you do," Hopalong replied, and then, suddenly: "Just where was it you shot at them snakes?"

Red told him and Hopalong wheeled as if to ride after them.

"Here, you!" cried Red, the horseless. "Where th' devil are you going so sudden?"

"Up to get them cow-lifters that you couldn't, of course," his companion replied. "I'm shore going to show you how easy it is when you know how."

"Like hell you are!" Red cried, springing up, his lariat in his hand. "Yo're going to stay right here with me, that's what yo're going to do! I've got something for you to do, you compact bundle of gall! You try to get away without me and I'll make you look like an interrupted spasm, you wart-head!"

"Do you want 'em to get plumb away?" cried the man in the saddle, concealing his mirth.

"I want you to stick right here an' tote me to a cayuse!" Red retorted, swinging the rope. "*I'm* going to be around when anybody goes after them Siwashes, an' don't you forget it. There ain't no hurry—we'll get 'em quick enough when we starts west. An' if you try any get-away play an' leave me out here on my two feet with all these contraptions, I'll pick you off'n that pie-bald like hell greased with calamity!"

Hopalong laughed heartily. "Why, I was only a-fooling, Red. Do you reckon I'd go away an' leave you standing out here like a busted-down pack mule?"

"I hoped you was only fooling, but I wasn't taking no chances with a cuss like you," Red replied, grinning. "Not with this load of woe, you bet."

"Say, it's too bad you didn't have my gun up there," Hopalong said, regretfully. "You could 'a got 'em both then, an' had two cayuses to ride home on."

"Well, *I* could 'a got 'em with it," Red replied, grinning, his good nature returning under the chaffing. "But you can't hit th' mesa with it over six hundred. They'd 'a got away from you without getting hit."

Hopalong laughed derisively and then sobered. "Yo're right, Red, yo're right. Now you get right up here behind me an' I'll take you to th' dam where th' Kid is. Pore feller," he sighed. "Well, I ain't a-wondering after all you've been through. It was enough to make a *strong*-minded man loco." He smiled reassuringly. "Now climb right up behind me, Reddie. Gimme yore little saddle an' yore no-account gun—Ouch!"

"I'll give you th' butt of it again if you don't act like you've made th' best of them gravy brains!" Red snorted. "Here, you lop-eared cow-wrastler—catch this!" throwing the saddle so sudden and hard that Hopalong almost lost his balance from the impact. "Now you gimme a little room in front of th' tail—I ain't no blasted fly."

Hopalong gave his friend a hand and Red landed across the horse's back, to the instant and strong dislike of that animal, which showed its displeasure by bucking mildly.

"Glory be!" cried Hopalong, laughing. "Riding double on a bucking hinge ain't no play, is it? Suppose he felt like pitching real strong—where would you be with that tail holt?"

"You bump my nose again with th' back of yore head an' you'll see how much play it is!" Red retorted. "Come on—pull out. We ain't glued fast. Th' world moves, all right, but if yo're counting on it sliding under you till th' dam comes around yo're way off; it ain't moving that way. Hey! Stop that spurring!"

"I'll hook 'em in you again if you don't shut up!" Hopalong promised, jabbing them into the horse, which gave one farewell kick, to Red's disgust, and cantered south with ears flattened.

"Whoop! I'm riding again!" Red exulted.

"I'm glad it wasn't Red Eagle they went an' killed," Hopalong remarked.

"Red Eagle!" snorted Red, indignantly. "What good is this cayuse, anyhow? Ginger was worth three like this."

"Well, if you don't like this cayuse you can get off an' hoof it, you know," Hopalong retorted. "But I'll tell you what you know a'ready; there ain't no cayuse in this part of th' country that can lose him in long-distance running.

He ain't no fancy parlor animal like Ginger was; he don't know how to smoke a cig or wash dishes, or do any of th' fool things yore cayuse did, but he's right on th' job when it comes to going hard an' long. An' it's them two things that tell how much a cayuse is worth, down here in this country. If I could 'a jumped on him up there when they made their get-away from you, me an' th' Sharps would 'a fixed 'em. They wouldn't be laughing now at how easy you was."

"They ain't laughing, not a bit of it—an' they won't even be able to swear after I get out to th' mesa," Red asserted. "Have you seen Buck, or anybody 'cept th' Kid?"

"Yes. I told Buck an' Frenchy about it, an' Skinny, too," Hopalong replied. "Buck an' Frenchy went north along th' west line to get th' boys from Number Two. Buck says we'll go after 'em just as soon as we can get ready, which most of us are now. Pore Lanky; he's got to stay home an' pet his wounds—Buck said he couldn't go."

"Did Buck say who was going an' who was going to stay home?"

"Yes; you, Johnny, Billy, Pete, Skinny, Frenchy, me, Buck, an' Pie Willis are going—th' rest will have to watch th' ranch. That makes nine of us. Wonder how many are up at the mesa?"

"There'll be plenty, don't you worry," Red replied. "When we go after anybody we generally has to mix up with a whole company. I wouldn't be a whole lot surprised if they give us an awful fight before they peter out. They'll be up in th' air a hundred feet. We'll have plenty to do, all right."

"Well, two won't be there, anyhow—Archer an' Juan. I bet we'll find most of th' people of Eagle up there waiting for us."

"Lord, I hope they are!" cried Red. "Then we can clean up everything at once, town an' all."

"There's th' Kid—see th' splash?" Hopalong laughed. "He shore is stuck on swimming. He don't care if there's cottonmouths in there with him. One of them snakes will get him some day, an' if one does, then we'll plant him, quick."

"Oh, I dunno. I ain't seen none at th' dam," Red replied. "They don't like th' sand there as much as they do th' mud up at th' other end, an' along th' sides. Gee! There's his cayuse!"

Johnny dove out of sight, turned over and came up again, happy as a lark, and saw his friends riding towards him, and he trod water and grinned. "Hullo, fellers. Coming in?—it's fine! Hey, Red. We're all going out to Thunder Mesa as soon as we can! But what are you riding double for? Where's yore cayuse?" Something in Red's expression made him suspicious of his friends' intentions and, fearing that he might have to do some walking, he made a few quick strokes and climbed out, dressing as rapidly as his wet skin would permit.

Red briefly related his experience and Johnny swore as he struggled through his shirt. "What are you going to do?" he asked, poking his head out into sight.

"I'm going to ride yore cayuse to th' line house—you ain't as tired as me," replied Red.

"Not while I'm alive, you ain't!" cried Johnny, running to his horse. Then he grinned and went back to his clothes. "You take him an' rope th' cayuse I saw down in that barranca—there's two of 'em there, both belonging to Meeker. But you be shore to come back!"

"Shore, Kid," Red replied, vaulting into the saddle and riding away.

Johnny fastened his belt around him and looked up. "Say, Hoppy," he laughed, "Buck said Cowan sent my new gun down to th' bunk house yesterday. He's going to bring it with him when he comes down to-morrow. But I only got fifty cartridges for it—will you lend me some of yourn if I run short?"

"Where did Cowan get it?"

"Why, don't you remember he said he'd get me one like yourn th' next time he went north? He got back yesterday—bought it off some feller up on th' XS. Cost me twenty-five dollars without th' cartridges. But I've got fifty empties I can load when I get time, so I'll be all right later on. Will you lend me some?"

"Fifty is enough, you chump," laughed Hopalong. "You won't get that many good chances out there."

"I know; but I want to practice a little. It'll shoot flatter than my Winchester," Johnny grinned, hardly able to keep from riding to the bunk house to get his new gun.

Red rode up leading a horse. "That's a good rope, Kid, 'though th' hondo is purty heavy," he said, saddling the captured animal. "Is Buck going to bring down any food an' cartridges when he comes?" he asked.

"Yes; three cayuses will pack 'em. We can send back for more if we stay out there long enough to need more. Buck says that freak spring up on top flows about half a mile through th' chaparral before it peters out. What do you know about it, Red?" Hopalong asked.

"Seems to me that he's right. I think it flows through a twisting arroyo. But there'll be water enough for us, all right."

"I got a .45–120 Sharps just like Hopalong's, Red," Johnny grinned. "He said he'd lend me fifty cartridges for it, didn't you, Hoppy?"

"Well, I'll be blamed!" exclaimed Hopalong. "First thing *I* knowed about it, if I did. I tell you you won't need 'em.

"Where'd you get it?" asked Red.

"Cowan got it. I told you all about it three weeks ago."

"Well, you better give it back an' use yore Winchester,"

replied Red. "It ain't no good, an' you'll shoot some of us with it, too. What do *you* want with a gun that'll shoot eighteen hundred? You can't hit anything now above three hundred."

"Yo're another—I can, an' you know it, too. Three hundred!" he snorted. "Huh! Here comes Skinny!"

Skinny rode up and joined them, all going to the Peak. Finally he turned and winked at Johnny.

"Hey, Kid. Hopalong ought to go right down to th' H2 while he's got time. He hadn't ought to go off fighting without saying good-bye to his girl, had he?"

"She'd keep him home—wouldn't let him take no chances of getting shot," Red asserted. "Anyhow, if he went down there he'd forget to come back."

"Ow-wow!" cried Johnny. "You hit him! You hit him! Look at his face!"

"He shore can't do no courting while he's away," Skinny remarked. "He wouldn't let Red go with him when he went to give Meeker th' shovel, an' I didn't know why till just now."

"You go to blazes, all of you!" exclaimed Hopalong, red and uncomfortable. "I ain't doing no courting, you chump! An' Red knows why I went down there alone.

"Yes; you gave me a fool reason, an' went alone," Red retorted. "An' if that ain't courting, for th' Lords sake what is it? Or is she doing all of it, you being bashful?"

"Yes, Hoppy; tell us what it is," asked Skinny.

"Oh, don't mind them, Hoppy; they're jealous," Johnny interposed. Don't you make no excuses, not one. Admit that yo're courting an' tell 'em that yo're going to keep right on a-doing it an' get all th' honey you can."

Red and Skinny grinned and Hopalong, swearing at Johnny, made a quick grab for him, but missed, for Johnny knew the strength of that grip. "I ain't courting! I'm only trying to—trying to be—sociable; that's all!"

"Sociable!" yelled Red. "Oh, Lord!"

"It must be nice to be sociable," replied Johnny. "Since you ain't courting, an' are only trying to be sociable, then you won't care if we go down an' try it!"

"You bet; an' I'm going down, too," asserted Red, who was very much afraid of women, and who wouldn't have called on Mary Meeker for a hundred dollars.

Hopalong knew his friend's weakness and he quickly replied: "Red, I dare you to do that. I dare you to go down there an' talk to her for five minutes. When I say talk, I don't mean stammer. I dare you!"

"Do you dare *me*?" asked Johnny, quickly, glancing at the sun to see how much time he had.

"Oh, I ain't got time," replied Red, grinning.

"You ain't got th' nerve, you mean," jeered Skinny.

"I dare you, Red," Hopalong repeated, grimly.

"I asked you if you dared *me*?" hastily repeated Johnny.

"*You*! Not on yore life, Kid. But you stay away from there!" Hopalong warned.

"Gee—wish you'd lend me them cartridges," sighed Johnny. "Mebbe Meeker has got some he ain't so stingy with," he added, thoughtfully.

"I'll lend you th' cartridges, Kid," Hopalong offered. "But you stay away from th' H2. D'y hear?"

XXV

♦

Antonio's Revenge

While Red had been trudging southward under his saddle and other possessions a scene was being enacted on a remote part of the H2 range which showed how completely a cowboy leased his very life to the man who paid him his monthly wage, one which serves to illustrate in a way how a ranchman was almost a feudal lord. There are songs of men who gave up their lives to save their fellows, one life for many, and they are well sung; but what of him who risks his life to save one small, insignificantly small portion of his employer's possessions, risks it without hesitation or fear, as a part of his daily work? What of the man who, not content with taking his share of danger in blizzard, fire, and stampede, on drive, roundup, and range-riding, leaps fearlessly at the risk of his life to save a paltry head or two of cattle to his ranch's tally sheet? Such men were the rule, and such a one was Curley, who, with all his faults, was a man as a man should be.

Following out his orders he rode his part of the range with alertness, and decided to explore the more remote southwestern angle of the ranch. Doc had left him an hour before to search the range nearer Eagle and would not be back again until time to return to the ranch house for the night. This was against Meeker's order, for they had been told to keep together for their own protection, but they had agreed that there was little risk and that it would be better to separate and cover more ground.

The day was bright and, with the exception of the heat, all he could desire. His spirits bubbled over in snatches of song, but all the time moving in the general direction of the little-ridden territory. On all sides stretched the same monotonous view, sage brush, mesquite, cactus, scattered tufts of grass, and the brown plain, endless, flat, wearying.

The surroundings did not depress him, but only gradually slowed the exultant surge of his blood and, as he hummed at random, an old favorite came to him out of the past, and he sung it joyously:

My taste is that of an aristocrat,
My purse that of a pauper:

I scorn the gold her parents hold—
But shore I love their daughter.
Hey de diddle de, hey de dee,
But shore I love their daughter.

When silvery nights my courting light
An' souls of flowers wander,
Then who's to blame if I loved th' game
An' did not pause to ponder?
Hey de diddle de, hey de dee,
An' did not pause to ponder.

Her eyes are blue, an' oh, so true—
Th' words were said ere thought, Lad.
Her father swore we'd meet no more—
But I am not distraught, Lad.
Hey de diddle de, hey de de—
But I am not distraught, Lad.

He ceased abruptly, rigidly erect, staring straight ahead as the significance of the well trodden trail impressed itself on his mind. He was close to the edge of a steep-walled basin; and leading to it was a narrow, steep gully, down which the beaten trail went. Riding closer he saw that two poles were set close to the wall of the gully, and from one of them dangled a short, frayed hempen rope. There was a water hole in the basin, surrounded by a muddy flat, and everywhere were the tracks of cattle.

As he hesitated to decide whether or not it would be worth while to ride through the depression he chanced to look south, and the question decided itself. Spurring savagely, he leaned forward in the saddle, the wind playing a stern song in his ears, a call to battle for his ranch, his pride, and his hatred for foul work. He felt the peculiar, compelling delight, the surging, irresistible intoxication of his kind for fighting, the ecstasy of the blood lust, handed down from his Saxon forefathers.

A mile ahead of him was a small herd of cattle, being driven west by two men. Did he stop to return to the ranch for assistance? Did he count the odds? Not he, for he saw the perpetrators of the insults he and his companions had chafed under—the way was clear, the quarry plain, and he asked naught else.

They saw him coming—one of them raised a pair of glasses to his eyes and looked closely at him and from him all around the plain. All the time they were driving the cattle harder, shouting and whipping about them with their rawhide quirts; and constantly nearer came the cowboy, now standing up in his stirrups and lashing his straining mount without mercy. Soon he thought he recognized one of the herders, and he flung the name on the whistling wind in one contemptuous shout: "*Antonio*! Damn his soul!" and fell to beating the horse all the harder.

It was Antonio, and a puff of smoke arose from the Mexican's shoulder, and streaked behind, soon followed by another. Curley knew the rifle, a .40–90 Sharps, and did not waste a shot, for he must be on equal terms before he could hope to cope with it. Another puff, then another and another, but still he was not hit. Now he drew his own rifle from his holster and hazarded a shot, but to no avail. Then the second herder, who had not as yet fired, snatching the rifle from Antonio's hands and, checking his horse, leaped off and rested the weapon across the saddle. Taking deliberate aim, he fired, and Curley pitched out of the saddle as his horse stumbled and fell. The rider scrambled to his feet, dazed and hurt, and ran to his horse, but one look told the story and he ended the animal's misery with a shot from his Colt.

The herder and the cattle were rapidly growing smaller in the distance but the Mexican rode slowly around the man on foot, following the circumference of a large circle and shooting with calm deliberation. The bullets hummed and whined viciously past the H2 puncher, kicking up the dust in little spurts, and cold ferocity filled his heart as he realized the rustler's purpose. He raised his own rifle and fired—and leaded the barrel. When he had fallen the barrel had become choked with sand and dust and he was at the mercy of his gloating enemy, who would now wipe out the insult put upon him at the bunk house. Slowly Antonio rode and carefully he fired and then, seeing that there was something wrong with Curley's rifle, which the puncher threw aside, he drew closer, determined to shoot him to pieces.

Curley was stung with rage now. He knew that it was only a question of waiting until the right bullet came, and scorning to hug the sand for the man he held in such contempt, and vaguely realizing that such an act would not change the result, he put all his faith in a dash. He ran swiftly towards his astonished enemy, who expected him to seek what cover the dead horse would give him, Colt in hand, cursing at every jump and hoping to be spared long enough to get within range with his six-shooter, if only for one shot. Antonio did not like this close work and cantered away, glancing back from time to time. When Curley finally was forced to stop because of exhaustion the rider also stopped and slipped off his horse to have a rest for the rifle. Curley emptied the Colt in a futile, enraged effort to make a lucky hit while his enemy had now aimed from across the saddle. Hastily reloading the Colt as he ran, the puncher dashed forward again, zig-zagging to avoid being hit. There was a puff of gray smoke, but Curley did not hear the report. He threw one arm half up as if to ward off the shot and pitched forward, face down in the dust, free from all pain and strife.

Antonio fired again and then cautiously drew nearer to his victim, the rifle at the ready. Turning shortly he made a quick grab at his horse, fearing that it might leave him on foot to be caught by some wandering H2 puncher. Springing into the saddle he rode forward warily to get a closer look at the man he had murdered, proud of his work, but fearful that Curley was playing dead.

When assured that he had nothing to fear from the prostrate form, he rode close. "Knock me down, will you!" he gritted, urging the horse to trample on the body, which the animal refused to do. "Come out looking for us, did you? Well, you found us, all right, but a hell of a lot of good it did you. You ain't saying a word, are you, you carrion? You ain't got no smart come-back now, an' you ain't throwing no wash water on me, are you?"

He started and looked around nervously, fearful that he might be caught and left lying on the sand as he had left Curley. One or two of the H2 outfit carried single-shot rifles which shot as far if not farther than his own, and the owners of them knew how to shoot. Wheeling abruptly he galloped after the herd, looking back constantly and thinking only of putting as great a distance as possible between himself and the scene of the killing.

A lizard crawled out of a hillock and stared steadily at the quiet figure and then, making a tentative sortie, disappeared under the sand; but the man who had sung so buoyantly did not mind it, he lay wrapped in the Sleep Eternal. He had died as he had lived, fearlessly and without a whimper.

Late in the afternoon Doc Riley, sweeping on a circling course, rode through chaparrals, alert even after his fruitless search, looking around on all sides, and wondered if Curley and he would meet before they reached the ranch proper. Suddenly something caught his eye and he stood up in the stirrups to see it better, a ready curse leaping from his lips. He could not make out who it was, but he had fears and he spurred forward as hard as he could go. Then he saw the horse and knew.

Riding close to the figure so as to be absolutely sure, he knew beyond a hope of mistake and looked around the plain, his expression malevolent and murderous.

"Curley! Curley!" he cried, leaping off his horse and placing a heavy, kindly hand on the broad, sloping shoulder of the man who had been his best friend for years. "So they got you, lad! They got you! In God's name, why did I leave you?" he cried in bitter self-condemnation. "It's my fault, it's my fault, lad!" He straightened up suddenly and glared around through tear-dimmed eyes. "*But by th' living God I'll pay them for this*, I'll pay them for this! Damn their murdering souls!"

He caught sight of an empty cartridge shell and snatched it up eagerly. "Forty–ninety, by God! That's Antonio's! Curley, my lad, I'll get him for you—an' when I *do*! I'll send his soul to th' blackest pit in hell, an' send it *slow*!"

He noticed and followed the tracks in the sand, reading them easily. He found the Winchester and quickly learned its story, which told him the whole thing. Returning to the body of his friend he sat by it quietly, looking down at it for several minutes, his sombrero in his hand.

"Well, wishing won't do no good," he muttered, dismounting. "I'll take you home, lad, an' see you put down too deep for coyotes to bother you. An' I'll square yore scores or join you trying."

He lifted the body across the withers of his horse and picked up the Colt. Mounting, he rode at a walk toward the bunk house, afire with rage and sorrow.

For the third time Meeker strode to the door of the bunk house and looked out into the darkness, uneasy and anxious. Chick sauntered over to him and leaned against the frame of the door. "They'll show up purty soon, Jim," he remarked.

"Yes. I reckon so—Salem!" the foreman called. "Put their grub where it'll keep warm."

"Aye, aye, sir. I was just thinking I ought to. They're late, ain't they, sir?" he asked. "An' it's dark, too," he added, gratis.

"Why, is it, Salem?" queried Dan, winking at Jack Curtis, but Salem disappeared into the gallery.

"Listen!—I hear 'em!" exclaimed Chick.

"You hear one of 'em," corrected Meeker, turning to the table to finish drinking his coffee. "Hey, Salem! Never mind warming that grub—rustle it in here. One of 'em's here, an' he'll be starved, too."

Suddenly Chick started back with an exclamation as Doc Riley loomed up in the light of the door, carrying a body over his shoulder. Stepping into the room while his friends leaped to their feet in amazement and incredulity, he lowered his burden to a bench and faced them, bloody and furious.

"What's th' matter?" exclaimed Meeker, the first to find his voice, leaping forward and dropping the cup to the floor. "Who did that?"

Doc placed his sombrero over the upturned face and ripped out a savage reply. "Antonio! Yore broncho-buster! Th' snake that's raising all th' devil on this range! Here—see for yoreself!" tossing the cartridge shell to his foreman, who caught it clumsily, looked at it, and then handed it to Dan. Exclamations and short, fierce questions burst from the others, who crowded up to see the shell.

"Tell me about it, Doc," requested Meeker, pacing from wall to wall.

"He was shot down like a dog!" Doc cried, his rage sweeping over him anew in all its savagery. "I saw th' whole thing in th' sand, plain as day. Antonio got his cayuse first an' then rode rings around him, keeping out of range of Curley's Colt, for Curley had leaded his rifle. It was Colt against Sharps at five hundred, that was what it was! He didn't have a show, not a measly show for his life! Shot down like a *dog*!"

"Where'd it happen?" asked Chick, breathlessly, while the low-voiced threats and imprecations swelled to an angry, humming chorus.

"Away down in th' southwest corner," replied Doc, and he continued almost inaudibly, speaking to himself and forgetful of the others. "Me an' him went to school together an' I used to lick every kid that bullied him till he got big enough to do it hisself. We run away together an' shared th' same hard luck. We went through that Sioux campaign together, side by side, an' to think that after he pulled out of *that* alive he had to be murdered by a yaller coward. If he'd been killed in fair fight it would be all right; but by that coyote—it don't seem possible, not noway. I licked th' feller that hurt him on his first day at school—I'm going to kill th' last!

"Meeker," he said, coming to himself and facing the angry foreman, "I'm quitting to-night. I won't punch no more till I get that murderer. I take up that trail at daylight an' push it to a finish. It's got to be him or me, now."

"You don't have to quit to do that, an' you *know* it! I don't care if yore gone for six months—yore pay goes on just th' same. He went down fighting for me, an' I'll be everlastingly condemned if I don't have a hand in squaring up for it. Yo're going on special duty for th' H2, Doc, an' yore orders are to get Antonio. Why, by th' Lord, I'll take up th' trail with you, Doc, an' with th' rest of th' boys behind me. This ranch can go galley-west an' crooked till we get that snake. Dan an' Salem stays with my girl an' to watch th' ranch—th' rest of us are with you—we're as anxious as you to push him Yonder, Doc."

"If I can get him alive, get my two hands on his skinny neck," Doc muttered, his fingers twitching. "I'll kill him slow, so he'll feel it longer, so he'll be shore to know why he's going. I want to *feel* his murdering soul dribble hell-wards, an' let him come back a couple of times so I can laugh in his yaller face when he begs! I want to get him—*so*!" and Chick shuddered as the knotted, steel-like fingers opened and shut, for Doc was half devil now. While Chick stared, the transformed man walked over to the bench and picked up the body in his brawny arms and strode into the blackness—Curley was going to lie in the open, with the stars and the sky and the sighing wind.

"God!" breathed Chick, looking around, "I never saw a man like *that* before!"

"I hope he gets what he wants!" exclaimed Dan, fiercely.

"You fellers get yore traps ready for a chase," Meeker ordered as he strode to the door of the gallery. "Fifty rounds for six-shooters an' fifty for rifle, an' plenty of grub. It's a whole lot likely that killer's headed for his gang, an' we've got to be ready to handle everything that comes up. Hey, Salem!" he shouted.

"Aye, aye, sir!" replied Salem, who had just come in from one of the corrals and knew nothing of what had occurred.

"Did you cure that beef I told you to?" demanded the foreman.

"Yes, sir; but it ain't had time to cure—th' weather's not been right. Howsomever, I smoked some. That'll be ship shape."

"Well, have it on our cayuses at daylight. Did you cut this beef in strips, or in twenty-pound chunks, like you did th' last?"

"Strips, *little* strips—I ain't trying to sun-cure no more big hunks, not me, sir."

Meeker turned and went towards the outer door.

"Don't waste no time, boys," he said. "Get all th' sleep you can to-night—you'll need it if I reckon right. Good-night," and he stepped out into the darkness. "Damn them dogs!" he muttered, disappearing in the direction of the kennels, from which came quavering, long-drawn howls.

XXVI

♦

Frisco Visits Eagle

Eagle did not thoroughly awaken until the sun began to set, for it was not until dark that its inhabitants, largely transient, cared to venture forth. Then it was that the town seethed, boldly, openly, restrained by nothing save the might of the individual.

Prosperity had blessed the town, for there had been an abrupt and pleasing change in local conditions since the disagreement between the two ranches north of the town had assumed warlike aspect. Men who heretofore had no standing with the proprietors of the town's places of amusement and who had seldom been able to pay for as much liquor as they were capable of drinking, now swaggered importantly where they pleased, and found welcome where formerly it had been denied them; for their hands were thrust deep into pockets from which came the cheerful and open-sesame clinking of gold. Even Big Sandy, who had earned his food by sweeping out the saloons and doing odd jobs about them, and was popularly believed to be too lazy to earn a better living by real work, now drank his fill and failed to recognize a broom when he saw it. While the inhabitants could not "get in" on the big plums which they were certain were being shaken down on the range, they could and did take care of the windfalls, and thrived well. They would stay in town until their money was gone and then disappear for a week, and return to spend recklessly. It is not out of place to state, in passing, that numerous small herds bearing strange brands frequently passed around the town at a speed greater than that common to drives, and left clouds of dust on the southeastern horizon.

The town debated the probable whereabouts of ten men who had suddenly disappeared in a body, along with Antonio of the H2. It was obvious what they were doing and the conjectures were limited as to their whereabouts and success. For a while after they had left one or two had ridden in occasionally to buy flour and other necessities, and at that time they had caused no particular thought. But now even these visits had ceased. It was common belief that Quinn knew all about them, but Quinn for good reasons was not urged to talk about the matter. Big Sandy acted as though he knew, which increased his importance for a time, and discredited him thereafter.

While the citizens had been able to rustle as they pleased they had given but little thought to the ten men, being too busy to trail. But now that the H2 punchers rode range with rifles across their arms rustling had become very risky and had fallen off. Then it was that the idlers renewed their conjectures about Shaw and his men and thrashed that matter over and over again. The majority being, as we have said, transients, knew nothing about Thunder Mesa, and those who did know of it were silent, for Shaw and some of his companions knew only one way to close a man's mouth, and were very capable.

So it happened that about noon of the day Curley lost his life six men met in the shadow cast by the front of the "Rawhide" a hundred yards from Quinn's, and exercised squatter sovereignty on the bench just outside the door, while inside the saloon Big Sandy and Nevada played cards close to the bar and talked in low tones. When they were aware of the presence of those on the bench they played silently and listened. The six men outside made up one of the groups of the town's society, having ridden in together and stuck together ever since they had arrived, which was wise.

Big Sandy and Nevada made a team more feared than any other combination. The former, while fair with weapons, was endowed with prodigious strength; by some it was hailed as being greater than that of Pete Wilson, the squat giant of the Bar-20, whose strength was proverbial, as it had good right to be. Nevada was the opposite type, short, wiry, and soft-spoken, but the quickest man in the draw and of uncertain temper.

Chet Bates, on the bench, replied to a companion and gave vent to his soft, Southern laugh. "Yuh still wondering 'bout thet man Shaw, an' th' othas?"

"Nothing else to do, is there?" retorted Dal Gilbert. "We can't run no more cattle, can we?"

"I reckon we can't."

"They're running a big game an' I want to get in it," remarked John Elder. "Frisco was allus friendly. We've got to go trailing for 'em."

"Yes; an' get shot," interposed George Lewis. "They're ten to our six. An' that ain't all of our troubles, neither. We'll find ourselves in a big fight some day, an' right here. Them ranches will wake up, patch up their troubles, an' come down here. You remember what Quinn said about th' time Peters led a lot of mad punchers agin Trendley an' his crowd, don't you? In a day he can raise men enough to wipe this town off th' map."

"Yuh forget, suh, that they are fighting foh principles, an' men who fight foh principles don't call truces," said Chet Bates.

"You've said that till it's old," laughed Sam Austin.

"*I* say we've got to keep our eyes open," warned Lewis.

"Th' devil with that!" broke in Con Irwin. "What *I* want to know is how we're going to get some of th' easy money Shaw's getting."

"We'll have to wait for one of his men to come to town an' trail him back," replied Gilbert.

"What do you say that we try to run one more good herd an' then scout for them, or their trails?" asked Irwin.

"Heah comes somebody," remarked Chet, listening.

The sound of galloping grew rapidly louder and soon they saw Frisco turn into the street and ride towards them. As they saw him a quiet voice was heard behind them and looking up, they saw Nevada smiling at them. "Get him drunk an' keep him away from Quinn's," he counselled.

They exchanged looks and then Elder stepped out into the street and held up his hand. "Hullo, Frisco!" he cried.

"Where yuh been keeping yuhself foh so long?" asked Chet, affably. "Holed up som'ers?"

"Hullo, fellers," grinned Frisco, drawing rein.

"Everybody have a drink on me," laughed Chet. "Ah'm pow'ful thirsty."

Frisco was escorted inside to the bar, where Chet did the honors, and where such a spirit of hospitality and joviality surrounded him that he forgot how many drinks he had taken. He dug up a handful of gold and silver and spread it out on the bar and waved at the bartender. "Bes' you got—ver' bes'," he grinned. "Me an' my fren's want th' ver' bes'; don't we, fellers? I got money—helluva lot of money—an' thersh more where it came from, ain't that so, boys?"

When the noise had subsided he turned around and levelled an unsteady finger at the bartender. "I never go—back onsh fren', never. An' we're all frensh—ain't we, fellers? Tha's right. I got s'more frensh—good fellesh, an' lots of money cached in sand."

"Ah'll bet yuh have!" cried Chet.

"You allus could find pay-dirt," marvelled Nevada, glancing warningly around him. "Yo're a fine prospector, all right."

Frisco stared for a moment and then laughed loudly and leaned against the bar for support. "Proshpector! Proshpector! W'y, we earned tha's money—run a helluva lot of risks. Mebbe tha's Bar-20 outfit'll jump us an' make us fight 'em. No; they can't jump us—they can't get up at us!"

"On a mesa, shore!" whispered Elder to Lewis.

"Wha's you shay?"

"Said they couldn't lick you."

"Who couldn't—lick us?"

"Th' Bar-20," explained Elder.

Frisco rubbed his head and drew himself up, suspicion percolating through his muddled brain. "Never shaid nozzing 'bout no Bar-Twensh!" he asserted, angrily. "Nozzing 'tall. I'm going out of here—don't like you! Gotta get some flour an' ozzer stuff. Never shaid nozzing 'bout—" he muttered, staggering out.

Nevada turned to Elder. "You go with him an' quiet his suspicions. Keep him away from Quinn, for that coyote'll hold him till he gets sober if you don't. This is the chance we've been wanting. Don't try to pump him—his trail will be all we need."

"Wonder what mesa they're on?" asked Lewis.

"Don't know, an' don't care," Nevada replied. "We'll find out quick enough. There's eight of us an' we can put up a stiff argument if they won't take us in. You know they ain't going to welcome us, don't you?"

"Hey, go out th' back way," growled Big Sandy interposing his huge hulk between Bates and the door. "An' don't let Frisco see you near a cayuse, neither," he added.

Nevada walked quickly over to his friend and said a few hurried words in a low voice and Big Sandy nodded. "Shore, Nevada; he might try that, but I'll watch him. If he tries to speak I'll let you know hasty. We're in this to stay," and he followed the others to the door.

Nevada turned and faced the bartender. "Mike, you keep quiet about what you saw an' heard to-day; understand? If you don't, me an' you won't fit in this town at th' same time."

Mike grinned. "I forgot how to talk after one exciting day up in Cheyenne, an' I ain't been drunk since, neither."

"Yo're a wise man," replied the other, stepping out by the back door and hastening up the street where he could keep watch over Quinn's saloon. It was an hour before he caught sight of Frisco, and he was riding west, singing at the top of his lungs. Then Quinn slipped into his corral and threw a saddle on a horse.

"Drop it!" said a quiet voice behind him and he turned to see Nevada watching him.

"What do you mean?" demanded Quinn, ominously.

"Let loose of that cayuse an' go back inside," was the reply.

"You get th' hell out of here an mind yore own—" Quinn leaped aside and jerked at his Colt; but was too late, and he fell, badly wounded. Nevada sprang forward and disarmed him and then, mounting, galloped off to join his friends.

XXVII

◆

Shaw Has Visitors

When Frisco reached the edge of the clearing around the mesa he saw Antonio and Shaw toiling cautiously up the steep, precarious trail leading to the top, and he hailed vociferously. Both looked around, Antonio scowling and his companion swearing at their friend's condition. Frisco's pack horse, which he had sense enough to bring back, was loaded down with bags and packages which had been put on recklessly, inasmuch as a slab of bacon hung from the animal's neck and swayed to and fro with each step; and the animal he rode had a bartender's apron hanging down before its shoulders.

"Had a rip-snorting time—rip-snorting time," he announced pleasantly, in a roar. "Salubrious—rip-snorting—helluva time!"

"Nobody'd guess it!" retorted Shaw. "Look at them bundles! An' him an expert pack-horse man, too. An' that cayuse with a shirt! For anybody that can throw as neat a diamond hitch as him, that pack horse is a howling disgrace!"

"Hang th' pack horse!" growled Antonio. "I bet th' whole town knows our business now! He ought to be shot. Where you going?"

"Down to help him up," Shaw replied. "He'll bust his fool neck if he wrestles with that trail alone. You go on up an' send a couple of th' boys down to bring up th' grub," he ordered, starting down the path.

"Let him bust his fool neck!" replied Antonio. "He should 'a done that before he left."

"What's th' ruction?" asked Clausen, looking down over the edge.

"Oh, Frisco's come back howling drunk. Go down an' help him tote th' grub up. Shaw said for somebody else to help you."

"Hey, Cavalry," cried Clausen. "Come on an' gimme a hand," and the two disappeared down the trail.

The leader returned, heralded by singing and swearing, and pushed Frisco over the mesa top to sprawl full-length on the ground. Shaw looked down at him with an expression of anger and anxiety and then turned abruptly on his heel as a quavering snore floated up from the other.

"Here, Manuel!" he called, sharply. "Take my glasses an' go out to yore lookout rock. Look towards Eagle an' call me if you see anybody."

Manuel moved away as Cavalry and Clausen, loaded down, appeared over the edge of the mesa wall and dropped their loads at Shaw's feet.

"What did you tell him to get?" asked Clausen, marvelling.

"What do you think I told him to get?" snapped Shaw.

"I don't know, seeing what he brought back," was the reply.

Shaw examined the pile. "God's name, what's all this stuff?" he roared. "Bacon! An' all th' meat we want is down below. Canned milk! Two bottles XXX Cough Syrup, four bottles of whiskey, bottle vaniller extract, plug tobacco, an' three harmonicas! Is *that* flour!" he yelled, glaring at a small bag. "Twenty pounds! Five pounds of salt!"

"I reckon he bought all th' cartridges in town," Cavalry announced, staggering into sight with a box on his shoulder. "Lord, but it's heavy!"

"Twenty pounds of flour to last nine men a month!"

Shaw shouted, kicking at the bag. "An' look at this coffee—two pounds! I'll teach him a lesson when he gets sober."

"Well, he made up th' weight in th' cartridges," Cavalry grinned. He grasped Shaw's arm. "What's got into Manuel?"

The leader looked and sprinted to the lookout rock, where Manuel was gesticulating, and took the glasses. Half a minute later he returned them and rejoined his companions near the pile of supplies.

"What is it?" asked Cavalry.

"Some of our Eagle friends. Mebby they want cards in this game, but we'll waste little time with 'em. Post th' fellers along th' edge, Clausen, an' you watch th' trail up. Keep 'em covered while I talks with 'em. Don't be slow to burn powder if they gets to pushing things."

"They trailed Frisco," growled Cavalry.

"Shore; oh, he was a great success!" snapped Shaw, going to the edge of the mesa to await the eight newcomers, his men finding convenient places along the top of the wall, their rifles ready for action.

They did not have long to wait for soon Nevada and Chet Bates rode into the clearing and made for the trail.

"That's far enough, Nevada!" shouted Shaw, holding up his hand.

"Why, hullo, Shaw!" cried the man below. "Yo're up a good tree, all right," he laughed.

"Yes."

"Can we ride up, or do we have to take shank's mare?"

"Neither."

"Well, we want some water after that ride," replied Nevada.

"Plenty of it below. Nobody asked you to take that ride. What do you want, anyhow?"

"Why, when Frisco said you was out here we thought we'd drop in on you an' pay you a little visit."

"You have paid us a little visit. Call again next summer."

"Running many cows?" asked Nevada.

"Nope; educating coyotes. Didn't see none, did you?"

Nevada exchanged a few words with his companion and then looked up again. "I reckon you need us, Shaw. Eight more men means twice as many cows; an' we can all fight a little if th' ranches get busy out here."

"We're crowded now. Better water up an' hit th' back trail. It's hard riding in th' dark."

"We didn't come out here for a drink," replied Nevada. "We came out to help you rustle, which same we'll do. I tell you that you need us, man!"

"When I need you I'll send for you. *Adios*."

"You ain't going to let us come up?"

"Not a little bit. Pull yore stakes an' hit th' back trail. *Adios*!"

"Well, we'll hang around to-night an' talk it over again tomorrow. Mebby you'll change yore mind. So long," and the two wheeled and disappeared into the chaparrals, Nevada chuckling. "I didn't spring that little joker, Chet, because it's a good card to play last. When we tell him that we won't let nobody come down off'n th' mesa it'll be after we can't do nothing else. No use making him mad."

Up on the mesa Shaw wheeled, scowling. "I knowed that fool would fire off something big! Why can't he get drunk out here, where it's all right?"

"That Nevada is a shore bad proposition," Clausen remarked.

"So'm I!" snapped Shaw. "He can't come up, an' pursooant to that idee I reckon you an' Hall better arrange to watch th' trail to-night."

He walked away and paced slowly along the edge of the wall, studying every yard of it. He had done this thing before and had decided that no man set a saddle who could scale the sheer hundred feet of rock which dropped so straight below him. But somehow he felt oppressed, and the sinking sun threw into bold relief the furrows of his weather-beaten, leathery face and showed the trouble marks which sat above his eyes. At one part of the wall he stopped and peered over, marshalling imaginative forces in attack after attack against it. But at the end he smiled and moved on—that was the weakest point in his defense, but he would consider himself fortunate if he should find no weaker defense in future conflicts. As he returned to the hut he glanced at the lookout rock and saw Manuel in his characteristic pose, unmoving, silent, watchful.

"I'm getting as bad as Cavalry and his desert," he grumbled. "Still, they can't lick us while we stay up here."

XXVIII

◆

Nevada Joins Shaw

Late in the forenoon of the day after Nevada had argued with Shaw, Manuel shifted his position on the lookout rock and turned to face the hut. "Señor! Señor Shaw! He ees here."

Shaw strode to the edge of the mesa and looked down, seeing Nevada sitting quietly on a horse and looking up at him. Manuel, his duty performed, turned and looked eastward, shrinking back as Shaw stepped close to him. Lying prone along the edge half a dozen men idly fingered rifles as they covered the man below, Antonio's face in particular showing intense aversion to any more recruits.

"Morning, Shaw," shouted Nevada. "Going to let us come up?"

The leader was about to reply when he felt a tug at his ankle and saw Manuel's lips moving. "What is it"

"Look, Señor, look!" whispered the frightened Mexican, pointing eastward. "Eet ees de Bar-20! They be here *poco tiempo!*"

"Shut up!" retorted Shaw in a whisper, glancing east, and what he saw changed his reply to the man below. "Well, Nevada, we are purty crowded up here as it is, but I'll ask th' boys about it. They ain't quite decided. Be back in a minute," and he stepped back out of sight of those below and waved his companions to him. Briefly stating the facts he asked that Nevada and his force be allowed up to help repulse the Bar-20, and the men who only a short time before had sworn that they would take in no partners nodded assent and talked over the new conditions while their leader again went to the edge.

"We can get along without you fellers," he called down, "but we don't reckon you'll cut any hole in our profits as long as you do yore share of work. If yo're willin' to share an' share alike, in work, grub, profits, an' fighting, why I reckon you can come up. But I'm leader here an' what I says goes: are you agreeable?"

"That's fair," Nevada replied. "Th' harder you work th' bigger th' pay—come on, boys," he cried, turning and waving his arm. "We're in!"

While the newcomers put their horses in the corral and toiled carefully up the steep trail Manuel stared steadily into the east and again saw the force that had filled him with fear. Hall, who was now watching with him, abruptly arose and returned to the hut, reporting: "Seven men out there—it's th' Bar-20, all right, I reckon;" and almost immediately afterward Manuel found a moving speck far to the east which Shaw's powerful glasses soon showed to be three pack horses driven by two men.

Nevada looked curiously about him as he gained his goal and then sought a place in the hut for his bunk. This, however, was full, and he cast around outside to find the best place for his blankets. Finding it, he stepped to the spring and had just quenched his thirst when he saw Shaw standing on a ledge of rock above him, looking down. "What is it, Shaw?" he asked.

"Well, you fellers shore enough raised hell, now didn't you!" demanded the leader, a rising anger in his voice. "Yo're a fine collection of fools, you are—"

"What do—"

"—Leading that Bar-20 gang out here by th' nice, plain trail you left," Shaw continued, sarcastically, not heeding the other's explosive interjection. "That's a nice thing to saddle us with! Damn it, don't you know you've queered th' game for good?"

"Yo're drunk!" retorted Nevada, heatedly. "We came up from th' south! How th' devil could that crowd hit *our* trail?"

"They must 'a hit southwest on a circle," lied Shaw. "Manuel just now saw 'em pass a clearing an' heading this way—nine of 'em!"

"Th' devil!" exclaimed Nevada. "How many are up here now?" he asked quickly.

"Sixteen."

"All right! Let 'em come!" cried the other. "Sixteen to nine—it's easy!" he laughed. "Look here; we can clean up them fellers an' then raid their ranch, for there's only four left at home. We can run off a whopping big herd, sell 'em, an' divvy even. Then we separates, savvy? Why, it couldn't be better!"

Shaw showed his astonishment and his companion

continued. "Th' H2 is shy men, an' th' C80 and th' Double Arrow is too far away to bother us. As soon as we lick this aggregation of trouble hunters, what's left will ride hell-bent for that valley. Then th' biggest herd ever rustled in these parts, a trip to a new range, an' plenty of money to spend there."

"That sounds good—but this pleasing cleaning-up is due to be full of knots," Shaw rejoined. "Them nine men come from th' craggiest outfit of high-toned gun-artists in these parts, an' you can bet that they are th' pick of th' crowd! Cassidy, Connors, Peters—an' they've got forty friends purty nigh as bad, an' eager to join in. I ain't no ways a quitter, but this looks to me like Custer's last stand, us being th' Custers."

"Ah, yo're loco!" retorted Nevada. "Look here! Send a dozen picked men down quick an' let 'em lose 'emselves in th' chaparral, far back. When th' terrible man-killers of th' great Bar-20 get plugging this way, our trouble-gang slips up behind an' it's all over! Go on, before it's too late! Or one of us will ride like th' devil to Eagle for help—but it's got to be quick! You say I got you in this, which I know well I didn't, but now I'll get you out an' put you in th' way of a barrel of money."

The crack of a rifle sounded from the plain and the next instant Clausen dashed up, crying, "Manuel tried to cut an' run, but somebody down below dropped him off'n th' trail. They're all around us!"

"Good for th' somebody!" cried Shaw. "I'll kill th' next man that tries to leave us—that goes, so pass it along." Then he turned to Nevada, a sneer on his face. "That means anybody riding for help, too!" and he backed away.

Hall turned the corner, looking Nevada squarely in the eyes. "Say, Shaw, wonder what's got into Archer? He's been gone a long time for that trip."

"Reckon he's got tired an' quit," replied Shaw.

"You know he ain't that kind!" Hall cried, angrily.

"All right, all right. If he comes back an' finds out what's up he'll probably hustle to Eagle for some of th' boys," Shaw responded. Neither would ever see Dick Archer again—his bones were whitening near a small water hole miles to the north, as Hopalong and Red could testify.

"As long as one of us is outside we've got a chance," Nevada remarked. "How're we fixed for grub, Hall?"

"Got enough jerked beef to last us a month," and Hall departed.

A shot hummed over Nevada's head and, ducking quickly, he followed Hall. Close behind him went Shaw, muttering. "Well, it had to come sometime—an' we're better fixed than I ever reckoned we'd be. Now we'll see who gets wiped out!"

XXIX

◆

Surrounded

Above, a pale, hot sky with only a wisp of cloud; below, a semi-arid "pasture," scant in grass, seamed by tortuous gullies and studded with small, compact thickets and bulky boulders. A wall of chaparral, appearing solid when viewed from a distance, fenced the pasture, and rising boldly from the southwest end of the clearing a towering mass of rock flung its rugged ramparts skyward. Nature had been in a sullen mood when this scene had been perpetrated and there was no need of men trying to heighten the gloomy aspect by killing each other. Yet they were trying and had been for a week, and they could have found no surroundings more in keeping with their occupation.

Minute clouds of smoke spurted from the top of the wall and from the many points of vantage on the pasture to hang wavering for an instant before lazily dissipating in the hot, close air. In such a sombre setting men had elected to joke and curse and kill, perhaps to die; men hot with passion and blood-lust plied rifles with deliberate intent to kill. On one side there was fierce, deep joy, an exultation in forcing the issue, much as if they had tugged vainly at a leash and suddenly found themselves free. They had been baited, tricked, robbed, and fired upon and now, their tormentors penned before them, there would be no cessation in their efforts to wipe out the indignities under which they had chafed for so long a time.

On the other side, high up on a natural fortress which was considered impregnable, lay those who had brought this angry pack about them. There was no joy there, no glad eagerness to force the battle, no jokes nor laughter, but only a grim desperation, a tenacious holding to that which the others would try to take. On one side aggression; on the other, defense. Fighters all, they now were inspired by the merciless end always in their minds; they were trapped like rats and would fight while mind could lay a plan or move a muscle. Of the type which had outroughed, out-fought for so long even the sturdy, rough men who had laid the foundation for an inland empire amid dangers superlative, they knew nothing of yielding; and to yield was to die. It was survivor against survivor in an even game.

"Ah, God!" moaned a man on the mesa's lofty rim, staggering back aimlessly before he fell, never to rise again. His companions regarded him curiously, stolidly, without sympathy, as is often the case where death is constantly expected. Dal Gilbert turned back to his rifle and the problems before him. "So you've gone, too. An' I reckon we'll follow"—such was Chet Bates' obituary.

In a thicket two hundred yards south of the mesa Red Connors worked the lever of his rifle, a frown on his face. "I got him, all right. Do you know who he is?"

"No; but I've seen him in Eagle," replied Hopalong, lowering the glasses. "What's worrying me is water—my throat's drying awful."

"You shouldn't 'a forgot it," chided Red. "Now we've got to go without it all day."

Hopalong ducked and swore as he felt of his bleeding face. "Purty close, that!"

"Mind what yo're doing!" replied Red. "Get off my hand."

"This scrap is shore slow," Hopalong growled. "Here we've been doing this for a whole week, all of us shot up, an' only got two of them fellers."

"Well, yo're right; but there ain't a man up there that ain't got a few bullet holes in him," Red replied. "But it is slow, that's shore."

"I've got to get a drink, an' that's all about it," Hopalong asserted. "I can crawl in that gully most of th' way, an' then trust a side-hopping dash. Anyhow, I'm tired of this place. Johnny's got th' place for *me*."

"You better stay here till it's dark, you fool."

"Aw, stay nothing—so long," and Hopalong, rifle in hand, crawled towards the gully. Red watched the mesa intently, hoping to be able to stop some of the firing his rash friend was sure to call forth.

Twenty minutes passed and then two puffs of smoke sailed against the sky, Red replying. Then half a dozen puffs burst into sight. A faint shout came to Red's ears and he smiled, for his friend was safe.

As Hopalong gained the chaparral he felt himself

heartily kicked and, wheeling pugnaciously, looked into Buck Peters' scowling face. "Yo're a healthy fool!" growled the foreman. "Ain't you got no sense at all? Hereafter you flit over that pasture after dark, d'y hear!"

"He's th' biggest fool I ever saw, an' th' coolest," said a voice in the chaparral at the left.

"Why, hullo, Meeker," Hopalong laughed, turning from Buck. "How do you like our little party now?"

"I'm getting tired of it, an' it's some costly for me," grumbled the H2 foreman. "Bet them skunks in Eagle have cleaned out every head I owned." Then he added as an afterthought: "But I don't care a whole lot if I can see this gang wiped out—*Antonio* is th' coyote *I'm* itching to stop."

"He'll be stopped," replied Hopalong. "Hey, Buck, Red's shore thirsty."

"He can stay thirsty, then. An' don't you try to take no water to him. You stay off that pasture during daylight."

"But it was all my fault—" Hopalong began, and then he was off like a shot across the open, leaping gullies and dodging around boulders.

"Here you!" roared Buck, and started to stare, Meeker at his side. A man was staggering in circles near a thicket which lay a hundred yards from them. He dropped and began to crawl aimlessly about, a good target for the eager rifles on the mesa. Bullets whined and shrilled and kicked up the dust on the plain, but still the rushing Bar-20 puncher was unhit. From the mesa came the faint cracking of rifle fire and clouds of smoke hovered over the cover sheltering Red Connors. Here and there over the pasture and along the chaparral's rim rifles cracked in hot endeavor to drive the rustlers from their positions long enough to save the reckless puncher. Buck and Meeker both were firing now, rapidly but carefully, muttering words of hope and anxiety as they worked the levers of their spurting guns. Then they saw Hopalong gain the prostrate man's side, drag him back to cover, and wave his arm. The fire from the mesa was growing weaker and as it stopped Hopalong, with the wounded man on his back, ran to the shelter of a gully and called for water.

"He's th' best man in this whole country!" cried Meeker, grabbing up a canteen and starting to go through the chaparral to give them water. "To do that for one of *my* men!"

"I've knowed that for nigh onto fifteen years," replied Buck.

Near the Eagle trail Billy Williams and Doc Riley lay side by side, friendly now.

"I tell you we've been shooting high," Doc grumbled. "It's no cinch picking range against that skyline."

"Hey! Look at Hopalong!" cried Billy, excited. "Blamed idiot—why, he's going out to that feller. Lord. Get busy!"

"That's Curtis out there!" ejaculated Doc, angrily. "They've got him, damn 'em!"

"My gun's jammed!" cursed Billy, in his excitement and anger standing up to tear at the cartridge. "I allus go an'—" he pitched sideways to the sand, where he lay quiet.

Doc dropped his rifle and leaped to drag his companion back to the shelter of the cover. As he did so his left arm was hit, but he accomplished his purpose and as he reached for his canteen the Bar-20 pessimist saved him the trouble by opening his eyes and staring around. "Oh, my head! It's shore burning up, Doc!" he groaned. "What th' devil happened that time, anyhow?"

"Here; swaller this," Doc replied, handing him the canteen.

"Who got me?" asked Billy, laying the vessel aside.

"How do I know? Whoever he was he creased you

nice. His friends got me in th' arm, too. You can help me fix it soon."

"Shore I will! We can lick them thieves, Doc," Billy expounded without much interest. "Yessir," he added.

"You make me tired," Doc retorted. "You talking about being careful when you stand up in plain sight of them fellers like you just did."

"Yes, I know. I was mad, an' sort of forgot about 'em being able to shoot me—but what happened out there, anyhow?"

Doc craned his neck. "There's Cassidy now, in that gully—Meeker's just joined him. Good men, both of 'em."

"You bet," replied Billy, satisfied. "Yessir, we can lick 'em—we've got to."

On the west side of the mesa, and out of sight of the rustlers, Pie Willis lay face down in the sand, quiet. Near him lay Frenchy McAllister, firing at intervals, aflame with anger and a desire to kill. Opposite him on the mesa, a scant three hundred yards away, two rustlers gloated and fired, eager to kill the other puncher, who shot so well.

"That other feller knows his business, Elder," remarked Nevada as a slug ricocheted past his head. "Wonder who he is."

"Wonder *where* he is," growled Elder, firing at a new place.

"He's been shifting a lot. Anyhow, we got one. There's so much smoke down there I can't seem to place him. Mebby—" he fell back, limp, his rifle clattering down a hundred feet of rock.

Nevada looked at him closely and now drew back to a more secure position. "We're even, stranger, but we ain't quits, by a good deal!" He swore. *Zing-ing-ing!* "Oh, you know I moved, do you!" he gritted. "Well, how's *that!*" *Spat!* a new, bright leaden splotch showed on the rock above his head and hot lead stung his neck and face as the bullets spattered. "I'll get you yet, you coyotc!" he muttered, changing his position again. "Ah, *hell!*" he sobbed and dropped his rifle to grasp his right elbow, shattered by a Winchester .45. Pain shot through every fibre of his body and weakened him so he could not crawl for shelter or assistance. He swayed, lost his balance and swayed further, and as his side showed beyond the edge of his rocky rampart he quivered and sank back, helpless, pain-racked, and bleeding to death from two desperate wounds.

"We was—tricked—up here!" he moaned. "That must—be Red—Connors out there. Ah!" *Spat! Chug! Spat!* But Nevada did not hear them now.

Down in the chaparral, Frenchy, getting no response to his shots, picked up his glasses and examined the mesa. A moment later he put them back in the case, picked up his rifle and crawled towards his companion.

"Pie!" he called, touching the body. "Pie, old feller! I got 'em both for you, Pie—got 'em—" Screened by the surrounding chaparral he stood up and shook a clenched fist at the sombre, smoke-wreathed pile of rock and shouted: "An' they won't be all! Do you hear, you thieves? *They won't be all!*"

Lying in a crack on the apex of a pinnacle of rock a hundred yards northwest of the mesa Johnny Nelson cursed the sun and squirmed around on the hot stone, vainly trying to find a spot comparatively cool, while two panic-stricken lizards huddled miserably as far back in the crack as they could force themselves. Long bright splotches marked the stone all around the youthful puncher and shrill whinings came to him out of the air, to hurtle away in the distance ten times as loud and high-pitched. For an hour he had not dared to raise his head to aim, and his sombrero, which he had used as a dummy, was shot full of holes. Johnny, at first elated because of his aerial position, now cursed it fervently and was filled with disgust. When he had begun firing at sunrise he had only one man to face. But the news went around among the rustlers that a fool had volunteered to be a target and now three good shots vied with each other to get the work over with quickly, and return to their former positions.

"I reckon I can squirm over th' edge an' drop down that split," Johnny soliloquized, eying a ragged, sharp edge in the rock close at hand. "Don't know where it goes to, or how far down, but it's cool, that's shore."

He wriggled over to it, flattened as much as possible, and looked over the edge, seeing a four-inch ledge ten feet below him. From the ledge it was ten feet more to the bottom, but the ledge was what interested him.

"Shore I can—just land on that shelf, hug th' wall an' they can't touch me," he grinned, slipping over and hanging for an instant until he stopped swinging. The rock bulged out between him and the ledge, but he did not give that any thought. Letting go he dropped down the face of the rock, shot out along the bulge and over his cherished ledge, and landed with a grunt on a mass of sand and debris twenty feet below. As he pitched forward to his hands he heard the metallic warning of a rattlesnake and all his fears of being shot were knocked out of his head by the sound. When he landed from his jump he was on the wrong side of the crevice and among hot lead. Ducking and dodging he worked back to the right side and then blew off the offending rattler's head with his Colt. Other rattlers now became prominent and Johnny, realizing that he was an unwelcome guest in a rattlesnake den, made good use of his eyes and Colt as he edged towards the mouth of the crevice. Behind him were rattlers; before him, rustlers who could and would shoot. To say that he was disgusted is to put it mildly.

"Cussed joint!" he grunted. "This is a measly place for me. If I stay I get bit to death; if I leave I get shot. Wonder if I can get to that ledge—ugh!" he cried as the tip of a rattler's tail hung down from it for an instant. "Come on! Bring 'em all out! Trot cut th' tarantulas, copper heads, an' Gilas! Th' more th' merrier! Blasted snake hangout!"

He glanced about him rapidly, apprehensively, and shivered. "No more of this for Little Johnny! I'll chance th' sharp-shooters," he yelled, and dashed out and around the pile so quickly as to be unhit. But he was not hit for another reason, also. Skinny Thompson and Pete Wilson, having grown restless, were encircling the mesa by keeping inside the chaparral and came opposite the pinnacle about the time Johnny discovered his reptilian neighbors. Hearing the noise they both stopped and threw their rifles to their shoulders. Here was a fine opportunity to lessen the numbers of the enemy, for the rustlers, careless for the moment, were peering over their breastwork to see what all the noise was about, not dreaming that two pairs of eyes three hundred yards away were calculating the range. Two puffs of smoke burst from the chaparral and the rustlers ducked out of sight, one of them hard hit. At that moment Johnny made his dash and caused smiles to flit across the faces of his friends.

"We might 'a knowed it was him!" laughed Skinny. "Nobody else would be loco enough to pick out that thing."

"Yes; but now what's he doing?" asked Pete, seeing Johnny poking around among the rocks, Colt in hand.

"Hunting rustlers, I reckon," Skinny replied. "Thinks they are tunnelling an' coming up under him. I suppose. Hey! Johnny!"

Johnny turned, peering at the chaparral.

"What are you doing?" yelled Skinny.

"Hunting snakes."

Skinny laughed and turned to watch the mesa, from which lead was coming.

"Can you cover me if I make a break?" shouted Johnny, hopefully.

"No; stay where you are!" shouted Pete, and then ducked.

"Stop yelling and move about some or you'll get us both hit," ordered Skinny. "Them fellers can *shoot*!"

"Come on; let's go ahead. Johnny can stay out there till dark an' hunt snakes," Pete was getting sarcastic. "Wonder if he reckons we came here to get shot at just to hunt snakes!"

"No; we'll help him in," Skinny replied. "You'll find th' rattlers made it too hot for him up there. Start shooting."

Johnny, hearing the rapid firing of his friends, ran backwards, keeping the pinnacle between him and his enemies as long as he could. Then, once out of its shelter, he leaped erratically over the plain and gained a clump of chaparral. He now had only about a hundred yards to go, and Johnny could sprint when need was. He sprinted. Joining his friends the three disappeared in the chaparral and two disgusted rustlers helped a badly wounded companion to the rough hospital in the hut at the top of the mesa trail.

Johnny and his friends had not gone far before Johnny, eager to find a rustler to shoot at, left them to go to the edge of the chaparral and while he was away his friends stumbled on the body of Pie Willis. Johnny, moving cautiously along the edge of the chaparral, soon met Buck and Hopalong, who were examining every square foot of the mesa wall for a way up.

"Hullo, Johnny!" cried Hopalong. "What you doing here? Thought you were plumb stuck on that freak rock up north."

"I was—an' *stuck*, for shore," grinned Johnny. "That rock is a nest of snakes, besides being a fine place to get plugged by them fellers. An' hot!"

"How'd you get away?"

"Pete an' Skinny drove 'em back an' I made my getaway. They're in th' chaparral somewhere close," Johnny replied. "But why are you telescoping at th' joker? Think you see money out there?"

"Looking for a place to climb it," Hopalong responded. "We're disgusted with this long-range squibbing. You didn't see no breaks in th' wall up where you was, did you?"

"Lemme see," and Johnny cogitated for a moment. Then his face cleared. "Shore I did; there's lots of cracks in it, running up an' down, an' a couple of ledges. I ain't so shore about th' ledges, though—you see I was too busy to look for ledges during th' first part of th' seance, and I dassn't look during th' last of it. There was three of 'em a-popping at me!"

"Hey, Johnny!" came a hail; "Johnny!"

"That's Pete an' Skinny—Hullo!" Johnny shouted.

"Come here—Pie Willis is done for!"

"What?"

"Pie—Willis—is—done—for!"

The three turned and hastened towards the voice, shouting questions. They found Skinny and Pete standing over the body and sombreros came off as the foreman knelt to examine it. Pie had been greatly liked by the members of the outfit he had lately joined, having been known to them for years.

"Clean temple shot," Buck remarked, covering the face and arising. "There's some fine shots up on that rock. Well, here's another reason why we've got to get up there an' wipe 'em out quick. Pie was square as a die and a good puncher—I wouldn't have asked for a better pard-

ner. You fellers take him to camp—we're going to find a
way to square things if there is one. No, Pete, you an'
Johnny carry him in—Skinny is going with us."

Buck, Hopalong, and Skinny returned to the edge of
the pasture and the foreman again swept the wall through
his glasses. "Hey! What's that? A body?"

Hopalong looked. "Yes, two of 'em! I reckon Pie died
game, all right."

"Well, come on—we've got to move along," and Buck
led the way north, Skinny bringing up the rear. Next to
Lanky Smith, at present nursing wounds at the ranch,
Skinny was the best man with a rope in the Bar-20 outfit
and the lariat he used so deftly was one hundred and fifty
feet in length, much longer than any used by those around
the mesa. Buck had asked him to go with them because
he wished to have his opinion as to the possibility of getting a rope up the mesa wall.

When they came opposite the rock which had sheltered Johnny they sortied to see if that part of the mesa
was guarded, but there was no sign of life upon it. Then,
separating, they dashed to the midway cover, the thicket,
which they reached without incident. From there they
continued to the pinnacle and now could see every rock
and seam of the wall with their naked eyes. But they
used the glasses and after a few minutes' examination
of the ledges Hopalong turned to his companions. "Just
as Johnny said. Skinny, do you reckon if you was under
them tonight that you could get yore rope fast to th' bottom one?"

"Shore; that's easy. But it won't be no cinch roping th'
other," Skinny replied. "She sticks out over th' first by
two feet. It'll be hard to jerk a rope from that narrow
foothold."

"Somebody can hang onto you so you can lean out,"
Buck replied. "Pete can hold you easy."

"But what'll he hold on to?"

Hopalong pointed. "See that spur up there, close to th' first ledge? He can hitch a rope around that an' hang on th' rope. I tell you it's *got* to be done. We can't lose no more men in this everlasting pot-shooting game. We've got to get close an' clean up!"

"Well, I ain't saying nothing different, am I?" snapped Skinny. "I'm saying it'll be hard, an' it will. Now suppose one of them fellers goes on sentry duty along this end; what then?"

"We'll solve that when we come to it," Hopalong replied. "I reckon if Red lays on this rock in th' moonlight that he can drop any sentry that stands up against th' sky at a hundred yards. We're got to try it, anyhow."

"Down!" whispered Buck, warningly. "Don't let 'em know we're here. Drop that gun, Hoppy!"

They dropped down behind the loose boulders while the rustler passed along the edge, his face turned towards the pinnacle. Then, deciding that Johnny had not returned, he swept the chaparral with a pair of glasses. Satisfied at length that all was well he turned and disappeared over a rocky ledge ten feet from the edge of the wall.

"I could 'a dropped him easy," grumbled Hopalong, regretfully, and Skinny backed him up.

"Shore you could; but I don't want them to think we are looking at this end," Buck replied. "We'll have th' boys raise th' devil down south till dark an' keep that gang away from this end."

"I reckon they read yore mind—hear th' shooting?" Skinny queried.

"That must be Red out there—I can see half of him from here," Hopalong remarked, lowering his glasses. "Look at th' smoke he's making! Wonder what's up? Hear th' others, too!"

"Come on—we'll get out of this," Buck responded.

"We'll go to camp an' plan for to-night, an' talk it over with th' rest. I want to hear what Meeker's going to do about it an' how we can place his men."

"By thunder! If we *can* get up there, half a dozen of us with Colts, an' sneak up on 'em, we'll have this fight tied up in a bag so quick they won't know what's up," Skinny remarked. "You can bet yore life that if there's any way to get a rope up that wall I'll do it!"

XXX

♦

Up the Wall

Pipes were glowing in the shadows away from the fire, where men lay in various attitudes of ease. A few were examining wounds while others cleaned rifles and saw that their revolvers were in good condition. Around the fire but well back from it four men sat cross-legged, two others stretched out on their elbows and stomachs near them.

"You say everything is all right on th' ranch?" asked Buck of a man who, covered with alkali, had just come from the Bar-20. "No trouble, hey?"

"Nope; no trouble at all," replied Cross, tossing his sombrero aside. "Lucas an' Bartlett each sent us four men to help out when they learned you had come out here. We shipped four of 'em right on to th' H2, which is too short-handed to do any damage to rustlers."

"Much obliged for that," spoke up Meeker, relief in his voice. "I'm blamed glad to hear things are quiet back home—but I don't know how long they'll stay that way with Eagle so close."

"Well, Eagle ain't a whole lot anxious to dip in no more,"

laughed Cross, looking at the H2 foreman. "Leastawise, that's what Lucas said. He sent a delegation down there which made a good impression. There was ten men in it an' they let it be known that if they came back again there would be ten more with 'em. In that case Eagle wouldn't be no more than a charred memory. Since Quinn died, being shot hard by Nevada, who I reckons is out here, th' town ain't got nobody to tell it how to do things right, which is shore pleasant."

"You bring blamed good news—I'm glad Lucas went down there," Buck replied. "I can't tell of good news about us out here, yet. We've had a hard time for a week. They got Pie to-day, an' most of us are shot up plentiful. Yo're just in time for th' festival, Cross—we're going to try to rush 'em to-night an' get it over. We reckon Skinny an' Pete can get us a way up that wall before dawn."

"Me for th' rush," laughed Cross. "I'm fresh as a daisy, which most of you fellers ain't. How many of 'em have you got so far? Are there many still up there?"

"We've got four of 'em that I knows of, an' how many of 'em died from their wounds I can't say," replied Hopalong. "But a whole lot of 'em have been plugged, an' plugged hard."

"But how many are up there still able to fight?"

"I should say about nine," Hopalong remarked, thoughtfully.

"Ten," corrected Red. "I've been watching th' positions an' I know."

"About nine or ten—they shift so nobody can really tell," Buck replied. "I reckon we've seen 'em all in Eagle, too."

"Frenchy got Nevada an' another to-day, on th' west side," Johnny interposed.

"I'm glad Nevada is gone—he's a terror in a mixup," Cross rejoined. "Best two-handed gun man in Eagle, he was."

"Huh!" snorted Johnny. "Stack him up against Hoppy an' see how long he'd last!"

"I said in Eagle!" retorted Cross.

Buck suddenly stood up and stretched. "You fellers all turn in now an' snatch some sleep. I'm going out to see how things are with Billy. I'll call you in time. Doc, you an' Curtis are too shot up to do any climbing—you turn in too. When I come back I'll wake you an' send you out to help Billy watch th' trail. Where's Red?"

"Over here—what do you want?" came from the shadows.

"Nothing, only get to sleep. I reckoned you might be off somewheres scouting. Skinny, where's yore rope? Got that manilla one? Good! Put three more hemp lariats out here where I can find 'em when I come back. Now don't none of you waste no time; turn in right now!" He started to walk away and then hesitated, turning around. "Doc, you an' Curtis better come with me now so you won't lose no time hunting Billy in th' dark when yore eyes are sleepy—it's hard enough to find him now in th' dark, when I'm wide awake. You can get yore sleep out there—he'll wake you when yo're needed."

The two punchers arose and joined him, Doc with his left arm bandaged and his companion with three bandages on him. When they joined Buck Doc protested. "Let me go with you an' th' rest of th' boys, Peters, when you go up that wall. I came out here to get th' man that murdered Curley, an' I hate to miss him now. If I can't climb th' boys will be glad to pull me up, an' it won't take no time to speak of. My gun arm is sound as a dollar—*I* want that murderer!"

Buck glanced at Meeker, who refused to give any sign of his thoughts on the matter. "Well, all right, Doc. But if we should have to fight as soon as we get up an' don't have no time to pull you after us, you'll miss everything. But you can do what you want."

"I'll just gamble on that. I ain't hurt much, an' if I can't climb I'll manage to get in th' scrap someway, even if I has to hunt up Billy," replied Doc, contentedly, returning to the fire.

Buck and his companion moved away into the darkness while those around the fire lay down to get a few hours' rest, which they needed badly. George Cross, who was not sleepy, remained awake in a shadow and kept guard, although none was needed.

Buck and Curtis found Billy by whistling and the wounded H2 puncher found a place to lie down and was soon asleep, while the foreman and his friend sat up, watching the faint glow on the mesa, the camp-fire of the besieged. Once they heard the clatter of a rifle from the head of the trail and later they saw a dim figure pass quickly across the lighted space. They were content to watch on such a night, for the air had cooled rapidly after the sun went down and the sky was one twinkling mass of stars.

Twice during the wait Buck disappeared into the black chaparral close at hand and struck a match under his coat to see the time, and on the last occasion he returned to Billy, remarking: "Got half an hour yet before I leave you. Are you sleepy?"

"No, not very; my head hurts too much to sleep," Billy replied, re-crossing his legs and settling himself in a more comfortable position. "When you leave I'll get up on my hoofs so I won't feel like dosing off. I won't wake Curtis unless I have to—he's about played out."

"You wake him when you think I've been gone half an hour," Buck ordered. "It'll take him some time to get his eyes open—we mustn't let any get away. They've got friends in Eagle, you know."

"Wish I could smoke," Billy remarked, wistfully.

"Why, you can," replied Buck, quickly. "Go back there

in th' chaparral an' get away with a pipeful. I'll watch things till you come back an' if I need you quick I can call. You've got near half an hour—make th' best of it."

"Here's th' gun—much obliged, Buck," and Billy disappeared, leaving the foreman to plan and watch. Buck glanced at the sleeping man occasionally when he heard him toss or mutter and wished he could let him sleep on undisturbed.

Suddenly a flash lighted up the top of the trail for an instant and the sharp report of a rifle rang out loudly on the still, night air. Buck, grabbing the Winchester, sprang to his feet as an excited chorus came from the rustlers' stronghold. Then he heard laughter and a few curses and quiet again ensued.

"What was that, Buck?" came a low, anxious hail from behind.

The foreman laughed softly and said: "Nothing, Billy, except that th' guard up there reckoned he saw something to shoot at. It's funny how staring at th' dark will get a feller seeing things that ain't. Why, had yore smoke so soon?" he asked in surprise as Billy sat down beside him.

"Shore," replied Billy. "Two of 'em. I reckon yore time is about up. Gimme th' gun now."

"Well, good luck, Billy. Better move up closer to th' trail if you can find any cover. You don't want to miss none. So long," and Billy was alone with his sleeping companion.

When the foreman returned to the camp he was challenged, and stopped, surprised. "It's Peters," he called.

"Oh, all right. Time to go yet?" asked Cross, emerging from the darkness.

"Purty near; but I thought I told you to go to sleep?"

"I know, but I ain't sleepy, not a bit. So I reckoned I'd keep watch over th' rest of th' gang."

"Well, since yo're wide awake, you help me knot these ropes an' let th' others have a few minutes more," Buck responded, picking up Skinny's fifty-foot lariat and placing it to one side. He picked up the three shorter ropes and threw one to his companion. "Put a knot every foot an' a half—make 'em tight an' big."

In a few minutes the work was finished and Buck awakened the sleeping men, who groped their way to the little stream close by and washed the sleep out of their tired eyes, grabbing a bit of food on their return to the fire.

"Now, fellers," said the foreman, "leave yore rifles here—it's Colts this trip, except in Red's case. Got plenty of cartridges? Everybody had a drink an' some grub? All right; single file after me an' don't make no noise."

When the moon came up an hour later Red Connors, lying full length on the apex of the pinnacle which Johnny had tried and found wanting, watched an indistinct blur of men in the shadow of the mesa wall. He saw one of them step out into the moonlight, lean back and then straighten up suddenly, his arm going above his head. The silence was so intense that Red could faintly hear the falling rope as it struck the ground. Another cast, and yet another, both unsuccessful, and then the fourth, which held. The puncher stepped back into the shadow again and another figure appeared, to go jerking himself up the face of the wall. While he watched the scaling operations Red was not missing anything on top of the mesa, where the moon bathed everything in a silvery light.

Then he saw another figure follow the first and kick energetically as it clambered over onto the ledge. Soon a rope fell to the plain and the last man up, who was Skinny, leaned far out and cast at the second ledge, Pete holding him. After some time he was successful and again he and his companion went up the wall. Pete climbed rapidly, his heavy body but small weight for the huge, mus-

cular arms which rose and fell so rapidly. On the second
ledge the same casting was gone through with, but it was
not until the eighth attempt that the rope stayed up. Then
Red, rising on his elbows, put his head closer to the stock
of his rifle and peered into the shadows back of the lighted
space on the rocky pile. He saw Pete pull his companion
back to safety and then, leaping forward, grasp the rope
and climb to the top. Already one of the others was part
way up the second rope while another was squirming
over the lower ledge, and below him a third kicked and
hauled, half way up the first lariat.

"String of monkeys," chuckled Red. "But they can't
none of 'em touch Pete in that sort of a game. Wonder
what Pete's doing?" he queried as he saw the man on the
top of the mesa bend, fumble around for a moment, and
then toss his arm out over the edge. "Oh, it's a knotted
rope—he's throwing it down for th' others. Well, Pete,
old feller, you was th' first man to get—*Lord*!"

He saw Pete wheel, leap forward into a shadow, and
then a heaving, twisting, bending bulk emerged into the
moonlight. It swayed back and forth, separated into two
figures and then became one again.

"They're fighting, rough an' tumble!" Red exclaimed.
"Lord have mercy on th' man who's closing with that Pete
of ourn!"

He could hear the scuffling and he knew that the others had heard it, too, for Skinny was desperately anxious
to wriggle over the edge, while down the line of ropes
the others acted like men crazed. Still the pair on the
mesa top swayed back and forth, this way and that, bending, twisting, and Red imagined he could hear their labored breathing. Then Skinny managed to pull himself
to the top of the wall and sprang forward, to sink down
from a kick in the stomach.

"God A'mighty!" cried Red excitedly. "Who is it that

can give Pete a fight like that? Well, I'm glad he's so busy he can't use his gun!"

Skinny was crawling around on his hands and knees as Buck's head arose over the edge. The foreman, well along in years, and heavy, was too tired to draw himself over the rim without a moment's rest. He had no fear for Pete, but he was worried lest some rustler might sound an alarm. Skinny now sat up and felt for his Colt, but the foreman's voice stopped him. "No shooting, yet! Want to tell 'em what's up! You let them fellers alone for a minute, an' give me a hand here."

Pete, his steel-like fingers darting in for hold after hold, managed to jerk his opponent's gun from its sheath and throw it aside, where Skinny quickly picked it up. He was astonished by the skill and strength of his adversary, who blocked every move, every attempt to get a dangerous hold. Pete, for a man reputed as being slow, which he was in some things, was darting his arms in and out with remarkable quickness, but without avail. Then, realizing that his cleaner living was standing him in good stead, and hearing the labored breathing of the rustler, he leaped in and clinched. By this time Hopalong and three more of the attacking force had gained the mesa top and were sent forward by the foreman, who was now intent upon the struggle at hand.

"It's Big Sandy!" Hopalong whispered to Skinny, pausing to watch for a moment before he disappeared into the shadows.

He was right, and Big Sandy, breathless and tired, was fighting a splendid fight for his life against a younger, fresher, and stronger man. The rustler tried several times for a throat hold but in vain; and in a fury of rage threw his weight against his opponent to bear him to the ground, incautiously bringing his feet close together as he felt the other yield. In that instant Pete dropped to a crouch, his vice-like hands tightened about Big Sandy's ankles, and with a sudden, great surge of his powerful back and shoulders he straightened up and Sandy plunged forward to a crashing fall on the very edge of the mesa, scrambled to his feet, staggered, lost his balance, and fell backwards a hundred feet to the rocks below.

The victor would have followed him but for Buck, who grasped him in time. Pete, steady on his feet again, threw Buck from him by one sweep of his arms and wheeled to renew the fight, surprise flashing across his face at not seeing his opponent.

"He's down below, Pete," Buck cried as Johnny, white-faced, crawled over the edge.

"What was that?" exclaimed the Kid. "Who fell?"

"Big Sandy," replied the foreman. "He—" the report of a shot cut him short. "Come on!" he called. "They're at it!" and he dashed away, closely followed by Johnny and Pete as Jim Meeker came into view. The H2 foreman slid over the mesa rim, leaped to his feet and sprinted forward, Colt in hand, to be quickly lost in the shadows, and after him came Red Connors, the last.

Down below Doc, hearing a thud not far from him, hurried around a spur of rock in the wall, sick at heart when he saw the body. Bending over quickly he recognized the mass as once having been Big Sandy, and he forthwith returned to the rope to be pulled up. When he at last realized that his friends had forgotten him there was loud, lurid cursing and he stamped around like a wild man, waving a Colt in his right hand. Finally he dropped heavily on a rock, too enraged to think, and called the attacking force, collectively and individually, every name that sprang to his lips. As he grew calmer he arose from the rock, intending to join Billy and Curtis at the other end of the pasture, and as he took a step in that direction he heard a sharp click and a pebble bounced past him.

He stepped backwards quickly and looked up, seeing a figure sliding rapidly down the highest rope. He was immediately filled with satisfaction and easily forgave his companions for the anxiety they had caused him, and as he was about to call out he heard something spoken in Spanish. Slipping quickly and noiselessly into the deeper shadow at the base of the wall he flattened himself behind the spur of rock close to the rope, where he waited tensely, a grim smile transforming his face. He knew that voice.

XXXI

♦

Fortune Snickers at Doc

Antonio was restless and could not sleep. He turned from side to side on the ground near the fire before the hut and was one of the first to run to the top of the trail when the guard there discharged his rifle at nothing. Returning to his blanket he tried to compose himself to rest, but was unsuccessful. Finally, he arose, picked up his rifle, and slouched off into the shadows to wander about from point to point.

Cavalry, coming in from his post to get a drink, caught sight of Antonio before he was swallowed up by the darkness and, suspicious as ever of Antonio, forgot the drink and followed.

After wandering about all unconscious of espionage Antonio finally drifted to the western edge and seated himself comfortably against a boulder, Cavalry not fifty feet away in a shadow. Time passed slowly and as Antonio was about to return to the fire he chanced to glance across the mesa along a moon-lighted path and stiffened at what he saw. A figure ran across the lighted space, silently, cautiously, Colt in hand, and then another, then two together, and he knew that the enemy had found a way up the wall and were hurrying forward to fight at close quarters, to effect a surprise on the unsuspecting men about the fire and in the hut. There remained, perhaps, time enough for him to escape and he arose and ran north, crouching as he zigzagged from cover to cover, cautious and alert.

Cavalry, because of his position, had not seen the flitting punchers and, his suspicions now fully aroused, he slipped after Antonio to find out just what he was going to do. When the firing burst out behind him he paused and stood up, amazed. As he struggled to understand what it meant he saw three men run past a boulder at his left and then he knew, and still hesitated. He was not a man who thought quickly and his first natural impulse, due to his army training, was to join his friends, but gradually the true situation came to him. How many men there were in the attacking force he did not know, but he had seen three after the fighting had begun; and it was evident that the cowmen would not rush into the lion's jaws unless they were strong enough to batter down all resistance. Four of his friends were dead, another had evidently deserted, and the remainder were all more or less severely wounded—there could be no hope of driving the ranchmen back, and small chance of him being able to work through their line to join his friends. There remained only one thing to be done, to save himself while he might.

As he moved forward slowly and cautiously to find a way down the wall he remembered Antonio's peculiar actions and wondered if he had a hand in helping the cowmen up.

Meanwhile Antonio, reaching the edge of the open

space where Pete and Big Sandy had fought, saw Red Connors appear over the rim and dash away to join in the fighting. Waiting long enough to assure himself that there were none following Red he ran to the edge and knelt by the rope. Leaving his rifle behind and seeing that the flap of his holster was fastened securely, he lowered himself over, sliding rapidly down to the first ledge. Here he spent a minute, a minute that seemed an eternity, hunting for the second rope in the shadows, found it and went on.

Sliding and bumping down the rough wall he at last reached the plain and, with a sigh of relief, turned to run. At that instant a figure leaped upon him from behind and a hand gripped his throat and jerked him over backwards. Antonio instinctively reached for his Colt with one hand while he tore at the gripping fingers with the other, but he found himself pinned down between two rocks in such a manner that his whole weight and that of his enemy was on the holster and made his effort useless. Then, terrified and choking for breath, he dug wildly at the vise-like fingers which not for a moment relaxed, but in vain, for he was growing weaker with each passing second.

Doc leaned forward, peering into the face before him, his fingers gripping with all their power, gripping with a force which made the muscles of the brawny forearm stand out like cords, his face malevolent and his heart full of savage joy. Here was the end of his hunt, here was the man who had murdered Curley in cold blood, cowardly, deliberately. The face, already dark, was turning black and the eyes were growing wide open and bulging out. He felt the surge of Antonio's pulse, steadily growing weaker. But he said no word as he watched and gloated, he was too intent to speak, too centered upon the man under him, too busy keeping his fingers tight-gripped. He would make good his threat, he would keep his word and kill the murderer of his best friend with his naked hands, as he had sworn.

Up above the two Cavalry, working along the edge, had come across Antonio's rifle and then as he glanced about, saw the rope. Here was where the cowmen had come up and here was where he could go down. From the way the shooting continued he knew that the fight was desperate and he believed himself to be cut off from his friends. He hated to desert in the face of the enemy, to leave his companions of a dangerous business to fight for their lives without him, but there was only one thing to do since he could not help them—he must save himself.

Dropping his rifle beside the other he lowered himself over the edge and slid rapidly down. When halfway down the last rope his burning hands slipped and he fell head over heels, and landed on Doc, knocking him over and partially stunning him. Cavalry's only idea now was to get from the men who, as he thought, were guarding the rope and, hastily picking himself up, he dashed towards the chaparral to the west as fast as he could run, every moment expecting to feel the hot sting of a bullet. At last, when the chaparral closed about him he plunged through it recklessly and ran until sheer exhaustion made him drop insensible to the sand. He had run far, much farther than he could have gone were it not for the stimulus of the fear which gripped him; and had he noticed where he was going he would have known that he was running up a slope, a slope which eventually reached a level higher than the top of the mesa. And when he dropped if he had been capable of observation he would have found himself in a chaparral which arose above his head, and seen the narrow lane through it which led to a great expanse of sand, tawney and blotched with ash-colored alkali, an expanse which stretched away to the desolate horizon.

Shortly after Cavalry's descent Antonio stirred, opened his eyes, stared vaguely about him and, feeling his bruised and aching throat, staggered to his feet and stumbled to the east, hardly conscious of what he was doing. As he proceeded his breath came easier and he began to remember having seen Doc lying quiet against a rock. He hesitated a moment as he wondered if Doc was dead and if so, who had killed him. Then he swore because he had not given him a shot to make sure that he would not rejoin his friends. Hesitating a moment he suddenly decided that he would be better off if he put a good distance between himself and the mesa, and ran on again, eager to gain the shelter of the chaparral.

When Doc opened his eyes and groped around he slowly remembered what had occurred and his first conscious act was to look to see if his expected victim were dead or alive. It did not take him long to realize that he was alone and his hand leaped for his Colt as he peered around. Limping out on the plain he caught sight of Antonio running, rapidly growing indistinct, and hazarded two shots after him. Antonio leaped into a new speed as though struck with a whip and cursed himself for not having killed the H2 puncher when he had the chance. A moment more and he was lost in the thickets. Doc tried to follow, but his leg, hurt by Cavalry's meteoric descent, was not equal to any great demand for speed and so, turning, he made his way towards the camp to get a horse and return to take up Antonio's trail.

He lost an hour in this, a feverishly impatient hour, punctuated with curses as he limped along and with an unsparing quirt once he was astride. What devilish Humpty Dumpty had cheated him this time? "All the king's horses and all the king's men couldn't put Humpty

Dumpty together again." He laughed grimly and swore
again as the cranky beast beneath him shied a pain into
his sore leg. "Go on, you!" he yelled, as he swept up to
where the ropes still dangled against the wall. The world
was not big enough to hide the murderer of Curley, to
save him from his just deserts. The two trails lay plain
before him in the brilliant moonlight and his pony sprang
forward toward the spot where Antonio had disappeared
in the chaparral.

XXXII

◆

Nature Takes a Hand

When Hopalong caught up with his four companions he was astonished by the conditions on the
mesa. Instead of a boulder-strewn, rocky plain as he had
believed it to be he found himself on a table-land cut and
barred by fissures which ran in all directions. At one
time these had been open almost to the level of the surrounding pasture but the winds had swept sand and debris into the gashes until now none were much more than
ten feet deep. Narrow alleyways which led in every direction, twisting and turning, now blocked and now
open for many feet in depth, their walls sand-beaten to
a smoothness baffling the grip of one who would scale
them, were not the same in a fight as a comparatively flat
plain broken only by miscellaneous boulders and hum-
mocks. There could be no concerted dash for the reason
that one group of the attacking force might be delayed
until after another had begun to fight. And it was possible,
even probable, that the turns in the alleyways might be
guarded; and once separated in the heat of battle it would

be easy enough to shoot each other. Instead of a dashing fight soon to be over, it looked as though it would be a deadly game of hide and seek to wear out the players and which might last for an indefinite length of time. It was disconcerting to find that what had been regarded as the hardest part of the whole affair, the gaining of the mesa top, was the easiest.

"Here, fellows!" Hopalong growled. "We'll stick together till we get right close, an' then if we have time an' these infernal gorges don't stop us, we may be able to spread out. We've got to move easy, too. If we go galloping reckless we'll run into some guard an' there won't be no surprise party on Thunder Mesa. We can count on having light, though not as much as we might have, for th' moon won't go back on us till th' sun fades it."

"It's light enough," growled Skinny. "Come on—we've got to go ahead an' every minute counts. *I* don't think we'd lose so much time roping them knobs an' getting up."

They moved forward cautiously in single file, alert and straining eyes and ears, and had covered half of the distance when a shot was heard ahead and they listened, expecting an uproar. Waiting a minute and hearing nothing further, they moved on again, angry and disgruntled. Then another shot rang out and they heard Billy and Curtis reply.

"Shooting before daylight, before they get their morning's grub," grumbled George Cross.

"Yes; sort of eye-opener, I reckon," softly laughed Chick Travers, who was nervous and impatient. "Get a move on an' let's start something," he added.

As they separated to take advantage of a spoke-like radiation of several intersecting fissures another shot rang out ahead and there was an angry *spat*! close to Hopalong's head. Another shot and then a rattling volley sent the punchers hunting cover on the run, but they were moving forward all the time. It was a case of getting close or be killed at a range too great for Colts, and their rifles were in the camp. Had the light been better the invaders might have paid dearly right there for the attack.

Confusion was rife among the defenders and the noise of the shouts and firing made one jumble of sound. Bullets whistled along the fissures in the dim light and hummed and whizzed as they ricochetted from wall to wall. As yet the attacking force had made no reply, being too busily occupied in getting close to lose time in wasting lead at that range, and being only five against an unknown number protected by a stone hut and who knew every boulder, crevice, and other points of vantage.

Hopalong slid over a boulder which choked his particular and personal fissure and saw Jim Meeker sliding down the wall in front of it. And as Meeker picked himself up Skinny Thompson slid down the other wall.

"Well, I'm hanged!" grunted Hopalong in astonishment.

"Same here," retorted Skinny. "What you doing 'way over here?"

"Thought you was going to lead th' other end of th' line!" rejoined Hopalong.

"This is it—yo're off yore range."

"Well, I reckon not!" Hopalong responded, indignantly.

"An' say, Meeker, how'd you get over here so quick?" Skinny asked, turning to the other. "You was down below when I saw you last."

"*Me*? Why, I just follered my nose, that's all," Meeker replied, surprised.

"You've got a blamed crooked nose, then," Skinny snorted, and turned to Hopalong. "Why don't you untangle yoreself an' go where you belong, you carrot-headed blunderer!"

"Hang it! I tell you—" Hopalong began, and then ducked quickly. "Lord, but somebody's got us mapped out good!"

"Well, some of our fellers have started up—hear 'em over there?" exclaimed Skinny as firing broke out on the east. "Them's Colts, all right. Mebby it's plumb lucky for us it *ain't* so blamed light, after all; we'll have time to pick our places before they can see us real good."

"Pick our places!" snorted Hopalong. "Get tangled up, you mean!" he added.

"Hullo! What you doing, fellers?" asked a pained and surprised voice above them. "Why ain't you in it?"

"For th' love of heaven—it's Frenchy!" cried Hopalong. "Skinny, I reckon them Colts you heard belonged to th' rustlers. *We're* all here but a couple."

"Didn't I leave you over east five minutes ago, Frenchy?" demanded Skinny, his mouth almost refusing to shut.

"Shore. I'm east—what's eating at you?" asked Frenchy.

"Come on—get out of this!" ordered Hopalong, scrambling ahead. "You foller me an' you'll be all right."

"We'll be back to th' ropes if we foller you," growled Skinny. "Of all th' locoed layouts I ever run up against this here mesa top takes th' prize," he finished in disgust.

Bullets whined and droned above them and frequently hummed down the fissure to search them out, the high, falsetto whine changing quickly to an angry *spang*! as they struck the wall a slanting blow. They seemed to spring away again with renewed strength as they sang the loud, whirring hum of the ricochette, not the almost musical, sad note of the uninterrupted bullet, but venomous, assertive, insistent. The shots could be distinguished now, for on one side were the sharp cracks of rifles; on the other a different note, the roar of Colts.

"This ain't no fit society for six-shooters," Meeker remarked in a low voice as they slid over a ridge, and dropped ten feet before they knew it.

"For th' Lord's sake!" ejaculated Hopalong as he arose to his feet. "Step over a rock an' you need wings! Foller a nice trail an you can't get out of th' cussed thing! Go west an' you land east, say 'solong' to a friend an' you meet him a minute later!"

"We ought to have rifles in this game," Meeker remarked, rubbing his knee-cap ruefully.

"Yes; an' ladders, ropes, an' balloons," snorted Skinny.

"Send somebody back for th' guns," suggested Frenchy.

"Who?" demanded Hopalong. "Will *you* go?"

"Me? Why, I don't want no rifle."

"Huh! Neither do I," remarked Skinny. "Here, Frenchy, give me a boost up this wall—take my hand."

"Well, don't wiggle so, you!"

"That's right! Walk backwards. I ain't no folding step-ladder! How do you think I'm going to grab that edge if you takes me ten feet away from it?"

Spang! Spang! Zing-ing-ing!

"Here, you! Lemme down! Want me to get plugged!" yelled Skinny, executing ungraceful and rapid contortions. "Lower me, you fool!"

"Let go that ridge, then!" retorted Frenchy.

During the comedy Hopalong had been crawling up a rough part of the wall and he fired before he lost his balance. As he landed on Meeker a yell rang out and the sound of a rifle clattering on rock came to them. "I got him, Skinny—go ahead now," he grunted, picking himself up.

It was not long until they were out of the fissure and crawling down a boulder-strewn slope. As they came to the bottom they saw a rustler trying to drag himself to cover and Meeker fired instantly, stopping the other short.

"Why, I thought *I* stopped him!" exclaimed Hopalong.

"Reckon you won't rustle no more cows, you thief," growled Meeker, rising to his knees.

Hopalong pulled him down again as a bullet whizzed through the space just occupied by his head. "Don't you get so curious," he warned. "Come on—I see Red. He's got his rifle, lucky cuss."

"Good for him! Wish I had mine," replied Meeker, grinning at Red, who wriggled an elbow as a salutation. In his position Red could hardly be expected to do much more, since two men were waiting for a shot at him.

"Well, you can get that gun down there an' have a rifle," Hopalong suggested, pointing to the Winchester lying close to its former owner. "You can do it, all right."

"Good idea—shoot 'em with their own lead," and the H2 foreman departed on his hands and knees for the weapon.

"I hit one—he's trying to put his shoulder together," hollered Red, grinning. "What makes you so late—I was th' last one up, an' I've been here a couple of hours."

"You're a sinful liar!" retorted Hopalong. "We stopped to pick blackberries back at that farm house," he finished with withering sarcasm.

"You fellers had time to get married an' raise a family," Red replied. He ducked and looked around. "Ah, you coyote—hit him, but not very hard, I reckon."

It was daylight when Pete, on the other end of the line, turned and scourged Johnny. "Ain't you got no sense in yore fool head? How can I see to shoot when you kick around like that an' fill my eyes with dirt! Come down from up there or I'll lick you!"

"Ah, shut up!" retorted Johnny with a curse. "You'd kick around if somebody nicked *yore* ear!"

"Well, it serves you right for being so unholy curious!" Pete replied. "You come down before he nicks yore eye!"

"Not before I get square—*Wow*!" and Johnny came down rapidly.

"Where'd he get you that time?"

"None of yore business!" growled Johnny.

"I told you to come—"

"Shut up!" roared Johnny, glaring at him. "Wish I had that new Sharps of mine!"

"Go an' get it, Kid. Yo're nimble," Pete responded. "An' bring up some of th' others, too, while yo're about it."

"But how long will this fight last, do you reckon?" the other asked, with an air of weighing something.

"All day with rifles—a week without 'em."

"Shore yo're right?"

"Yes; go ahead. There'll be some of th' scrap left for you when you get back."

"All right—but don't you get that feller. I want him for what he did to me," and Johnny hastened away. He returned in fifteen minutes with two rifles and gave one of them to his companion.

"They're .45–70's—an' full, too," he remarked. "But I ain't got no more cartridges for 'em."

"How'd you get 'em so quick?"

"Found 'em by th' rope where we came up—didn't have to stop; just picked 'em up an' came right back," Johnny laughed. "But I wonder how they got there?"

"Bet four dollars an' a tooth-pick they means that two thieves got away down thcm ropes. Where's Doc?"

"Don't know—but I don't think anybody pulled him up here."

"Then he might 'a stopped them two what owned th' rifles—he would be mad enough to stay there a month if Red forgot him."

"Yes; waiting to lick Red when he came down," and Johnny crawled up again to his former position. "Now, you cow-stealing coyote, watch out!" As he settled down he caught sight of his foreman. "Hullo, Buck! What yo doing?"

"Stringing beads for my night shirt," retorted Buck. "You get down from up there, you fool!"

"Can't. I got to pay for—" He ducked, and then fired twice. "Just missed th' other ear, Pete. But I made him jump a foot—plugged him where he sits down. He was moving away."

"Yes; an' you took two shots to do it, when cartridges are so scarce," Pete grumbled.

At first several of the rustlers had defended the hut but the concentrated fire of the attacking force had poured through its north window from so many angles that evacuation became necessary. This was accomplished through the south window, which opened behind the natural breastwork, and at a great cost, for Con Irwin and Sam Austin were killed in the move.

The high, steep ridge which formed the rear wall of the hut and overlooked the roof of the building ran at right angles to the low breastwork and extended from the north end of the hut to the edge of the mesa, a distance of perhaps fifty feet. On the side farthest from the breastwork it sloped to the stream made by the spring and its surface was covered with boulders. The rustlers, if they attempted to scale its steep face, would be picked off at short range, but they realized that once the enemy gained its top their position would be untenable except around the turn in the breastwork at the other side of the mesa. In order to keep the punchers from gaining this position they covered the wide cut which separated the ridge from the enemy's line and so long as they could command this they were safe.

After wandering from point to point Hopalong finally came to the edge of the cut and found Red Connors en-

sconced in a narrow, shallow depression on a comparatively high hummock. While they talked his eyes rested
on the ridge across the cut and took in the possibilities
that holding it would give.

"Say, Red, if we could get up on that hill behind th'
shack we'd have this fight over in no time—see how it
overlooks everything?"

"Yes," slowly replied Red. "But we can't cross this
barranca—they sweep it from end to end. I tried to get
over there, an' I know."

"But we can try again," Hopalong replied. "You cover
me."

"Now don't be a fool, Hoppy!" his friend retorted.
"We can't afford to lose you for no gang of rustlers. It's
shore death to try it."

"Well, you can bet I ain't going to be fool enough to
run twenty yards in th' open," Hopalong replied, starting
away. "But I'm going to look for a way across, just th'
same. Keep me covered."

"All right, I'll do my best—but don't you try no dash!"

But the rustlers had not given up the idea of holding
the ridge themselves, and there was another and just as
important reason why they must have it; their only water
was in the hut and the spring. To enter the building was
certain death, but if they could command the ridge it
would be possible to get water, for the spring and rivulet
lay on the other side at its base. Hall, well knowing the
folly of trying to scale the steep bank under fire, set
about finding another way to gain the coveted position.
He found a narrow ledge on the face of the mesa wall, at
no place more than eight inches wide, and he believed
that it led to the rear of the ridge. Finding that the wall
above the narrow foothold was rough and offered precarious finger holds, he began to edge along it, a hundred
feet above the plain. When he had almost reached the

end of his trying labors he was discovered by Billy and Curtis, who lay four hundred yards away in the chaparral, and at once became the target for their rifles. Were it not for the fact that they could not shoot at their best because of their wounds Hall would never have finished his attempt, and as it was the bullets flattened against the wall so close to him that on two occasions he was struck by spattering lead and flecks of stone. Then he moved around the turn and was free from that danger, but found that he must get fifty yards north before he could gain the plateau again. To make matters worse the ledge he was on began to grow narrower and at one place disappeared altogether. When he got to the gap he had to cling to the rough wall and move forward inch by inch, twice narrowly missing a drop to the plain below. But he managed to get across it and strike the ledge again and in a few minutes more he stepped into a crevice and sat down to rest before he pushed on. When he looked around he found that the crevice led northeast and did not run to the ridge, and he swore as he realized that he must go through the enemy's line to gain the position. He would not risk going back the way he had come, for he was pretty well tired out. He thought of trying to get to the other end of the mesa so as to escape by the way the attacking force had come up, but immediately put it out of his mind as being too contemptible for further consideration. He arose and moved forward, seeking a way up the wall of the crevice—and turning a corner, bumped into Jim Meeker.

There was no time for weapons and they clinched. Meeker scorned to call for help and Hall dared make no unnecessary noise while in the enemy's line and so they fought silently. Both tried to draw their Colts, Meeker to use his either as a gun or a club, Hall as a club only, and neither succeeded. Both were getting tired when Hall slipped and fell, the H2 foreman on top of him. At that

instant Buck Peters peered down at them from the edge
of the fissure and then dropped lightly. He struck Hall
over the head with the butt of his Colt and stepped back,
grinning.

"There'll be a lot more of these duets if this fight drags
out very long," Buck said. "This layout is shore loco with
all its hidden trails. Have you got a rope, Jim? We'll tie
this gent so he won't hurt hisself if you can find one."

"No. Much obliged, Peters," Meeker replied. "Why,
yes I have, too. Here, use this," and he quickly untied his
neck-kerchief and gave it to his friend. Buck took the one
from around Hall's neck and the two foremen gave a deft
and practical exhibition of how to tie a man so he cannot
get loose. Meeker took the Winchester from Hall's back,
the Colt and the cartridge belt, and gave them to Buck,
laughing.

"Seventy-three model; .44 caliber," he explained.
"You'll find it better than th' six-shooter, an' you'll have
plenty of cartridges for it, too."

"But don't you want it?" asked Buck, hesitating.

"Nope. I left one around th' corner here. I can get
along with it till I get my own from th' camp."

"All right, Jim. I'll be glad to keep this—it'll come in
handy."

"Tough luck, finding them fellers in such a strong layout," Meeker growled, glancing around at the prisoner.
"Ah, got yore eyes open, hey?" he ejaculated as Hall
glared at him. "How many of you fellers are up here,
anyhow?"

"Five thousand!" snapped Hall. "It took two of you to
get me!" he blazed. "Got my guns, too, ain't you? Hope
they bust an' blow yore cussed heads off!"

"Thanks, stranger, thanks," Buck replied, turning to
leave. "But Meeker had you licked good—I only hurried
it to save time. Coming, Jim?"

"Shore. But do you think this thief can get loose?"

Buck paused, searching his pockets, and smiled as he brought to light a small, tight roll of rawhide thongs. "Here, this'll keep him down," and when they had finished their prisoner could move neither hands nor feet. They looked at him critically and then went away towards the firing, the rustler cursing them heartily.

"What's the matter, Meeker?" asked Buck suddenly, noticing a drawn look on his companion's face.

"Oh, I can't help worrying about my girl. She ain't scared of nothing an' she likes to ride. She's too pretty to go breezing over a range that's covered with rustling skunks. I told her to stay in th' house, but—"

"Well, why in thunder don't you go back where you can take care of her?" Buck demanded, sharply. "She's worth more than all th' cows an' rustlers on earth. You ain't needed bad out here, for we can clean this up, all right. You know as long as there are fellers like us to handle a thing like this no man with a girl depending on him has really got any right to take chances. I never thought of it before, or I'd 'a told you so. You cut loose for home to-day, an' leave us to finish this."

"Well, I'll see how things go to-morrow, then. I can pull out th' next morning if everything is all right out here." He hesitated a moment, looking Buck steadily in the eyes, a peculiar expression on his face. "Peters, yo're a good man, one of th' best I ever met, an' you've got a good outfit. I don't reckon we'll have no more trouble about that line of yourn, not nohow. When we settle down to peace an' punching again I'm going to let you show me how to put down some wells at th' southern base of yore hills, like you said one day. If I can get water, a half as much as you got in th' Jumping Bear, I'll be fixed all right. But I want to ask you a fair question, man to man. I ain't no real fool an' I've seen more than I'm supposed to, but I want to be shore about this, dead shore. What kind of a man is Hopalong Cassidy when it comes to women?"

Buck looked at him frankly. "If I had a daughter I wouldn't want a better man for her."

XXXIII

♦

Doc Trails

Doc had not gone far into the chaparral before he realized that his work was going to be hard. The trail was much fainter than it would have been if the man he followed were mounted; the moonlight failed to penetrate the chaparral except in irregular patches which made the surrounding shadows all the deeper by contrast; what little he saw of the trail led through places far too small and turning too sharply to permit being followed by a man on horseback, and lastly, he expected every minute to be fired upon, and at close range. He paused and thought a while—Antonio would head for Eagle, that being the only place where he could get assistance, and there he would find friends. Doc picked his way out of the labyrinth of tortuous alleys and finally came to a comparatively wide lane leading southeast. He rode at a canter now and planned how he would strike the fugitive's trail further down, and after he had ridden a few miles he was struck by a thought that stopped him at once.

"Hang it all, he might 'a headed for them construction camps or for one of th' north ranches, to steal a cayuse," he muttered. "Th' only safe thing for me to do is to jump his trail an' stop guessing, an' even then mebby he'll get me before I get him. That's a clean gamble, an' so here goes," wheeling and retracing his course. When he again found the trail at the place he had quit in, he dismounted and crawled along on his hands and knees in order to follow the foot-prints among the shadows. Then some animal bounded up in front of him and leaped away, and as he turned to look after it he caught sight of his horse standing on its hind legs, and the next instant it was crashing through the chaparral. Drawing his Colt and cursing he ran back in time to see the horse gain an alleyway and gallop off. Angered thoroughly he sent a shot after it and then followed it, finally capturing it in a blind alley. Roundly cursing the frightened beast he led it back to where he had left the trail and, keeping one hand on the reins, continued to follow the foot-prints. Day broke when he had reached the edge of the chaparral and he mounted with a sigh of relief and rode forward along the now plainly marked trail.

As he cantered along he kept his eyes searching every possible cover ahead of and on both sides of him, watching the trail as far ahead as he could see it, for Antonio might have doubled back to get a pursuer as he rode past. After an hour of this caution he slapped his thigh and grinned at his foolishness.

"Now ain't I a cussed fool!" he exclaimed. "A regular, old-woman of a cow-puncher! He won't do no doubling back or ambushing. He'll shore reckon on being trailed by a bunch an' not by a locoed, prize-winning idiot. Why, he's making th' best time he can, an' that's aplenty, too. Besides he ain't got no rifle. Lift yore feet, you four-legged sage hen," he cried, spurring his horse into a lope. He mechanically felt at the long rifle holster at the saddle flap and then looked at it quickly. "An' no rifle for *me*, neither! Oh, well, that's all right, too. I don't need any better gun than he's got, th' coyote. Canteen full of water an' saddle flaps stuffed with grub. Why, old cayuse, if you can do without drinking till we get back to th' mesa we'll be plumb happy. Wonder when you was watered last?"

The trail had been swinging to the north more and more and when Doc noted this fact he grinned again.

"Nice fool I'd 'a been hunting for these tracks down towards Eagle, wouldn't I? But I wonder where he reckons he's going, anyhow?"

Sometime later he had his answers for he found himself riding towards a water hole and then he knew the reason for the trail swinging north. He let his mare drink its fill and while he waited he noticed a torn sombrero, then a spur, and further away the skeleton of a horse. Looking further he saw the skeleton of a man, all that the coyotes had left of the body of Dick Archer, the man killed by Red on the day when he and Hopalong had discovered that Thunder Mesa was inhabited. He pushed around the water hole and then caught sight of something in the sand. Edging his mount over to it he leaned down from the saddle and picked up a Colt's revolver, fully leaded and as good as the day Archer died. That air contained no moisture. As he slipped it in a saddle bag he spurred forward at top speed, for on the other side of a hummock he saw the head and then the full figure of a man plodding away from him, and it was Antonio.

The fugitive, hearing hoof-beats, looked back and then dropped to one knee, his rifle going to his shoulder with the movement.

"Where in the hell did *he* get a rifle?" ejaculated Doc, forcing his horse to buck-jump and pitch so as to be an erratic target. "He didn't have none when *I* grabbed him! Th' devil! That cussed skeleton back there gave *me* a six-shooter, an' *him* a rifle!"

There was a dull smothered report and he saw Antonio drop the gun and rock back and forth, apparently in agony, and he rode forward at top speed. Jerking his horse to its haunches he leaped off it just as Antonio wiped the blood from his eyes and jerked loose his Remington six-shooter. But his first shot missed and before he could fire again Doc grappled with him.

This time it was nearly an even break and Doc found that the slim figure of his enemy was made up of muscles of steel, that the lazy rider of the H2 ranch was, when necessary, quick as a cat and filled with the courage of desperation. It required all of Doc's attention and skill to keep himself from being shot by the other's gun and when he finally managed to wrest the weapon loose he was forced to drop it quickly and grab the same hand, which by some miracle of speed and dexterity now held a knife, a weapon far more deadly in hand-to-hand fighting. Once when believing himself to be gone the buckle of his belt stayed the slashing thrust and he again fought until the knife was above his head. Then, suddenly, two fingers flashed at his eyes and missed by so close a margin that Doc's eyebrows were torn open and his eyes blinded with blood. Instinct stronger than the effect of the disconcerting blindness made him hold his grip on the knife hand, else he would have been missing when his foreman looked for him at the mesa. He dug the fingers of his left hand, that had gripped around the waist, into his enemy's side and squeezed the writhing man tighter to him, wiping the blood from his eyes on the shirt of the other. As he did so he felt Antonio's teeth sink into his shoulder and a sudden great burst of rage swept over him and turned a man already desperate into a berserker, a mad man.

The grip tightened and then the brawny, bandaged left arm quickly slipped up and around Antonio's neck, pressing against the back of it with all the power of the swelling, knotted muscles. A smothered cry sobbed into his chest and he bent the knife hand back until the muscles were handicapped by their unnatural position and then, suddenly releasing both neck and hand, leaped back a step and the next instant his heavy boot thudded into the other's stomach and he watched the gasping, ghastly-faced rustler sink down in a nerveless heap, fighting desperately for the breath that almost refused to return.

Doc wiped his eyes free of blood and hastily bound his neck-kerchief around the bleeding eyebrows. As he knotted the bandage he stepped forward and picked up both the revolver and knife and threw them far from him. Glancing at the rifle he saw that it had burst and knew that the greased, dirty barrel had been choked with sand. He remembered how Curley's rifle had been leaded by the same cause and fierce joy surged through him at this act of retributive justice. He waited patiently, sneering and taunting him until the desperate man had gained his feet.

Doc stepped back a pace, tossing the burst rifle from him, and grinned malignantly. "Take yore own time. Get all yore wind an' strength. *I* ain't no murderer—I don't ride circles around a man an' potshoot him. I'm going to kill you fair, with my hands, like I said. Th' stronger you are th' better I'll feel when I leave you. An' if you should leave me out here on th' sand, all right—but it's got to be fair."

When fully recovered Antonio began the struggle by leaping forward, thinking his enemy unprepared. Doc faced him like a flash and bent low, barely escaping the other's kick. They clinched and swayed to and fro, panting, straining, every ounce of strength called into play. Then Doc got the throat hold again and took a shower of blows unflinchingly. His eyebrows, bleeding again, blinded him, but he could feel if he could not see. Slowly the resistance weakened and finally Doc wrestled Antonio to his knees, bending, and slowly tightening his grip; and the man who had murdered Curley went through all he had felt at the base of the mesa wall, at last paying with his life for his career of murder, theft, fear, and hypocrisy.

Doc arose and went to his horse. Leading the animal back to the scene of the struggle he stood a while, quietly watching for any sign of life, although he knew there would be none.

"Well, bronc, Curley's squared," he muttered, swinging into the saddle and turning the animal's head. "Come on, get out of this!" he exclaimed, quirting hard. As he passed the water hole he bowed to the broken skeleton. "Much obliged, stranger, whoever you was. Yore last play was a good one."

XXXIV

♦

Discoveries

When the two foremen entered the firing line again they saw Red Connors and they cautiously went towards him. As they came within twenty feet of him Buck chanced to glance across the cut and what he saw brought a sudden smile to his face.

"Meeker, Red has got that spring under his gun!" he exclaimed in a low voice. "They can't get within ten feet of it or within ten feet of th' water at any point along its course. This is too good to bungle—wait for me," and he ran out of sight around a bend in the crevice, Meeker staring across at the spring, his eyes following the rivulet until it flowed into the deep, narrow cut it had worn in the side of the mesa.

Red looked around. "Why, hullo, Meeker! Where's

Buck? Thought I heard him a minute ago. If you have any water to spare I can use some of it. Some thief drilled my canteen when I went fooling along this barranca, an' I ain't got a drop left."

Meeker began to move closer to him, Red warning him to be careful, and adding, "Three of them fellers ain't doing nothing but watch this cut. Scared we'll get across it an' flank 'em, I reckon."

"Do you know that yo're covering their water supply?" Meeker asked, handing his canteen to his thirsty companion. "They can't get to it as long as you stay here. That's why they're after you so hard."

Red wiped his lips on his sleeve and sighed contentedly. "It's blamed hot, but it's wet. But is that right? Am I keeping 'em thirsty? Where's th' water?"

"Shore you are! It's right over there—see that little ditch?" Meeker replied, pointing.

Bing! Spat!

The H2 foreman dropped his arm and grinned. "They're watching us purty close, ain't they? Didn't miss me far, at that," showing his companion a torn sleeve and a lead splotch on the rock behind him.

"Not a whole lot. Two of them fellers can shoot like blazes. Yo're plumb lucky," Red responded. "If you'd showed more'n your sleeve that time they'd 'a hit you." He looked across the cut and puckered his brow. "Well, if that's where their water is they don't get none. Mebby we can force 'em out if we watches that spring right smart."

"Here comes Buck now, with Skinny."

"It's too good a card to lose, Skinny," the Bar-20 foreman was saying as he approached. "You settle some place near there where you can pot anybody that tries for a drink. Mebby this little trick wins th' game for us—*quien sabe*? Hullo, Red; where's yore side pardner?"

"Oh, he went prospecting along this barranca to see if he could get across," Red replied. "He wants to get up on top of that ridge behind th' shack. Says if he can do it th' fight won't last long. See how it overlooks their layout?"

Buck looked and his eyes glistened. "An' he's right, too, like he is generally. That's th' key, an' it lies between them an' th' spring. Beats all how quick that feller can size up a hand. If he could play poker as well as he can fight he could quit working for a living."

"Yes; yo're shore right," Red replied.

Several shots rang out from the breastwork and the bullets hummed past them down the cut. A burst of derisive laughter replied fifty yards to their right and a taunt followed it. More shots were fired and answered by another laugh and taunt, inducing profanity from the marksman, and then Hopalong called to Red. "Six out of seven went plumb through my sombrero, Red, when I poked it out to find out if they was looking. They was. Purty good for 'em, eh?"

"Too blamed good to suit me—lucky yore head wasn't in it," Red replied.

Hopalong, singing in stentorian voice an original version of "Mary and Her Little Lamb" in which it seemed he aspired to be the lamb, finally came into view with a perforated sombrero in his hand, which he eyed ruefully. "A good roof gone up, but I didn't reckon everybody was looking my way," he grumbled. "Somebody shore has got to pay for that lid, too," then he glanced up, saw Meeker, and looked foolish. "Howd'y, Meeker; what's new, Buck?"

"Hey, Hoppy! Did you know I was covering their drinking water?" asked Red, triumphantly.

"I knowed you was covering some of it, but you needn't take on no airs about it, for you didn't know it," Hopalong retorted. "What *I* want to know is why you wasn't cover-

ing *me*, like you said you would! It's all yore fault that
my Stetson's bust wide open, an' that being so, we'll just
swap, right now, too!" suiting the action to the words.

"Hey! Gimme that war-bonnet, you bunch of gall!"
yelled Red kicking at his tormentor and missing. "Gimme
that, d'y hear!"

"Give you a punch in th' eye, you sheep!" retorted Hopalong, backing away. "Think you can get away with a
play like that after saying you was going to cover me? *I*
ain't no papoose, you animated carrot!"

"Gimme that Stetson!" Red commanded, starting to
rise. There was a sharp hum and he dropped back again,
blood flowing from his cheek, that being the extent of
his person he had so inadvertently exposed. "There,
blank you! See what you made me do! Going to drop
that hat?"

"Why don't you give 'em a good shot at you? That
ain't no way to treat 'em—but honest, Red, you shouldn't
get so excited over a little thing like that," Hopalong replied. "Now, I'll leave it to Meeker, here—hadn't I ought
to take his roof?"

Meeker laughed. "Th' Court reserves its decision, but
possession is nine points in law."

"Huh! Possession is everything. Since I can keep it,
why, then, according to th' Court, th' hat belongs to me.
Hear that, Red?"

"Yes, I hear it! An' if I wasn't so cussed busy I'd show
you how long you'd keep it," Red rejoined. "I'll bet you a
hat you don't keep it a day after we get this off'n our
hands. Bow-legged cuss, you!"

"Done—then I'll have two hats; one for work an' one
to wear when I'm visiting." Hopalong laughed. "But
you've got th' best of th' swap, anyhow. That new lid of
yourn, holes an' all, is worth twice as much as this wool
thing I'm getting for it. My old one is a *hat*!"

Red refused to lower his dignity by replying and soon fired. "Huh! Reckon that feller won't shoot no more with his right hand."

"Say, I near forgot to tell you Meeker captured one of them fellers out back; got him tied up now," Buck remarked, relating the incident, Meeker interrupting to give the Bar-20 foreman all the credit.

"Good!" exclaimed Red. "It's a rope necktie for him. An' one less to shoot at me."

"An' *you* here, Buck!" cried Hopalong in surprise. "Come on, lead th' way! How do you know he was th' only one to get behind us! Good Lord!"

"Gosh, yo're right!" Buck exclaimed, running off. "Come on, Jim. We're a pair of fools, after all!"

At the other end of the line Chick Travers and George Cross did as well as they could with their Colts, but found their efforts unavailing. Their positions were marked by the rustlers and they had several narrow escapes, both being wounded, Cross twice. Ten yards west of them Frenchy McAllister was crawling forward a foot at a time from cover to cover and so far he had not been hit. His position also had been marked and he was now trying to find a new one unobserved, where he could have a chance to shoot once without instantly being fired upon. Pete and Johnny had separated, the latter having given up his attempt to make the rustler pay for his wounded ear. He had emptied the magazine of the rifle he had found and now only used his Colt. As he worked along the firing line he saw Frenchy ten yards in front of him, covered nicely by a steep rise in the ground.

"How are you doing out there, Frenchy?" he asked in a low voice.

"Not very good; wish I had my rifle," came the soft-spoken reply.

"I had one that I found, but I used up all th' cartridges there was in th' magazine."

"What kind an' caliber?"

"Forty-five–seventy Winchester. I found it by th' ropes. Pete says he reckoned some rustler must have left it behind an' got away down th'—"

"Get it for me, Kid, will you?" interrupted Frenchy, eagerly. "I plumb forgot to leave my belt of rifle cartridges back in th' camp. Got it on now, an' it's chock full, too. Hurry up, an' I'll work back to you for it."

"What luck! In a second," Johnny exulted, disappearing. Returning with the rifle he handed it to his friend and gazed longingly at the beltful of rifle cartridges. "Say, Frenchy," he began. "You know we'll all have our rifles to-night, an' you've got more cartridges for that than you can use before then. It won't be more than three hours before we send for ours. Suppose you gimme some of them for Pete—he's got th' mate to that gun, an' can't use it no more because it's empty."

"Shore, Kid," and Frenchy slipped a handful of cartridges out of his belt and gave them to Johnny. "With my compliments to Pete. What was that you was saying about rustlers an' th' ropes?"

Johnny told of Pete's deductions regarding the finding of the rifles and Frenchy agreed with them, and also that Doc had taken care of the owners of the weapons when they had reached the plain.

"Well, I'm going further away from them thieves now that I've got something to shoot with," Frenchy asserted. "They won't be looking for any of us a hundred yards or more farther back. Mebbe I can catch some of 'em unawares."

"I'll chase off an' give Pete these pills," Johnny replied. "He'll be tickled plumb to death. He was cussing bad when I left him."

George Cross, crawling along a steep, smooth rock barely under the shelter of a boulder, endeavored to grasp the top, but under-reached and slipped, rolling down to the bottom and in plain sight of the rustlers. As his companion, Chick Travers, tried to help him two shots rang out and Cross, sitting up with his hands to his head, toppled back to arise no more. Chick leaped up and fired twice at one of the marksmen, and missed. His actions had been so sudden and unexpected that he escaped the return shot which passed over him by a foot as he dropped back to cover. Somehow the whole line seemed to feel that there had been a death among them, as evidenced by the burst of firing along it. And the whole line felt another thing; that the cartridges of the rustlers were getting low, for they seemed to be saving their shots. But it was Hopalong who found the cause of the diminishing fire. After hunting fruitlessly with the two foremen and finding that Hall was the only man to get back of the firing line he left his two companions in order to learn the condition of his friends. As he made his way along the line he chanced to look towards the hut and saw four rifles on the floor of it, and back of them, piled against the wall, was the rustlers' main supply of ammunition. Calling out, he was answered by Pete, who soon joined him.

"Pete, you lucky devil, turn that rifle through th' door of th' shack an' keep it on them cartridges," he ordered. "They ain't been shooting as fast as they was at first, an' there's th' reason for it. Oh, just wait till daylight tomorrow! They won't last long after that!"

"They won't get them cartridges, anyhow," Pete replied with conviction.

"Hey, fellers," cried a voice, and they looked around to see Chick Travers coming towards them. "Yore man Cross has passed. He rolled off his ledge an' couldn't stop. They got him when he hit th' bottom of it."

"Damn 'em!" growled Hopalong. "We'll square our accounts to-morrow morning. Pete, you watch them cartridges."

"Shore—" *Bang!* "Did you see that?" Pete asked, frantically pumping the lever of his rifle.

"Yes!" cried Chick. "Some feller tried to get in that south window! Bet he won't try again after that hint. Hear him cuss? There—Red must 'a fired then, too!"

"Good boy, Pete!—keep 'em out. We'll have somebody in there after dark," Hopalong responded. "They've got th' best covers now, but we'll turn th' table on 'em when th' sun comes up to-morrow."

"Here comes Buck an' Meeker," remarked Chick. "Them two are getting a whole lot chummy lately, all right. They're allus together."

"That's good, too. They're both of 'em all right," Hopalong replied, running to meet them. Chick saw the three engage in a consultation and look towards the hut and the ridge behind it, Buck and Meeker nodding slowly at what Hopalong was saying. Then they moved off towards the west where they could examine the building at closer range.

XXXV

◆

Johnny Takes the Hut

As the day waned the dropping shots became less and less frequent and the increasing darkness began to work its magic. The unsightly plain with its crevices and boulders and scrawny vegetation would soon be changed into one smooth blot, to be lighted with the lurid flashes of rifles as Red and Pete fired at irregular intervals through the south windows of the hut to keep back any rustler who tried to get the ammunition within its walls. Two were trying and had approached the window just as a bullet hummed through it. They stopped and looked at each other and moved forward again. Then a bullet from Pete's rifle, entering through the open door, hummed out the window and struck against the rocky ridge.

"Say! Them coyotes can see us through that windy," remarked Clausen. 'Th' sky at our backs is too light yet."

"They can't see us standing here," objected Shaw.

"Then what are they shooting at?"

"Cuss me if I know. Looks like they was using th' winder for a target. Reckon we better wait till it gets darker."

"If we wait till it's dark we can sneak in through th' door," suggested Clausen. "If we go in crawling we ain't likely to stop no shot high enough to go through that windy."

"You can if you wants, but I ain't taking no chances like that, none whatever."

Another shot whined through the window and stopped with an angry spat against the ridge. Shaw scratched his head reflectively. "It shore beats me why they keeps that up. There ain't no sense to it," he declared in aggrieved tones. "They don't know nothing about them cartridges in there."

"That's it!" exclaimed Clausen, excitedly. "I bet a stack of blues they do know. An' they're covering somebody going in to steal 'em. Oh, hell!" and he slammed his hat to the ground in bitter anger. "An' us a-standing here like a couple of mired cows! I'm going to risk it."

"Wait," advised Shaw. "Let's try a hat an' see if they plug it."

"Wait be damned! My feet are growing roots right now. I'm going in," and Clausen broke away from his friend

and ran towards the hut, a crouching run, comical to look
at but effective because it kept his head below the level
of the window; without pausing in his stride his body
lengthened into a supple curve as he plunged head foremost through the window, landing on the cabin floor with
hands and feet bunched under him, his passing seen only
as a fleeting puzzling shadow, by the watchful eyes outside.

Across the cut Johnny was giving Red instructions
and turned to leave. "Th' cut is full of shadows an' th'
moon ain't up yet. Now, remember, one more shot through
that window—I'm going to foller it right in. Get word to
Pete as soon as you can, though I won't pass th' door. He's
only got three cartridges left an' he'll be getting some
anxious about now. So long."

"So long, an' good luck, Kid," Red replied.

Johnny wriggled across the cut on his stomach, picking out the shadows and gaining the shelter of the opposite bank, stood up, and ran to the hut. Red fired and then
Johnny cautiously climbed through the window and
dropped to the floor.

He had anticipated Clausen by the fraction of a second. As his feet touched the floor the noise of Clausen's
arrival saluted him and the startled Johnny jerked his
gun loose and sent a shot in the other's direction, leaping
aside on the instant. The flash of the discharge was gone
too quickly for him to distinguish anything and the
scrambling sound that followed mystified him further.
That there had been no return shot did not cause him to
dance with joy, far otherwise; it made him drop silently
to his stomach and hunt the darkest part of the hut, the
west wall. He lay still for a minute, eyes and ears strained
for a sound to tell him where to shoot. Then Red called
to him and wanted an answer, whereupon Johnny thought
of things he ached to call Red. Then he heard a low voice

outside the south window, and it called: "Clausen, Clausen—what happened? Why don't you answer?"

"Oh, so my guest is Clausen, hey?" Johnny thought. "Wonder if Clausen can see in th' dark?" Nother damned fool wanting an answer! I'll bet Clausen is hugging th' dark spots, too. Wonder if I scared him as much as he scared me?"

The suspense was becoming too much of a strain and, poking his Colt out in front of him, he began to move forward, his eyes staring ahead of him at the place where Clausen ought to be.

Inch by inch he advanced, holding his breath as well as he could, every moment expecting to have Clausen salute him in the face with a hot .45. Johnny was scared, and well scared, but it only proves courage to go on when scared stiff, and Johnny went on and along the wall he thought Clausen was using for a highway.

"Wonder how it feels to have yore brains blowed out," he shivered. "For God's sake, Clausen, make a noise— sneeze, cough, choke, yell, anything!" he prayed, but Clausen remained ominously silent. Johnny pushed his Colt out farther and poked it all around. Touching the wall it made a slight scraping sound and Johnny's blood froze. Still no move from Clausen, and his fright went down a notch—Clausen was evidently even more scared than he was. That was consoling. Perhaps he was so scared that he couldn't pull a trigger, which would be more consoling.

"Johnny! Johnny! Answer, can't you!" came Red's stentorian voice, causing Johnny to jump a few inches off the floor.

"Clausen! Clausen!" came another voice.

"For God sake, answer, Clausen! Tell 'em yo're here!" prayed Johnny. "Yo're damned unpolite, anyhow."

By this time he was opposite the door and he wondered if Pete had been told not to bombard it. He stopped and looked, and stared. What was that thing on the floor? Or was it anything at all? He blinked and moved closer. It looked like a head, but Johnny was taking no chances. He stared steadily into the blackest part of the hut for a moment and then looked again at the object. He could see it a little plainer now, for it was not quite as dark outside as it was in the building; but he was not sure about it.

"Can't fool me, you coyote," he thought. "Yo're hugging this wall as tight as a tick on a cow, a blamed sight tighter than I am, an' in about a minute I'm going to shoot along it about four inches from th' floor. I'd just as soon get shot as be scared to death, anyhow. Mebby we've passed each other! An' Holy Medicine! Mebby there's two of 'em!"

He regarded the object again. "That shore looks like a head, all right." He felt a pebble under his hand and drawing back a little he covered the questionable object and then tossed the pebble at it. "Huh, if it's a head, why in thunder didn't it move?"

There were footsteps outside the south window and he listened, the Colt ready to stop any one rash enough to look in, Clausen or no Clausen.

"Where's Clausen, Shaw?" said a voice, and the reply was so low Johnny could not make it out.

"Yes; that's just what I want to know," and Johnny stared in frowning intentness at the supposed head. He moved closer to the object and by dint of staring thought he saw the head and shoulders of a man face down in a black, shallow pool. Then his hand became wet and he jerked it back and wiped it on his sleeve; he could hardly believe his senses. As he grasped the significance of his discovery he grinned sheepishly and moved back to the north wall, where no rustler's bullet could find him. "Lord! An' I got him th' first crack! Got him shooting by ear!"

"Johnny! Johnny!" came Red's roar, anxious and quer-ulous.

Johnny wheeled and shook his Colt out of the window, for the moment forgetting the peril of losing sight of the opening in the other wall. "I'll Johnny *you*, you blankety-blank fool!" he shouted. Then he heard a curse at the south window and turned quickly, his Colt covering the opening. "An' I'll Johnny you too, you cow-stealing coy-otes! Stick yore thieving heads in that windy an' holler for yore Clausen! *I* can show you where he is, an' send you after him if you'll just take a look! Want them car-tridges, hey? Well, come an' get 'em!"

A bullet, fired at an angle through the window, was the reply and several hummed through the open door and glanced off the steep sides of the ridge. Waiting until they stopped coming he dropped and wriggled forward along the west wall, feeling in front of him until he touched a box. Grasping it he dragged the important car-tridges to him and then backed to the north window with them.

He fell to stuffing his pockets with the captured am-munition and then stopped short and grinned happily. "Might as well *hold* this shack an' wait for somebody to look in that windy. They can't get me."

He dropped the box and walked to the heavy plank door, slamming it shut. He heard the thud of bullets in it as he propped it, and laughed. "Can't shoot through them planks, they're double thick." He smelled his sticky fin-gers. "An' they're full of resin, besides."

He stopped suddenly and frowned as a fear entered his mind; and then smiled, reassured. "Nope; no rustling snake can climb up that ridge—not with Red an' Pete watching it."

XXXVI

♦

The Last Night

Fifty yards behind the firing line of the besiegers a small fire burned brightly in a steep-walled basin, casting grotesque shadows on the rock walls as men passed and re-passed. Overhead a silvery moon looked down at the cheerful blaze and from the cracks and crevices of the plain came the tuneful chorus of Nature's tiny musicians, sounding startlingly out of place where men were killing and dying. A little aside from the others three men in consultation reached a mutual understanding and turned to face their waiting friends just as Pete Wilson ran into the lighted circle.

"Hey, Johnny is in th' hut with th' cartridges," he exclaimed, telling the story in a few words.

"Good for th' Kid!"

"It's easy now, thanks to him."

"Why didn't he tell us he was going to try that?" demanded Buck. "Taking a chance like that on his own hook!"

"Scared you wouldn't let him," Pete laughed. "Red an' me backed him up with our rifles th' best we could. He had a fight in there, too, judging from th' shot. He had me an' Red worried, thinking he might 'a been hit, but he was cussing Red when I left."

"Well, that helps us a lot," Buck replied. "Now I want three of you to go to camp an' bring back grub, rifles, an' cartridges. Pete, Skinny, Chick—yo're th' ones. Leave yore canteens here an' hustle! Hopalong, you an' Meeker go off somewhere an' get some sleep. I'll call you before it gets light. Frenchy, me an' you will take all th' canteens at hand an' fill 'em while we've got time. They won't be able to see us now. We'll pass Red an' get his, too. Come on."

When they returned they dropped the dripping vessels and began cleaning their Colts. That done they filled their pipes and sat cross-legged, staring into the fire. A snatch of Johnny's exultant song floated to them and Buck smiled, laying his pipe aside and rising. "Well, Frenchy, things'll happen in chunks when th' sun comes up. Something like old times, eh? There ain't no Deacon Rankin or Slippery Trendley here—" He stopped, having mentioned a name he had promised himself never to say in Frenchy's presence, and then continued in a sub-dued voice, bitterly scourging himself for his blunder. "They're stronger than I thought, an' they've shot us up purty well, killed Willis an' Cross, an' made fools of us for weeks on th' range; but this is th' end of it all. *We* deal to-morrow, an' we cut th' cards to-night."

Frenchy was strangely silent, staring fixedly at the fire. Buck glanced at him in strong sympathy, for he knew what his slip of the tongue had awakened in his friend's heart. Frenchy had adored his young wife and since the day he had found her murdered in his cabin on the Double Y he had been another man. When the mo-ment of his vengeance had come, when he had her mur-derer in his power and saw his friends ride away to leave him alone with Trendley that day over in the Panhandle, to exact what payment he wished, then he had become his old self for a while, but it was not long before he again sank into his habitual carelessness, waiting patiently for death to remove his burden and make him free. His ven-geance did not bring him back his wife.

Buck shook his head slowly and affectionately placed a heavy hand on his friend's shoulder. "Frenchy, won't you ever forget it? It hurts me to see you this way so much.

It's over twenty years now an' day after day I've grieved
to see you so unhappy. You paid him for it in yore own
way. Can't you forget it now?"

"Yes; I killed him, an' slow. He never thought a man
could make th' payment so hard, not even his black heart
could realize it till he felt it," Frenchy replied, slowly and
calmly. "He took th' heart out of me; he killed my wife
and made my life a living hell. All I had worth living for
went that day, an' if I could kill him over again every day
for a year it wouldn't square th' score. I reckon I ain't
built like other men. You never heard me whimper. I
kept my poison to myself an' tried to do the best that was
in me. An' you ain't never heard me say what I'm going
to tell you now. I never believed in hunches, but something tells me that I'll leave all this behind me before
another day passes. I felt it somehow when we left th'
ranch an' it's been growing stronger every hour since. If
I do pass out to-morrow, I want you to be glad of it, same
as I would be if I could know. I'm going back to th' line
now an' watch them fellers. So long."

The two men, bosom friends for thirty years, looked
in each other's eyes as they grasped hands, and it was
Buck's eyes that grew moist and dropped first. "So long,
Frenchy—an' good luck, as you see it."

The foreman watched his friend until lost in the darkness and he thought he heard him singing, but of this he
was not sure. He turned and stared at the fire for a minute, silent, immovable, and then breathed heavily.

"I never saw anybody carry a grief so long, never. I
reckon it sort of turned his brain, coming so sudden an'
in such a damnable way. I know it made me see red for a
week. If I had only stayed there that day! When he got
Trendley in th' Panhandle I hoped he would change, an'
he did for a while, but that was all. He lived for that alone,
an' since then I reckon he's felt he hadn't nothing to do

with his life. He has been mixed up in a bunch of gun-arguments since then; but he didn't have no luck. Well, Frenchy, I hate to lose a friend like you, but here's better luck to-morrow, luck as you see it, friend!"

He kicked the fire together and was about to add fuel when he heard two quick shots and raised his head to listen. Then a ringing whoop came from the front and he recognized Johnny's voice. He heard Red call out and Johnny reply and he smiled grimly as he went towards the sounds. "Reckon somebody tried to get in that shack, like a fool. He must 'a been disgusted. How that Kid shore does love to fight!"

> *Joyous Joe got a juniper jag,*
> *A jogging out of Jaytown,*

came down the wind.

"Did you get him, Kid?" cried Buck from the firing line.

"Nope; got his hat, though—but I shore got Clausen an' all of their cartridges!"

"Can you keep them shells alone?"

"*Can I? Wow,* ask th' other fellers! An' I'm eating jerked beef—sorry I can't give you some."

"Shut up about eating, you pig!" blazed Red, who was hungry.

"You'll eat hot lead to-morrow, all of you!" jeered a rustler's voice.

Red fired at the sound. "Take yourn now!" he shouted.

"You can't hit a cow!" came the taunt, while other strange voices joined in.

Buck found Red and ordered him to camp to get some sleep before Pete and the others returned, feeling that he and Frenchy were enough to watch. Red demurred sleep-ily and finally compromised by lying down at Buck's side, where he would be handy in case of trouble. Buck waited patiently, too heavily laden with responsibility to feel the need of rest, and when he judged that three hours had passed began to worry about the men he had sent to camp. Drawing back into a crevice he struck a match and looked at him.

"Twelve o'clock!" he muttered. "I'll wake Red an' see how Frenchy is getting on. Time them fellers were back too."

Frenchy changed his position uneasily and peered at the distant breastwork, hearing the low murmur of voices behind it. All night he had heard their curses, but a new note made him sit up and watch more closely. The moon was coming up now and he could see better. Suddenly he caught the soft flash of a silver sombrero buckle and fired instantly. Curses and a few shots replied and a new, querulous voice was added to the murmur, a voice expressing pain.

"I reckon you got him," remarked a quiet voice at his side as Buck lay down beside him. The foreman had lost some time in wandering along the whole line of defense and was later than he had expected.

"Yes; I reckon so," Frenchy replied without interest, and they lapsed into silence, the eloquent silence of men who understand each other. They heard a shot from below and knew that Billy or Curtis was about and smiled grimly at the rising murmur it caused among the rustlers. Buck glanced at the sky and frowned. "There can't be more'n five or six left by now, an' if it wasn't for th' moon I'd get th' boys together an' rush that bunch." He was silent for a moment and then added, half to himself, "but it won't be long now, an' we can wait."

Distant voices heralded the return of Pete and his companions and the foreman arose. "Frenchy, I'm going to place th' boys an' start things right away. We've been quiet too long."

"Might as well," Frenchy replied, "I'm getting sleepy—straining my eyes too much, I reckon, trying to see a little better than I can."

"Here's th' stuff, Buck," Skinny remarked as the foreman entered the circle of light. "Two day's fighting rations, fifty rounds for th' rifles an' fifty for th' Colts. Chick is coming back there with th' rifles."

"Good. Had yore grub yet?" Buck asked. "All right—didn't reckon you'd wait for it. What kept you so long? You've been gone over three hours."

"We was talking to Bill an' Curtis," Skinny remarked. "They're anxious to have it over. They've been spelling each other an' getting some sleep. We saw Doc's saddle piled on top of th' grub when we got to camp. It wasn't there when we all left th' other night. Billy says Doc came running past last night, saddled up an' rode off. He got back this afternoon wearing a bandage around his head. He didn't say where he had been, but now he is at th' bottom of th' trail waiting for a shot, so Billy says. Pete reckons he went after somebody that got down last night, one of them fellers that left their rifles up here by th' ropes."

"Mebby yo're right," replied Buck, hurriedly. "Get ready to fight. I ain't going to wait for daylight when this moonlight will answer. Pete, Skinny, Chick—you get settled out on th' east end, where me an' Frenchy will join you. We'll have this game over before long."

He strode away and returned with Hopalong and Meeker, who hastily ate and drank and, filling their belts with cartridges and taking their own rifles from the pile Chick had brought, departed toward the cut with orders for Red to come in.

Pete and his companions moved away as Frenchy, shortly followed by Red, came in and reported.

"Eat an' drink, lively. Red, you get back to yore place

an' take care of th' cut," Buck ordered. "Frenchy, you come out east with th' rest. There's cartridges for you both an' there's yore own rifle, Frenchy."

"Glad yo're going to start things," chewed Red through a mouthful of food. "It's about time we show them fellers we can live up to our reputation. Any of 'em coming my way won't go far."

Frenchy filled his pipe and lighted it from a stick he took out of the fire and as it began to draw well he stepped quickly forward and held out his hand. "Good luck, Red. They can't fight long."

"Same to you, Frenchy. You look plumb wide awake, like Buck—how'd you do it?"

Frenchy laughed and strode after his foreman, Red watching him. "He's acting funny—reckon it's th' sleep he's missed. Well, here goes," and he, too, went off to the firing line.

> —An' aching thoughts pour in on me,
>   Of Whiskey Bill,

came Johnny's song from the hut—and the fight began again.

XXXVII

♦

Their Last Fight

A figure suddenly appeared on the top of the flanking ridge, outlined against the sky, and flashes of flame spurted from its hands, while kneeling beside it was another, rapidly working a rifle, the roar of the guns deafening because of the silence which preceded it. Shouts, curses, and a few random, futile shots replied from the breastworks, its defenders, panic-stricken by the surprise and the deadly accuracy of the two marksmen, scurrying around the bend in their fortifications, so busy in seeking shelter that they failed to make their shots tell. Two men, riddled by bullets, lay where they had fallen and the remaining three, each of them wounded more than once, crouched under cover and turned their weapons against the new factors; but these had already slid down the face of the ridge and were crawling along the breastwork, alert and cautious.

In front of the rustlers heavy firing burst out along the cowmen's line and Red Connors, from his old position above the cut, swung part way around and turned his rifle against the remnant of the defenders at another angle, and fired at every mark, whether it was hand, foot, or head; while Johnny, tumbling out of the south window of the hut, followed in the wake of Hopalong and Meeker. The east end of the line was wrapped in smoke, where Buck and his companions labored zealously.

Along the narrow trail up the mesa's face a man toiled heavily and it was not long before Doc Riley opened fire from the rear. The three rustlers, besieged from all sides, found their positions to be most desperate and knew then that only a few minutes intervened between them and eternity. They had three choices—to surrender, to die fighting, or to leap from the mesa to instant death below.

Shaw, to his credit, chose the second and like a cornered wolf goaded to despair leaped up and forward to take a gambler's chance of gaining the hut. Before him were Hopalong, Meeker, Johnny, and Doc. Doc was hastily reloading his Colt, Johnny was temporarily out of sight as he crawled around a boulder, and Hopalong was greatly worried by ricochettes and wild shots from the rifles of his friends which threatened to end his career.

Meeker alone was watching at that moment but his attention was held by the rustler near the edge of the mesa who was trying to shrink himself to fit the small rock in front of him and to use his gun at the same time.

Shaw sprang from his cover and straight at the H2 foreman, his foot slipping slightly as he fired. The bullet grazed Meeker's waist, but the second, fired as the rustler was recovering his balance, bored through Meeker's shoulder. The H2 foreman, bending forward for a shot at the man behind the small rock, was caught unawares and his balance, already strained, was destroyed by the shock of the second bullet, and he flopped down to all fours. Shaw sprang over him just as Hopalong and Johnny caught sight of him and he swung his revolver on Hopalong at the moment when the latter's bullet crashed through his brain.

Buck Peters, trying for a better position, slipped on the rock which had been the cause of the death of George Cross and before he could gain his feet a figure leaped down in front of him and raised a Colt in his defense, but spun half way around and fell, shot through the head. A cry of rage went up at this and a rush was made against the breastworks from front and side. Frenchy McAllister's forebodings had come true.

Sanchez, finding his revolver empty and no time to reload, held up his hands. Frisco, blinded by blood, wounded in half a dozen places, desperate, snarling, and still unbeaten, wheeled viciously, but before he could pull his trigger, Hopalong grasped him and hurled him down, Johnny going with them. Doc, a second too late, waved his sombrero. "Come on, it's all over!"

In another second the rushing punchers from the front slid and rolled and plunged over the breastwork and eyed the results of their fire.

Meeker staggered around the corner and leaned

against Buck for support. "My God! This is awful! I didn't think we were doing so much damage."

"I did!" retorted Buck. "I know what happens when my outfit burns powder. Where's Red?" he asked anxiously.

"Here I am," replied a voice behind him.

"All right; take that feller to the hut," the foreman ordered. "Johnny, you an Pete take the other," pointing to Frisco. "He's th' one that killed Frenchy. Hopalong, take Red, an' bring in that feller me an' Meeker tied up in that crevice, if he ain't got away."

Hopalong and Red went off to bring in Hall and Buck turned to the others. "You fellers doctor yore wounds. Meeker, yo're hard hit," he remarked, more closely looking at the H2 foreman.

"Yes. I know it—loss of blood, mostly," Meeker replied. "An' if it hadn't been for Cassidy I'd been hit a damned sight harder. Where's Doc? He knows what to do—*Doc!*"

"Coming," replied a voice and Doc turned the corner. He had a limited knowledge of the work he was called upon to do, and practice, though infrequent, had kept it more or less fresh.

"Reckon yo're named about right, Doc," Buck remarked as he passed the busy man. "You got me beat an' I ain't no slouch."

"I'd 'a been a real Doc if I hadn't left college like a fool—you've got to keep still, Jim," he chided.

"Hey, Buck," remarked Hopalong, joining the crowd and grinning at the injured, "we've got that feller in th' shack. When th' feller I grabbed out here saw him he called him Hall. Th' other is Frisco. How you feeling, Meeker? That was Shaw plugged you."

"Feeling better'n him," Meeker growled. "Yo're a good man to work with, Cassidy."

"Well, Cassidy, got any slugs in you?" affably asked

Doc, the man Hopalong had wounded on the line a few weeks before. Doc brandished a knife and cleaning rod and appeared to be anxious to use them on somebody else.

"No; but what do you do with them things?" Hopalong rejoined, feeling of his bandage.

"Take out bullets," Doc grinned.

"Oh, I see; you cut a hole in th' back an' then push 'em right through," Hopalong laughed. "Reckon I'd rather have 'em go right through without stopping. Who's that calling?"

"Billy an' Curtis. Tell 'em to come up," Buck replied, walking towards the place where Frenchy's body lay.

Hopalong went to the edge and replied to the shouts and it was not long before they appeared. When Doc saw them he grinned pleasantly and drew them aside, trying to coax them to let him repair them. But Billy, eyeing the implements, side-stepped and declined with alacrity; Curtis was the victim.

"After *him* th' undertaker," Billy growled, going towards the hut.

XXXVIII

♦

A Disagreeable Task

Two men, Hall and Frisco, sat with their backs against the wall of the hut, weaponless, wounded, nervous, one sullen and enraged, the other growling querulously to himself about his numerous wounds. The third prisoner, was pacing to and fro with restless strides, vicious and defiant, his burning eyes quick, searching, calculating. It seemed as though he was filled with a tremendous amount of energy which would not let him remain quiet. When his companions spoke to him he flashed them a quick glance but did not answer; thinking, scheming, plotting, he missed not the slightest movement of those about him. Wounded as he was he did not appear to know it, so intent was he upon his thoughts.

Hall, saved from the dangers of the last night's fight, loosed his cumulative rage frequently in caustic and profane verbal abuse of his captors, his defeat, his companions, and the guard. Frisco, courageous as any under fire, was dejected because of the wait; merely a difference of temperament.

The guard, seated carelessly on a nearby rock, kept watch over the three and cogitated upon the whole affair, his Colt swinging from a hand between his knees. Twenty paces to his right was a stack of rifles and Sanchez, lengthening his panther stride with barely perceptible effort, drew nearer to them on each northward lap. He typified the class of men who never give up hope, and as he gained each yard he glanced furtively at the guard and then estimated the number of leaps necessary to reach the coveted rifles. His rippling muscles were bunching up for the desperate attempt when the guard interfered, the sharp clicks of his Colt bringing the Mexican to an abrupt stop. Sanchez shrugged his shoulders and wheeling, resumed his restless walk, being careful to keep it within safe limits.

Hall, lighting his pipe, blew a cloud of smoke into the air and looked at the guard, who was still cogitating.

"How did you fools finally figger we was out here?"

Hopalong looked up and smiled. "Oh, we just figgered you fools would be here, and would stay up here. Yore friend Antonio worked too hard."

Hall carefully packed his pipe and puffed quietly. "I knowed he'd bungle it."

"What happened to Cavalry an' Antonio?" asked Hall. "Did you get 'em when you came up?"

"They got down th' way we came up—Doc trailed Antonio an' got him at that water hole up north," Hopalong replied. "Don't know nothing about th' other feller. Reckon he got away, but one don't make much difference, anyhow. He'll never come back to this country."

"Say, how much longer will it take yore friends to do th' buryin' act?" asked Frisco irritably. "I'm plumb tired of waiting—these wounds hurt like blazes, too."

"Reckon they're coming now," was the reply. "I hear— yes, here they are."

"I owe you ten dollars, Hall," Frisco remarked, trivial thing now entering his mind. "Reckon you won't get it, neither."

"Oh, pay me in hell!" Hall snapped.

"Yes," Buck was saying, "He knowed he was going an' he went like th' man he was—saving a friend. 'Tain't th' first time Frenchy McAllister's saved my life, neither."

Frisco glanced around and his face flashed with a look of recognition, but he held his tongue; not so with Curtis, who stared at him in surprise and stepped forward.

"Good God! It's Davis! What ever got you into this?"

"Easy money an' a gun fight," Davis, alias Frisco, replied.

"Tough luck, tough luck," Curtis muttered slowly.

"Damn tough, if you asks me," Frisco growled.

"What happened to th' others?" Curtis asked, referring to three men with whom he and Frisco had punched and prospected several years before.

"Little Dan went out in that same gun fight, Joe Baird was got by th' posse next day, an' George Wild an' I got into th' mountains an' was separated. I got free after a sixty-mile chase, but I don't know how George made out. We had stuck up a gold caravan an' killed two men what was with it. They was th' only fellers to pull their guns against us."

"Well, I'm damned!" ejaculated Curtis. "An' so that crowd went bad!"

"Say, for th' Lord's sake, get things moving," cried Hall, angrily. "If we've got to die make it quick. Wish I'd a' gone with Shaw 'stead of waiting for my own funeral."

Buck surveyed them. "Got anything to say?"

"Not me—I've had mine," replied Frisco, toying with a bandage. Then he started to say something but changed his mind. "Oh, well what's th' use! Go ahead."

"Don't drag it out," growled Hall. "Say, you got *my* rope there?" he demanded suddenly, eyeing the coils slung over Skinny's shoulder. "No, you ain't, I want my own, savvy?"

"Oh, we ain't got time to hunt for no ropes," rejoined Skinny. "One's as good as another, ain't it."

"Yes, I reckon so—hustle it through," Hall replied, sullenly.

"Go ahead, you fellers," ordered Hopalong as some of his friends went first down the trail after the two sent to the camp for the horses. "Come, on, Sanchez! Fall in there!"

When the procession reached the bottom of the trail Buck halted it to wait for the horses and his prisoners took one more look around.

"Say, Peters, where's th' cayuses we had in that corral?" asked Hall, surprised.

"Oh, we got them out th' first night—we wasn't taking no chances," replied the foreman. "They're somewhere near th' camp now."

As the horse herd was driven up Sanchez made his last play. All were intent upon tightening cinches, the more intent because of the impending and disagreeable task, when he slipped like a shadow through the group and throwing himself across a pinto, headed in a circular track for the not too distant chaparral.

"*Take* him, Red!" shouted Buck, who was the first to recover.

Red's rifle leaped to his shoulder and steadied; in three more jumps the speedy pinto would have shielded Sanchez, clinging like a burr to the further side; but the rifle spoke once and he dropped and lay quiet on the sand.

Hopalong rode out to him and glancing at the still form, wheeled and returned. "Got him clean, Red."

A group of horsemen rode eastward towards the chaparral and as it was about to enclose them one of the riders bringing up the rear turned in his saddle and looked back at two dangling forms outlined against the darker background of the frowning mesa, two where he had expected to see three.

"Well, th' rustling is over," he remarked.

XXXIX

♦

Thirst

The stars grow dim and a streak of color paints the eastern sky, sweeping through the upper reaches of the darkness and tingeing the earth's curtain until the dim gray light outlines spectral yuccas and twisted, grotesque cacti leaning in the hushed air like drunken sentries of some monstrous army. The dark carpet which stretched away on all sides begins to show its characteristics and soon develops into greasewood brush. As if curtains were drawn aside objects which a moment before were lost to sight in the darkness emerge out of the light like ghosts, bulky, indistinct, grotesque, and array themselves to complete the scene.

The silence seems to deepen and become strained, as if in fear of what is to come; the dark ground is now gray and tawny in places and the vegetation is plain to the eye. Then out of the east comes a flash and a red, coppery sun flares above the horizon, molten, quivering, blinding; the cool of the night swiftly departs and a caldron-like heat bursts upon the plain. The silence seems almost to shrink and become portentous with evil, the air is hushed, the plants stand without the movement of a leaf, and nowhere is seen any living creature. The whole is unreal, a panorama, with vegetation of wax and a painted, faded blue sky, the only movement being the shortening shadows and the rising sun.

Across the sand is an erratic trail of shoe prints, coming from the east. For a dozen yards it runs evenly and straight, then a few close prints straggle to and fro, zigzagging for a distance, finally going on straight again. But the erratic prints grow more frequent and become more pronounced as they go on, circling and weaving, crossing, recrossing and doubling back as their maker staggered hopelessly on his way, urged only by the instinct of thirst, to find water, if it were only a mouthful. The trail is here blurred, for he fell, and the prints of his hands and knees and shoe-tips tell how he went on for some distance. He gained his feet here and threw away his Colt, and later his holster and belt.

The sun is overhead now and the sand shimmers, the heated air quivering and glistening, and the desolate void takes on an air of mystery and fear, and death. No living thing moves across the heat-cursed sand, but here is a tangled mass of sand and clay and greasewood twigs, in the heart of which mice sleep and wait for night, and over there is a hillock sheltering lizards. Stay! Under that greasewood bush a foolish gray wolf is waiting for night—but he has little to fear, for he can cover forty miles between dark and dawn, and his instinct is infallible; no wandering trail will mark his passing, but one as straight as the flight of a bullet. The shadows shrink close to the stems of the plants and the thin air dances with heat.

Behind that clump of greasewood, back beyond those crippled cacti, a man staggers on and on. His hair is matted, his fingers bleeding from digging frantically in the sand for water; his lips, cracked and bleeding and swollen, hide the shrivelled, stiff tongue which clicks against his teeth at every painful step. His eyelids are stiff and the staring, unblinking eyes are set and swollen. He clutches at his throat time and time again—a drowning sensation is there. Ha! He drops to his knees and digs frantically again, for the sand is moist! A few days ago a water hole lay there. He throws off his shirt and finally staggers on again.

His tongue begins to swell and forces itself beyond the swollen, festering lips; the eyelids split and the protruding eyeballs weep tears of blood. His skin cracks and curls up, the clefts going constantly deeper into the flesh, and the exuding blood quickly dries and leaves a tough coating over the wounds. Wherever the exudation touches it stings and burns, and the cracks and clefts, irritated more and more each minute, deepen and widen and lengthen, smarting and nerve-racking with their pain.

There! A grove of beautiful green trees is before him, and in it a fountain splashes with musical babbling. He yells and dances and then, casting aside the rest of his clothes, staggers towards it. Water, water, at last! Water and shade! It grows indistinct, wavers—and is gone! But it must be there. It was there only a moment ago—and on and on he runs, hands tearing at his choking, drowning throat. Here is water—close at hand—a purling, cold brook, whispering and tinkling over its rocky bed—he jumps into it—it moved! It's over there, ten paces to his right. On and on he staggers, the stream just ahead. He falls more frequently and wavers now. Oh, for just a canteen of water, just a swallow, just a drop! The gold of the world would not buy it from him—just a drop of water!

He is dying from within, from the inside out. The liquids of his body exude through the clefts and evaporate. His brain burns and bands of white-hot steel crush his throbbing head and his burning lungs. No amount of water will save him now—only death, merciful death can end his sufferings.

Water at last! Real water, a pool of stagnant liquid lies at the bottom of a slight depression, the dregs of a larger pool concentrated by evaporation. Around it are the prints of many kinds of feet. It is water, water!—he plunges forward into it and lies motionless, half submerged. A gray-back lizard darts out of the greasewood near at hand, blinks rapidly and darts back again, glad to escape the intolerable heat.

Cavalry had escaped.

XL

◆

Changes

With the passing of the weeks the two ranches had settled down to routine duty. On the H2 conditions were changed greatly for the better and Meeker gloated over his gushing wells and the dam which gave him a reservoir on his north range, the early completion of which he owed largely to the experience and willing assistance of Buck and the Bar-20 outfit.

It was getting along towards fall when a letter came to the Bar-20 addressed to John McAllister. Buck looked at it long and curiously. "Wonder who's writing to Frenchy?" he mused. "Well, I've got to find out," and he opened the envelope and looked at the signature; it made him stare still more and he read the letter carefully. George McAllister, through the aid of the courts, had gained possession of the old Double Y in the name of its owners and was going to put an outfit on the ground to evict and hold off those who had jumped it. He knew nothing about ranching and wanted Frenchy McAllister, who owned half of it, to take charge of it and to give him the address of Buck Peters the other half-owner. He advised that Peters' share be bought because the range was near a railroad and was growing more valuable every day.

Buck's decision was taken instantly. Much as he disliked to leave the old outfit here was the chance he had been waiting for without knowing it. He would never have set foot on the Double Y during Frenchy's lifetime because of loyalty to his old friend. Had he at any time desired possession of the property he and his friends could have taken it and left court actions to the other side. But Frenchy was gone, and he still owned half of a valuable piece of property and one that he could make pay well. He was getting on in years and it would be pleasant to have his cherished dream come true, to be the over-lord and half-owner of a good cattle ranch and to know that when he became too old to work with any degree of pleasure he need not worry about his remaining years. If he left the Bar-20 one of his friends would take his place and he was sure it would be Hopalong. The advancement in pay and authority would please the man whom he had looked upon as his son. And perhaps it would bring to Hopalong that which now kept his eyes turned towards the H2. Yes, it was time to go to his own

and let another man come into *his* own; to move along
and give a younger man a chance.

He replied to George McAllister at length, covering
everything, and took the letter to the bunk house to have
it mailed.

"Billy," he said, "here's a letter to go to Cowan's first
thing to-morrow. Don't forget."

Buck started the fall work early and pushed it harder
than usual for he wished to have everything done before
the new foreman took charge. The beef roundup and drives
were over with quickly, considering the time and labor involved, and when the chill blasts of early winter swept
across the range and whined around the ranch buildings
Buck smiled with the satisfaction which comes with work
well done. George McAllister, failing to buy Buck's interest, now implored him to go to the Double Y at once and
take charge, which he had promised to do in time to become familiar with conditions on the winterbound northern range before the new herds were driven to it.

As yet he had told his men nothing of his plans for fear
they would persuade him to stay where he was, but he
could tell Meeker, and one crisp morning he called at the
H2 and led its foreman aside. When he had finished
Meeker grasped his hand, told him how sorry he was to
lose so good a friend and neighbor, and how glad he was
at the friend's good fortune.

"I hope Cassidy *is* th' man to take yore place, Peters,"
he remarked, thoughtfully. "He's a good man, th' best in
th'country, strong, square, and nervy. I've had my eyes
on him for some time an' I'll back him to bust anything
he throws his rope on. He can handle that ranch easy an'
well."

"Yo're right," replied Buck, slowly. "He ain't never
failed to make good yet. Whoever th' boys pick out to be
foreman will be foreman, for th' owners have left that

question with me. But Meeker, it's like pulling teeth for me to go up to Montana without him. I can't take him 'less I take 'em all, an' I've got reasons why I can't do that. An' I ain't quite shore he'd go with me now—yore ranch holds something that ties him tight to this range. He'll be lonely up in our ranch house, an' it's plenty big enough for two," he finished, smiling interrogatively at his companion.

"Well, I reckon it'll not be lonely if he wants to change it," laughed Meeker. "Leastawise, them's th' symptoms plentiful enough down here. I was dead set agin it at first, but now I don't want nothing else but to see my girl fixed for life. An' when I pass out, all I have is hers."

XLI

◆

Hopalong's Reward

Seven men loitered about the line house on Lookout Peak, wondering why they, the old outfit, had been told to await their foreman there. Why were the others, all good fellows, excluded? What could it mean? Foreboding grew upon them as they talked the matter over and when Buck approached they waited eagerly for him to speak.

He dismounted and looked at them with pride and affection and a trace of sorrow showed in his voice and face when he began to talk.

"Boys," he said, slowly, "We've got things ready for snow when it comes. Th' cattle are strong an' fat, there's plenty of grass curing on th' range, an' th' biggest drive ever sent north from this ranch has been taken care of. There's seven of you here, two on th' north range, an' four more good men coming next week; an' thirteen men can handle this ranch with some time to spare.

"I've been with you for a long time now. Some of you I've had for over twelve years, an' no man ever had a better outfit. You've never turned back on any game, an' you've never had no trouble among yoreselves. You've seen me sending an' getting letters purty regular for some time, an' you've been surprised at how I've pushed you to get ready for winter. I'm going to tell you all about it now, an' when I've finished I want you to vote on something," and they listened in dumb surprise and sorrow while he told them of his decision. When he had finished they crowded about him and begged him to stay with them, telling him they would not allow him to leave. But if he must go, then they, too, must go and help him whip a wild and lawless range into submission. He would need them badly in Montana, and nowhere could he get men who would work and fight so hard and cheerfully for him as his old outfit. They would not let him talk and he could not if they would, for there was something in his throat which choked and pained him. Johnny Nelson and Hopalong were tugging at his shoulders and the others stormed and pleaded and swore, tears in the eyes of all. He wavered and would have thrown away all his resolutions, when he thought of Hopalong and the girl. Pushing them back he told them he could not stay and begged them, as they loved him to consider his future. They looked at one another strangely and then realized how selfish they were, and said so profanely.

"*Now* yo're my old outfit," he cried, striking while the iron was hot. "I've told you why I must go, an' why I can't take *all* of you with me, an' why I won't take a few an' leave th' rest. Don't think I don't want you! Why, with you at my back I'd buck that range into shape in no time, an' chase th' festive gunfighters off th' earth. Mebby some day you can come up to me, but not now. Now I want th' new foreman of th' Bar-20 to be one of th' men who worked so hard an' loyally an' long for me an' th' ranch. I want one of you to take my place. Th' owners have left th' choice to me, an' say th' man I appoint will be their choice; an' I ain't a-going to do it—I can't do it. One last favor, boys; go in that house an' pick yore foreman. Go now, an' I'll wait for you here."

"We'll do it right here—Red Connors!" cried Hopalong.

"Hopalong!" yelled Red and Johnny in the same voice, and only a breath ahead of the others. "Hopalong! Hopalong!" was the cry, his own voice lost, buried, swept under. He tried to argue, but he could make no headway, for his exploits were shouted to convince him. As fast as he tried to speak someone remembered something else he had done—they ranged over a period of ten years and from Mexico to Cheyenne; from Dodge City and Leavenworth to the Rockies.

Buck laughed and clapped his hands on Hopalong's shoulders. "I appoint you foreman, an' you can't get out of it, nohow! Lemme shake hands with th' new foreman of th' Bar-20—I'm one of th' boys now, an' glad to get rid of th' responsibility for a while. Good luck, son!"

"No you ain't going to get rid of 'em," laughed Hopalong, but serious withal. "Yo're th' foreman of this ranch till you leave us—ain't he, boys?" he appealed.

Buck put his hands to his ears and yelled for less noise. "All right, I'll play at breaking you in—'though th' Lord knows I can't show you nothing you don't know now. My first order under these conditions is that you ride south, Hopalong, an' tell th' news to Meeker, an' to his girl. An' tell 'em separate, too. An' don't forget I want to see you hobbled before I leave next month—tell her to make it soon!"

Hopalong reddened and grinned under the rapid-fire advice and chaffing of his friends and tried to retort.

Johnny sprang forward. "Come on, fellers! Put him on his cayuse an' start him south! We've got to have *some* hand in his courting, anyhow!"

"Right!"

"Good idea!"

"Look out! *Grab* him, Red!"

"Up with him!"

"We ought to escort him on his first love trail," yelled Skinny above the uproar. "Come on! *Saddles*, boys!"

"Like hell!" cried Hopalong, spurring forward his nettlesome mount. "You've got to grow wings to catch me an' Red Eagle! *Go, bronc!*" and he shot forward, cheers and good wishes thundering after him.

Buck moved about restlessly in his sleep and then awakened suddenly and lay quiet as a hand touched his shoulder. "What is it? Who are you?" he demanded, ominously.

"I reckoned you'd like to know that yo're going to be best man in two weeks, Buck," said a happy voice. "She said a month, but I told her you was going away before then, an' you *might*, you know. I shore feel joyous!"

The huge hand of the elder man closed over his in a grip which made him wince. "Good boy, an' good luck, Hoppy! It was due you. Good luck, an' happiness, son!"

Bar-20
Days

◆

Affectionately Dedicated
to
"M. D."

I

♦

On a Strange Range

Two tired but happy punchers rode into the coast town and dismounted in front of the best hotel. Putting up their horses as quickly as possible they made arrangements for sleeping quarters and then hastened out to attend to business. Buck had been kind to delegate this mission to them and they would have it over with first of all; then they would feel free to enjoy what pleasures the town might afford. While at that time the city was not what it is now, nevertheless it was capable of satisfying what demands might be made upon it by two very active and zealous cow-punchers. Their first experience began as they left the hotel.

"Hey, you cow-wrastlers!" said a not unpleasant voice, and they turned suspiciously as it continued: "You've shore got to hang up them guns with th' hotel clerk while you cavorts around on this range. This is *fence* country."

They regarded the speaker's smiling face and twinkling eyes and laughed. "Well, yo're th' foreman if you owns that badge," grinned Hopalong, cheerfully. "We don't need no guns, nohow, in this town, we don't. Plumb forgot we was toting them. But mebby you can tell us where lawyer Jeremiah T. Jones grazes in daylight?"

"Right over yonder, second floor," replied the marshal. "An' come to think of it, mebby you better leave most of yore cash with th' guns—somebody'll take it away from you if you don't. It'd be an awful temptation, an' flesh is weak."

"Huh!" laughed Johnny, moving back into the hotel to leave his gun, closely followed by Hopalong. "Anybody that can turn that little trick on me an' Hoppy will shore earn every red cent; why, we've been to Kansas City!"

As they emerged again Johnny slapped his pocket, from which sounded a musical jingling. "If them weak people try anything on us, we may come between them and *their* money!" he boasted.

"From th' bottom of my heart I pity you," called the marshal, watching them depart, a broad smile illuminating his face. "In about twenty-four hours they'll put up a holler for me to go git it back for 'em," he muttered. "An' I almost believe I'll do it, too. I ain't never seen none of that breed what ever left a town without empty pockets an' aching heads—an' th' smarter they think they are th' easier they fall." A fleeting expression of discontent clouded the smile, for the lure of the open range is hard to resist when once a man has ridden free under its sky and watched its stars. "An' I wish I was one of 'em again," he muttered, sauntering on.

Jeremiah T. Jones, Esq., was busy when his door opened, but he leaned back in his chair and smiled pleasantly at their bow-legged entry, waving them towards two chairs. Hopalong hung his sombrero on a letter press and tipped his chair back against the wall; Johnny hung grimly to his hat, sat stiffly upright until he noticed his companion's pose, and then, deciding that everything was all right, and that Hopalong was better up in etiquette than himself, pitched his sombrero dexterously over the water pitcher and also leaned against the wall. Nobody could lose him when it came to doing the right thing.

"Well, gentlemen, you look tired and thirsty. This is

considered good for all human ailments of whatsoever nature, degree, or wheresoever located, in part or entirety, *ab initio*," Mr. Jones remarked, filling glasses. There was no argument and when the glasses were empty, he continued: "Now what can I do for you? From the Bar-20? Ah, yes; I was expecting you. We'll get right at it," and they did. Half an hour later they emerged on the street, free to take in the town, or to have the town take them in,—which was usually the case.

"What was that he said for us to keep away from?" asked Johnny with keen interest.

"Sh! Not so loud," chuckled Hopalong, winking prodigiously.

Johnny pulled tentatively at his upper lip but before he could reply his companion had accosted a stranger.

"Friend, we're pilgrims in a strange land, an' we don't know th' trails. Can you tell us where th' docks are?"

"Certainly; glad to. You'll find them at the end of this street," and he smilingly waved them towards the section of the town which Jeremiah T. Jones had specifically and earnestly warned them to avoid.

"Wonder if you're as thirsty as me?" solicitously inquired Hopalong of his companion.

"I was just wondering th' same," replied Johnny. "Say," he confided in a lower voice, "blamed if I don't feel sort of lost without that Colt. Every time I lifts my right laig she goes too high—don't feel natural, nohow."

"Same here; I'm allus feeling to see if I lost it," Hopalong responded. "There ain't no rubbing, no weight, nor nothing."

"Wish I had something to put in its place, blamed if I don't."

"Why, now yo're talking—mebby we can buy something," grinned Hopalong, happily. "Here's a hardware store—come on in."

The clerk looked up and laid aside his novel. "Good-morning, gentlemen; what can I do for you? We've just got in some fine new rifles," he suggested.

The customers exchanged looks and it was Hopalong who first found his voice. "Nope, don't want no rifles," he replied, glancing around. "To tell th' truth, I don't know just what we do want, but we want something, all right— got to have it. It's a funny thing, come to think of it; I can't never pass a hardware store without going in an' buying something. I've been told my father was th' same way, so I must inherit it. It's th' same with my pardner, here, only he gets his weakness from his whole family, and it's different from mine. He can't pass a saloon with-out going in an' buying something."

"Yo're a cheerful liar, an' you know it," retorted Johnny. "You know th' reason why I goes in saloons so much— you'd never leave 'em if I didn't drag you out. He inherits that weakness from his grandfather, twice removed," he confided to the astonished clerk, whose expression didn't know what to express.

"Let's see: a saw?" soliloquized Hopalong. "Nope; got lots of 'em, an' they're all genuine Colts," he mused thoughtfully. "Axe? Nails? Augurs? Corkscrews? Can we use a corkscrew, Johnny? Ah, thought I'd wake you up. Now, what was it cookie said for us to bring him? Bacon? Got any bacon? Too bad—oh, don't apologize; it's all right. Cold chisels—that's th' thing if you ain't got no bacon. Let me see a three-pound cold chisel about as big as that,"—extending a huge and crooked forefinger,— "an' with a big bulge at one end. Straight in th' middle, circling off into a three-cornered wavy edge on the other side. What? Look here! You can't tell us nothing about saloons that we don't know. I want a three-pound cold chisel, any kind, so it's cold."

Johnny nudged him. "How about them wedges?"

"Twenty-five cents a pound," explained the clerk, groping for his bearings.

"They might do," Hopalong muttered, forcing the article mentioned into his holster. "Why, they're quite hocus-pocus. You take th' brother to mine, Johnny."

"Feels good, but I dunno," his companion muttered. "Little wide at th' sharp end. Hey, got any loose shot?" he suddenly asked, whereat Hopalong beamed and the clerk gasped. It didn't seem to matter whether they bought bacon, cold chisels, wedges, or shot; yet they looked sober.

"Yes, sir; what size?"

"Three pounds of shot, I said!" Johnny rumbled in his throat. "Never mind what size."

"We never care about size when we buy shot," Hopalong smiled. "But, Johnny, wouldn't them little screws be better?" he asked, pointing eagerly.

"Mebby; reckon we better get 'em mixed—half of each," Johnny gravely replied. "Anyhow, there ain't much difference."

The clerk had been behind that counter for four years, and executing and filling orders had become a habit with him; else he would have given them six pounds of cold chisels and corkscrews, mixed. His mouth was still open when he weighed out the screws.

"Mix 'em! Mix 'em!" roared Hopalong, and the stunned clerk complied, and charged them for the whole purchase at the rate set down for screws.

Hopalong started to pour his purchase into the holster which, being open at the bottom, gayly passed the first instalment through to the floor. He stopped and looked appealingly at Johnny, and Johnny, in pain from holding back screams of laughter, looked at him indignantly. Then a guileless smile crept over Hopalong's face and he stopped the opening with a wad of wrapping paper and disposed of the shot and screws, Johnny following his laudable example. After haggling a moment over the bill they paid it and walked out, to the apparent joy of the clerk.

"Don't laugh, Kid; you'll spoil it all," warned Hopalong, as he noted signs of distress on his companion's face. "Now, then; what was it we said about thirst? Come on; I see one already."

Having entered the saloon and ordered, Hopalong beamed upon the bartender and shoved his glass back again. "One more, kind stranger; it's good stuff."

"Yes, feels like a shore-enough gun," remarked Johnny, combining two thoughts in one expression, which is brevity.

The bartender looked at him quickly and then stood quite still and listened, a puzzled expression on his face.

Tic—tickety-tick—tic-tic, came strange sounds from the other side of the bar. Hopalong was intently studying a chromo on the wall and Johnny gazed vacantly out of the window.

"What's that? What in the deuce is that?" quickly demanded the man with the apron, swiftly reaching for his bung-starter.

Tickety-tic-tic-tic-tic-tic, the noise went on, and Hopalong, slowly rolling his eyes, looked at the floor. A screw rebounded and struck his foot, while shot were rolling recklessly.

"Them's making th' noise," Johnny explained after critical survey.

"Hang it! I knowed we ought to 'a' got them wedges!" Hopalong exclaimed, petulantly, closing the bottom of the sheath. "Why, I won't have no gun left soon 'less I holds it in." The complaint was plaintive.

"Must be filtering through th' stopper," Johnny remarked. "But don't it sound nice, especially when it hits that brass cuspidor!"

The bartender, grasping the mallet even more firmly,

arose on his toes and peered over the bar, not quite sure of what he might discover. He had read of infernal machines although he had never seen one. "What th' blazes!" he said in almost a whisper; and then his face went hard. "You get out of here, quick! You've had too much already! I've seen drunks, but—G'wan! Get out!"

"But we ain't begun yet," Hopalong interposed hastily. "You see—"

"Never mind what I see! I'd hate to see what you'll be seein' before long. God help you when you finish!" rather impolitely interrupted the bartender. He waved the mallet and made for the end of the counter with no hesitancy and lots of purpose in his stride. "G'wan, now! Get out!"

"Come on, Johnny; I'd shoot him only we didn't put no powder with th' shot," Hopalong remarked sadly, leading the way out of the saloon and towards the hardware store.

"You better get out!" shouted the man with the mallet, waving the weapon defiantly. "An' don't you never come back again, neither," he warned.

"Hey, it leaked," Hopalong said pleasantly as he closed the door of the hardware store behind him, whereupon the clerk jumped and reached for the sawed-off shotgun behind the counter. Sawed-off shotguns are great institutions for arguing at short range, almost as effective as dynamite in clearing away obstacles.

"Don't you come no nearer!" he cried, white of face. "You git out, or I'll let *this* leak, an' give you *all* shot, an' more than you can carry!"

"Easy! Easy there, pardner; we want them wedges," Hopalong replied, somewhat hurriedly. "Th' others ain't no good; I choked on th' very first screw. Why, I wouldn't hurt you for th' world," Hopalong assured him, gazing interestedly down the twin tunnels.

Johnny leaned over a nail keg and loosed the shot and

screws into it, smiling with childlike simplicity as he listened to the tintinnabulation of the metal shower among the nails. "It *does* drop when you let go of it," he observed.

"Didn't I tell you it would? I allus said so," replied Hopalong, looking back to the clerk and the shotgun. "Didn't I, stranger?"

The clerk's reply was a guttural rumbling, ninety per cent profanity, and Hopalong, nodding wisely, picked up two wedges. "Johnny, here's yore gun. If this man will stop talking to hisself and drop that lead-sprayer long enough to take our good money, we'll wear 'em."

He tossed a gold coin on the table, and the clerk, still holding tightly to the shotgun, tossed the coin into the cash box and cautiously slid the change across the counter. Hopalong picked up the money and, emptying his holster into the nail keg, followed his companion to the street, in turn followed slowly by the suspicious clerk. The door slammed shut behind them, the bolt shot home, and the clerk sat down on a box and cogitated.

Hopalong hooked his arm through Johnny's and started down the street. "I wonder what that feller thinks about us, anyhow. I'm glad Buck sent Red over to El Paso instead of us. Won't he be mad when we tell him all th' fun we've had?" he asked, grinning broadly.

They were to meet Red at Dent's store on the way back and ride home together.

They were strangely clad for their surroundings, the chaps glaringly out of place in the Seaman's Port, and winks were exchanged by the regular *habitués* when the two punchers entered the room and called for drinks. They were very tired and a little under the weather, for they had made the most of their time and spent almost all of their money; but any one counting on robbing them would have found them sober enough to look out for themselves. Night had found them ready to go to the hotel, but on the way they felt that they must have one more bracer, and finish their exploration of Jeremiah T. Jones' tabooed section. The town had begun to grow wearisome and they were vastly relieved when they realized that the rising sun would see them in the saddle and homeward bound, headed for God's country, which was the only place for cow-punchers after all.

"Long way from th' home port, ain't you, mates?" queried a tar of Hopalong. Another seaman went to the bar to hold a short, whispered consultation with the bartender, who at first frowned and then finally nodded assent.

"Too far from home, if that's what yo're driving at," Hopalong replied. "Blast these hard trails—my feet are shore on th' prod. Ever meet my side pardner? Johnny, here's a friend of mine, a saltwater puncher, an' he's welcome to th' job, too."

Johnny turned his head ponderously and nodded. "Pleased to meet you, stranger. An' what'll you all have?"

"Old Holland, mate," replied the other, joining them.

"All up!" invited Hopalong, waving them forward. "Might as well do things right or not at all. Them's my sentiments, which I holds as proper. Plain rye, general, if you means me," he replied to the bartender's look of inquiry.

He drained the glass and then made a grimace. "Tastes a little off—reckon it's my mouth; nothing tastes right in this cussed town. Now, up on our—" he stopped and caught at the bar. "Holy smoke! That's shore alcohol!"

Johnny was relaxing and vainly trying to command his will power. "Something's wrong; what's th' matter?" he muttered sleepily.

"Guess you meant beer; you ain't used to drinking whiskey," grinned the bartender, derisively, and watching him closely.

"I can—drink as much whiskey as—" and, muttering, Johnny slipped to the floor.

"That wasn't whiskey!" cried Hopalong, sleepily. "That liquor was *fixed!*" he shouted, sudden anger bracing him. "An I'm going to fix *you*, too!" he added, reaching for his gun, and drawing forth a wedge. His sailor friend leaped at him, to go down like a log, and Hopalong, seething with rage, wheeled and threw the weapon at the man behind the bar, who also went down. The wedge, glancing from his skull, swept a row of bottles and glasses from the shelf and, carroming, went through the window.

In an instant Hopalong was the vortex of a mass of struggling men and, handicapped as he was, fought valiantly, his rage for the time neutralizing the effects of the drug. But at last, too sleepy to stand or think, he, too, went down.

"By th' Lord, that man's a fighter!" enthusiastically remarked the leader, gently touching his swollen eye. "George must 'a' put an awful dose in that grog."

"Lucky for us he didn't have no gun—th' wedge was bad enough," groaned a man on the floor, slowly sitting up. "Whoever swapped him that wedge for his gun did us a good turn, all right."

A companion tentatively readjusted his lip. "I don't envy Wilkins his job breaking in that man when he gets awake."

"Don't waste no time, mates," came the order. "Up with 'em an' aboard. We've done our share; let th' mate do his, an' be hanged. Hullo, Portsmouth; coming around, eh?" he asked the man who had first felt the wedge. "I was scared you was done for that time."

"No more shanghaing hair pants fer me, no more!" thickly replied Portsmouth. "Oh, my head, it's bust open!"

"Never mind about th' bartender—let him alone; we

can't waste no time with him now!" commanded the leader sharply. "Get these fellers on board before we're caught with 'em. We want our money after that."

"All clear!" came a low call from the lookout at the door, and soon a shadowy mass surged across the street and along a wharf. There was a short pause as a boat emerged out of the gloom, some whispered orders, and then the squeaking of oars grew steadily fainter in the direction of a ship which lay indistinct in the darkness.

II

♦

The Rebound

A man moaned and stirred restlessly in a bunk, muttering incoherently. A stampeded herd was thundering over him, the grinding hoofs beating him slowly to death. He saw one mad steer stop and lower its head to gore him and just as the sharp horns touched his skin, he awakened. Slowly opening his bloodshot eyes he squinted about him, sick, weak, racking with pain where heavy shoes had struck him in the *mêlée*, his head reverberating with roars which seemed almost to split it open. Slowly he regained his full senses and began to make out his surroundings. He was in a bunk which moved up and down, from side to side, and was never still. There was a small, round window near his feet—thank heaven it was open, for he was almost suffocated by the foul air and the heat. Where was he? What had happened? Was there a salty odor in the air, or was he still dreaming? Painfully raising himself on one elbow he looked around and caught sight of a man in a bunk across the aisle. It was Johnny Nelson! Then, bit by bit, the whole thing came to him and he cursed heartily as he reviewed it and reached the only possible conclusion. He was at sea! He, Hopalong Cassidy, the best fighting unit of a good fighting outfit, shanghaied and at sea! Drugged, beaten, and stolen to labor on a ship!

Johnny was muttering and moaning and Hopalong slowly climbed out of the narrow bunk, unsteadily crossed the moving floor, and shook him. "Reckon he's in a stampede, too!" he growled. "They shore raised hell with us. Oh, what a beating we got! But we'll pass it along with trimmings."

Johnny's eyes opened and he looked around in confusion. "Wha', Hopalong!"

"Yes; it's me, th' prize idiot of a blamed good pair of 'em. How'd you feel?"

"Sleepy an' sick. My eyes ache an' my head's splitting. Where's Buck an' th' rest?"

Hopalong sat down on the edge of the bunk and swore luridly, eloquently, beautifully, with a fervor and polish which left nothing to be desired in that line, and caused his companion to gaze at him in astonishment.

"I had a mighty bad dream, but you must 'a' had one a whole lot worse, to listen to you," Johnny remarked. "Gee, you're going some! What's th' matter with you? You sick, too?"

Thereupon Hopalong unfolded the tale of woe and when Johnny had grasped its import and knew that his dream had been a stern reality he straightway loosed his vocabulary and earned a draw. "Well, I'm going back again," he finished, with great decision, arising to make good his assertion.

"Swim or walk?" asked Hopalong nonchalantly.

"Huh! Oh, Lord!"

"Well, I ain't going to either swim or walk," Hopalong soliloquized. "I'm just going to stay right here in this one-by-nothing cellar an' spoil th' health an' good looks of any pirate that comes down that ladder to get me out." He looked around, interested in life once more, and his trained eye grasped the strategic worth of their position. "Only one at a time, an' down that ladder," he mused, thoughtfully. "Why, Johnny, we owns this range as long as we wants to. They can't get us out. But, say, if we only had our guns!" he sighed, regretfully.

"You're right as far as you go; but you don't go to th' eating part. We'll starve, an' we ain't got no water. I can drink about a bucketful right now," moodily replied his companion.

"Well, yo're right; but mebby we can find food an' water."

"Don't see no signs of none. Hey!" Johnny called out, smiling faintly in his misery. "Let's get busy an' burn th' cussed thing up! Got any matches?"

"First you want to drown yoreself swimming, an' now you want to roast th' pair of us to death," Hopalong retorted, eying the rear wall of the room. "Wonder what's on th' other side of that partition?"

Johnny looked. "Why, water; an' lots of it, too."

"Naw; th' water is on th' other sides."

"Then how do I know?—sh! I hear somebody coming on th' roof."

"Tumble back in yore bunk—quick!" Hopalong hurriedly whispered. "Be asleep—if he comes down here it'll be our deal."

The steps overhead stopped at the companionway and a shadow appeared across the small patch of sunlight on the floor of the forecastle. "Tumble up here, you blasted loafers!" roared a deep voice.

No reply came from the forecastle—the silence was unbroken.

"If I have to come down there I'll—" the first mate

made promises in no uncertain tones and in very impolite language. He listened for a moment, and having very good ears and hearing nothing, made more promises and came down the ladder quickly and nimbly.

"*I*'ll bring you to," he muttered, reaching a brawny hand for Hopalong's nose, and missing. But he made contact with his own face, which stopped a short-arm blow from the owner of the aforesaid nose, a jolt full of enthusiasm and purpose. Beautiful and dazzling flashes of fire filled the air and just then something landed behind his ear and prolonged the pyrotechnic display. When the sky-rockets went up he lost interest in the proceedings and dropped to the floor like a bag of meal.

Hopalong cut another piece from the rope in his hand and watched his companion's busy fingers. "Tie him good, Johnny; he's th' only ace we've drawn in this game so far, an' we mustn't lose him."

Johnny tied an extra knot for luck and leaned forward, his eyes riveted on the bump under the victim's coat. His darting hand brought into sight that which pleased him greatly. "Oh, joy! Here, Hoppy; you take it."

Hopalong turned the weapon over in his hand, spun the cylinder and gloated, the clicking sweet music to his ears. "Plumb full, too! I never reckoned I'd ever be so tickled over a snub-nosed gun like this—but I feel like singing!"

"An' I feel like dying," grunted Johnny, grabbing at his stomach. "If th' blamed shack would only stand still!" he groaned, gazing at the floor with strong disgust. "I don't reckon I've ever been so blamed sick in all my—" the sentence was unfinished, for the open porthole caught his eye and he leaped forward to use it for a collar.

Hopalong gazed at him in astonishment and sudden pity took possession of him as his pallid companion left the porthole and faced him.

"You ought to have something to eat, Kid—I'm purty hungry myself—what th' blazes!" he exclaimed, for Johnny's protesting wail was finished outside the port. Then a light broke upon him and he wondered how soon it would be his turn to pay tribute to Neptune.

"Mr. Wilkins!" shouted a voice from the deck, and Hopalong moved back a step. "Mr. Wilkins!" After a short silence the voice soliloquized: "Guess he changed his mind about it; I'll get 'em up for him," and feet came into view. When halfway down the ladder the second mate turned his head and looked blankly down a gun barrel, while a quiet but angry voice urged him further: "Keep a-coming, keep a-coming!" The second mate complained, but complied.

"Stick 'em up higher—now, Johnny, wobble around behind the nice man an' take *his* toy gun—you shut yore yap! I'm bossing this trick, not you. Got it, Kid? There's th' rope—that's right. Nobody'd think you sick to see you work. Well, that's a good draw; but it's only a pair of aces against a full, at that. Wonder who'll be th' next. Hope it's th' foreman."

Johnny, keeping up by sheer grit, pointed to the rear wall. "What about that?"

For reply his companion walked over to it, put his shoulder to it and pushed. He stepped back and hurled his weight against it, but it was firm despite its squeaking protest. Then he examined it foot by foot and found a large knot, which he drove in by a blow of the gun. Bending, he squinted through the opening for a full minute and then reported:

"Purty black in there at this end, but up at th' other there's light from a hole in th' roof, an' I could see boxes an' things like that. I reckon it's th' main cellar."

"If we could get out at th' other end with that gun you've got we could raise blazes for a while," suggested Johnny.

"Anyhow, mebby they can come at us that way when they find out what we've gone an' done."

"Yo're right," Hopalong replied, looking around. Seeing an iron bar he procured it and, pushing it through the knot hole in the partition, pulled. The board, splitting and cracking under the attack, finally broke from its fastenings with a sharp report, and Hopalong, pulling it aside, stepped out of sight of his companion. Johnny was grinning at the success of his plan when he was interrupted.

"Ahoy, down there!" yelled a stentorian voice from above. "Mr. Wilkins! What th' devil are you doing so long?" and after a very short wait other feet came into sight. Just then the second mate, having managed to slip off the gag, shouted warning:

"Look out, Captain! They've got us and our guns! One of them has—" but Johnny's knee thudded into his chest and ended the sentence as a bullet sent a splinter flying from under the captain's foot.

"Hang these guns!" Johnny swore, and quickly turned to secure the gag in the mouth of the offending second mate. "You make any more yaps like that an' I'll wing you for keeps with yore own gun!" he snapped. "We're caught in yore trap an' we'll fight to a finish. You'll be th' first to go under if you gets any smart."

"Ahoy, men!" roared the captain in a towering rage, dancing frantically about on the deck and shouting for the crew to join him. He filled the air with picturesque profanity and stamped and yelled in passion at such rank mutiny.

"Hand grenades! Hand grenades!" he cried. Then he remembered that his two mates were also below and would share in the mutineers' fate, and his rage increased at his galling helplessness. When he had calmed sufficiently to think clearly he realized that it was certain

death for any one to attempt going down the ladder, and
that his must be a waiting game. He glanced at his crew,
thirteen good men, all armed with windlass bars and be-
laying pins, and gave them orders. Two were to watch the
hatch and break the first head to appear, while the others
returned to work. Hunger and thirst would do the rest.
And what joy would be his when they were forced to surrender!

Hopalong groped his way slowly towards the patch of
light, barking his shins, stumbling and falling over the
barrels and crates and finally, losing his footing at a critical moment, tumbled down upon a box marked "Cotton." There was a splintering crash and the very faint
clink of metal. Dazed and bruised, he sat up and felt of
himself—and found that he had lost his gun in the fall.

"Now, where in blazes did it fly to?" he muttered angrily, peering about anxiously. His eyes suddenly opened
their widest and he stared in surprise at a field gun which
covered him; and then he saw parts of two more.

"Good Lord! Is this a gunboat!" he cried. "Are we up
against blue jackets an' Uncle Sam?" He glanced quickly
back the way he had come when he heard Johnny's shot,
but he could see nothing. He figured that Johnny had
sense enough to call for help if he needed it, and put
that possibility out of his mind. "Naw, this ain't no gunboat—th' Government don't steal men; it enlists 'em. But
it's a funny pile of junk, all th' same. Where in blazes is
that toy gun? *Well*, I'll be hanged!" and he plunged toward the "Cotton" box he had burst in his descent, and
worked at it frantically.

"Winchesters! Winchesters!" he cried, dragging out
two of them. "Whoop! Now for th' cartridges—there
shore must be some to go with these guns!" He saw a
keg marked "Nails," and managed to open it after great
labor—and found it full of army Colts. Forcing down the

desire to turn a handspring, he slipped one of the six-shooters in his empty holster and patted it lovingly. "Old friend, I'm shore glad to see you, all right. You've been used, but that don't make no difference." Searching further, he opened a full box of *machetes*, and soon after found cartridges of many kinds and calibres. It took him but a few minutes to make his selection and cram his pockets with them. Then he filled two Colts and two Winchesters—and executed a short jig to work off the dangerous pressure of his exuberance.

"But what an unholy lot of weapons," he soliloquized on his way back to Johnny. "An' they're all second-hand. Cannons, too—an' *machetes!*" he exclaimed, suddenly understanding. "Jumping Jerusalem!—a filibustering expedition bound for Cuba, or one of them wildcat republics down south! Oh, ho, my friends; I see where you have bit off more'n you can chew." In his haste to impart the joyous news to his companion, he barked his shins shamefully.

"'Way down south in th' land o' cotton, cinnamon seed an'"—whoa, blast you!" and Hopalong stuck his head through the opening in the partition and grinned. "Heard you shoot, Kid; I reckoned you might need me—an' these!" he finished, looking fondly upon the weapons as he shoved them into the forecastle.

Johnny groaned and held his stomach, but his eyes lighted up when he saw the guns, and he eagerly took one of each kind, a faint smile wreathing his lips. "Now we'll show these water snakes what kind of men they stole," he threatened.

Up on the deck the choleric captain still stamped and swore, and his crew, with well-concealed mirth, went about their various duties as if they were accustomed to have shanghaied men act this way. They sympathized with the unfortunate pair, realizing how they themselves would feel if shanghaied to break bronchos.

Hogan, A. B., stated the feelings of his companions very well in his remarks to the men who worked alongside: "In me hear-rt I'm dommed glad av it, Yensen. I hope they bate th' old man at his own game. 'Tis a shame in these days fer honest men to be took in that unlawful way. I've heard me father tell of th' press gangs on th' other side, an' 't is small business."

Yensen looked up to reply, chanced to glance aft, and dropped his calking iron in his astonishment. "Yumping Yimminy! Luk at dat fallar!"

Hogan looked. "Th' deuce! That's a man after me own hear-rt! Kape yore pagan mouth shut! If ye take a hand agin 'em I'll swab up th' deck wid yez. G'wan wor-rking like a sane man, ye ijit!"

"Ay ent ban fight wit dat fallar! Luk at th' gun!"

A man had climbed out of the after hatch and was walking rapidly towards them, a rifle in his hands, while at his thigh swung a Colt. He watched the two seamen closely and caught sight of Hogan's twinkling blue eyes, and a smile quivered about his mouth. Hogan shut and opened one eye and went on working.

As soon as Hopalong caught sight of the captain, the rifle went up and he announced his presence without loss of time. "Throw up yore hands, you pole-cat! I'm running this ranch from now on!"

The captain wheeled with a jerk and his mouth opened, and then clicked shut as he started forward, his rage acting galvanically. But he stopped quickly enough when he looked down the barrel of the Winchester and glared at the cool man behind it.

"What th' blank are you doing?" he yelled.

"Well, I ain't kidnapping cow-punchers to steal my boat," replied Hopalong. "An' you fellers stand still or I'll drop you cold!" he ordered to the assembled and restless crew. "Johnny!" he shouted, and his companion popped up through the hatch like a jack-in-the-box. "Good boy, Johnny. Tie this coyote foreman like you did th' others," he ordered. While Johnny obeyed, Hopalong looked around the circle, and his eyes rested on Hogan's face, studying it, and found something there which warmed his heart. "Friend, do you know th' back trail? Can you find that runt of a town we left?"

"Aye, aye."

"Shore, you; who'd you think I was talking to? Can you find th' way back, th' way we came?"

"Shure an' I can that, if I'm made to."

"You'll swing for mutiny if you do, you bilge-wallering pirate!" roared the trussed captain. "Take that gun away from him, d'ye hear!" he yelled at the crew. "I'm captain of this ship, an' I'll hang every last one of you if you don't obey orders! This is mutiny!"

"You won't do no hanging with that load of weapons below!" retorted Hopalong. "Uncle Sam is looking for filibusters—this here gun is 'cotton,'" he said, grinning. He turned to the crew. "But you fellers are due to get shot if you sees her through," he added.

"I'm captain of this ship—" began the helpless autocrat.

"You shore look like it, all right," Hopalong replied, smiling. "If yo're th' captain you order her turned around and headed over th' back trail, or I'll drop you overboard off yore own ship!" Then fierce anger at the thought of the indignities and injuries he and his companion had suffered swept over him and prompted a one-minute speech which left no doubt as to what he would do if his demand was not complied with. Johnny, now free to watch the crew, added a word or two of endorsement, and he acted a little as if he rather hoped it would not be complied with: he itched for an excuse.

The captain did some quick thinking; the true situation could not be disguised, and with a final oath of rage he gave in. "'Bout ship, Hogan; nor' by nor'west," he growled, and the seaman started away to execute the command, but was quickly stopped by Hopalong.

"Hogan, is that right?" he demanded. "No funny business, or we'll clean up th' whole bunch, an' blamed quick, too!"

"That's th' course, sor. That's th' way back to town. I can navigate, an' me orders are plain. Ye're Irish, by th' way av ye, and 't is back to town ye go, sor." He turned to the crew: "Stand by, me boys." And in a short time the course was nor' by nor'west.

The return journey was uneventful and at nightfall the ship lay at anchor off the low Texas coast, and a boat loaded with men grounded on the sandy beach. Four of them arose and leaped out into the mild surf and dragged the boat as high up on the sand as it would go. Then the two cowpunchers followed and one of them gave a low-spoken order to the Irishman at his side.

"Yes, sor," replied Hogan, and hastened to help the captain out onto the sand and to cut the ropes which bound him. "Do ye want th' mates, too, sor?" he asked, glancing at the trussed men in the boat.

"No; th' foreman's enough," Hopalong responded, handing his weapons to Johnny and turning to face the captain, who was looking into Johnny's gun as he rubbed his arms to restore perfect circulation.

"Now, you flat-faced coyote, yo're going to get th' beating of yore life, an' I'm going to give it to you!" Hopalong cried, warily advancing upon the man whom he held to be responsible for the miseries of the past twenty-four hours. "You didn't give me a square deal, but I'm man enough to give you one! When you drug an' steal any more cow-punchers—" action stopped his words.

It was a great fight. A filibustering sea captain is no

more peaceful than a wild boar and about as dangerous; and while this one was not at his best, neither was Hopalong. The latter luckily had acquired some knowledge of the rudiments of the game and had the vigor of youth to oppose to the captain's experience and his infuriated but well-timed rushes. The seamen, for the honor of their calling and perhaps with a mind to the future, cheered on the captain and danced up and down in their delight and excitement. They had a lot of respect for the prowess of their master, and for the man who could stand up against him in a fair and square fist fight. To give assistance to either in a fair fight was not to be thought of, and Johnny's gun was sufficient after-excuse for noninterference.

The *sop! sop!* of the punishing blows as they got home and the steady circling of Hopalong in avoiding the dangerous attacks, went on minute after minute. Slowly the captain's strength was giving out, and he resorted to trickery as his last chance. Retreating, he half raised his arms and lowered them as if weary, ready as a cat to strike with all his weight if the other gave an opening. It ought to have worked—it had worked before—but Hopalong was there to win, and without the momentary hesitation of the suspicious fighter he followed the retreat and his hard hand flashed in over the captain's guard a fraction of a second sooner than that surprised gentleman anticipated. The ferocious frown gave way to placid peace and the captain reclined at the feet of the battered victor, who stood waiting for him to get up and fight. The captain lay without a sign of movement and as Hopalong wondered, Hogan was the first to speak.

"Fer th' love av hiven, let him be! Ye needn't wait—he's done: I know by th' sound av it!" he exclaimed, stepping forward. "'T was a purty blow, an' 't was a gr-rand foight ye put up, sor! A gr-rand foight, but any more av that is murder! 'T is an Irishman's game, sor, an' ye did yersilf proud. But now let him be—no man, least av all a Dootchman, iver tuk more than that an' lived!"

Hopalong looked at him and slowly replied between swollen lips, "Yo're right, Hogan; we're square now, I reckon."

"That's right, sor," Hogan replied, and turned to his companions. "Put him in th' boat; an' mind ye handle him gintly—we'll be sailing under him soon. Now, sor, if it's yer pleasure, I'll be after sayin' good-bye to ye, sor; an' to ye, too," he said, shaking hands with both punchers. "Fer a sick la-ad ye're a wonder, ye are that," he smiled at Johnny, "but ye want to kape away from th' water fronts. Good-bye to ye both, an' a pleasant journey home. Th' town is tin miles to me right, over beyant them hills."

"Good-bye, Hogan," mumbled Hopalong gratefully. "Yo're square all th' way through; an' if you ever get out of a job or in any kind of trouble that I can help you out of, come up to th' Bar-20 an' you won't have to ask twice. Good luck!" And the two sore and aching punchers, wiser in the ways of the world, plodded doggedly towards the town, ten miles away.

The next morning found them in the saddle, bound for Dent's hotel and store near the San Miguel Canyon. When they arrived at their destination and Johnny found there was some hours to wait for Red, his restlessness sent him roaming about the country, not so much "seeking what he might devour" as hoping something might seek to devour him. He was so sore over his recent kidnapping that he longed to find a salve. He faithfully promised Hopalong that he would return at noon.

III

♦

Dick Martin Starts Something

Dick Martin slowly turned, leaned his back against the bar, and languidly regarded a group of Mexicans at the other end of the room. Singly, or in combinations of two or more, each was imparting all he knew, or thought he knew about the ghost of San Miguel Canyon. Their fellow-countryman, new to the locality, seemed properly impressed. That it was the ghost of Carlos Martinez, murdered nearly one hundred years before at the big bend in the canyon, was conceded by all; but there was a dispute as to why it showed itself only on Friday nights, and why it was never seen by any but a Mexican. Never had a Gringo seen it. The Mexican stranger was appealed to: Did this not prove that the murder had been committed by a Mexican? The stranger affected to consider the question.

Martin surveyed them with outward impassiveness and inward contempt. A realist, a cynic, and an absolute genius with a Colt .45, he was well known along the border for his dare-devil exploits and reckless courage. The brainiest men in the Secret Service, Lewis, Thomas, Sayre, and even Old Jim Lane, the local chief, whose fingers at El Paso felt every vibration along the Rio Grande, were not as well known—except to those who had seen the inside of Government penitentiaries—and they were quite satisfied to be so eclipsed. But the Service knew of the ghost, as it knew everything pertaining to the border, and gave it no serious thought; if it took interest in all the ghosts and superstitions peculiar to the Mexican temperament it would have no time for serious work. Martin once, in a spirit of savage denial, had wasted the better part of several successive Friday nights in the San Miguel, but to no avail. When told that the ghost showed itself only to Mexicans he had shrugged his shoulders eloquently and laughed, also eloquently.

"A Mexican," he replied, "is one-half fear and superstition, an' th' other half imagination. There ain't no ghosts, but I know th' Mexicans have seen 'em, all right. A Mexican can see anything scary if he makes up his mind to. If *I* ever see one an' he keeps on being one after I shoot, I'll either believe in ghosts, or quit drinking." His eyes twinkled as he added: "An' of th' two, I think I'd *prefer* to see ghosts!"

He was flushed and restless with deviltry. His fifth glass always made him so; and to-night there was an added stimulus. He believed the strange Mexican to be Juan Alvarez, who was so clever that the Government had never been able to convict him. Alvarez was fearless to recklessness and Martin, eager to test him, addressed the group with the blunt terseness for which he was famed, and hated.

"Mexicans are cowards," he asserted quietly, and with a smile which invited excitement. He took a keen delight in analyzing the expressions on the faces of those hit. It was one of his favorite pastimes when feeling coltish.

The group was shocked into silence, quickly followed by great unrest and hot, muttered words. Martin did not move a muscle, the smile was set, but between the half-closed eyelids crouched Combat, on its toes. The Mexicans knew it was there without looking for it—the tone of his voice, the caressing purr of his words, and his unnatural languor were signs well known to them. Not a criminal sneaking back from voluntary banishment in Mexico who had seen those signs ever forgot them, if he lived. Martin watched the group cat-like, keenly scrutinizing each face, reading the changing emotions in every shifting expression; he had this art down so well that he could tell when a man was debating the pull of a gun, and beat him on the draw by a fraction of a second.

"De señor ees meestak," came the reply, as quiet and caressing as the words which provoked it. The strange Mexican was standing proudly and looking into the squinting eyes with only a grayness of face and a tigerish litheness to tell what he felt.

"None go through th' canyon after dark on Fridays," purred Martin.

"*I* go tro' de canyon nex' Friday night. Eef I do, then you mak' apology to me?"

"I'll limit my remark to all but one Mexican."

The Mexican stepped forward. "I tak' thees gloove an' leave eet at de Beeg Ben', for you to fin' in daylight," he said, tapping one of Martin's gauntlets which lay on the bar. "You geev' me eet befo' I go?"

"Yes; at nine o'clock to-morrow night," Martin replied, hiding his elation. He was sure that he knew the man now.

The Mexican, cool and smiling, bowed and left the room, his companions hastening after him.

"Well, I'll bet twenty-five dollars he flunks!" breathed the bartender, straightening up.

Martin turned languidly and smiled at him. "I'll take that, Charley," he replied.

Johnny Nelson was always late, and on this occasion he was later than usual. He was to have joined Hopalong and Red, if Red had arrived, at Dent's at noon the day before, and now it was after nine o'clock at night as he rode through San Felippe without pausing and struck east for the canyon. The dropping trail down the can-

yon wall was serious enough in broad daylight, but at
night to attempt its passage was foolhardy, unless one
knew every turn and slant by heart, which Johnny did
not. He was thirty-three hours late now, and he was
determined to make up what he could in the next three.

When Johnny left Hopalong at Dent's he had given his
word to be back on time and not to keep his companions
waiting, for Red might be on time and he would chafe if
he were delayed. But, alas for Johnny's good intentions,
his course took him through a small Mexican hamlet in
which lived a señorita of remarkable beauty and rebel-
lious eyes; and Johnny tarried in the town most of the
day, riding up and down the streets, practising the nice
things he would say if he met her. She watched him from
the heavily draped window, and sighed as she wondered
if her dashing Americano would storm the house and
carry her off like the knights of old. Finally he had to turn
away with heavy and reluctant heart, promising himself
that he would return when no petulant and sarcastic companions were waiting for him. Then—ah! what dreams
youth knows.

Half an hour ahead of him on another trail rode Juan,
smiling with satisfaction. He had come to San Felippe to
get a look at the canyon on Friday nights, and Martin had
given him an excuse entirely unexpected. For this he was
truly grateful, even while he knew that the American
had tried to pick a quarrel with him and thus rid the border of a man entirely too clever for the good of customs
receipts; and failing in that, had hoped the treacherous
canyon trail would gain that end in another manner. Old
Jim Lane's fingers touched wires not one whit more sensitive than those which had sent Juan Alvarez to look
over the San Miguel—and Lane's wires had been slow
this time. When Juan had left the saloon the night before
and had seen Manuel slip away from the group and ride

off into the north, he had known that the ghost would show itself the following night.

But Juan was to be disappointed. He was still some distance from the canyon when a snarling bulk landed on the haunches of his horse. He jerked loose his gun and fired twice and then knew nothing. When he opened his eyes he lay quietly, trying to figure it out with a head throbbing with pain from his fall. The cougar must have been desperate for food to attack a man. He moved his foot and struck something soft and heavy. His shots had been lucky, but they had not saved him his horse and a sprained arm and leg. There would be no gauntlet found at the Big Bend at daylight.

When Johnny Nelson reached the twin boulders marking the beginning of the sloping run where the trail pitched down, he grinned happily at sight of the moon rising over the low hills and then grabbed at his holster, while every hair in his head stood up curiously. A wild, haunting, feminine scream arose to a quavering soprano and sobbed away into silence. No words can adequately describe the unearthly wail in that cry and it took a full half-minute for Johnny to become himself again and to understand what it was. Once more it arose, nearer, and Johnny peered into the shadows along a rough backbone of rock, his Colt balanced in his half-raised hand.

"You come 'round me an' you'll get hurt," he muttered, straining his eyes to peer into the blackness of the shadows. "Come on out, Soft-foot; th' moon's yore finish. You an' me will have it out right here an' now—I don't want no cougar trailing me through that ink-black canyon on a two-foot ledge—" he thought he saw a shadow glide across a dim patch of moonlight, but when his smoke rifted he knew he had missed. "Damn it! You've got a mate 'round here somewhere," he complained.

"Well, I'll have to chance it, anyhow. Come on, bronch! Yo're shaking like a leaf—get out of this!"

When he began to descend into the canyon he allowed his horse to pick its own way without any guidance from him, and gave all of his attention to the trail behind him. The horse could get along better by itself in the dark, and it was more than possible that one or two lithe cougars might be slinking behind him on velvet paws. The horse scraped along gingerly, feeling its way step by step, and sending stones rattling and clattering down the precipice at his left to tinkle into the stream at the bottom.

"Gee, but I wish I'd not wasted so much time," muttered the rider uneasily. "This here canyon-cougar combination is th' worst *I* ever butted up against. I'll never be late again, not never; not for all th' girls in th' world. Easy, bronch," he cautioned, as he felt the animal slip and quiver. "Won't this trail ever start going up again?" he growled petulantly, taking his eyes off the black back trail, where no amount of scrutiny showed him anything, and turned in the saddle to peer ahead—and a yell of surprise and fear burst from him, while chills ran up and down his spine. An unearthly, piercing shriek suddenly rang out and filled the canyon with ear-splitting uproar and a glowing, sheeted half-figure of a man floated and danced twenty feet from him and over the chasm. He jerked his gun and fired, but only once, for his mount had its own ideas about some things and this particular one easily headed the list. The startled rider grabbed reins and pommel, his blood congealed with fear of the precipice less than a foot from his side, and he gave all his attention to the horse. But scared as he was he heard, or thought that he heard, a peculiar sound when he fired, and he would have sworn that he hit the mark—the striking of the bullet was not drowned in the uproar and he would never forget the sound of that impact. He rounded Big Bend as if he were coming up to the judge's stand, and when he struck the upslant of the emerging trail he had made a record. Cold sweat beaded his forehead and he was trembling from head to foot when he again rode into the moonlight on the level plain, where he tried to break another record.

IV

◆

Johnny Arrives

Meanwhile, Hopalong and Red quarrelled petulantly and damned the erring Johnny with enthusiastic abandon, while Dent smiled at them and joked; but his efforts at levity made little impression on the irate pair. Red, true to his word, had turned up at the time set, in fact, he was half an hour ahead of time, for which miracle he endeavored to take great and disproportionate credit. Dent was secretly glad about the delay, for he found his place lonesome. He thoroughly enjoyed the company of the two gentlemen from the Bar-20, whose actions seemed to be governed by whims and who appeared to lack all regard for consequences; and they squabbled so refreshingly, and spent their money cheerfully. Now, if they would only wind up the day by fighting! Such a finish would be joy indeed. And speaking of fights, Dent was certain that Mr. Cassidy *had* been in one recently, for his face bore marks that could only be acquired in that way.

After supper the two guests had relapsed into a silence which endured only as long as the pleasing fulness. Then the squabbling began again, growing worse until they fell silent from lack of adequate expression. Finally Red once again spoke of their absent friend.

"We oughtn't get peevish, Hoppy—he's only thirty-six hours late," suggested Red. "An' he might be a week," he added thoughtfully, as his mind ran back over a long list of Johnny's misdeeds.

"Yes; he might. An' won't he have a fine cock-an'-bull tale to explain it," growled Hopalong, reminiscently. "His excuses are th' worst part of it generally."

"Eh, does he—make excuses?" asked Dent, mildly surprised.

"He does to *us*," retorted Red savagely. "He's worse than a woman; take him all in all an' you've got th' toughest proposition that ever wore pants. But he's a good feller, at that."

"Well, you've got a lot of nerve, you have!" retorted Hopalong. "You don't want to say anything about th' Kid—if there's anybody that can beat him in being late an' acting th' fool generally, it's you. An' what's more, you know it!"

Red wheeled to reply, but was interrupted by a sudden uproar outside, fluent swearing coming towards the house. The door opened with a bang, admitting a white-faced, big-eyed man with one leg jammed through the box he had landed on in dismounting.

"Gimme a drink, quick!" he shouted wildly, dragging the box over to the bar with a cheerful disregard for chairs and other temporary obstructions. "Gimme a drink!" he reiterated.

"Give you six hops in th' neck!" yelled Red, missing and almost sitting down because of the enthusiasm he had put into his effort. Johnny side-stepped and ducked, and as he straightened up to ask for whys and wherefores, Red's eyes opened wide and he paused in his further intentions to stare at the apparition.

"Sick?" queried Hopalong, who was frightened.

"Gimme that drink!" demanded Johnny feverishly, and when he had it he leaned against the bar and mopped his face with a trembling hand.

"What's th' matter with you, anyhow?" asked Red, with deep anxiety.

"Yes; for God's sake, what's happened to you?" demanded Hopalong.

Johnny breathed deeply and threw back his shoulders as if to shake off a weight. "Fellers, I had a cougar soft-footing after me in that dark canyon, my cayuse ran away on a two-foot ledge up th' wall,—*an'*—*I*—*saw*—*a*—*ghost!*"

There was a most respectful silence. Johnny, waiting a reasonable length of time for replies and exclamations, flushed a bit and repeated his frank and candid statement, adding a few adjectives to it. "*A real, screeching, flying ghost!* An' I'm going *home*, an' I'm going to *stay* there. I ain't never coming back no more, not for anything. Damn this border country, *anyhow*!"

The silence continued, whereupon Johnny grew properly indignant. "You act like I told you it was going to rain! Why don't you say something? Didn't you hear what I said, you fools?" he asked pugnaciously. "Are you in th' habit of having a thing like that told you? Why don't you show some interest, you dod-blasted, thick-skulled wooden-heads?"

Red looked at Hopalong, Hopalong looked at Red, and then they both looked at Dent, whose eyes were fixed in a stare on Johnny.

"Huh!" snorted Hopalong, warily arising. "Was that all?" he asked, nodding at Red, who also arose and began to move cautiously toward their erring friend. "Didn't you see no more'n one ghost? Anybody that can see one ghost, an' no more, is wrong somewhere. Now, stop an' think: didn't you see *two*?" He was advancing carefully while he talked, and Red was now behind the man who saw one ghost.

"Why, you—" there was a sudden flurry and Johnny's words were cut short in the *mêlée*.

"Good, Red! Ouch!" shouted Hopalong. "Look out! Got any rope, Dent? Well, hurry up: there ain't no telling what he'll do if he's loose. Th' mescal they sells down in this country ain't liquor—it's poison," he panted. "An' he can't even stand whiskey!"

Finding the rope was easier than finding a place to put it, and the unequal battle raged across the room and into the next, where it sounded as if the house were falling down. Johnny's voice was shrill and full of vexation and his words were extremely impolite and lacked censoring. His feet appeared to be numerous and growing rapidly, judging from the amount of territory they covered and defended, and Red joyfully kicked Hopalong in the *mêlée*, which in this instance also stands for stomach; Red always took great pains to do more than his share in a scrimmage. Dent hovered on the flanks, his hands full of rope, and begged with great earnestness to be allowed to apply it to parts of Johnny's thrashing anatomy. But as the flanks continued to change with bewildering swiftness he begged in vain, and began to make suggestions and give advice pleasing to the three combatants. Dent knew just how it should be done, and was generous with the knowledge until Johnny zealously planted five knuckles on his one good eye, when the engagement became general.

The table skidded through the door on one leg and carromed off the bar at a graceful angle, collecting three chairs and one sand-box cuspidor on the way. The box on Johnny's leg had long since departed, as Hopalong's shin could testify. One chair dissolved unity and distributed itself lavishly over the room, while the bed shrunk silently and folded itself on top of Dent, who bucked it up and down with burning zeal, and finally had sense enough to crawl from under it. He immediately celebrated his liberation by getting a strangle hold on two legs, one of which happened to be the personal property of Hopalong Cassidy; and the battle raged on a lower plane. Red raised one hand as he carefully traced a neck to its own proper head and then his steel fingers opened and swooped down and shut off the dialect. Hopalong pushed Dent off him and managed to catch Johnny's flaying arm on the third attempt, while Dent made tentative sorties against Johnny's spurred boots.

"Phew! Can he fight like that when he's sober?" reverently asked Dent, seeing how close his fingers could come to his gaudy eye without touching it. "I won't be able to see at all in an hour," he added, gloomily.

Hopalong, seated on Johnny's chest, soberly made reply as he tenderly flirted with a raw shin. "It's th' mescal. I'm going to slip some of that stuff into Pete's cayuse some of these days," he promised, happy with a new idea. Pete Wilson had no sense of humor.

"That ghost was plumb lucky," grunted Red, "an' so was th' sea-captain," he finished as an afterthought, limping off toward the bar, slowly and painfully followed by his disfigured companions. "One drink; then to bed."

After Red had departed, Hopalong and Dent smoked a while and then, knocking the ashes out of his pipe, Hopalong arose. "An' yet, Dent, there are people that believe in ghosts," he remarked, with a vast and settled contempt.

Dent gave critical scrutiny to the scratched bar for a moment. "Well, th' Mexicans all say there *is* a ghost in th' San Miguel, though I never saw it. But some of them have seen it, an' no Mexicans ride that trail no more."

"Huh!" snorted Hopalong. "Some Mexicans must have filled th' Kid up on ghosts while he was filling himself up on mescal. Ghosts? R-a-t-s!"

"It shows itself only to Mexicans, an' then only on Friday nights," explained Dent, thoughtfully. This was Friday night. Others had seen that ghost, but they were all Mexicans; now that a man of Johnny's undisputed calibre had been so honored Dent's skepticism wavered and he had something to think about for days to come. True, Johnny was not a Mexican; but even ghosts might make mistakes once in a while.

Hopalong laughed, dismissing the subject from his mind as being beneath further comment. "Well, we won't argue—I'm too tired. An' I'm sorry you got that eye, Dent."

"Oh, that's all right," hastily assured the storekeeper, smiling faintly. "I was just spoiling for a fight, an' now I've had it. Feels sort of good. Yes, first thing in th' morning—breakfast'll be ready soon as you are. Goodnight."

But the proprietor couldn't sleep. Finally he arose and tiptoed into the room where Johnny lay wrapped in the sleep of the exhausted. After cautious and critical inspection, which was made hard because of his damaged eye, he tiptoed back to his bunk, shaking his head slowly. "He wasn't drunk," he muttered. "He saw that ghost, all right; an' I'll bet everything I've got on it!"

At daybreak three quarrelling punchers rode homeward and after a monotonous journey arrived at the bunk house and reported. It took them two nights adequately to describe their experiences to an envious audience. The morning after the telling of the ghost story things began to happen, Red starting it by erecting a sign.

NOTICE—NO GHOSTS ALLOWED

An exuberant handful of the outfit watched him drive the last nail and step back to admire his work, and the running fire of comment covered all degrees of humor, and promised much hilarity in the future at the expense of the only man on the Bar-20 who had seen a ghost.

In a week Johnny and his acute vision had become a bye-word in that part of the country and his friends had made it a practice to stop him and gravely discuss spirit manifestations of all kinds. He had thrashed Wood Wright and been thrashed by Sandy Lucas in two beautiful and memorable fights and was only waiting to recover from the last affair before having the matter out with Rich Finn. These facts were beginning to have the effect he strove for; though Cowan still sold a new concoction of gin, brandy, and whiskey which he called "Flying Ghost," and which he proudly guaranteed would show more ghosts per drink than any liquor south of the Rio Grande—and some of his patrons were eager to back up his claims with real money.

This was the condition of affairs when Hopalong Cassidy strolled into Cowan's and forgot his thirst in the story being told by a strange Mexican. It was Johnny's ghost, without a doubt, and when he had carelessly asked a few questions he was convinced that Johnny had really seen something. On the way home he cogitated upon it and two points challenged his intelligence with renewed insistence: the ghost showed itself only on Friday, and then only to "Mexicans." His suspicious mind would not rest until he had viewed the question from all sides, and his opinion was that there was something more than spiritual about the ghost of the San Miguel—and a cold, practical reason for it.

When he rode into the corral at the ranch he saw that another sign had been put on the corral wall. He had destroyed the first, speaking his mind in full at the time. He swept his gloved hand upward with a rush, tore the flimsy board from its fastenings, broke it to pieces across his saddle, and tossed the fragments from him. He was angry, for he had warned the outfit that they were carrying the joke too far, that Johnny was giving way to hysterical rage more frequently, and might easily do something that they all would regret. And he felt sorry for the Kid; he knew what Johnny's feelings were and he made up his mind to start a few fights himself if the persecution did not cease. When he stepped into the bunk house and faced his friends they listened to a three-minute speech that made them squirm, and as he finished talking the deep voice of the foreman endorsed the promises he had just heard made, for Buck had entered the gallery without being noticed. The joke had come to an end.

When Johnny rode in that evening he was surprised to find Hopalong waiting for him a short distance from the corral and he replied to his friend's gesture by riding over to him. "What's up now?" he asked.

"Come along with me. I want to talk to you for a few minutes," and Hopalong led the way toward the open, followed by Johnny, who was more or less suspicious. Finally Hopalong stopped, turned, and looked his companion squarely in the eyes. "Kid, I'm in dead earnest. This ain't no fool joke—now you tell me what that ghost looked like, how he acted, an' all about it. I mean what I say, because now I know that you saw *something*. If it wasn't a ghost it was made to look like one, anyhow. Now go ahead."

"I've told you a dozen times already," retorted Johnny, his face flushing. "I've begged you to believe me an' told you that I wasn't fooling. How do I know you ain't now? I'm not going to tell—"

"Hold on; yes, you are. You're going to tell it slow, an' just like you saw it," Hopalong interrupted hastily. "I know

I've doubted it, but who wouldn't! Wait a minute—I've done a heap of thinking in th' last few days an' I know that you saw a ghost. Now, everybody knows that there ain't no such thing as ghosts; then what was it you saw? There's a game on, Kid, an' it's a dandy; an' you an' me are going to bust it up an' get th' laugh on th' whole blasted crowd, from Buck to Cowan."

Johnny's suspicions left him with a rush, for his old Hoppy was one man in a thousand, and when he spoke like that, with such sharp decision, Johnny knew what it meant. Hopalong listened intently and when the short account was finished he put out his hand and smiled.

"We're th' fools, Kid; not you. There's something crooked going on in that canyon, an' I know it! But keep mum about what we think."

Johnny lost his grouch so suddenly and beamed upon his friends with such a superior air that they began to worry about what was in the wind. The suspense wore on them, for with Hopalong's assistance, Johnny might spring some game on them all that would more than pay up for the fun they had enjoyed at his expense; and the longer the suspense lasted the worse it became. They never lost sight of him while he was around and Hopalong had to endure the same surveillance; and it was no uncommon thing to see small groups of the anxious men engaged in deep discussion. When they found that Buck must have been told and noticed that his smile was as fixed as Hopalong's or Johnny's, they were certain that trouble of some nature was in store for them.

Several weeks later Buck Peters drew rein and waited for a stranger to join him.

"Howd'y. Is yore name Peters?" asked the newcomer, sizing him up in one trained glance.

"Well, who are you, an' what do you want?"

"I want to see Peters, Buck Peters. That yore name?"

"Yes; what of it?"

"My name's Fox. Old Jim Lane gave me a message for you," and the stranger spoke earnestly to some length. "There; that's th' situation. We've got to have shrewd men that they don't know an' won't suspect. Lane wants to pay a couple of yore men their wages for a month or two. He said he was shore he could count on you to help him out."

"He's right; he can. I don't forget favors. I've got a couple of men that—there's one of 'em now. Hey, Hoppy! Whoop-e, Hoppy!"

Mr. Cassidy arrived quickly, listened eagerly, named Red and Johnny to accompany him, overruled his companions by insisting that if Johnny didn't go the whole thing was off, carried his point, and galloped off to find the lucky two, his eyes gleaming with anticipation and joy. Fox laughed, thanked the foreman, and rode on his way north; and that night three cow-punchers rode south, all strangely elated. And the friends who watched them go heaved sighs of relief, for the reprisals evidently were to be postponed for a while.

V

♦

The Ghost of the San Miguel

Juan Alvarez had not been in San Felippe since Dick Martin left, which meant for over a month. Martin was down the river looking for a man who did not wish to be found; and some said that Martin cared nothing about international boundaries when he wanted any one real bad. And there was that geologist who wore blue glasses and was always puttering around in the canyon and hammering chips of rock off the steep walls; he must have slipped one noon, because his body was found on a flat boulder at the edge of the stream. Manuel had found it and wanted to be paid for his trouble in bringing it to town—but Manuel was a fool. Who, indeed, would pay good money for a dead Gringo, especially after he was dead? And there were three cow-punchers holding a herd of 6-X cattle up north, an hour or so from the town. They wanted to buy steers from Señor Rodriguez, but said that he was a robber and threatened to cut his ears off. Cannot a man name his own price? These cow-punchers liked to get drunk and gallop through San Felippe, shooting like crazy men. They got drunk one Friday night and went shouting and singing to the Big Bend in the canyon to see the flying ghost, and they called it names and fired off their pistols and sang loudly; and for a week they insulted all the Mexicans in town by calling them liars and cowards. Was it the fault of any one that the ghost would show itself only to Mexicans? Oh, these Gringos—might the good God punish them for their sins!

Thus the peons complained to the padre while they kept one eye open for the advent of the rowdy cow-punchers, who always wanted to drink, and then to fight with some one, either with fists or pistols. Why should any one fight with them, especially with such things as fists?

"Let them fight among themselves. What have you to do with heretics?" reproved the good padre, who ostracized himself from the pleasant parts of the wide world that he might make easier the life and struggles of his ignorant flock. "God is not hasty—He will punish in His own way when it best suits Him. And perhaps you will profit much if you are more regular to mass instead of wasting the cool hours of the morning in bed. Think well of what I have said, my children."

But the cow-punchers were not punished and they swore they would not leave the vicinity until they had all the steers they wanted, and at their own price. And one night their herd stampeded and was checked only in time to save it from going over the canyon's edge. And for some reason Sanchez kept out of the padre's way and did not go to confess when he should, for the padre spoke plainly and set hard obligations for penance.

The cow-punchers swore that it had been done by some Mexican and said that they would come to town some day soon and kill three Mexicans unless the guilty one was found and brought to them. Then the padre mounted his donkey and went out to them to argue and they finally told him they would wait for two weeks. But the padre was too smart for them—he sent a messenger to find Señor Dick Martin, and in one week Señor Martin came to town. There was no fight. The Gringo rowdies were cowards at heart and Martin could not shoot them down in cold blood, and he could not arrest them, because he was not a policeman or even a sheriff, but only a revenue officer, which was a most foolish law. But he watched them all the time and wanted them to fight— there was no more shooting or drunkenness in town. Nobody wanted to fight Señor Martin, for he was a great man. He even went so far as to talk with them about it and wave his arms, but they were as frightened at him as little children might be.

So the Mexicans gossiped and exulted, some of the bolder of them even swaggering out to the Gringo camp; but Martin drove them back again, saying he would not allow them to bully men who could not retaliate, which was right and fair. Then, afraid to go away and leave the mad cow-punchers so close to town, he ordered them to drive their herd farther east, nearer to Dent's store, and never to return to San Felippe unless they needed the padre; and they obeyed him after a long talk. After seeing them settled in their new camp, which was on Monday morning, Martin returned to San Felippe and told the padre where he could be found and then rode away again. San Felippe celebrated for a whole day and two Mexican babies were christened after Señor Dick Martin, which was honor all around.

Friday, when Manuel went over to spy upon the cowpunchers in their new camp, he found them so drunk that they could not stand, and before he crept away at dusk two of them were sleeping like gorged snakes and the third was firing off his revolver at random, which diversion had not a little to do with Manuel's departure.

When Manuel crept away he headed straight for a crevice near the wall of the canyon at the Big Bend and, reaching it, looked all around and then dropped into it. Not long thereafter another Mexican appeared, this one from San Felippe, and also disappeared into the crevice. As darkness fell Manuel reappeared with something under his jacket and a moment later a light gleamed at the base of a slender sapling which grew on the edge of the canyon wall and leaned out over the abyss. It was cleverly placed, for only at one spot on the Mexican side of the distant Rio Grande could it be seen—the high canyon walls farther down screened it from any one who might be riding on the north bank of the river. In a moment there came an answering twinkle and Manuel, covering the lantern with a blanket, was swallowed up in the darkness of the crevice.

Without a trace of emotion, Dick Martin, from his place of concealment, caught the answering gleam, and he watched Manuel disappear. "Cassidy was right in every point; Lewis or Sayre couldn't 'a' done this better. I hope he won't be late," he muttered, and settled himself more comfortably to wait for the cue for action, smiling as the moon poked its rim over the low hills to his right. "This means promotion for me, or I'm very much mistaken," he chuckled.

Hopalong was not late and as soon as it was dark he and his companions stole into the canyon on foot. They felt their way down the east end of the trail, not far from Dent's, toward the Big Bend, which they gained without a mishap. Johnny was sent up to a place they had noticed and marked in their memories at the time they had rioted down to defy the ghost. He was to stop any one trying to escape up the San Felippe end of the canyon trail, and his confidence in his ability to do this was exuberant. Hopalong and Red slowly and laboriously worked their way down the perilous path leading to the bottom, forded the stream, and crept up the other side, where they found cover not far from a wide crack in the canyon wall. Upon the occasion of their hilarious visit to the Big Bend they had observed that a faint trail led to the crack and had cogitated deeply upon this fact.

Three hours passed before the watchers in and above the canyon were rewarded by anything further; and then a light flickered far down the canyon and close to the edge of the stream. Immediately strange noises were heard and suddenly the ghost swung out of the opening in the rock wall near Hopalong and Red and danced above their heads, while the shrieking which had so frightened Johnny and his horse filled the canyon with uproar and sent Martin wriggling nearer to the crevice which he had watched so closely. The noise soon ceased, but the ghost danced on, and the sound of men stumbling along the rocky ledge bordering the stream became more and more audible. Four were in the party and they all carried bulky loads on their backs and grunted with pleasure and relief as they entered the entrance in the wall. When the last man had disappeared and the noise of their passing had died out, Johnny's rope sailed up and out, and the ghost swayed violently and then began to sag in an unaccountable manner towards the trail as the owner of the rope hitched its free end around a spur of rock and made it fast. Then he feverishly scrambled down the steep path to join his friends.

Hopalong and Red, wriggling on their stomachs towards the crack in the wall, paused in amazement and stared across the canyon; and then the former chuckled and whispered something in his companion's ear. "That was why he lugged his rope along! He's just idiot enough to want a souveneer an' plaything at th' risk of losing th' game. Come on!—they'll tumble to what's up an' get away if we don't hustle."

When the two punchers cautiously and noiselessly entered the crack and felt their way along its rock walls they heard fluent swearing in Spanish by the man who worked the ghost, and who could not understand its sudden ambition to take root. It was made painfully clear to him a moment later when a pair of brawny hands reached out of the darkness behind him and encircled his throat a hand's width below his gleaming cigarette. Another pair used cords with deftness and despatch and he was left by himself to browse upon the gag when all his senses returned.

Hopalong, with Red inconsiderately stepping on his heels, felt his way along the wall of the crevice, alert and silent, his Colt nestling comfortably in his right hand, while the left was pushed out ahead feeling for trouble. As they worked farther away from the canyon distant voices could be heard and they forthwith proceeded even more cautiously. When Hopalong came to the second bend in the narrow passage he peered around it and stopped so abruptly that Red's nose almost spread itself over the back of his head. Red's indignation was all the harder to bear because it must bloom unheard.

In a huge, irregular room, whose roof could not be discerned in the dim light of the few candles, five men were resting in various attitudes of ease as they discussed the events of the night and tried to compute their profits. They were secure, for Manuel, having by this time put away the ghost and megaphone, was on duty at the mouth of the crevice, and he was as sensitive to danger as a hound.

"The risk is not much and the profits are large," remarked Pedro, in Spanish. "We must burn a candle for the repose of the soul of Carlos Martinez. It is he that made our plans safe. And a candle is not much when we—"

"Hands up!" said a quiet voice, followed by grim commands. The Mexicans jumped as if stung by a scorpion, and could just discern two of the rowdy Gringo cow-punchers in the heavy shadows of the opposite wall, but the candle light glinted in rings on the muzzles of their six-shooters. Had Manuel betrayed them? But they had little time or inclination for cogitation regarding Manuel.

"Easy there!" shouted Red, and Pedro's hand stopped when half way to his chest. Pedro was a gambler by nature, but the odds were too heavy and he sullenly obeyed the command.

"Stick 'em up! Stick 'em up! Higher yet, an' hold 'em there," purred a soft voice from the other end of the room, where Dick Martin smiled pleasantly upon them and wondered if there was anything on earth harder to pound good common sense into than a "Mexican's" head. His gun was blue, but it was, nevertheless, the most prominent part of his make-up, even if the light were poor.

One of the Mexicans reached involuntarily for his gun, for he was a gun-man by training; while his companions felt for their knives, deadly weapons in a *mêlée*. Martin, crying, "Watch 'em, Cassidy!" side-stepped and lunged forward with the speed and skill of a boxer, and his hard left hand landed on the point of Juan Alvarez's jaw with a force and precision not to be withstood. But to make more certain that the Mexican would not take part in any possible demonstration of resistance, Martin's right circled up in a short half-hook and stopped against Juan's short ribs. Martin weighed one hundred and eighty pounds and packed no fat on his well-knit frame.

At this moment a two-legged cyclone burst upon the scene in the person of Johnny Nelson, whose rage had been worked up almost to the weeping point because he had lost so much time hunting for the crevice where it was not. Seeing Juan fall, and the glint of knives, he started in to clean things up, yelling, "I'm a ghost! I'm a ghost! Take 'em alive! Take 'em alive!"

Hopalong and Red felt that they were in his way, and taking care of one Mexican between them, while Martin knocked out another, they watched the exits,—for anything was possible in such a chaotic mix-up,—and gave Johnny plenty of room. The latter paused, triumphant, looked around to see if he had missed any, and then advanced upon his friends and shoved his jaw up close to Hopalong's face. "Tried to lose me, didn't you! Wouldn't wait for me, eh! For seven cents an' a toothbrush I'd give you what's left!"

Red grabbed him by trousers and collar and heaved him into the passageway. "Go out an' play with yore souveneer or we'll step on you!"

Johnny sat up, rubbed certain portions of his anatomy, and grinned. "Oh, I've got it, all right! I'm shore

going to take that ghost home an' make some of them
fools *eat* it!"

Martin smiled as he finished tying the last prisoner.
"That's right, Nelson; you've got it on 'em this time. Make
'em chew it."

VI

♦

Hopalong Loses a Horse

For a month after their return from the San Miguel,
Hopalong and his companions worked with renewed zest, and told and retold the other members of the
outfit of their unusual experiences near the Mexican border. Word had come up to them that Martin had secured
the conviction of the smugglers and was in line for immediate advancement. No one on the range had the heart
to meet Johnny Nelson, for Johnny carried with him a
piece of the ghost, and became pugnacious if his once-
jeering friends and acquaintances refused to nibble on it.
Cowan still sold his remarkable drink, but he had yielded
to Johnny's persuasive methods and now called it "Nelson's Pet."

One bright day the outfit started rounding up a small
herd of three-year-olds, which Buck had sold, and by the
end of the week the herd was complete and ready for the
drive. This took two weeks and when Hopalong led his
drive outfit through Hoyt's Corners on its homeward
journey he felt the pull of the town of Grant, some miles
distant, and it was too strong to be resisted. Flinging a
word of explanation to the nearest puncher, he turned to
lope away, when Red's voice checked him. Red wanted
to delay his home-going for a day or two and attend to a

purely personal matter at a ranch lying to the west. Hopalong, knowing the reason for Red's wish, grinned and told him to go, and not to propose until he had thought the matter over very carefully. Red's reply was characteristic, and after arranging a rendezvous and naming the time, the two separated and rode toward their destinations, while the rest of the outfit kept on towards their ranch.

"A man owes something to *all* his friends," Hopalong mused. In this case he owed a return game of draw poker to certain of Grant's leading citizens, and he liked to pay his obligations when opportunity offered.

It was mid-forenoon when he topped a rise and saw below him the handful of shacks making up the town. A look of pleased interest flickered across his face as he noticed a patched and dirty tent pitched close up to the nearest shack. "Show!" he shouted. "Now, ain't that luck! I'll shore take it in. If it's a circus, mebby it has a trick mule to ride—I'll never forget that one up in Kansas City," he grinned. But almost instantly a doubt arose and tempered the grin. "Huh! Mebby it's th' branding chute of some gospel sharp." As he drew near he focussed his eyes on the canvas and found that his fears were justified.

"All Are Welcome," he spelled out slowly. "Shore they are!" he muttered. "I never nowhere saw such hard-working, all-embracing rustlers as them fellers. They'll stick their iron on anything from a wobbly calf or dying dogie to a staggering-with-age mosshead, an' shout 'tally one' with th' same joy. Well, not for mine, *this* trip. I'm going to graze loose an' buck-jump all I wants. Anyhow, if I did let him brand me I'd only backslide in a week," and Hopalong pressed his pony to a more rapid gait as two men emerged from the tent. "There's th' sky-pilot now," he muttered—"an' there's Dave!" he shouted, waving his arm. "Oh, Dave! Dave!"

Dave Wilkes looked up, and his grin of delight threatened to engulf his ears. "Hullo, Cassidy! Glad to see you! Keep right on for th' store—I'll be with you in a minute." When Dave told his companion the visitor's name the evangelist held up his hands eloquently and spoke.

"I know all about him!" he said sorrowfully. "If I can lead him out of his wickedness I will rest content though I save no more souls this fortnight. Is it all true?"

"Huh? What true?"

"All that I have heard about him."

"Well, I dunno what you've heard," replied Dave, with grave caution, "but I reckon it might be if it didn't cover lying, stealing, cowardice, an' such coyote traits. He's shore a holy terror with a short gun, all right, but lemme tell you something mebby you *ain't* heard: There ain't a square man in this part of th' country that won't feel some honored an' proud to be called a friend of Hopalong Cassidy. Them's th' sentiments rampaging hereabouts. I ain't denying that he's gone an' killed off a lot of men first an' last—but th' only trouble there is that he didn't get 'em soon enough. They all had lived too blamed long when they went an' stacked up agin him an' that lightning short gun of hissn. But, say, if yo're calculating to tackle him at yore game, lead him gentle—don't push none. He comes to life real sudden when he's shoved. So long; see you later, mebby."

The revivalist looked after him and mused, "I hope I was informed wrong, but this much I have to be thankful for: The wickedness of most of these men, these overgrown children, is manly, stalwart, and open; few of them are vicious or contemptible. Their one great curse is drink."

When Hopalong entered the store he was vociferously welcomed by two men, and the proprietor joining them, the circle was complete. When the conversation threatened to repeat itself cards were brought and the next two hours passed very rapidly. They were expensive hours to the Bar-20 puncher, who finally arose with an apologetic grin and slapped his thigh significantly.

"Well, you've got it all; I'm busted wide open, except for a measly dollar, an' I shore hopes you don't want that," he laughed. "You play a whole lot better than you did th' last time I was here. I've got to move along. I'm going east an' see Wallace an' from there I've got to meet Red an' ride home with him. But you come down an' see us when you can—it's *me* that wants revenge this time."

"Huh; you'll be wanting it worse than ever if we do," smiled Dave.

"Say, Hoppy," advised Tom Lawrence, "better drop in an' hear th' sky-pilot's palaver before you go. It'll do you a whole lot of good, an' it can't do you no harm, anyhow."

"You going?" asked Hopalong suspiciously.

"Can't—got too much work to do," quickly responded Tom, his brother Art nodding happy confirmation.

"Huh; I reckoned so!" snorted Hopalong sarcastically, as he shook hands all around. "You all know where to find us—drop in an' see us when you get down our way," he invited.

"Sorry you can't stay longer, Cassidy," remarked Dave, as his friend mounted. "But come up again soon—an' be shore to tell all the boys we was asking for 'em," he called.

Considering the speed with which Hopalong started for Wallace's, he might have been expecting a relay of "quarter" horses to keep it going, but he pulled up short at the tent. Such inconsistency is trying to the temper of the best-mannered horse, and this particular animal was not in the least good-mannered, wherefore its rider was obliged to soothe its resentment in his own peculiar way, listening meanwhile to the loud and impassioned voice of the evangelist haranguing his small audience.

"I wonder," said Hopalong, glancing through the door, "if them friends of mine reckon I'm any ascared to go in that tent? Huh, I'll just show 'em, anyhow!" whereupon he dismounted, flung the reins over his horse's head, and strode through the doorway.

The nearest seat, a bench made by placing a bottom board of the evangelist's wagon across two up-ended boxes, was close enough to the exhorter and he dropped onto it and glanced carelessly at his nearest neighbor. The carelessness went out of his bearing as his eyes fastened themselves in a stare on the man's neck-kerchief. Hopalong was hardened to awful sights and at best his was not an artistic soul, but the villainous riot of fiery crimson, gaudy yellow, and pugnacious and domineering green which flaunted defiance and insolence from the stranger's neck caused his breath to hang over one count and then come doubly strong at the next exhalation. "Gee whiz!" he whispered.

The stranger slowly turned his head and looked coldly upon the impudent disturber of his reverent reflections. "Meaning?" he questioned, with an upward slant in his voice. The neck-kerchief seemed to grow suddenly malignant and about to spring. "Meaning?" repeated the other with great insolence, while his eyes looked a challenge.

While Hopalong's eyes left the scrambled color-insult and tried to banish the horrible afterimage, his mind groped for the rules of etiquette governing free fist fights in gospel tents, and while he hesitated as to whether he should dent the classic profile of the color-bearer or just twist his nose as a sign of displeasure, the voice of the evangelist arose to a roar and thundered out. Hopalong ducked instinctively.

"—Stop! Stop before it is too late, before death takes

you in the wallow of your sins! Repent and gain salvation—"

Hopalong felt relieved, but his face retained its expression of childlike innocence even after he realized that he was not being personally addressed; and he glanced around. It took him ninety-seven seconds to see everything there was to be seen, and his eyes were drawn irresistibly back to the stranger's kerchief. "Awful! Awful thing for a drinking man to wear, or run up against unexpectedly!" he muttered, blinking. "Worse than snakes," he added thoughtfully.

"Look ahere, you—" began the owner of the offensive decoration, if it might be called such, but the evangelist drowned his voice in another flight of eloquence.

"—*Peace! Peace* is the message of the Lord to His children," roared the voice from the upturned soap box, and when the speaker turned and looked in the direction of the two men-with-a-difference he found them sitting up very straight and apparently drinking in his words with great relish; whereupon he felt that he was making gratifying progress toward the salvation of their spotted souls. He was very glad, indeed, that he had been so grievously misinformed about the personal attributes of one Hopalong Cassidy,—glad and thankful.

"Death cometh as a thief in the night," the voice went on. "Think of the friends who have gone before; who were well one minute and gone the next! And it must come to all of us, to all of us, to me and to you—"

The man with the afflicted neck started rocking the bench.

"Something is coming to somebody purty soon," murmured Hopalong. He began to sidle over towards his neighbor, his near hand doubled up into a huge knot of protuberant knuckles and white-streaked fingers; but as he was about to deliver his hint that he was greatly displeased at the antics of the bench, a sob came to his ears. Turning his head swiftly, he caught sight of the stranger's face, and sorrow was marked so strongly upon it that the sight made Hopalong gape. His hand opened slowly and he cautiously sidled back again, disgruntled, puzzled, and vexed at himself for having strayed into a game where he was so hopelessly at sea. He thought it all over carefully and then gave it up as being too deep for him to solve. But he determined one thing: He was not going to leave before the other man did, anyhow.

"An' if I catch that howling kerchief outside," he muttered, smacking his lips with satisfaction at what was in store for it. His visit to Wallace was not very important, anyway, and it could wait on more important events.

"There sits a sinner!" thundered out the exhorter, and Hopalong looked stealthily around for a sight of the villain. "God only has the right to punish. 'Vengeance is mine,' saith the Lord, and whosoever takes the law into his own hands, whosoever takes human life, defies the Creator. There sits a man who has killed his fellow-men, his brothers! Are you not a sinner, *Cassidy*?"

Cassidy jumped clear of the bench as he jerked his head around and stared over the suddenly outstretched arm and pointing finger of the speaker and into his accusing eyes.

"Answer me! Are you not a sinner?"

Hopalong stood up, confused, bewildered, and then his suspended thoughts stirred and formed. "Guilty, I reckon, an' in th' first degree. But they didn't get no more'n what was coming to 'em, no more'n they earned. An' that's straight!"

"How do you know they didn't? How do you know they earned it? How do you *know*?" demanded the evangelist, who was delighted with the chance to argue with a sinner. He had great faith in "personal contact," and his was the assurance of training, of the man well rehearsed and fully prepared. And he knew that if he should be pinned into a corner by logic and asked for *his* proofs, that he could squirm out easily and take the offensive again by appealing to faith, the last word in sophistry, and a greater and more powerful weapon than intelligence. *This* was his game, and it was fixed; he could not lose if he could arouse enough interest in a man to hold him to the end of the argument. He continued to drive, to crowd. "What right have you to think so? What right have you to judge them? Have you divine insight? Are you inspired? 'Judge not lest ye be judged,' saith the Lord, and you *dare* to fly in the face of that great command!"

"You've got me picking th' pea in *this* game, all right," responded Hopalong, dropping back on the bench. "But lemme tell you one thing: Command or no command, devine or not devine, I know when a man has lived too long, an' when he's going to try to get me. An' all th' gospel sharps south of heaven can't stop me from handing a thief what he's earned. Go on with th' show, but count me out."

While the evangelist warmed to the attack, vaguely realizing that he had made a mistake in not heeding Dave Wilkes' tip, Hopalong became conscious of a sense of relief stealing over him and he looked around wonderingly for the cause. The man with the kerchief had "folded his tents" and departed; and Hopalong, heaving a sigh of satisfaction, settled himself more comfortably and gave real attention to the discourse, although he did not reply to the warm and eloquent man on the soap box. Suddenly he sat up with a start as he remembered that he had a long and hard ride before him if he wished to see Wallace, and arising, strode towards the exit, his chest up and his chin thrust out. The only reply he made to the excited and personal remarks of the revivalist was to stop at the door and drop his last dollar into the yeast box before passing out.

For a moment he stood still and pondered, his head too full of what he had heard to notice that anything out of the ordinary had happened. Although the evangelist had adopted the wrong method he had gained more than he knew and Hopalong had something to take home with him and wrestle out for himself in spare moments; that is, he would have had but for one thing: As he slowly looked around for his horse he came to himself with a sharp jerk, and hot profanity routed the germ of religion incubating in his soul. His horse was missing! Here was a pretty mess, he thought savagely; and then his expression of anger and perplexity gave way to a flickering grin as the probable solution came to his mind.

"By th' Lord, I never saw such a bunch to play jokes," he laughed. "Won't they never grow up? They was watching me when I went inside an' sneaked up and rustled my cayuse. Well, I'll get it back again without much trouble, all right. They ought to know me better by this time.

"Hey, stranger!" he called to a man who was riding past, "have you seen anything of a skinny roan cayuse fifteen han's high, white stocking on th' near foreleg, an' a bandage on th' off fetlock, Bar-20 being th' brand?"

The stranger, knowing the grinning inquisitor by sight, suspected that a joke was being played; he also knew Dave Wilkes and that gentleman's friends. He chuckled and determined to help it along a little. "Shore did, pardner; saw a man leading him real cautious. Was he yourn?"

"Oh, no; not at all. He belonged to my great-great-grandfather, who left him to my second cousin. You see, I borrowed it," he grinned, making his way leisurely towards the general store, kept by his friend Dave, the joker. "Funny how everybody likes a joke," he muttered, opening the door of the store. "Hey, Dave," he called.

Mr. Wilkes wheeled suddenly and stared. "Why, I thought you was half-way to Wallace's by now!" he exclaimed. "Did you come back to lose that lone dollar?"

"Oh, I lost that too. But yo're a real smart cuss, now ain't you?" queried Hopalong, his eyes twinkling and his face wreathed with good humor. "An' how innocent you act, too. Thought you could scare me, didn't you? Thought I'd go tearing 'round this fool town like a house afire, hey? Well, I reckon you can guess again. Now, I'm owning up that th' joke's on me, so you hand over my cayuse, an' I'll make up for lost time."

Dave Wilkes' face expressed several things, but surprise was dominant. "Why, I ain't even seen yore ol' cayuse, you chump! Last time I saw it you was on him, goin' like th' devil. Did somebody pull you off it an' take it away from you?" he demanded with great sarcasm. "Is somebody abusing you?"

Hopalong bit into a generous handful of dried apricots, chewed complacently for a moment, and replied: "'At's aw right; I wan' my c'use." Swallowing hastily, he continued: "I want it, an' I've come to th' right place for it, too. Hand it over, David."

"Dod blast it, I tell you I ain't got it!" retorted Dave, beginning to suspect that something was radically wrong. "I ain't seen it, an' I don't know nothing about it."

Hopalong wiped his mouth with his sleeve. "Well, then, Tom or Art does, all right."

"No, they don't, neither; I watched 'em leave an' they rode straight out of town, an' went th' other way, same as they allus do." Dave was getting irritated. "Look here, you; are you joking or drunk, or both, or is that animule of yourn really missing?"

"Huh!" snorted Hopalong, trying some new prunes. "'Ese prunes er purty good," he mumbled, in grave congratulation. "I don' get prunes like 'ese very of'n."

"I reckon you don't! They ought to be good! Cost me thirty cents a half-pound," Dave retorted with asperity, anxiously shifting his feet. It didn't take much of a loss to wipe out a day's profits with him.

"An' I don't reckon you paid none too much for 'em, at that," Mr. Cassidy responded, nodding his head in comprehension. "Ain't no worms in 'em, is there?"

"Shore there is!" exploded Dave. "Plumb full of 'em!"

"You don't say! Hardly know whether to take a chance with th' worms or try th' apricots. Ain't no worms in them, anyhow. But when am I going to get my cayuse? I've got a long way to go, an' delay is costly—how much did you say these yaller fellers cost?" he asked significantly, trying another handful of apricots.

"On th' dead level, cross my heart an' hope to die, but I ain't seen yore cayuse since you left here," earnestly replied Dave. "If you don't know where it is, then somebody went an' lifted it. It looks like it's up to you to do some hunting, 'stead of cultivating a belly-ache at *my* expense. *I* ain't trying to keep you, God knows!"

Hopalong glanced out of the window as he considered, and saw, entering the saloon, the same puncher who had confessed to seeing his horse. "Hey, Dave; wait a minute!" and he dashed out of the store and made good time towards the liquid refreshment parlor. Dave promptly nailed the covers on the boxes of prunes and apricots and leaned innocently against the cracker box to await results, thinking hard all the while. It looked like a plain case of horse-stealing to him.

"Stranger," cried Hopalong, bouncing into the barroom, "where did you see that cayuse of mine?"

"Th' ancient relic of yore fambly was aheading towards Hoyt's Corners," the stranger replied, grinning broadly. "It's a long walk. Have something before you starts?"

"Damn th' walk! Who was riding him?"

"Nobody at all."

"What do you mean?"

"He wasn't being rid when I saw him."

"Hang it, man; that cayuse was stole from me!"

"Somewhat in th' nature of a calamity, now ain't it?" smiled the stranger, enjoying his contributions to the success of the joke.

"You bet yore life it is!" shouted Hopalong, growing red and then pale. "You tell me who was leading him, understand?"

"Well, I couldn't see his face, honest I couldn't," replied the stranger. "Every time I tried it I was shore blinded by th' most awful an' horrible neck-kerchief I've ever had th' hard luck to lay my eyes on. Of all th' drunks I ever met, them there colors was— Hey! Wait a minute!" he shouted at Hopalong's back.

"Dave, gimme yore cayuse an' a rifle—quick!" cried Hopalong from the middle of the street as he ran towards the store. "Hypocrite son-of-a-hoss-thief went an' run mine off. Might 'a' knowed nobody but a thief could wear such a kerchief!"

"I'm with you!" shouted Dave, leading the way on a run towards the corral in the rear of his store.

"No, you ain't with me, neither!" replied Hopalong, deftly saddling. "This ain't no plain hoss-thief case—it's a private grudge. See you later, mebby," and he was pacing a cloud of dust towards the outskirts of the town.

Dave looked after him. "Well, that feller has shore got a big start on you, but he can't keep ahead of that Doll of mine for very long. She can out-run anything in these parts. 'Sides, Cassidy's cayuse looked sort of done up, while mine's as fresh as a bird. That thief will get what's coming to him, all right."

VII

♦

Mr. Cassidy Cogitates

While Hopalong tried to find his horse, Ben Ferris pushed forward, circling steadily to the east and away from the direction of Hoyt's Corners, which was as much a menace to his health and happiness as the town of Grant, twenty miles to his rear. If he could have been certain that no danger was nearer to him than these two towns, he would have felt vastly relieved, even if his horse were not fresh. During the last hour he had not urged it as hard as he had in the beginning of his flight and it had dropped to a walk for minutes at a stretch. This was not because he felt that he had plenty of time, but for the reason that he understood horses and could not afford to exhaust his mount so early in the chase. He glanced back from time to time as if fearing what might be on his trail, and well he might fear. According to all the traditions and customs of the range, both of which he knew well, somewhere between him and Grant was a posse of hard-riding cow-punchers, all anxious and eager for a glance at him over their sights. In his mind's eye he could see them, silent, grim, tenacious, reeling off the miles on that distance-eating lope. He had stolen a horse, and that meant death if they caught him. He loosened his gaudy kerchief and gulped in fear, not of what pursued, but of what was miles before him. His own saddle, strapped behind the one he sat in, bumped against him with each reach of the horse and had already made his back sore—but he must endure it for a time. Never in all his life had minutes been so precious.

Another hour passed and the horse seemed to be doing

well, much better than he had hoped—he would rest it for a few minutes at the next water while he drank his fill and changed the bumping saddle. As he rounded a turn and entered a heavily grassed valley he saw a stream close at hand and, leaping off, fixed the saddle first. As he knelt to drink he caught a movement and jumped up to catch his mount. Time after time he almost touched it, but it evaded him and kept up the game, cropping a mouthful of grass during each respite.

"All right!" he muttered as he let it eat. "I'll get my drink while you eat an' then I'll get you!"

He knelt by the stream again and drank long and deep. As he paused for breath something made him leap up and to one side, reaching for his Colt at the same instant. His fingers found only leather and he swore fiercely as he remembered—he had sold the Colt for food and kept the rifle for defence. As he faced the rear a horseman rounded the turn and the fugitive, wheeling, dashed for the stolen horse forty yards away, where his rifle lay in its saddle sheath. But an angry command and the sharp hum of a bullet fired in front of him checked his flight and he stopped short and swore.

"I reckon th' jig's up," remarked Mr. Cassidy, balancing the up-raised Colt with nicety and indifference.

"Yes; I reckon so," sullenly replied the other, tears coming into his eyes.

"Well, I'm damned!" snorted Hopalong with cutting contempt. "Cryin' like a li'l baby! Got nerve enough to steal my cayuse, an' then go an' beller like a lost calf when I catch you. Yo're a fine specimen of a hoss-thief, I don't think!"

"Yo're a liar!" retorted the other, clenching his fists and growing red.

Mr. Cassidy's mouth opened and then clicked shut as his Colt swung down. But he did not shoot; something inside of him held his trigger finger and he swore instead. The idea of a man stealing his horse, being caught red-handed and unarmed, and still possessed of sufficient courage to call his captor a name never tolerated or overlooked in that country! And the idea that he, Hopalong Cassidy, of the Bar-20, could not shoot such a thief! "Damn that sky pilot! He's shore gone an' made me loco," he muttered, savagely, and then addressed his prisoner. "Oh, you ain't crying? Wind got in yore eyes, I reckon, an' sort of made 'em leak a little—that it? Or mebby them unholy green roses an' yaller grass on that blasted fool neck-kerchief of yourn are too much for *your* eyes, too!"

"Look ahere!" snapped the man on the ground, stepping forward, one fist upraised. "I came nigh onto licking you this noon in that gospel sharp's tent for making fun of that scarf, an' I'll do it yet if you get any smart about it! You mind yore own business an' close yore fool eyes if you don't like my clothes!"

"Say! You ain't no cry-baby after all. Hanged if I even think yo're a real genuine hoss-thief!" enthused Mr. Cassidy. "You act like a twin brother; but what th' devil ever made you steal that cayuse, anyhow?"

"An' that's none of yore business, neither; but I'll tell you, just th' same," replied the thief. "I had to have it; that's why. I'll fight you rough-an'-tumble to see if I keep it, or if you take th' cayuse an' shoot me besides: is it a go?"

Hopalong stared at him and then a grin struggled for life, got it, and spread slowly over his tanned countenance. "Yore gall is refreshing! Damned if it ain't worse than th' scarf. Here, you tell me what made you take a chance like stealing a cayuse this noon—I'm getting to like you, bad as you are, hanged if I ain't!"

"Oh, what's th' use?" demanded the other, tears again

coming into his eyes. "You'll think I'm lying an' trying to crawl out—an' I won't do neither."

"*I* didn't say *you* was a liar," replied Hopalong. "It was th' other way about. Reckon you can try me, anyhow; can't you?"

"Yes; I s'pose so," responded the other, slowly, and in a milder tone of voice. "An' when I called you that I was mad an' desperate. I was hasty—you see, my wife's dying, or dead, over in Winchester. I was riding hard to get to her before it was too late when my cayuse stepped into a hole just th' other side of Grant—you know what happened. I shot th' animal, stripped off my saddle an' hoofed it to town, an' dropped into that gospel dealer's layout to see if he could make me feel any better—which he could not. I just couldn't stand his palaver about death an' slipped out. I was going to lay for you an' lick you for th' way you acted about this scarf—had to do something or go loco. But when I got outside there was yore cayuse, all saddled an' ready to go. I just up an' threw my saddle on it, followed suit with myself an' was ten miles out of town before I realized just what I'd done. But th' realizing part of it didn't make no difference to me—I'd 'a' done it just th' same if I had stopped to think it over. That's flat, an' straight. I've got to get to that li'l woman as quick as I can, an' I'd steal all th' cayuses in th' whole damned country if they'd do me any good. That's all of it—take it or leave it. I put it up to you. That's yore cayuse, but you ain't going to get it without fighting me for it! If you shoot me down without giving me a chance, all right! I'll cut a throat for that wore-out bronch!"

Hopalong was buried in thought and came to himself just in time to cover the other and stop him not six feet away. "Just a minute, before you make me shoot you! I want to think about it."

"Damn that gun!" swore the fugitive, nervously shifting his feet and preparing to spring. "We'd 'a' been fighting by this time if it wasn't for that!"

"You stand still or I'll blow you apart," retorted Hopalong, grimly. "A man's got a right to think, ain't he? An' if I had somebody here to mind these guns so you couldn't sneak 'em on me I'd fight you so blamed quick that you'd be licked before you knew you was at it. But we ain't going to fight—*stand still!* You ain't got no show at all when yo're dead!"

"Then you gimme that cayuse—my God, man! Do you know th' hell I've been through for th' last two days? Got th' word up at Daly's Crossing an' ain't slept since. I'll go loco if th' strain lasts much longer! She asking for me, begging to see me: an' me, like a damned idiot, wasting time out here talking to another. Ride with me, behind me—it's only forty miles more—tie me to th' saddle an' blow me to pieces if you find I'm lying—do anything you wants; but let me get to Winchester before dark!"

Hopalong was watching him closely and at the end of the other's outburst threw back his head. "I reckon I'm a plain fool, a jackass; but I don't care. I'll rope that cayuse for you. You come along to save time," Hopalong ordered, spurring forward. His borrowed rope sailed out, tightened, and in a moment he was working at the saddle. "Here, you; I'm going to swap mounts with you—this one is fresher an' faster." He had his own saddle off and the other on in record time, and stepped back. "There; don't stand there like a fool—wake up an' hustle! I might change my mind—that's th' way to move! Gimme that neck-kerchief for a souveneer, an' get out. Send that cayuse back to Dave Wilkes, at Grant—it's hissn. Don't thank me; just gimme that scarf an' ride like th' devil."

The other, already mounted, tore the kerchief from his

throat and handed it quickly to his benefactor. "If you ever want a man to take you out of hell, send to Winchester for Ben Ferris—that's me. So long!"

Mr. Cassidy sat on his saddle where he had dropped it after making the exchange and looked after the galloping horseman, and when a distant rise had shut him from sight, turned his eyes on the scarf in his hand and cogitated. Finally, with a long-drawn sigh he arose, and, placing the scarf on the ground, caught and saddled his horse. Riding gloomily back to where the riot of color fluttered on the grass he drew his Colt and sent six bullets through it with a great amount of satisfaction. Not content with the damage he had inflicted, he leaned over and swooped it up. Riding further he also swooped up a stone and tied the kerchief around it, and then stood up in his stirrups and drew back his arm with critical judgment. He sat quietly for a time after the gaudy missile had disappeared into the stream and then, wheeling, cantered away. But he did not return to the town of Grant—he lacked the nerve to face Dave Wilkes and tell his childish and improbable story. He would ride on and meet Red as they had agreed; a letter would do for Mr. Wilkes, and after he had broken the shock in that manner he could pay him a personal visit sometime soon. Dave would never believe the story and when it was told Hopalong wanted to have the value of the horse in his trousers pocket. Of course, Ben Ferris *might* have told the truth and he might return the horse according to directions. Hopalong emerged from his reverie long enough to appeal to his mount:

"Bronch, I've been thinking: am I or am I not a jackass?"

VIII

♦

Red Brings Trouble

After a night spent on the plain and a cigarette for his breakfast, Hopalong, grouchy and hungry, rode slowly to the place appointed for his meeting with Red, but Mr. Connors was over two hours late. It was now mid-forenoon and Hopalong occupied his time for a while by riding out fancy designs on the sand; but he soon tired of this makeshift diversion and grew petulant. Red's tardiness was all the worse because the erring party to the agreement had turned in his saddle at Hoyt's Corners and loosed a flippant and entirely uncalled-for remark about his friend's ideas regarding appointments.

"Well, that red-headed Romeo is shore late this time," Hopalong muttered. "Why don't he find a girl closer to home, anyhow? Thank th' Lord I ain't got no use for shell games of any kind. Here I am, without anything to eat an' no prospects of anything, sitting up on this locoed layout like a sore thumb, an' can't move without hitting myself! An' it'll be late to-day before I can get any grub, too. Oh, well," he sighed, "I ain't in love, so things might be a whole lot worse with me. An' he ain't in love, neither, only he won't listen to reason. He gets mad an' calls me a sage hen an' says I'm stuck on myself because some fool told me I had brains."

He laughed as he pictured the object of his friend's affections. "Huh; anybody that got one good, square look at her wouldn't ever accuse him of having brains. But he'll forget her in a month. That was th' life of his last hobbling fit an' it was th' worst he ever had."

Grinning at his friend's peculiarly human characteristics he leaned back in the saddle and felt for tobacco and papers. As he finished pouring the chopped alfalfa into the paper he glanced up and saw a mounted man top the skyline of the distant hills and shoot down the slope at full speed.

"I knowed it: started three hours late an' now he's trying to make it up in th' last mile," Hopalong muttered, dexterously spreading the tobacco along the groove and quickly rolling the cigarette. Lighting it he looked up again and saw that the horseman was wildly waving a sombrero.

"Huh! Wigwagging for forgiveness," laughed the man who waited. "Old son-of-a-gun, I'd wait a week if I had some grub, an' he knows it. Couldn't get mad at him if I tried."

Mr. Connors' antics now became frantic and he shouted something at the top of his voice. His friend spurred his mount. "Come on, bronch; wake up. His girl said 'yes' an' now he wants me to get him out of his trouble." Whereupon he jogged forward. "What's that?" he shouted, sitting up very straight. "What's that?"

Red energetically swept the sombrero behind him and pointed to the rear. "War-whoops! W-a-r w-h-o-o-p-s! Injuns, you chump!" Mr. Connors appeared to be mildly exasperated.

"Yes?" sarcastically rejoined Mr. Cassidy in his throat, and then shouted in reply: "Love an' liquor don't mix very well in you. Wake up! Come out of it!"

"That's straight—I mean it!" cried Mr. Connors, close enough now to save the remainder of his lungs. "It's a bunch of young bucks on their first war-trail, I reckon. 'T ain't Geronimo, all right; I wouldn't be here now if it was. Three of 'em chased me an' th' two that are left are coming hot-foot somewhere th' other side of them hills. They act sort of mad, too."

"Mebby they ain't acting at all," cheerily replied his

companion. "An' then that's th' way you got that graze, eh?" pointing to a bloody furrow on Mr. Connors' cheek. "But just th' same it looks like th' trail left by a woman's finger nail."

"Finger nail nothing," retorted Mr. Connors, flushing a little. "But, for God's sake, are you going to sit here like a wart on a dead dog an' wait for 'em?" he demanded with a rising inflection. "Do you reckon yo're running a dance, or a party, or something like that?"

"How many?" placidly inquired Mr. Cassidy, gazing intently towards the high sky-line of the distant hills.

"Two—an' I won't tell you again, neither!" snapped the owner of the furrowed cheek. "Th' others are 'way behind now—but we're standing *still!*"

"Why didn't you say there was others?" reproved Hopalong. "Naturally I didn't see no use of getting all het up just because two sprouted papooses feel like crowding us a bit; it wouldn't be none of *our* funeral, would it?" and the indignant Mr. Cassidy hurriedly dismounted and hid his horse in a nearby chaparral and returned to his companion at a run.

"Red, gimme yore Winchester an' then hustle on for a ways, have an accident, fall off yore cayuse, an' act scared to death, if you know how. It's that little trick Buck told us about, an' it shore ought to work fine here. We'll see if two infant feather-dusters can lick th' Bar-20. Get a-going!"

They traded rifles, Hopalong taking the repeater in place of the single-shot gun he carried, and Red departed as bidden, his face gradually breaking into an enthusiastic grin as he ruminated upon the plan. "Level-headed old cuss; he's a wonder when it comes to planning or fighting. An' lucky,—well, I reckon!"

Hopalong ran forward for a short distance and slid down the steep bank of a narrow arroyo and waited, the repeater thrust out through the dense fringe of grass and shrubs which bordered the edge. When settled to his complete satisfaction and certain that he was effectually screened from the sight of any one in front of him, he arose on his toes and looked around for his companion, and laughed. Mr. Connors was bending very dejectedly apparently over his prostrate horse, but in reality was swearing heartily at the ignorant quadruped because it strove with might and main to get its master's foot off its head so it could arise. The man in the arroyo turned again and watched the hills and it was not long before he saw two Indians burst into view over the crest and gallop towards his friend. They were not to be blamed because they did not know the pursued had joined a friend, for the second trail was yet some distance in front of them.

"Pair of budding warriors, all right; an' awful important. Somebody must 'a' told *them* they had brains," Mr. Cassidy muttered. "They're just at th' age when they knows it all an' have to go 'round raising hell all th' time. Wonder when they jumped th' reservation."

The Indians, seeing Mr. Connors arguing with his prostrate horse, and taking it for granted that he was not stopping for pleasure or to view the scenery, let out a yell and dashed ahead at greater speed, at the same time separating so as to encircle him and attack him front and rear at the same time. They had a great amount of respect for cowboys.

This maneuver was entirely unexpected and clashed violently with Mr. Cassidy's plan of procedure, so two irate punchers swore heartily at their rank stupidity in not counting on it. Of course everybody that knew anything at all about such warfare knew that they would do just such a thing, which made it all the more bitter. But Red had cultivated the habit of thinking quickly and he saw at once that the remedy lay with him; he astonished

the exultant savages by straddling his disgruntled horse
as it scrambled to its feet and galloping away from them,
bearing slightly to the south, because he wished to lure
his pursuers to ride closer to his anxious and eager friend.

This action was a success, for the yelling warriors,
slowing perceptibly because of their natural astonishment at the resurrection and speed of an animal regarded
as dead or useless, spurred on again, drawing closer together, and along the chord of the arc made by Mr. Connors' trail. Evidently the fool white man was either crazy
or had original and startling ideas about the way to rest a
horse when hard pressed, which pleased them much,
since he had lost so much time. The pleasures of the war-
trail would be vastly greater if all white men had similar
ideas.

Hopalong, the light of fighting burning strong in his
eyes, watched them sweep nearer and nearer, splendid
examples of their type and seeming to be a part of their
mounts. Then two shots rang out in quick succession and
a cloud of pungent smoke arose lazily from the edge of
the arroyo as the warriors fell from their mounts not sixty
yards from the hidden marksman.

Mr. Connors' rifle spat fire once to make assurance
doubly sure and he hastily rejoined his friend as that person climbed out of the arroyo.

"Huh! They must have been half-breeds!" snorted Red
in great disgust, watching his friend shed sand from his
clothes. "I allus opined that 'Paches was too blamed slick
to bite on a game like that."

"Well, they are purty 'lusive animals, 'Paches; but there
are exceptions," replied Hopalong, smiling at the success
of their scheme. "Them two ain't 'Paches—they're th' exceptions. But let me tell you that's a good game, just th'
same. It is as long as they don't see th' second trail in
time. Didn't Buck and Skinny get two that way?"

"Yes, I reckon so. But what'll we do now? What's th' next play?" asked Red, hurriedly, his eyes searching the sky-line of the hills. "Th' rest of th' coyotes will be here purty soon, an' they'll be madder than ever now. An' you better gimme back that gun, too."

"Take yore old gun—who wants th' blamed thing, anyhow?" Hopalong demanded, throwing the weapon at his friend as he ran to bring up the hidden horse. When he returned he grinned pleasantly. "Why, we'll go on like we was greased for calamity, that's what we'll do. Did you reckon we was going to play leap-frog around here an' wait for th' rest of them paintshops, like a blamed fool pair of idiots?"

"I didn't know what *you* might do, remembering how you acted when I met you," retorted Red, shifting his cartridge belt so the empty loops were behind and out of the way. "But I shore knowed what we ought to do, all right."

"Well, mebby you also know how many's headed this way; do you?"

"You've got me stumped there; but there's a round dozen, anyway," Red replied. "You see, th' three that chased me were out scouting ahead of th' main bunch; an' I didn't have no time to take no blasted census."

"Then we've got to hit th' home trail, an' hit it hard. Wind up that four-laigged excuse of yourn, an' take my dust," Hopalong responded, leading the way. "If we can get home there'll be a lot of disgusted braves hitting th' high spots on th' back trail trying to find a way out. Buck an' th' rest of th' boys will be a whole lot pleased, too. We can muster thirty men in two hours if we gets to Buckskin, an' that's twenty more than we'll need."

"Tell you one thing, Hoppy; we can get as far as Powers' old ranch house, an' that's shore," replied Red, thoughtfully.

"Yas!" exploded his companion in scorn and pity.
"That old sieve of a shack ain't good enough for *me* to
die in, no matter what you think about it. Why, it's as
full of holes as a stiff hat in a *mêlée*. Yo're on th' wrong
trail: think again."

Mr. Cassidy objected not because he believed that
Powers' old ranch house was unworthy of serious consideration as a place of refuge and defence, but for the
reason that he wished to reach Buckskin so his friends
might all get in on the treat. Times were very dull on the
ranch, and this was an occasion far too precious to let
slip by. Besides, he then would have the pleasure of leading his friends against the enemy and battling on even
terms. If he sought shelter he and Red would have to
fight on the defensive, which was a game he hated cordially because it put him in a relatively subordinate position and thereby hurt his pride.

"Let me tell you that it's a whole lot better than thin
air with a hard-working circle around us—an' you know
what that means," retorted Mr. Connors. "But if you don't
want to take a chance in th' shack, why mebby we can
make Wallace's, or th' Cross-O-Cross. That is, if we don't
get turned out of our way."

"We don't head for no Cross-O-Cross or Wallace's,"
rejoined his friend with emphasis, "an' we won't waste
no time in Powers' shack, neither; we'll push right through
as hard as we can go for Buckskin. Let them fellers find
their own hunting—our outfit comes first. An' besides
that'll mean a detour in a country fine for ambushes.
We'd never get through."

"Well, have it yore own way, then!" snapped Red.
"You allus was a hard-headed old mule, anyhow." In his
heart Red knew that Hopalong was right about Wallace's
and the Cross-O-Cross.

Some time after the two punchers had quitted the

scene of their trap, several Apaches loped up, read the story of the tragedy at a glance, and galloped on in pursuit. They had left the reservation a fortnight before under the able leadership of that veteran of many wartrails—Black Bear. Their leader, chafing at inaction and sick of the monotony of reservation life, had yielded to the entreaties of a score of restless young men and slipped away at their head, eager for the joys of raiding and plundering. But instead of stealing horses and murdering isolated whites as they had expected, they met with heavy repulses and were now without the mind of their leader. They had fled from one defeat to another and twice had barely eluded the cavalry which pursued them. Now two more of their dwindling force were dead and another had been found but an hour before. Rage and ferocity seethed in each savage heart and they determined to get the puncher they had chased, and that other whose trail they now saw for the first time. They would place at least one victory against the string of their defeats, and at any cost. Whips rose and fell and the warparty shot forward in a compact group, two scouts thrown ahead to feel the way.

Red and Hopalong rode on rejoicing, for there were three less Apaches loose in the Southwest for the inhabitants to swear about and fear, and there was an excellent chance of more to follow. The Southwest had no toleration for the Government's policy of dealing with the Indians and derived a great amount of satisfaction every time an Apache was killed. It still clung to the timehonored belief that the only good Indian was a dead one. Mr. Cassidy voiced his elation and then rubbed an empty stomach in vain regret,—when a bullet shrilled past his head, so unexpectedly as to cause him to duck instinctively and then glance apologetically at his red-haired friend; and both spurred their mounts to greater speed.

Next Mr. Connors grabbed frantically at his perforated sombrero and grew petulant and loquacious.

"Both them shots was lucky, Hoppy; th' feller that fired at me did it on th' dead run; but that won't help us none if one of 'em connects with us. You gimme that Sharps—got to show 'em that they're taking big chances crowding us this way." He took the heavy rifle and turned in the saddle. "It's an even thousand, if it's a yard. He don't look very big, can't hardly tell him from his cayuse; an' th' wind's puffy. Why don't you dirty or rust this gun? Th' sun glitters all along th' barrel. Well, here goes."

"Missed by a mile," reproved Hopalong, who would have been stunned by such a thing as a hit under the circumstances, even if his good-shooting friend had made it.

"Yes! Missed th' coyote I aimed for, but I got th' cayuse of his off pardner; see it?"

"Talk about luck!"

"That's all right: it takes blamed good shooting to miss that close in this case. Look! It's slowed 'em up a bit, an' that's about all I hoped to do. Bet they think I'm a real, shore-'nuff medicine-man. Now gimme another cartridge."

"I will not; no use wasting lead at this range. We'll need all th' cartridges we got before we get out of this hole. You can't do nothing without stopping—an' that takes time."

"Then I'll stop! Th' blazes with th' time! Gimme another, d 'ye hear?"

Mr. Cassidy heard, complied, and stopped beside his companion, who was very intent upon the matter at hand. It took some figuring to make a hit when the range was so great and the sun so blinding and the wind so capricious. He lowered the rifle and peered through the smoke at the confusion he had caused by dropping the nearest warrior. He was said to be the best rifle shot in the Southwest, which means a great deal, and his enemies did not deny it. But since the Sharps shot a special cartridge and was reliable up to the limit of its sight gauge, a matter of eighteen hundred yards, he did not regard the hit as anything worthy of especial mention. Not so his friend, who grinned joyously and loosed his admiration.

"Yo're a shore wonder with that gun, Red! Why don't you lose that repeater an' get a gun like mine? Lord, if I could use a rifle like you, I wouldn't have that gun of yourn for a gift. Just look at what you did with it! Please get one like it."

"I'm plumb satisfied with th' repeater," replied Red. "I don't miss very often at eight hundred with it, an' that's long enough range for most anybody. An' if I do miss, I can send another that won't, an' right on th' tail of th' first, too."

"Ah, th' devil! You make me disgusted with yore fool talk about that carbine!" snapped his companion, and the subject was dropped.

The merits of their respective rifles had always been a bone of contention between them and one well chewed, at that. Red was very well satisfied with his Winchester, and he was a good judge.

"You did stop 'em a little," asserted Mr. Cassidy some time later as he looked back. "You stopped 'em coming straight, but they're spreading out to work up around us. Now, if we had good cayuses instead of these wooden wonders, we could run away from 'em dead easy, draw their best mounted warriors to th' front an' then close with 'em. Good thing their cayuses are well tired out, for as it is we've got to make a stand purty soon. Gee! They don't like you, Red; they're calling you names in th' sign language. Just look at 'em cuss you!"

"How much water have you got?" inquired his friend with anxiety.

"Canteen plumb full. How're you fixed?"

"I got th' same, less one drink. That gives us enough for a couple of days with some to spare, if we're careful," Mr. Connors replied. New Mexican canteens are built on generous lines and are known as life-preservers.

"Look at that glory-hunter go!" exclaimed Red, watching a brave who was riding half a mile to their right and rapidly coming abreast of them. "Wonder how he got over there without us seeing him."

"Here; stop him!" suggested Hopalong, holding out his Sharps. "We can't let him get ahead of us and lay in ambush—that's what he's playing to do."

"My gun's good, and better, for me, at this range; but you know, I can't hit a jack-rabbit going over rough country as fast as that feller is," replied his companion, standing up in his stirrups and firing.

"Huh! Never touched him! But he's edging off a-plenty. See him cuss you. What's he calling you, anyhow?"

"Aw, shut up! How th' devil do *I* know? I don't talk with my arms."

"Are you superstitious, Red?"

"No! Shut up!"

"Well, I am. See that feller over there? If he gets in front of us it's a shore sign that somebody's going to get hurt. He'll have plenty of time to get cover an' pick us off as we come up."

"Don't you worry— his cayuse is deader'n ours. They must 'a' been pushing on purty hard th' last few days. See it stumble?—what'd I tell you!"

"Yes; but they're gaining on us slow but shore. We've got to make a stand purty soon—how much further do you reckon that infernal shack is, anyhow?" Hopalong asked sharply.

" 'T ain't fur off—see it any minute now."

"Here," remarked Hopalong, holding out his rifle, "stencil yore mark on his hide; catch him just as he strikes th' top of that little rise."

"Ain't got time—that shack can't be much further."

And it wasn't, for as they galloped over a rise they saw, half a mile ahead of them, an adobe building in poor state of preservation. It was Powers' old ranch house, and as they neared it, they saw that there was no doubt about the holes.

"Told you it was a sieve," grunted Hopalong, swinging in on the trail of his companion. "Not worth a hang for anything," he added bitterly.

"It'll answer, all right," retorted Red grimly.

IX

♦

Mr. Holden Drops In

Mr. Cassidy dismounted and viewed the building with open disgust, walking around it to see what held it up, and when he finally realized that it was self-supporting his astonishment was profound. Undoubtedly there were shacks in the United States in worse condition, but he hoped their number was small. Of course he knew that the building would make a very good place of defence, but for the sake of argument he called to his companion and urged that they be satisfied with what defence they could extemporize in the open. Mr. Connors hotly and hastily dissented as he led the horses into the building, and straightway the subject was arbitrated with much feeling and snappy eloquence. Finally Hopalong thought that Red was a chump, and said so out loud, whereat Red said unpleasant things about his good friend's pedigree, attributes, intelligence, *et al.*, even going so far as to prognosticate his friend's place of eternal abode. The remarks were fast getting to be somewhat personal in tenor when a whine in the air swept up the scale to a vicious shriek as it passed between them, dropped rapidly to a whine again and quickly died out in the distance, a flat report coming to their ears a few seconds later. Invisible bees seemed to be winging through the air, the angry and venomous droning becoming more pronounced each passing moment, and the irregular cracking of rifles grew louder rapidly. An angry *s-p-a-t!* told of where a stone behind them had launched the ricochet which hurtled skyward with a wheezing scream. A handful of 'dobe dust sprang from the corner of the building and sifted down upon them, causing Red to cough.

"That ricochet was a Sharps!" exclaimed Hopalong, and they lost no time in getting into the building, where the discussion was renewed as they prepared for the final struggle. Red grunted his cheerful approval, for now he was out of the blazing sun and where he could better appreciate the musical tones of the flying bullets; but his companion, slamming shut the door and propping it with a fallen roof-beam, grumbled and finally gave rein to his rancor by sneering at the Winchester.

"It shore gets me that after all I have said about that gun you will tote it around with you and force yoreself into a suicide's grave," quoth Mr. Cassidy, with exuberant pugnacity. "I ain't in no way objecting to th' suicide part of it, but I can't see that it's at all fair to drag *me* onto th' edge of everlasting eternity with you. If you ain't got no regard for yore own life you shore ought to think a little about yore friend's. Now you'll waste all yore catridges an' then come snooping around me to borrow my gun. Why don't you lose th' damned thing?"

"What I pack ain't none of yore business, which same I'll uphold," retorted Mr. Connors, at last able to make himself heard. "You get over on yore own side an' use yore Colt; I've wondered a whole lot where you ever got th' sense to use a Colt—*I* wouldn't be a heap surprised to see you toting a pearl-handled .22, like th' kids use. Now you 'tend to yore grave-yard aspirants, an' lemme do th' same with mine."

"Th' Lord knows I've stood a whole lot from you because you just can't help being foolish, but I've got plumb weary and sick of it. It stops right here or you won't get no 'Paches," snorted Hopalong, peering intently through a hole in the shack. The more they squabbled the better they liked it,—controversies had become so common that they were merely a habit; and they served to take the grimness out of desperate situations.

"Aw, you can't lick one side of me," averred Red loftily. "You never did stop anybody that was anything," he jeered as he fired from his window. "Why, you couldn't even hit th' bottom of th' Grand Canyon if you leaned over th' edge."

"You could, if you leaned too far, you red-headed wart of a half-breed," snapped Hopalong. "But how about th' Joneses, Tarantula Charley, Slim Travennes, an' all th' rest? How about them, hey?"

"Huh! You couldn't 'a' got any of 'em if they had been sober," and Mr. Connors shook so with mirth that the Indian at whom he had fired got away with a whole skin and cheerfully derided the marksman. "That 'Pache shore reckons it was you shooting at him, I missed him so far. Now, you shut up—I want to get some so we can go home. I don't want to stay out here all night an' th' next day as well," Red grumbled, his words dying slowly in his throat as he voiced other thoughts.

Hopalong caught sight of an Apache who moved cautiously through a chaparral lying about nine hundred yards away. As long as the distant enemy lay quietly he could not be discerned, but he was not content with assured safety and took a chance. Hopalong raised his rifle to his shoulder as the Indian fired and the latter's bullet, striking the edge of the hole through which Mr. Cassidy peered, kicked up a generous handful of dust, some of which found lodgment in that individual's eyes.

"Oh! Oh! Oh! Wow!" yelled the unfortunate, dancing blindly around the room in rage and pain, and dropping his rifle to grab at his eyes. "Oh! Oh! Oh!"

His companion wheeled like a flash and grabbed him as he stumbled past. "Are you plugged bad, Hoppy? Where did they get you? Are you hit bad?" and Red's heart was in his voice.

"No, I ain't plugged bad!" mimicked Hopalong. "I ain't plugged at all!" he blazed, kicking enthusiastically at his solicitous friend. "Get me some water, you jackass! Don't stand there like a fool! I ain't going to fall down. Don't you know my eyes are full of 'dobe?"

Red, avoiding another kick, hastily complied, and as hastily left Mr. Cassidy to wash out the dirt while he returned to his post by the window. "Anybody'd think you was full of red-eye, th' way you act," muttered Red peevishly.

Hopalong, ridding his eyes of the dirt, went back to the hole in the wall and looked out. "Hey, Red! Come over here an' spill that brave's conceit. I can't keep my eyes open long enough to aim, an' it's a nice shot, too. It'd serve him right if you got him!"

Mr. Connors obeyed the summons and peered out cautiously. "I can't see him, nohow; where is th' coyote?"

"Over there in that little chaparral; see him now? *There!* See him moving. Do you mean to tell me—"

"Yep; I see him, all right. You watch," was the reply.

"He's just over nine hundred—where's yore Sharps?" He took the weapon, glanced at the Buffington sight, which he found to be set right, and aimed carefully.

Hopalong blinked through another hole as his friend fired and saw the Indian flop down and crawl aimlessly about on hands and knees. "What's he doing, now, Red?"

"Playing marbles, you chump; an' here goes for his agate," replied the man with the Sharps, firing again. "There! Gee!" he exclaimed, as a bullet hummed in through the window he had quitted for the moment, and thudded into the wall, making the dry adobe fly. It had missed him by only a few inches and he now crept along the floor to the rear of the room and shoved his rifle out among the branches of a stunted mesquite which grew before a fissure in the wall. "You keep away from that windy for a minute, Hoppy," he warned as he waited.

A terror-stricken lizard flashed out of the fissure and along the wall where the roof had fallen in and flitted into a hole, while a fly buzzed loudly and hovered persistently around Red's head, to the rage of that individual. "Ah, ha!" he grunted, lowering the rifle and peering through the smoke. A yell reached his ears and he forthwith returned to his window, whistling softly.

Evidently Mr. Cassidy's eyes were better and his temper sweeter, for he hummed "Dixie" and then jumped to "Yankee Doodle," mixing the two airs with careless impartiality, which was a sign that he was thinking deeply. "Wonder what ever became of Powers, Red. Peculiar feller, he was."

"In jail, I reckon, if drink hasn't killed him."

"Yes; I reckon so," and Mr. Cassidy continued his medley, which prompted his friend quickly to announce his unqualified disapproval.

"You can make more of a mess of them two songs

than anybody I ever heard murder 'em! *Shut up!*"—and the concert stopped, the vocalist venting his feelings at an Indian, and killing the horse instead.

"Did you get him?" queried Red.

"Nope; but I got his cayuse," Hopalong replied, shoving a fresh cartridge into the foul, greasy breech of the Sharps. "An' here's where I get him—got to square up for my eyes some way," he muttered, firing. "Missed! Now, what do you think of that!" he complained.

"Better take my Winchester," suggested Red, in a matter-of-fact way, but he chuckled softly and listened for the reply.

"Aw, you go to th' devil!" snapped Mr. Cassidy, firing again. "Whoop! Got him that time!"

"Where?" asked his companion, with strong suspicion.

"None of yore business!"

"Aw, darn it! Who spilled th' water?" yelled Red, staring blankly at the overturned canteen.

"Pshaw! Reckon I did, Red," apologized his friend ruefully. "Now of all th' cussed luck!"

"Oh, well; we've got another, an' you had to wash out yore eyes. Lucky we each had one—*Holy smoke!* It's most all gone! Th' top is loose!"

Heartfelt profanity filled the room and the two disgusted punchers went sullenly back to their posts. It was a calamity of no small magnitude, for, while food could be dispensed with for a long time if necessary, going without water was another question. It was as necessary as cartridges.

Then Hopalong laughed at the ludicrous side of the whole affair, thereby revealing one of the characteristics which endeared him to his friends. No matter how desperate a situation might be, he could always find in it something at which to laugh. He laughed going into danger and coming out of it, with a joke or a pleasantry always trembling on the end of his tongue.

"Red, did it ever strike you how cussed thirsty a feller gets just as soon as he knows he can't have no drink? But it don't make much difference, nohow. We'll get out of this little scrape just as we've allus got out of trouble. There's some mad war-whoops outside that are worse off than we are, because they are at th' wrong end of yore gun. I feel sort of sorry for 'em."

"Yo're shore a happy idiot," grinned Red. "Hey! Listen!"

Galloping was heard and Hopalong, running to the door, looked out through a crack as sudden firing broke out around the rear of the shack, and fell to pulling away the props, crying, "It's a puncher, Red; he's riding this way! Come on an' help him in!"

"He's a blamed fool to ride this way! I'm with you!" replied Red, running to his side.

Half a mile from the house, coming across the open space as fast as he could urge his horse, rode a cowboy, and not far behind him raced about a dozen Apaches, yelling and firing.

Red picked up his companion's rifle, and steadying it against the jamb of the door, fired, dropping one of the foremost of the pursuers. Quickly reloading again, he fired and missed. The third shot struck another horse, and then taking up his own gun he began to fire rapidly, as rapidly as he could work the lever and yet make his shots tell. Hopalong drew his Colt and ran back to watch the rear of the house, and it was well that he did so, for an Apache in that direction, believing that the trapped punchers were so busily engaged with the new developments as to forget for the moment, sprinted towards the back window; and he had gotten within twenty paces of the goal when Hopalong's Colt cracked a protest. Seeing that the warrior was no longer a combatant,

Mr. Cassidy ran back to the door just as the stranger fell from his horse and crawled past Red. The door slammed shut, the props fell against it, and the two friends turned to the work of driving back the second band, which, however, had given up all hope of rushing the house in the face of Red's telling fire, and had sought cover instead.

The stranger dragged himself to the canteens and drank what little water remained, and then turned to watch the two men moving from place to place, firing coolly and methodically. He thought he recognized one of them from the descriptions he had heard, but he was not sure.

"My name's Holden," he whispered hoarsely, but the cracking of the rifles drowned his voice. During a lull he tried again. "My name's Holden," he repeated weakly. "I'm from th' Cross-O-Cross, an' can't get back there again."

"Mine's Cassidy, an' that's Connors, of th' Bar-20. Are you hurt very bad?"

"No; not very bad," lied Holden, trying to smile. "Gee, but I'm glad I fell in with you two fellers," he exclaimed. He was but little more than a boy, and to him Hopalong Cassidy and Red Connors were names with which to conjure. "But I'm plumb sorry I went an' brought you more trouble," he added regretfully.

"Oh, pshaw! We had it before you came—you needn't do no worrying about that, Holden; besides, I reckon you couldn't help it," Hopalong grinned facetiously. "But tell us how you came to mix up with that bunch," he continued.

Holden shuddered and hesitated a moment, his companions alertly shifting from crack to crack, window to window, their rifles cracking at intervals. They appeared to him to act as if they had done nothing else all their lives but fight Indians from that shack, and he braced up a little at their example of coolness.

"It's an awful story, awful!" he began. "I was riding towards Hoyt's Corners an' when I got about half way there I topped a rise an' saw a nester's house about half a mile away. It wasn't there th' last time I rode that way, an' it looked so peaceful an' home-like that I stopped an' looked at it a few minutes. I was just going to start again when that war-party rode out of a barranca close to th' house an' went straight for it at top speed. It seemed like a dream, 'cause I thought Apaches never got so far east. They don't, do they? I thought not—these must 'a' got turned out of their way an' had to hustle for safety. Well, it was all over purty quick. I saw 'em drag two women an'—an'—purty soon a man. He was fighting like fury, but he didn't last long. Then they set fire to th' house an' threw th' man's body up on th' roof. I couldn't seem to move till th' flames shot up, but then I must 'a' went sort of loco, because I emptied my gun at 'em, which was plumb foolish at that distance, for me. Th' next thing I knowed was that half of 'em was coming my way as hard as they could ride, an' I lit out instanter; an' here I am. I can't get that sight outen my head nohow—it'll drive me loco!" he screamed, sobbing like a child from the horror of it all.

His auditors still moved around the room, growing more and more vindictive all the while and more zealously endeavoring to create a still greater deficit in one Apache war-party. They knew what he had looked upon, for they themselves had become familiar with the work of Apaches in Arizona. They could picture it vividly in all its devilish horror. Neither of them paid any apparent attention to their companion, for they could not spare the time, and, also, they believed it best to let him fight out his own battles unassisted.

Holden sobbed and muttered as the minutes dragged along, at times acting so strangely as to draw a covert side-glance from one or both of the Bar-20 punchers. Then Mr. Connors saw his boon companion suddenly lean out of a window and immediately become the target for the hardworking enemy. He swore angrily at the criminal recklessness of it. "Hey, you! Come in out of that! Ain't you got no brains at all, you blasted idiot! Don't you know that we need every gun?"

"Yes; that's right. I sort of forgot," grinned the reckless one, obeying with alacrity and looking sheepish. "But you know there's two thundering big tarantulas out there fighting like blazes. You ought to see 'em jump! It's a sort of a leap-frog fight, Red."

"Fool!" snorted Mr. Connors belligerently. "*You'd* 'a' jumped if one of them slugs had 'a' got you! Yo're th' damnedest fool that ever walked on two laigs, you blasted sage hen!" Mr. Connors was beginning to lose his temper and talk in his throat.

"Well, they didn't get me, did they? What you yelling about, anyhow?" growled Hopalong, trying to brazen it out.

"An' *you* talking about suicide to me!" snapped Mr. Connors, determined to rub it in and have the last word.

Mr. Holden stared, open-mouthed, at the man who could enjoy a miserable spider fight under such distressing circumstances, and his shaken nerves became steadier as he gave thought to the fact that he was a companion of the two men about whose exploits he had heard so much. Evidently the stories had not been exaggerated. What must they think of him for giving away as he had? He arose to his feet in time to see a horse blunder into the open on Red's side of the house, and after it blundered its owner, who immediately lost all need of earthly conveyances. Holden laughed from the joy of being with a man who could shoot like that, and he took up his rifle and turned to a crack in the wall, filled with the determination to let his companions know that he was built of the right kind of timber after all, wounded as he was.

Red's only comment, as he pumped a fresh cartridge into the barrel, was, "He must 'a' thought he saw a spider fight, too."

"Hey, Red," called Hopalong. "Th' big one is dead."

"What big one?"

"Why, don't you remember? That big tarantula I was watching. One was bigger than th' other, but th' little feller shore waded into him an'—"

"Go to th' devil!" shouted Red, who had to grin, despite his anger.

"Presently, presently," replied Hopalong, laughing.

So the day passed, and when darkness came upon them all of the defenders were wounded, Holden desperately so.

"Red, one of us has got to try to make th' ranch," Hopalong suddenly announced, and his friend knew he was right. Since Holden had appeared upon the scene they had known that they could not try a dash; one of them had to stay.

"We'll toss for it; heads, I go," Red suggested, flipping a coin.

"Tails!" cried Hopalong. "It's only thirty miles to Buckskin, an' if I can get away from here I'm good to make it by eleven to-night. I'll stop at Cowan's an' have him send word to Lucas an' Bartlett, so there'll be enough in case any of our boys are out on th' range in some line house. We can pick 'em up on th' way back, so there won't be no time lost. If I get through you can expect excitement on th' outside of this sieve by daylight. You an' Holden can hold her till then, because they never attack at night. It's th' only way out of this for us—we ain't got cartridges or water enough to last another day."

Red, knowing that Hopalong was taking a desperate chance in working through the cordon of Indians which surrounded them, and that the house was safe when compared to running such a gantlet, offered to go through the danger line with him. For several minutes a wordy war raged and finally Red accepted a compromise; he was to help, but not to work through the line.

"But what's th' use of all this argument?" feebly demanded Holden. "Why don't you both go? I ain't a-going to live, nohow, so there ain't no use of anybody staying here with me, to die with me. Put a bullet through me so them devils can't play with me like they do with others, an' then get away while you've got a chance. Two men can get through as easy as one." He sank back, exhausted by the effort.

"No more of that!" cried Red, trying to be stern. "I'm going to stay with you an' see things through. I'd be a fine sort of a coyote to sneak off an' leave you for them fiends. An', besides, I can't get away; my cayuse is hit too hard an' yourn is dead," he lied cheerfully. "An' yo're going to get well, all right. I've seen fellers hit harder than you are pull through."

Hopalong walked over to the prostrate man and shook hands with him. "I'm awful glad I met you, Holden. Yo're pure grit all th' way through, an' I like to tie to that kind of a man. Don't you worry about nothing; Red can handle this proposition, and we'll have you in Buckskin by tomorrow night; you'll be riding again in two weeks. So long."

He turned to Red and shook hands silently, led his horse out of the building and mounted, glad that the moon had not yet come up, for in the darkness he had a chance.

"Good luck, Hoppy!" cried Red, running to the door. "Good luck!"

"You bet—an' lots of it, too," groaned Holden, but he

was gone. Then Red wheeled. "Holden, keep yore eyes an' ears open. I'm going out to see that he gets off. He may run into a—" and he, too, was gone.

Holden watched the door and windows, striving to resist the weak, giddy feeling in his head, and ten minutes later he heard a shot and then several more in quick succession. Shortly afterward Red called out, and almost immediately the Bar-20 puncher crawled in through a window.

"Well?" anxiously cried the man on the floor. "Did he make it?"

"I reckon so. He got away from th' first crowd, anyhow. I wasn't very far behind him, an' by th' time they woke up to what was going on he was through an' riding like blazes. I heard him call 'em half-breeds a moment later an' it sounded far off. They hit me,—fired at my flash, like I drilled one of them. But it ain't much, anyhow. How are you feeling now?"

"Fine!" lied the other. "That Cassidy is shore a wonder—he's all right, an' so are you. I'll never see him again, but I shore hope he gets through!"

"Don't be foolish. Here, you finish th' water in yore canteen—I picked it up outside by yore cayuse. Then go to sleep," ordered Red. "I'll do all th' watching that's necessary."

"I will if you'll call me when you get sleepy."

"Why, shore I will. But don't you want th' rest of th' water? I ain't a bit thirsty—I had all I could hold just before you came," Red remarked as his companion pushed the canteen against him in the dark. He was choking with thirst. "Well, then; all right," and Red pretended to drink. "Now, then, you go to sleep; a good snooze will do you a world of good—it's just what you need."

X

◆

Buck Takes a Hand

Cowan's saloon, club, and place of general assembly
for the town of Buckskin and the nearby ranches,
held a merry crowd, for it was pay-day on the range, and
laughter and liquor ran a close race. Buck Peters, his hands
full of cigars, passed through the happy-go-lucky, do-
as-you-please crowd and invited everybody to smoke,
which nobody refused to do. Wood Wright, of the C-80,
turned his fiddle anew and swung into a rousing quick-
step. Partners were chosen, the "women" wearing hand-
kerchiefs on their arms to indicate the fact, and the room
shook and quivered as the scraping of heavy boots filled
the air with a cloud of dust. "Allaman left!" cried the
prompter, and then the dance stopped as if by magic. The
door had crashed open and a blood-stained man staggered
in and towards the bar, crying, "Buck! Red's hemmed in
by 'Paches!"

"Good God!" roared the foreman of the Bar-20, leaping
forward, the cigars falling to the floor to be crushed and
ground into powder by careless feet. He grasped his
puncher and steadied him while Cowan slid an extra generous glassful of brandy across the bar for the wounded
man. The room was in an uproar, men grabbing rifles
and running out to get their horses, for it was plain to be
seen that there was hard work to be done, and quickly.
Questions, threats, curses filled the air, those who remained inside to get the story listening intently to the
jerky narrative; those outside, caring less for the facts of
an action past than for the action to come, shouted impatiently for a start to be made, even threatening to go on

and tackle the proposition by themselves if there were not more haste. Hopalong told in a graphic, terse manner all that was necessary, while Buck and Cowan hurriedly bandaged his wounds.

"Come on! Come on!" shouted the mounted crowd outside, angry, and impatient for a start, the prancing of horses and the clinking of metal adding to the noise. "Get a move on! *Will* you hurry up!"

"Listen, Hoppy!" pleaded Buck, in the furore. "Shut up, you outside!" he yelled. "You say they know that you got away, Hoppy?" he asked. "All right—*Lanky!*" he shouted. *"Lanky!"*

"All right, Buck!" and Lanky Smith roughly pushed his way through the crowd to his foreman's side. "Here I am."

"Take Skinny and Pete with you, an' a lead horse apiece. Strike straight for Powers' old ranch house. Them Injuns'll have pickets out looking for Hoppy's friends. You three get th' pickets nearest th' old trail though that arroyo to th' southeast, an' then wait for us. We'll come along th' high bank on th' left. Don't make no noise doing it, neither, if you can help it. Understand? Good! Now ride like th' devil!"

Lanky grabbed Pete and Skinny on his way out and disappeared into the corral; and very soon thereafter hoof-beats thudded softly in the sandy street and pounded into the darkness of the north, soon lost to the ear. An uproar of advice and good wishes crashed after them, for the game had begun.

"It's Powers' old shack, boys!" shouted a man in the door to the restless force outside, which immediately became more restless. "Hey! Don't go yet!" he begged. "Wait for me an' th' rest. Don't be a lot of idiots!"

Excited and impatient voices replied from the darkness, vexed, grouchy, and querulous. "Then get a move on—*whoa!*—it'll be light before we get there if you don't hustle!" roared one voice above the confusion. "You know what *that* means!"

"Come on! Come on! For God's sake, are you tied to th' bar?"

"Yo're a lot of old grandmothers! Come on!"

Hopalong appeared in the door. "I'll show you th' way, boys!" he shouted. "Cowan, put my saddle on yore cayuse—*pronto!*"

"Good for you, Hoppy!" came from the street. "We'll wait!"

"You stay here; yo're hurt too much!" cried Buck to his puncher, as he grabbed up a box of cartridges from a shelf behind the bar. "Ain't you got no sense? There's enough of us to take care of this without you!"

Hopalong wheeled and looked his foreman squarely in the eyes. "Red's out there, waiting for me—I'm going! I'd be a fine sort of a coyote to leave him in that hell hole an' not go back, wouldn't I!" he said, with quiet determination.

"Good fer you, Cassidy!" cried a man who hastened out to mount.

"Well, then, come on," replied Buck. "There's blamed few like you," he muttered, following Hopalong outside.

"Here's th' cayuse, Cassidy," cried Cowan, turning the animal over to him. "*Wait*, Buck!" and he leaped into the building and ran out again, shoving a bottle of brandy and a package of food into the impatient foreman's hand.

"Mebby Red or Hoppy'll need it—so long, an' good luck!" and he was alone in a choking cloud of dust, peering through the darkness along the river trail after a black mass that was swallowed up almost instantly. Then, as he watched, the moon pushed its rim up over the hills and he laughed joyously as he realized what its light would mean to the crowd. "There'll be great doings when *that* gang cuts loose," he muttered with savage elation. "Wish I was with 'em. Damn Injuns, anyhow!"

Far ahead of the main fighting force rode the three special-duty men, reeling off the miles at top speed and constantly distancing their friends, for they changed mounts at need, thanks to the lead horses provided by Mr. Peters' cool-headed foresight. It was a race against dawn, and every effort was made to win—the life of Red Connors hung in the balance and a minute might turn the scale.

In Powers' old ranch house the night dragged along slowly to the grim watcher, and the man huddled in the corner stirred uneasily and babbled, ofttimes crying out in horror at the vivid dreams of his disordered mind. Pacing ceaselessly from window to window, crack to crack, when the moon came up, Mr. Connors scanned the bare, level plain with anxious eyes, searching out the few covers and looking for dark spots on the dull gray sand. They never attacked at night, but still—. Through the void came the quavering call of a coyote, and he listened for the reply, which soon came from the black chaparral across the clearing. He knew where two of them were hiding, anyhow. Holden was muttering and tried to answer the calls, and Red looked at him for the hundredth time that night. He glanced out of the window again and noticed that there was a glow in the eastern sky, and shortly afterwards dawn swiftly developed.

Pouring the last few drops of the precious water between the wounded man's parched and swollen lips, he tossed the empty canteen from him and stood erect.

"Pore devil," he muttered, shaking his head sorrowfully, as he realized that Holden's delirium was getting worse all the time. "If you was all right we could give them wolves hell to dance to. Well, you won't know nothing about it if we go under, an' that's some consolation." He examined his rifle and saw that the Colt at his thigh was fully loaded and in good working order. "An' they'll pay us for their victory, by God! They'll pay for it!" He stepped closer to the window, throwing the rifle into the hollow of his arm. "It's about time for th' rush; about time for th' game—"

There was movement by that small chaparral to the south! To the east something stirred into bounding life and action; a coyote called twice—and then they came, on foot and silently as fleeting shadows, leaning forward to bring into play every ounce of energy in the slim, red legs. Smoke filled the room with its acrid sting. The crashing of the Winchester, worked with wonderful speed and deadly accuracy by the best rifle shot in the Southwest, brought the prostrate man to his feet in an instinctive response to the call to action, the necessity of defence. He grasped his Colt and stumbled blindly to a window to help the man who had stayed with him.

On Red's side of the house one warrior threw up his arms and fell forward, sprawling with arms and legs extended; another pitched to one side and rolled over twice before he lay still; the legs of the third collapsed and threw him headlong, bunched up in a grotesque pile of lifeless flesh; the fourth leaped high into the air and turned a somersault before he struck the sand, badly wounded, and out of the fight. Holden, steadying himself against the wall, leaned in a window on the other side of the shack and emptied his Colt in a dazed manner—doing his very best. Then the man with the rifle staggered back with a muttered curse, his right arm useless, and dropped the weapon to draw his Colt with the other hand.

Holden shrieked once and sank down; wagging his head slowly from side to side, blood oozing from his mouth and nostrils; and his companion, goaded into a frenzy of blood-lust and insane rage at the sight, threw himself against the door and out into the open, to die under the clear sky, to go like the man he was if he must die. "Damn you! It'll cost you more yet!" he screamed, wheeling to place his back against the wall.

The triumphant yells of the exultant savages were cut short and turned to howls of dismay by a fusillade which thundered from the south, where a crowd of hard-riding, hard-shooting cow-punchers tore out of the thicket like an avalanche and swept over the open sand, yelling and cursing, and then separated to go in hot pursuit of the sprinting Apaches. Some stood up in their stirrups and fired down at a slant, making a short, chopping motion with their heavy Colts; others leaned forward, far over the necks of their horses, and shot with stationary guns; while yet others, with reins dangling free, worked the levers of blue Winchesters so rapidly that the flashes seemed to merge into a continuous flame.

"Thank God! Thank God—an' Hoppy!" groaned the man at the door of the shack, staggering forward to meet the two men who had lost no time in pursuit of the enemy, but had ridden straight to him.

"I was scared stiff you was done fer!" cried Hopalong, leaping off his horse and shaking hands with his friend, whose hand-clasp was not as strong as usual. "How's Holden?" he demanded, anxiously.

"He passed. It was a close—" began Red, weakly, but his foreman interposed.

"Shut up, an' drink this!" ordered Buck, kindly but sternly. "We'll do th' talking for a while; you can tell us all about it later on. Why, *hullo!*" he cried as Lanky Smith and his two happy companions rode up. "Reckon you must 'a' got them pickets."

"Shore we did! Stalked 'em on our bellies, didn't we,

Skinny?" modestly replied Mr. Smith, the roping expert of the Bar-20. "Ropes an' clubbed guns did th' rest. Anyhow, there was only two anywhere near th' trail."

"We didn't see you," responded the foreman, tying the knot of a bandage on Mr. Connors' arm. "An' we looked sharp, too."

"Reckon we were hunting for more; we sort of forgot what you said about waiting for you," Mr. Smith replied, grinning broadly.

"An' you've got a good memory now," smiled Mr. Peters.

"We didn't find no more, though," offered Mr. Pete Wilson, with grave regret. "An' we looked good, too. But we got Red, an' that's th' whole game. Red, you old son-of-a-gun, you can lick yore weight in powder!"

"It's too bad about Holden," muttered Red, sullenly.

XI

♦

Hopalong Nurses a Grouch

After the excitement incident to the affair at Powers' shack had died down and the Bar-20 outfit worked over its range in the old, placid way, there began to be heard low mutterings, and an air of peevish discontent began to be manifested in various childish ways. And it was all caused by the fact that Hopalong Cassidy had a grouch, and a big one. It was two months old and growing worse daily, and the signs threatened contagion. His foreman, tired and sick of the snarling, fidgety, petulant atmosphere that Hopalong had created on the ranch, and driven to desperation, eagerly sought some chance to get rid of the "sore-thumb" temporarily and give him an opportunity to shed his generous mantle of the blues. And at last it came.

No one knew the cause for Hoppy's unusual state of mind, although there were many conjectures, and they covered the field rather thoroughly; but they did not strike on the cause. Even Red Connors, now well over all ill effects of the wounds acquired in the old ranch house, was forced to guess; and when Red had to do that about anything concerning Hopalong he was well warranted in believing the matter to be very serious.

Johnny Nelson made no secret of his opinion and derived from it a great amount of satisfaction, which he admitted with a grin to his foreman.

"Buck," he said, "Hoppy told me he went broke playing poker over in Grant with Dave Wilkes and them two Lawrence boys, an' that shore explains it all. He's got pack sores from carrying his unholy licking. It was due to come to him, an' Dave Wilkes is just th' boy to deliver it. That's th' whole trouble, an' I know it, an' I'm damned glad they trimmed him. But he ain't got no right of making *us* miserable because he lost a few measly dollars."

"Yo're wrong, son; dead, dead wrong," Buck replied. "He takes his beatings with a grin, an' money never did bother him. No poker game that ever was played could leave a welt on him like th' one we all mourn, an' cuss. He's been doing something that he don't want us to know—make a fool of hisself some way, most likely, an' feels so ashamed that he's sore. I've knowed him too long an' well to believe that gambling had anything to do with it. But this little trip he's taking will fix him up all right, an' I couldn't 'a' picked a better man—or one that I'd ruther get rid of just now."

"Well, lemme tell you it's blamed lucky for him that you picked him to go," rejoined Johnny, who thought more of the woful absentee than he did of his own skin.

"I was going to lick him, shore, if it went on much longer. Me an' Red an' Billy was going to beat him up good till he forgot his dead injuries an' took more interest in his friends."

Buck laughed heartily. "Well, th' three of you might 'a' done it if you worked hard an' didn't get careless, but I have my doubts. Now look here—you've been hanging around th' bunk house too blamed much lately. Henceforth an' hereafter you've got to earn yore grub. Get out on that west line an' hustle."

"You know I've had a toothache!" snorted Johnny with a show of indignation, his face as sober as that of a judge.

"An' you'll have a stomach ache from lack of grub if you don't earn yore right to eat purty soon," retorted Buck. "You ain't had a toothache in yore whole life, an' you don't know what one is. G'wan, now, or I'll give you a backache that'll ache!"

"Huh! Devil of a way to treat a sick man!" Johnny retorted, but he departed exultantly, whistling with much noise and no music. But he was sorry for one thing: he sincerely regretted that he had not been present when Hopalong met his Waterloo. It would have been pleasing to look upon.

While the outfit blessed the proposed lease of range which took him out of their small circle for a time, Hopalong rode farther and farther into the northwest, frequently lost in abstraction which, judging by its effect upon him, must have been caused by something serious. He had not heard from Dave Wilkes about that individual's good horse which had been loaned to Ben Ferris, of Winchester. Did Dave think he had been killed or was still pursuing the man whose neck-kerchief had aroused such animosity in Hopalong's heart? Or had the horse actually been returned? The animal was a good one, a successful contender in all distances from one to five miles, and had earned its owner and backers much money—and Hopalong had parted with it as easily as he would have borrowed five dollars from Red. The story, as he had often reflected since, was as old as lying—a broken-legged horse, a wife dying forty miles away, and a horse all saddled which needed only to be mounted and ridden.

These thoughts kept him company for a day and when he dismounted before Stevenson's "Hotel" in Hoyt's Corners he summed up his feelings for the enlightenment of his horse.

"Damn it, bronch! I'd give ten dollars right now to know if I was a jackass or not," he growled. "But he was an awful slick talker if he lied. An' I've got to go up an' face Dave Wilkes to find out about it!"

Mr. Cassidy was not known by sight to the citizens of Hoyt's Corners, however well versed they might be in his numerous exploits of wisdom and folly. Therefore the *habitués* of Stevenson's Hotel did not recognize him in the gloomy and morose individual who dropped his saddle on the floor with a crash and stamped over to the three-legged table at dusk and surlily demanded shelter for the night.

"Gimme a bed an' something to eat," he demanded, eying the three men seated with their chairs tilted against the wall. "Do I get 'em?" he asked, impatiently.

"You do," replied a one-eyed man, lazily arising and approaching him. "One dollar, now."

"An take th' rocks outen that bed—I want to sleep."

"A dollar per for every rock you find," grinned Stevenson, pleasantly. "There ain't no rocks in *my* beds," he added.

"Some folks likes to be rocked to sleep," facetiously remarked one of the pair by the wall, laughing contentedly at his own pun. He bore all the ear-marks of being regarded as the wit of the locality—every hamlet has one; I have seen some myself.

"Hee, hee, hee! Yo're a droll feller, Charley," chuckled Old John Ferris, rubbing his ear with unconcealed delight. "That's a good un."

"One drink, now," growled Hopalong, mimicking the proprietor, and glaring savagely at the "droll feller" and his companion. "An' mind that it's a good one," he admonished the host.

"It's better," smiled Stevenson, whereat Old John crossed his legs and chuckled again. Stevenson winked.

"Riding long?" he asked.

"Since I started."

"Going fur?"

"Till I stop."

"Where do you belong?" Stevenson's pique was urging him against the ethics of the range, which forbade personal questions.

Hopalong looked at him with a light in his eye that told the host he had gone too far. "Under my sombrero!" he snapped.

"Hee, hee, hee!" chortled Old John, rubbing his ear again and nudging Charley. "He ain't no fool, eh?"

"Why, I don't know, John; he won't tell," replied Charley.

Hopalong wheeled and glared at him, and Charley, smiling uneasily, made an appeal: "Ain't mad, are you?"

"Not yet," and Hopalong turned to the bar again, took up his liquor and tossed it off. Considering a moment he shoved the glass back again, while Old John tongued his lips in anticipation of a treat. "It is good—fill it again."

The third was even better and by the time the fourth and fifth had joined their predecessors Hopalong began to feel a little more cheerful. But even the liquor and an exceptionally well-cooked supper could not separate him from his persistent and set grouch. And of liquor he had already taken more than his limit. He had always boasted, with truth, that he had never been drunk, although there had been two occasions when he was not far from it. That was one doubtful luxury which he could not afford for the reason that there were men who would have been glad to see him, if only for a few seconds, when liquor had dulled his brain and slowed his speed of hand. He could never tell when and where he might meet one of these.

He dropped into a chair by a card table and, baffling all attempts to engage him in conversation, reviewed his troubles in a mumbled soliloquy, the liquor gradually making him careless. But of all the jumbled words his companions' diligent ears heard they recognized and retained only the bare term "Winchester"; and their conjectures were limited only by their imaginations.

Hopalong stirred and looked up, shaking off the hand which had aroused him. "Better go to bed, stranger," the proprietor was saying. "You an' me are th' last two up. It's after twelve, an' you look tired and sleepy."

"Said his wife was sick," muttered the puncher. "Oh, what you saying?"

"You'll find a bed better'n this table, stranger—it's after twelve an' I want to close up an' get some sleep. I'm tired myself."

"Oh, that all? Shore I'll go to bed—like to see anybody stop me! Ain't no rocks in it, hey?"

"Nary a rock," laughingly reassured the host, picking up Hopalong's saddle and leading the way to a small room off the "office," his guest stumbling after him and growling about the rocks that lived in Winchester. When Stevenson had dropped the saddle by the window and departed, Hopalong sat on the edge of the bed to close his eyes for just a moment before tackling the labor of removing his clothes. A crash and a jar awakened him and he found himself on the floor with his back to the bed. He was hot and his head ached, and his back was skinned a little—and how hot and stuffy and choking the room had become! He thought he had blown out the light, but it still burned, and three-quarters of the chimney was thickly covered with soot. He was stifling and could not endure it any longer. After three attempts he put out the light, stumbled against his saddle and, opening the window, leaned out to breathe the pure air. As his lungs filled he chuckled wisely and, picking up the saddle, managed to get it and himself through the window and on the ground without serious mishap. He would ride for an hour, give the room time to freshen and cool off, and come back feeling much better. Not a star could be seen as he groped his way unsteadily towards the rear of the building, where he vaguely remembered having seen the corral as he rode up.

"Huh! Said he lived in Winchester an 's name was Bill—no, Ben Ferris," he muttered, stumbling towards a noise he knew was made by a horse rubbing against the corral fence. Then his feet got tangled up in the cinch of his saddle, which he had kicked before him, and after great labor he arose, muttering savagely, and continued on his wobbly way. "Goo' Lord, it's darker'n cats in— *oof!*" he grunted, recoiling from forcible contact with the fence he sought. Growling words unholy he felt his way along it and finally his arm slipped through an opening and he bumped his head solidly against the top bar of the gate. As he righted himself his hand struck the nose of a horse and closed mechanically over it. Cowponies look alike in the dark and he grinned jubilantly as he complimented himself upon finding his own so unerringly.

"Anything is easy, when you know how. Can't fool me, ol' cayuse," he beamed, fumbling at the bars with his free hand and getting them down with a fool's luck. "You can't do it—I got you firs', las', an' always; an' I got you good. Yessir, I got you good. Quit that rearing, you ol' fool! Stan' still, can't you?" The pony sidled as the saddle hit its back and evoked profane abuse from the indignant puncher as he risked his balance in picking it up to try again, this time successfully. He began to fasten the girth, and then paused in wonder and thought deeply, for the pin in the buckle would slide to no hole but the first. "Huh! Gettin' fat, ain't you, piebald?" he demanded with withering sarcasm. "You blow yoreself up any more'n I'll bust you wide open!" heaving with all his might on the free end of the strap, one knee pushing against the animal's side. The "fat" disappeared and Hopalong laughed. "Been learnin' new tricks, ain't you? Got smart since you been travellin', hey?" He fumbled with the bars again and got two of them back in place and then, throwing himself across the saddle as the horse started forward as hard as it could go, slipped off, but managed to save himself by hopping along the ground. As soon as he had secured the grip he wished he mounted with the ease of habit and felt for the reins. "G'wan, now, an' easy—it's plumb dark an' my head's bustin'."

When he saddled his mount at the corral he was not aware that two of the three remaining horses had taken advantage of their opportunity and had walked out and made off in the darkness before he replaced the bars, and he was too drunk to care if he had known it.

The night air felt so good that it moved him to song, but it was not long before the words faltered more and more and soon ceased altogether and a subdued snore rasped from him. He awakened from time to time, but only for a moment, for he was tired and sleepy.

His mount very quickly learned that something was wrong and that it was being given its head. As long as it could go where it pleased it could do nothing better than head for home, and it quickened its pace towards Winchester. Some time after daylight it pricked up its ears and broke into a canter, which soon developed signs of irritation in its rider. Finally Hopalong opened his heavy eyes and looked around for his bearings. Not knowing where he was and too tired and miserable to give much thought to a matter of such slight importance, he glanced around for a place to finish his sleep. A tree some distance ahead of him looked inviting and towards it he rode. Habit made him picket the horse before he lay down and as he fell asleep he had vague recollections of handling a strange picket rope some time recently. The horse slowly turned and stared at the already snoring figure, glanced over the landscape, back to the queerest man it had ever met, and then fell to grazing in quiet content. A slinking coyote topped a rise a short distance away and stopped instantly, regarding the sleeping man with grave curiosity and strong suspicion. Deciding that there was nothing good to eat in that vicinity and that the man was carrying out a fell plot for the death of coyotes, it backed away out of sight and loped on to other hunting grounds.

XII

♦

A Friend In Need

Stevenson, having started the fire for breakfast, took a pail and departed towards the spring; but he got no farther than the corral gate, where he dropped the pail and stared. There was only one horse in the enclosure where the night before there had been four. He wasted no time in surmises, but wheeled and dashed back towards the hotel, and his vigorous shouts brought Old John to the door, sleepy and peevish. Old John's mouth dropped open as he beheld his habitually indolent host marking off long distances on the sand with each falling foot.

"What's got inter you?" demanded Old John.

"Our bronchs are gone! Our bronchs are gone!" yelled Stevenson, shoving Old John roughly to one side as he dashed through the doorway and on into the room he had assigned to the sullen and bibulous stranger. "I knowed it! I knowed it!" he wailed, popping out again as if on springs. "He's gone, an' he's took our bronchs with him, th' measly, low-down dog! I knowed he wasn't no good! I could see it in his eye; an' he wasn't drunk, not by a darn sight. Go out an' see for yoreself if they ain't gone!" he snapped in reply to Old John's look. "Go on out, while I throw some cold grub on th' table—won't have no time this morning to do no cooking. He's got five hours' start on us, an' it'll take some right smart riding to get him before dark; but we'll do it, an' hang him, too!"

"What's all this here rumpus?" demanded a sleepy voice from upstairs. "Who's hanged?" and Charley entered the room, very much interested. His interest increased remarkably when the calamity was made known and he lost no time in joining Old John in the corral to verify the news.

Old John waved his hands over the scene and carefully explained what he had read in the tracks, to his companion's great irritation, for Charley's keen eye and good training had already told him all there was to learn; and his reading did not exactly agree with that of his companion.

"Charley, he's gone and took our cayuses; an' that's th' very way he came—'round th' corner of th' hotel. He got all tangled up an' fell over there, an' here he bumped inter th' palisade, an' dropped his saddle. When he opened th' bars he took my roan gelding because it was th' best an' fastest, an' then he let out th' others to mix us up on th' tracks. See how he went? Had to hop four times on one foot afore he could get inter th' saddle. An' that proves he was sober for no drunk could hop four times like that without falling down an' being drug to death. An' he left his own critter behind because he knowed it wasn't no good. It's all as plain as th' nose on yore face, Charley," and Old John proudly rubbed his ear. "Hee, hee, hee! You can't fool Old John, even if he is gettin' old. No, sir, b'gum."

Charley had just returned from inside the corral, where he had looked at the brand on the far side of the one horse left, and he waited impatiently for his companion to cease talking. He took quick advantage of the first pause Old John made and spoke crisply.

"I don't care what corner he come 'round, or what he bumped inter; an' any fool can see that. An' if he left that cayuse behind because he thought it wasn't no good, he *was* drunk. That's a Bar-20 cayuse, an' no hoss-thief ever worked for that ranch. He left it behind because he stole it; that's why. An' he didn't let them others out because he wanted to mix us up, neither. How'd he know if we couldn't tell th' tracks of our own animals? He did that to make us lose time; that's what he did it for. An' he couldn't tell what bronch he took last night—it was too dark. He must 'a' struck a match an' seen where that Bar-20 cayuse was an' then took th' first one nearest that wasn't it. An' now you tell me how th' devil he knowed yourn was th' fastest, which it ain't," he finished, sarcastically, gloating over a chance to rub it into the man he had always regarded as a windy old nuisance.

"Well, mebby what you said is—"

"Mebby nothin'!" snapped Charley. "If he wanted to mix th' tracks would he 'a' hopped like that so we couldn't help tellin' what cayuse he rode? He knowed we'd pick his trail quick, an' he knowed that every minute counted; that's why he hopped—why, yore roan was goin' like th' wind afore he got in th' saddle. If you don't believe it, look at them toe-prints!"

"H'm; reckon yo're right, Charley. My eyes ain't nigh as good as they once was. But I heard him say something 'bout Winchester," replied Old John, glad to change the subject. "But he's goin' over there, too. He won't get through that town on no critter wearin' my brand. Everybody knows that roan, an'—"

"Quit guessin'!" snapped Charley, beginning to lose some of the tattered remnant of his respect for old age. "He's a whole lot likely to head for a town on a stolen cayuse, now ain't he! But we don't care where he's heading; we'll foller th' trail."

"Grub pile!" shouted Stevenson, and the two made haste to obey.

"Charley, gimme a chaw of yore tobacker," and Old John, biting off a generous chunk, quietly slipped it into his pocket, there to lay until after he had eaten his breakfast.

All talk was tabled while the three men gulped down a cold and uninviting meal. Ten minutes later they had finished and separated to find horses and spread the news; in fifteen more they had them and were riding along the plain trail at top speed, with three other men close at their heels. Three hundred yards from the corral they pounded out of an arroyo, and Charley, who was leading, stood up in his stirrups and looked keenly ahead. Another trail joined the one they were following and ran with and on top of it. This, he reasoned, had been made by one of the strays and would turn away soon. He kept his eyes looking well ahead and soon saw that he was right in his surmise, and without checking the speed of his horse in the slightest degree he went ahead on the trail of the smaller hoof-prints. In a moment Old John spurred forward and gained his side and began to argue hot-headedly.

"Hey! Charley!" he cried. "Why are you follerin' this track?" he demanded.

"Because it's his; that's why."

"Well, here; wait a minute!" and Old John was getting red from excitement. "How do you know it is? Mebby he took th' other!"

"He started out on th' cayuse that made these little tracks," retorted Charley, "an' I don't see no reason to think he swapped animules. Don't you know th' prints of your own cayuse?"

"Lawd, no!" answered Old John. "Why, I don't hardly ride th' same cayuse th' second day, straight hand-runnin'. I tell you we ought to foller that other trail. He's just cute enough to play some trick on us."

"Well, you better do that for us," Charley replied, hoping against hope that the old man would chase off on the other and give his companions a rest.

"He ain't got sand enough to tackle a thing like that single-handed," laughed Jed White, winking to the others.

Old John wheeled. "Ain't, hey! I am going to do that same thing an' prove that you are a pack of fools. I'm too old to be fooled by a common trick like that. An' I don't need no help—I'll ketch him all by myself, an' hang him, too!" And he wheeled to follow the other trail, angry and outraged. "Young fools," he muttered. "Why, I was fightin' all around these parts afore any of 'em knowed th' difference between day an' night!"

"Hard-headed old fool," remarked Charley, frowning, as he led the way again.

"He's gittin' old an' childish," excused Stevenson. "They say there warn't nobody in these parts could hold a candle to him in his prime."

Hopalong muttered and stirred and opened his eyes to gaze blankly into those of one of the men who were tugging at his hands, and as he stared he started his stupefied brain sluggishly to work in an endeavor to explain the unusual experience. There were five men around him and the two who hauled at his hands stepped back and kicked him. A look of pained indignation slowly spread over his countenance as he realized beyond doubt that they were really kicking him, and with sturdy vigor. He considered a moment and then decided that such treatment was most unwarranted and outrageous and, furthermore, that he must defend himself and chastise the perpetrators.

"Hey!" he snorted, "what do you reckon yo're doing, anyhow? If you want to do any kickin', why, kick each other an' I'll help you! But I'll lick th' whole blasted bunch of you if you don't quit maulin' me. Ain't you got no manners? Don't you know anything? Come 'round wakin' a feller up an' man-handling—"

"Get up!" snapped Stevenson, angrily.

"Why, ain't I seen you before? Somewhere? Sometime?" queried Hopalong, his brow wrinkling from intense concentration of thought. "I ain't dreamin'; I've seen a one-eyed coyote som'ers, lately, ain't I?" he appealed, anxiously, to the others.

"Get up!" ordered Charley, shortly.

"An' I've seen you, too. Funny, all right."

"You've seen me, all right," retorted Stevenson. "Get up, damn you! Get up!"

"Why, I can't—my han's are tied!" exclaimed Hopalong in great wonder, pausing in his exertions to cogitate deeply upon this most remarkable phenomenon. "Tied up! Now what th' devil do you think—"

"Use yore feet, you thief!" rejoined Stevenson roughly, stepping forward and delivering another kick. "Use yore feet!" he reiterated.

"Thief! Me a thief! Shore I'll use my feet, you yaller dog!" yelled the prostrate man, and his boot heel sank into the stomach of the offending Mr. Stevenson with sickening force and laudable precision. He drew it back slowly, as if debating shoving it farther. "Call me a thief, hey! Come pokin' 'round kickin' hones' punchers an' callin' 'em names! Anybody want th' other boot?" he inquired with grave solicitation.

Stevenson sat down forcibly and rocked to and fro, doubled up and gasping for breath, and Hopalong squinted at him and grinned with happiness. "Hear him sing! Reg'lar ol' brass band. Sounds like a cow pullin' its hoofs outen th' mud. Called me a thief, he did, jus' now. An' I won't let nobody kick me an' call me names. He's a liar, jus' a plain, squaw's dog liar, he—"

Two men grabbed him and raised him up, holding him tightly, and they were not over careful to handle him gently, which he naturally resented. Charley stepped in front of him to go to the aid of Stevenson and caught the other boot in his groin, dropping as if he had been shot. The man on the prisoner's left emitted a yell and loosed his hold to sympathize with a bruised shinbone, and his companion promptly knocked the bound and still intoxicated man down. Bill Thomas swore and eyed the prostrate figure with resentment and regret. "Hate to hit a man who can fight like that when he's loaded an' tied. I'm glad, all th' same, that he ain't sober an' loose."

"An' you ain't going to hit him no more!" snapped Jed White, reddening with anger. "I'm ready to hang him, 'cause that's what he deserves, an' what we're here for, but I'm damned if I'll stand for any more mauling. I don't blame him for fightin', an' they didn't have no right to kick him in th' beginning."

"Didn't kick him in th' beginning," grinned Bill. "Kicked him in th' ending. Anyhow," he continued seriously, "I didn't hit him hard—didn't have to. Just let him go an' shoved him quick."

"I'm just naturally goin' to clean house," muttered the prisoner, sitting up and glaring around. "Untie my han's an' gimme a gun or a club or anythin', an' watch yoreselves get licked. Called me a thief! What are you fellers, then?—stickin' me up an' 'busing me for a few measly dollars. Why didn't you take my money an' lemme sleep, 'stead of wakin' me up an' kickin' me? I wouldn't 'a' cared then."

"Come on now; get up. We ain't through with you yet, not by a whole lot," growled Bill, helping him to his feet and steadying him. "I'm plumb glad you kicked 'em; it was comin' to 'em."

"No, you ain't; you can't fool me," gravely assured Hopalong. "Yo're lyin', an' you know it. What you goin' to do now? Ain't I got money enough? Wish I had an even break with you fellers! Wish my outfit was here!"

Stevenson, on his feet again, walked painfully up and shook his fist at the captive, from the side. "You'll find out what we want of you, you damned hoss-thief!" he cried. "We're goin' to tie you to that there limb so yore feet'll swing above th' grass, that's what we're goin' to do."

Bill and Jed had their hands full for a moment and as they finally mastered the puncher, Charley came up with a rope. "Hurry up—no use draggin' it out this way. I want to get back to th' ranch some time before next week."

"W'y *I* ain't no hoss-thief, you liar!" Hopalong yelled. "My name's Hopalong Cassidy of th' Bar-20, an' w'en I tell my friends about what you've gone an' done they'll make you hard to find! You gimme any kind of a chance an' I'll do it all by myself, sick as I am, you yaller dogs!"

"Is that yore cayuse?" demanded Charley, pointing.

Hopalong squinted towards the animal indicated. "W'ich one?"

"There's only one there, you fool!"

"Tha' so?" replied Hopalong, surprised. "Well, I never seen it afore. My cayuse is—is—where th' devil *is* it?" he asked, looking around anxiously.

"How'd you get that one, then, if it ain't yours?"

"Never had it—'t ain't mine, nohow," replied Hopalong, with strong conviction. "Mine was a *hoss*."

"You stole that cayuse las' night outen Stevenson's corral," continued Charley, merely as a matter of form. Charley believed that a man had the right to be heard before he died—it wouldn't change the result and so could not do any harm.

"Did I? W'y—" his forehead became furrowed again, but the events of the night before were vague in his memory and he only stumbled in his soliloquy. "But *I* wouldn't swap my cayuse for that spavined, saddle-galled, ring-boned boneyard! Why, it interferes, an' it's got th' heaves somethin' awful!" he finished triumphantly, as if an appeal to common sense would clinch things. But he made no headway against them, for the rope went around his neck almost before he had finished talking and a flurry of excitement ensued. When the dust settled he was on his back again and the rope was being tossed over the limb.

The crowd had been too busily occupied to notice anything away from the scene of their strife and were greatly surprised when they heard a hail and saw a stranger sliding to a stand not twenty feet from them. "What's this?" demanded the newcomer, angrily.

Charley's gun glinted as it swung up and the stranger

swore again. "What you doin'?" he shouted. "Take that gun off'n me or I'll blow you apart!"

"Mind yore business an' sit still!" Charley snapped. "You ain't in no position to blow anything apart. We've got a hoss-thief an' we're shore goin' to hang him regardless."

"An' if there's any trouble about it we can hang two as well as we can one," suggested Stevenson, placidly. "You sit tight an' mind yore own affairs, stranger," he warned.

Hopalong turned his head slowly. "He's a liar, stranger; just a plain, squaw's dog of a liar. An' I'll be much obliged if you'll lick hell out'n 'em an' let—*why, hullo, hoss-thief!*" he shouted, at once recognizing the other. It was the man he had met in the gospel tent, the man he had chased for a horse-thief and then swapped mounts with. "Stole any more cayuses?" he asked, grinning, believing that everything was all right now. "Did you take that cayuse back to Grant?" he finished.

"Han's up!" roared Stevenson, also covering the stranger. "So yo're another one of 'em, hey? We're in luck to-day. Watch him, boys, till I get his gun. If he moves, drop him quick."

"You damned fool!" cried Ferris, white with rage. "He ain't no thief, an' neither am I! My name's Ben Ferris an' I live in Winchester. Why, that man you've got is Hopalong Cassidy—Cassidy, of th' Bar-20!"

"Sit still—you can talk later, mebby," replied Stevenson, warily approaching him. "Watch him, boys!"

"Hold on!" shouted Ferris, murder in his eyes. "Don't you try that on me! I'll get one of you before I go; I'll shore get one! You can listen a minute, an' I can't get away."

"All right; talk quick."

Ferris pleaded as hard as he knew how and called attention to the condition of the prisoner. "If he did take th' wrong cayuse he was too blind drunk to know it! Can't you *see* he was?" he cried.

"Yep; through yet?" asked Stevenson, quietly.

"No! I ain't started yet!" Ferris yelled. "He did me a good turn once, one that I can't never repay, an' I'm going to stop this murder or go with him. If I go I'll take one of you with me, an' my friends an' outfit'll get th' rest."

"Wait till Old John gets here," suggested Jed to Charley. "He ought to know this feller."

"For th' Lord's sake!" snorted Charley. "He won't show up for a week. Did you hear that, fellers?" he laughed, turning to the others.

"Stranger," began Stevenson, moving slowly ahead again. "You give us yore guns an' sit quiet till we gets this feller out of th' way. We'll wait till Old John Ferris comes before doing anything with you. He ought to know you."

"He knows me all right; an' he'd like to see me hung," replied the stranger. "I won't give up my guns, an' you won't lynch Hopalong Cassidy while I can pull a trigger. That's flat!" He began to talk feverishly to gain time and his eyes lighted suddenly. Seeing that Jed White was wavering, Stevenson ordered them to go on with the work they had come to perform, and he watched Ferris as a cat watches a mouse, knowing that he would be the first man hit if the stranger got a chance to shoot. But Ferris stood up very slowly in his stirrups so as not to alarm the five with any quick movement, and shouted at the top of his voice, grabbing off his sombrero and waving it frantically. A faint cheer reached his ears and made the lynchers turn quickly and look behind them. Nine men were tearing towards them at a dead gallop and had already begun to forsake their bunched-up formation in favor of an extended line. They were due to arrive in a very few minutes and caused Mr. Ferris' heart to overflow with joy.

"Me an' my outfit," he said, laughing softly and waving

his hand towards the newcomers, "started out this morning to round up a bunch of cows, an' we've got jackasses instead. Now lynch him, damn you!"

The nine swept up in skirmish order, guns out and ready for anything in the nature of trouble that might zephyr up. "What's th' matter, Ben?" asked Tom Murphy ominously. As under-foreman of the ranch he regarded himself as spokesman. And at that instant catching sight of the rope, he swore savagely under his breath.

"Nothing, Tom; nothing now," responded Mr. Ferris. "They was going to hang my friend there, Mr. Hopalong Cassidy, of th' Bar-20. He's th' feller that lent me his cayuse to get home on when Molly was sick. I'm going to take him back to th' ranch when he gets sober an' introduce him to some very good friends of hissn that he ain't never seen. Ain't I, Cassidy?" he demanded with a laugh.

But Mr. Cassidy made no reply. He was sound asleep, as he had been since the advent of his very good and capable friend, Mr. Ben Ferris, of Winchester.

XIII

♦

Mr. Townsend, Marshal

Mr. Cassidy went to the ranch and lived like a lord until shame drove him away. He had no business to live on cake and pie and wonderful dishes that Mrs. Ferris and her sister literally forced on him, and let Buck's mission wait on his convenience. So he tore himself away and made up for lost time as he continued his journey on his own horse, for which Tom Murphy and three men had faced down the scowling population of Hoyt's Corners. The rest of his journey was without incident until, on his return home along another route, he rode into Rawhide and heard about the marshal, Mr. Townsend.

This individual was unanimously regarded as an affliction upon society and there had been objections to his continued existence, which had been overruled by the object himself. Then word had gone forth that a substantial reward and the undying gratitude of a considerable number of people awaited the man who would rid the community of the pest who seemed to be ubiquitous. Several had come in response to the call, one had returned in a wagon, and the others were now looked upon as martyrs, and as examples of asinine foolhardiness. Then it had been decided to elect a marshal, or perhaps two or three, to preserve the peace of the town; but this was a flat failure. In the first place, Mr. Townsend had dispersed the meeting with no date set for a new one; in the second, no man wanted the office; and as a finish to the comedy, Mr. Townsend cheerfully announced that hereafter and henceforth he was the marshal, self-appointed and self-sustained. Those who did not like it could easily move to other localities.

With this touch of office-holding came ambition, and of stern stuff. The marshal asked himself why he could not be more officers than one and found no reasons. Thereupon he announced that he was marshal, town council, mayor, justice, and pound-keeper. He did not go to the trouble of incorporating himself as the Town of Rawhide, because he knew nothing of such immaterial things; but he was the town, and that sufficed.

He had been grievously troubled about finances in the past, and he firmly believed that genius such as his should be above such petty annoyances as being "broke." That was why he constituted himself the keeper of the public pound, which contented him for a short time; but later, feeling that he needed more money than the pound was giving him, he decided that the spirit of the times demanded public improvements, and therefore, as the executive head of the town, he levied taxes and improved the town by improving his wardrobe and the manner of his living. Each saloon must pay into the town treasury the sum of one hundred dollars per year, which entitled it to police protection and assured it that no new competitors would be allowed to do business in Rawhide.

Needless to say he was not furiously popular, and the crowds congregated where he was not. His tyranny was based upon his uncanny faculty of anticipating the other man's draw. The citizens were not unaccustomed to seeing swift death result to the slower man from misplaced confidence in his speed of hand—that was in the game—an even break; but to oppose an individual who *always* knew what you were going to do before you knew it yourself—this was very discouraging. Therefore, he flourished and waxed fat.

Of late, however, he had been very low in finances and could expect no taxes to be paid for three months. Even the pound had yielded him nothing for over a week, the old patrons of Rawhide's stores and saloons preferring to ride twenty miles farther in another direction than to redeem impounded horses. Perhaps his prices had been too high, he thought; so he assembled the town council, the mayor, the marshal, and the keeper of the public pound to consult upon the matter. He decided that the prices were too high and at once posted a new notice announcing the cut. It was hard to fall from a dollar to "two bits," but the treasury was low—the times were panicky.

As soon as he had changed the notice he strolled up to the Paradise to inform the bartender that impounding fines had been cut to bargain prices and to ask him to make the fact generally known through his patrons. As he came within sight of the building he jumped with pleasure, for a horse was standing dejectedly before the door. Joy of joys, trade was picking up—a stranger had come to town! Hastening back to the corral, he added a cipher to the posted figure, added a decimal point, and changed the cents sign to that of the dollar. Two dollars and fifty cents was now the price prescribed by law. Returning hastily to the Paradise, he led the animal away, impounded it, and then sat down in front of the corral gate with his Winchester across his knees. Two dollars and fifty cents! Prosperity had indeed returned!

"Where th' CG ranch is I dunno, but I do know where one of their cayuses is," he mused, glancing between two of the corral posts at the sleepy animal. "If I has to auction it off to pay for its keep and th' fine, th' saddle will bring a good, round sum. I allus knowed that a dollar wasn't enough, nohow."

Nat Fisher, punching cows for the CG and tired of his job, leaned comfortably back in his chair in the Paradise and swapped lies with the all-wise bartender. After a while he realized that he was hopelessly outclassed at this diversion and he dug down into his pocket and brought to light some loose silver and regarded it thoughtfully. It was all the money he had and was beginning to grow interesting.

"Say, was you ever broke?" he asked suddenly, a trace of sadness in his voice.

The bartender glanced at him quickly, but remained judiciously silent, smelling the preamble of an attempt to "touch."

"Well, I have been, am now, an' allus will be, more or less," continued Fisher, in soliloquy, not waiting for an answer to his question. "Money an' me don't ride th' same range, not any. Here I am fifty miles away from my ranch, with four dollars and ninety-five cents between me an' starvation an' thirst, an' me not going home for three days yet. I was going to quit th' CG this month, but now I gotta go on workin' for it till another payday. I don't even own a cayuse. Now, just to show you what kind of a prickly pear I am, I'll cut th' cards with you to see who owns this," he suggested, smiling brightly at his companion.

The bartender laughed, treated on the house, and shuffled out from behind the bar with a pack of greasy playing cards. "All at once, or a dollar a shot?" he asked, shuffling deftly.

"Any way it suits you," responded Fisher, nonchalantly. He knew how a sport should talk; and once he had cut the cards to see who should own his full month's pay. He hoped he would be more successful this time.

"Don't make no difference to me," rejoined the bartender.

"All right; all at once, an' have it over with. It's a kid's game, at that."

"High wins, of course?"

"High wins."

The bartender pushed the cards across the table for his companion to cut. Nat did so, and turned up a deuce. "Oh, don't bother," he said, sliding the four dollars and ninety-five cents across the table.

"Wait," grinned the bartender, who was a stickler for rules. He reached over and turned up a card, and then laughed. "Matched, by George!"

"Try again," grinned Fisher, his face clearing with hope.

The bartender shuffled, and Fisher turned a five, which proved to be just one point shy when his companion had shown his card.

"Now," remarked Fisher, watching his money disappear into the bartender's pocket, "I'll put up my gun agin ten of yore dollars if yo're game. How about it?"

"Done—that's a good weapon."

"None better. Ah, a jack!"

"I say queen—nope, *king!*" exulted the dispenser of liquids. "Say, mebby you can get a job around here when you quit th' CG," he suggested.

"That's a good idee," replied Fisher. "But let's finish this while we're at it. I got a good saddle outside on my cayuse—go look it over an' tell me how much you'll put up agin it. If you win it an' can't use it, you can sell it. It's first class."

The bartender walked to the door, looked carefully around for a moment, his eyes fastening upon a trail in the sandy street. Then he laughed. "There ain't no saddle out here," he reported, well knowing where it could be found.

"What! Has that ornery piebald—well, what do you think of that!" exclaimed Fisher, looking up and down the street. "This is th' first time that ever happened to me. Why, some coyote stole it! Look at th' tracks!"

"No; it ain't stolen," the bartender responded. He considered a moment and then made a suggestion. "Mebby th' marshal can tell you where it is—he knows everything like that. Nobody can take a cayuse out of this town while th' marshal is up an' well."

"Lucky town, all right," chirped Fisher. "An' where is th' marshal?"

"You'll find him down th' back way a couple of hundred yards; can't miss him. He allus hangs out there when there are cayuses in town."

"Good for him! I'll chase right down an' see him; an' when I get that piebald—!"

The bartender watched him go around the corner and shook his head sadly. "Yes; hell of a lucky town," he snorted bitterly, listening for the riot to begin.

The marshal still sat against the corral gate and stroked

the Winchester in beatific contemplation. He had a fine
job and he was happy. Suddenly leaning forward to look
up the road, he smiled derisively and shifted the gun. A
cow-puncher was coming his way rapidly, and on foot.

"Are you th' marshal of this flea of a town?" politely
inquired the newcomer.

"I am th' same," replied the man with the rifle. "Anything I kin do for you?"

"Yes; have you seen a piebald cayuse straying around
loose-like, or anybody leadin' one—CG being th' brand?"

"I did; it was straying."

"An' which way did it go?"

"Into th' town pound."

"What! Pond! What'n blazes is it doin' with a pond?
Couldn't it drink without gettin' in? Where's th' pond?"

"Right here. It's eating its fool head off. I said pound,
not pond. P-o-u-n-d; which means that it's pawned, in
hock, for destroyin' th' vegetation of Rawhide, an' disturbin' th' public peace.

"Good joke on th' piebald, all right; it was never
locked up before," laughed Fisher, trying to read a sign
that faced away from him at a slight angle. "Get it out for
me an' I'll disturb *its* peace. Sorry it put you to all that
trouble," he sympathized.

"Two dollars an' four bits, an' a dollar initiation fee—it
wasn't never in th' pound before. That makes three an' a
half. Got th' money with you?"

"What!" yelled Fisher, emerging from his trance.
"What!" he yelled again.

"I ain't none deaf," placidly replied the marshal. "Got
th' money, th' three an' a half?"

"If you think yo're goin' to skin me outen three-fifty,
one-fifty, or one measly cent, you need some medicine,
an' I'll give it to you in pill form! You'd make a bum-
lookin' angel, so get up an' hand over that cayuse, *an' do
it damned quick!*"

"Three-fifty, an' two bits extry for feed. It'll cost you 'bout a dollar a day for feed. At th' end of th' week I'll sell that cayuse at auction to pay its bills if you don't cough up. Got th' money?"

"I've got a lead slug for you if I can borrow my gun for five minutes!" retorted Fisher, seeing double from anger.

"Five dollars more for contempt of court," pleasantly responded Mr. Townsend. "As Justice of th' Peace of this community I must allow no disrespect, no contempt of th' sovereign law of this town to go unpunished. That makes it eight-seventy-five."

"An' to think I lost my gun!" shouted Fisher, dancing with rage. "I'll get that cayuse out an' I won't pay a cent, not a damned cent! An' I'll get you at th' same time!"

"Now you dust around for fifteen dollars even an' stop yore contempt of court an' threats or I'll drill you just for luck!" rejoined Mr. Townsend, angrily. "If you keep on workin' yore mouth like that there won't be nothin' co-min' to you when I sell that cayuse of yourn. Turn around an' strike out or I'll put you with yore ancestors!"

XIV

◆

The Stranger's Plan

Fisher, wild with rage, returned to the Paradise and profanely unfolded the tale of his burning wrongs to the bartender and demanded the loan of his gun, which the bartender promptly refused. The present owner of the gun liked Fisher very much for being such a sport and sympathized with him deeply, but he did not want to have such a pleasing acquaintance killed.

"Now, see here: you cool down an' I'll lend you fifteen dollars on that saddle of yourn. You go up an' get that cayuse out before th' price goes up any higher—you don't know that man like I do," remarked the man behind the bar earnestly. "That feller Townsend can shoot th' eyes out of a small dog at ten miles, purty nigh. Do you savvy my drift?"

"I won't pay him a cussed cent, an' when he goes to sell that piebald at auction, I'll be on hand with a gun; I'll get one somewhere, all right, even if I have to steal it. Then I'll shoot out *his* eyes at ten paces. Why, he's a two-laigged hold-up! That man would—" he stopped as a stranger entered the room. "Hey, stranger! Don't you leave that cayuse of yourn outside all alone or that coyote of a marshal will steal it, shore. He's th' biggest thief I ever knowed. He'll lift yore animal quick as a wink!" Fisher warned, excitedly.

The stranger looked at him in surprise and then smiled. "Is it usual for a marshal to steal cayuses? Somewhat out of line, ain't it?" he asked Fisher, glancing at the bartender for light.

"I don't care what's th' rule—that marshal just stole my cayuse; an' he'll take yourn, too, if you ain't careful," Fisher replied.

"Well," drawled the stranger, smiling still more, "I reckon I ain't goin' to stay out there an' watch it, an' I can't bring it in here. But I reckon it'll be all right. You see, I carry 'big medicine' agin hoss-thieves," he replied, tapping his holster and smiling as he remembered the time, not long past, when he himself had been accused of being one. "I'll take a chance if he will—what'll you all have?"

"Little whiskey," replied Fisher, uneasily, worrying because he could not stand for a return treat. "But, say; you keep yore eye on that animal, just th' same," he added, and then hurriedly gave his reasons. "An' th' worst part of th' whole thing is that I ain't got no gun, an' can't seem to borrow none, neither," he added, wistfully eying the stranger's Colt. "I gambled mine away to th' bartender here, an' he won't lemme borrow it for five minutes!"

"Why, I never heard tell of such a thing before!" exclaimed the stranger, hardly believing his ears, and aghast at the thought that such conditions could exist. "Friend," he said, addressing the bartender, "how is it that this sort of thing can go on in this town?" When the bartender had explained at some length, his interested listener smote the bar with a heavy fist and voiced his outraged feelings. "I'll shore be plumb happy to spread that coyote marshal all over his cussed pound! Say, come with me; I'm going down there right now an' get that cayuse, an' if th' marshal opens his mouth to peep I'll get him, too. I'm itching for a chance to tunnel a man like him. Come on an' see th' show!"

"Not much!" retorted Fisher. "While I am some pleased to meet you, an' have a deep an' abiding gratitude for yore noble offer, I can't let you do it. He put it over on me, an' I'm th' one that's got to shoot him up. He's mine, my pudding; an' I'm hogging him all to myself. That is one luxury I can indulge in even if I am broke: an' I'm sorry, but I can't give you cards. Seein', however, as you are so friendly to th' cause of liberty an' justice, suppose you lend me yore gun for about three minutes by th' watch. From what I've been told about this town such an act will win for you th' eternal love an' gratitude of a downtrodden people; yore gun will blaze th' way to liberty an' light, freedom an' th' right to own yore own property, an' keep it. All I ask is that I be th' undescrvin' medium."

"A-men," sighed the bartender. "Deacon Jones will now pass down th' aisle an' collect th' buttons an' tin money."

"Stranger," continued Fisher, warming up, when he saw that his words had not produced the desired result, "King James th' Twelfth, on th' memorable an' blood-soaked field of Trafalgar, gave men their rights. On that great day he signed th' Magnet Charter, and proved himself as great a liberator as th' sainted Lincoln. You, on this most auspicious occasion, hold in yore strong right hand th' destiny of this town—th' women an' children in this cursed community will rise up an' bless you forever an' pass yore name down to their ancestors as a man of deeds an' honor! Let us pause to consider this—"

"Hold that pause!" interrupted the astounded bartender hurriedly, and with shaking voice. "String it out till I get untangled! I ain't up much on history, so I won't take no chance with that; but I want to tell our eloquent guest that there ain't no women *or* children in this town. An' if there was, I sort of reckon their ancestors would be born first. What do you think about it—"

"Let us pause to consider th' shameful an' burnin' in*dig*nity perpetrated upon us to-day!" continued Fisher, unheeding the bartender's words. "I, a peaceful, law-abidin' *citi*zen of this *glor*ious Commonwealth, a free an' equal member of a liberty-lovin' nation, a nation whose standard is, *now* and forever, 'Gimme liberty or gimme det', a *na*tion that stands for all th' conceivable benefits that mankind may enjoy, a *na*tion that scintillates pyrotechnically over the prostitution of power—"

Bang! went the bartender's fist on the counter. "Hey! Pause again! Wait a minute! Go back to 'shameful an' burnin',' an' gimme a chance!"

"—that stands for an even break, I, Nathaniel G. Fisher, have been deprived of one of my inalienable rights, th' right of locomotion to distant an' other parts. *An'* I say, right here an' now, that I won't allow no spavined individual with thieving prehensils to—"

"Has that pound-keeper got a rifle?" calmly interrupted the stranger, without a pang of remorse.

"He has. Thus has it allus been with tyrants—well armed, fortified by habit an' tradition—"

"Then you won't get my gun, savvy? We'll find another way to get that cayuse as long as you feel that th' marshal is yore hunting. Besides, this man's gall deserves some respect; it is genius, an' to pump genius full of cold lead is to act rash. Now, suppose you tell me when this auction is due to come off."

"Oh, not for a week; he wants to run up th' board an' keep expenses. Tyrants, such as him—"

"Shore," interposed the bartender, "he'll make th' expenses equal what he gets for th' cayuse, no matter what it comes to. An' he's th' whole town, an' th' justice of th' peace, besides. What he says goes."

"Well, I'm th' Governor of th' State an' I've got th' Supreme Court right here in my holster, so I reckon I can reverse his official acts an' fill his legal opinions full of holes," the stranger replied, laughing heartily. "Bartender, will you help me play a little joke on His Honor, th' Town,—just a little harmless joke?"

"Well, that all depends whether th' joke is harmless on *me*. You see, he can shoot like th' devil—he allus knows when a man is going to draw, an' gets his gun out first. I ain't got no respect for him, but I take off my hat to his gunplay, all right."

The stranger smiled. "Well, I can shoot a bit myself. But I shore wish he'd hold that auction quick—I've got to go on home without losing any more time. Fisher, suppose you go down to th' pound and dare that tumble-bug to hold th' auction this afternoon. Tell him that you'll shoot him full of holes if he goes pulling off any auction today, an' dare him to try it. I want it to come off before night, an' I reckon that'll hustle it along."

"I'll do anything to get th' edge on that thief," replied Fisher, quickly, "but don't you reckon I'd better tote a gun, goin' down an' beardin' such a thief in his own den? You know I allus like to shoot when I'm bein' shot at."

"Well, I don't blame you; it's only a petty weakness," grinned the stranger, hanging onto his Colt as if fearing that the other would snatch it and run. "But you'll do better without any gun—me an' th' bartender don't want to have to go down there an' bring you back on a plank."

"All right, then," sighed Fisher, reluctantly, "but he'll jump th' price again. He'll fine me for contempt of court an' make me pay money I ain't got for disturbin' him. But I'm game—so long."

When he had gained the street, the stranger turned to the bartender. "Now, friend, you tell me if this man of gall, this Mr. Townsend, has got many friends in town— anybody that'll be likely to pot shoot from th' back when things get warm. I can't watch both ends unless I know what I'm up against."

"*No!* Every man in town hates him," answered the bartender, hastily, and with emphasis.

"Ah, that's good. Now, I wonder if you could see 'most everybody that's in town now an' get 'em to promise to help me by lettin' me run this all by myself. All I want them to do is not to say a word. It ain't hard to keep still when you want to."

"Why, I reckon I might see 'em—there ain't many here this time of day," responded the bartender. "But what's yore game, anyhow?" he asked, suddenly growing suspicious.

"It's just a little scheme I figgered out," the stranger replied, and then he confided in the bartender, who jigged a few fancy steps to show his appreciation of the other's genius. His suspicions left him at once, and he hastened out to tell the inhabitants of the town to follow his instructions to the letter, and he knew they would obey, and be glad, hilariously glad, to do so. While he was hurrying around giving his instructions, the CG puncher returned to the hotel and reported.

"Well, it worked, all right," Fisher growled. "I told him what I'd do to him if he tried to auction that cayuse off an' he retorted that if I didn't shut up an' mind my own business, that he'd sell th' horse this noon, at twelve o'clock, in th' public square, wherever that is. I told him he was a coyote and dared him to do it. Told him I'd pump him full of air ducts if he didn't wait till next week. Said I had th' promise of a gun an' that it'd give me great pleasure to use it on him if he tried any auctioneering at my expense this noon. Then he fined me five dollars more, swore that he'd show me what it meant to dare the marshal of Rawhide an' insult th' dignity of th' court an' town council, an' also that he'd shoot my liver all through my system if I didn't leave him to his reflections. Now, look here, stranger; noon is only two hours away an' I'm due to lose my outfit: what are *you* going to do to get me out of this mess?" he finished anxiously, hands on hips.

"You did real well, very fine, indeed," replied the stranger, smiling with content. "An' don't you worry about that outfit—I'm going to get it back for you an' a little bit more. So, as long as you don't lose nothin', you ain't got no kick coming, have you? An' you ain't got no interest in what I'm going to do. Just sit tight an' keep yore eyes an' ears open at noon. Meantime, if you want something to do to keep you busy, practise makin' speeches—you ought to be ashamed to be punchin' cows an' workin' for a living when you could use yore talents an' get a lot of graft besides. Any man who can say as much on nothing as you can ought to be in th' Senate representing some railroad company or water power steal—you don't have to work there, just loaf an' take easy money for cheating th' people what put you there. Now, don't get mad—I'm only stringing you: I wouldn't be mean enough to call you a senator. To tell th' truth, I think yo're too honest to even think of such a thing. But go ahead an' practise—*I* don't mind it a bit."

"Huh! I couldn't go to Congress," laughed Fisher. "I'd have to practise by gettin' elected mayor of some town an' then go to th' Legislature for th' finishing touches."

"Mr. Townsend would beat you out," murmured the stranger, looking out of the window and wishing for noon. He sauntered over to a chair, placed it where he could see his horse, and took things easy. The bartender returned with several men at his heels, and all were grinning and joking. They took up their places against the bar and indulged in frequent fits of chuckling, not letting their eyes stray from the man in the chair and the open street through the door, where the auction was to be held. They regarded the stranger in the light of a would-be public benefactor, a martyr, who was to provide the town with a little excitement before he followed his predecessors into the grave. Perhaps he would *not* be killed, perhaps he would shoot the pound-keeper and general public nuisance—but ah, this was the stuff of which dreams were made: the marshal would never be killed, he would thrive and outlive his fellow-townsmen, and die in bed at a ripe old age.

One of the citizens, dangling his legs from the card table, again looked closely at the man with the plan, and then turned to a companion beside him. "I've seen that there feller som'ers, sometime," he whispered. "I *know* I have. But I'll be teetotally dod-blasted if I can place him."

"Well, Jim; I never saw him afore, an' I don't know who he is," replied the other, refilling his pipe with elaborate care, "but if he can kill Townsend to-day, I'll be so plumb joyous I won't know what to do with m'self."

"I'm afraid he won't, though," remarked another, lolling back against the bar. "Th' marshal was born to hang—nobody can beat him on th' draw. But, anyhow, we're going to see some fun."

The first speaker, still straining his memory for a clue to the stranger's identity, pulled out a handful of silver and placed it on the table. "I'll bet that he makes good," he offered, but there were no takers.

The stranger now lazily arose and stepped into the doorway, leaning against the jamb and shaking his holster sharply to loosen the gun for action. He glanced quickly behind him and spoke curtly: "Remember, now—*I* am to do all th' talking at this auction; you fellers just look on."

A mumble of assent replied to him, and the townsmen craned their necks to look out. A procession slowly wended its way up the street, led by the marshal, astride a piebald horse bearing the crude brand of the CG. Three men followed him and numerous dogs of several colors, sizes, and ages roamed at will, in a listless, bored way, between the horse and the men. The dust arose sluggishly and slowly dissipated in the hot, shimmering air, and a fly buzzed with wearying persistence against the dirty glass in the front window.

The marshal, peering out from under the pulled-down brim of his Stetson, looked critically at the sleepy horse standing near the open door of the Paradise and sought its brand, but in vain, for it was standing with the wrong side towards him. Then he glanced at the man in the door, a puzzled expression over his face. He had known that man once, but time and events had wiped him nearly out of his memory and he could not place him. He decided that the other horse could wait until he had sold the one he was on, and, stopping before the door of the Paradise, he raised his left arm, his right arm lying close to his side, not far from the holster on his thigh.

"Gentlemen an' feller-citizens," he began: "As marshal of this boomin' city, I am about to offer for sale to th' highest bidder this A Number 1 piebald, pursooant to th' decree of th' local court an' with th' sanction of th' town council an' th' mayor. This same sale is for to pay th' town for th' board an' keep of this animal, an' to square th' fine in such cases made an' provided. It's sound in wind an' limb, fourteen han's high, an' in all ways a beautiful piece of hoss-flesh. Now, gentlemen, how much am I bid for this cayuse? Remember, before you make me any offer, that this animal is broke to punchin' cows an' is a first-class cayuse."

The crowd in the Paradise had flocked out into the street and oozed along the front of the building, while the stranger now leaned carelessly against his own horse, critically looking over the one on sale. Fisher, uneasy and worried, squirmed close at hand and glanced covertly from his horse and saddle to the guns in the belts on the members of the crowd.

It was the stranger who broke the silence: "Two bits I bid—two bits," he said, very quietly, whereat the crowd indulged in a faint snicker and a few nudges.

The marshal looked at him and then ignored him. "How much, gentlemen?" he asked, facing the crowd again.

"Two bits," repeated the stranger, as the crowd remained silent.

"Two bits!" yelled the marshal, glaring at him angrily: "*Two bits!* Why, th' *look* in this cayuse's eyes is worth four! Look at th' spirit in them eyes, look at th' intelligence! Th' saddle alone is worth a clean forty dollars of any man's money. I am out here to sell this animal to th' highest bidder; th' sale's begun, an' I want bids, not jokes. Now, who'll start it off?" he demanded, glancing around; but no one had anything to say except the terse stranger, who appeared to be getting irritated.

"You've got a starter—I've given you a bid. I bid two bits—t-w-o b-i-t-s, twenty-five cents. Now go ahead with yore auction."

The marshal thought he saw an attempt at humor, and since he was feeling quite happy, and since he knew that good humor is conducive to good bidding, he smiled, all the time, however, racking his memory for the name of the humorist. So he accepted the bid: "All right, this gentleman bids two bits. Two bits I am bid—two bits. Twenty-five cents. Who'll make it twenty-five dollars? Two bits—who says twenty-five dollars? Ah, did *you* say twenty-five dollars?" he snapped, levelling an accusing and threatening fore-finger at the man nearest him, who squirmed restlessly and glanced at the stranger. "*Did you say twenty-five dollars?*" he shouted.

The stranger came to the rescue. "He did not. He hasn't opened his mouth. But *I* said twenty-five *cents*," quietly observed the humorist.

"Who'll gimme thirty? Who'll gimme thirty dollars? Did I hear thirty dollars? Did I hear twenty-five dollars bid? Who said thirty dollars? Did *you* say twenty-five dollars?"

"How could he when he was talkin' politics to th' man behind him?" asked the stranger. "I said two bits," he added complacently, as he watched the auctioneer closely.

"I want twenty-five dollars—an' you shut yore blasted mouth!" snapped the marshal at the persistent twenty-five-cent man. He did not see the fire smouldering in the squinting eyes so alertly watching him. "Twenty-five dollars—not a cent less takes this cayuse. Why, gentlemen, he's worth twenty in *cans!* Gimme twenty-five dollars, somebody. *I* bid twenty-five. I want thirty. I want thirty, gentlemen; you must gimme thirty. *I* bid twenty-five dollars—who's going to make it thirty?"

"Show us yore twenty-five an' she's yourn," remarked the stranger, with exasperating assurance, while Fisher grew pale with excitement. The stranger was standing clear of his horse now, and alert readiness was stamped all over him. "You accepted my bid—show yore twenty-five dollars or take my two bits."

"You close that face of yourn!" exploded the marshal, angrily. "I don't mind a little fun, but you've got altogether too damned much to say. You've queered th' biddin', an' now you shut up!"

"I said two bits an' I mean just that. You show yore twenty-five or gimme that cayuse on my bid," retorted the stranger.

"By th' pants of Julius Caesar!" shouted the marshal. "I'll put you to sleep so you'll never wake up if I hears any more about you an' yore two bits!"

"Show me, Rednose," snapped the other, his gun out in a flash. "I want that cayuse, an' I want it quick. You show me twenty-five dollars or I'll take it out from under you on my bid, you yaller dog! *Stop it!* Shut up! That's suicide, that is. Others have tried it an' failed, an' yo're no sleight-of-hand gun-man. This is th' first time I ever paid a hoss-thief in *silver*, or bought stolen goods, but everything has to have a beginnin'. You get nervous with that hand of yourn an' I'll cure you of it! Git off that piebald, an' quick!"

The marshal felt stunned and groped for a way out, but the gun under his nose was as steady as a rock. He sat there stupidly, not knowing enough to obey orders.

"Come, get off that cayuse," sharply commanded the stranger. "An' I'll take yore Winchester as a fine for this high-handed business you've been carryin' on. You may be th' local court an' all th' town officials, but I'm th' Governor, an' here's my Supreme Court, as I was saying to th' boys a little while ago. Yo're overruled. Get off that cayuse, an' don't waste no more time about it, neither!"

The marshal glared into the muzzle of the weapon and felt a sinking in the pit of his stomach. Never before had he failed to anticipate the pull of a gun. As the stranger said, there must always be a beginning, a first time. He was thinking quickly now; he was master of himself again, but he realized that he was in a tight place unless he obeyed the man with the drop. Not a man in town would help him; on the other hand, they were all against him, and hugely enjoying his discomfiture. With some men he could afford to take chances and jerk at his gun even when at such a disadvantage, but—

"Stranger," he said slowly, "what's yore name?"

The crowd listened eagerly.

"My *friends* call me Hopalong Cassidy; other people, other things—you gimme that cayuse an' that Winchester. Here! Hand th' gun to Fisher, so there won't be no lamentable accidents; I don't want to shoot you, 'less I have to."

"They're both yourn," sighed Mr. Townsend, remembering a certain day over near Alameda, when he had seen Mr. Cassidy at gun-play. He dismounted slowly and sorrowfully. "Do I—do I get my two bits?" he asked.

"You shore do—yore gall is worth it," said Mr. Cassidy, turning the piebald over to its overjoyed owner, who was already arranging further gambling with his friend, the bartender.

Mr. Townsend pocketed the one bid, surveyed glumly the hilarious crowd flocking in to the bar to drink to their joy in his defeat, and wandered disconsolately back to the pound. He was never again seen in that locality, or by any of the citizens of Rawhide, for between dark and dawn he resumed his travels, bound for some locality far removed from limping, red-headed drawbacks.

XV

◆

Johnny Learns Something

For several weeks after Hopalong got back to the ranch, full of interesting stories and minus the grouch, things went on in a way placid enough for the most peacefully inclined individual that ever sat a saddle. And then trouble drifted down from the north and caused a look of anxiety to spoil Buck Peters' pleasant expression, and began to show on the faces of his men. When one finds the carcasses of two cows on the same day, and both are skinned, there can be only one conclusion. The killing and skinning of two cows out of herds that are numbered by thousands need not, in themselves, bring lines of worry to any foreman's brow; but there is the sting of being cheated, the possibility of the losses going higher unless a sharp lesson be given upon the folly of fooling with a very keen and active buzz-saw,—and it was the determination of the outfit of the Bar-20 to teach that lesson, and as quickly as circumstances would permit.

It was common knowledge that there was a more or less organized band of shiftless malcontents making its headquarters in and near Perry's Bend, some distance up the river, and the deduction in this case was easy. The Bar-20 cared very little about what went on at Perry's Bend—that was a matter which concerned only the ranches near that town—as long as no vexatious happenings sifted too far south. But they had so sifted, and Perry's Bend, or rather the undesirable class hanging out there, was due to receive a shock before long.

About a week after the finding of the first skinned

cows, Pete Wilson tornadoed up to the bunk house with a perforated arm. Pete was on foot, having lost his horse at the first exchange of shots, which accounts for the expression describing his arrival. Pete hated to walk, he hated still more to get shot, and most of all he hated to have to admit that his rifle-shooting was so far below par. He had seen the thief at work and, too eager to work up close to the cattle skinner before announcing his displeasure, had missed the first shot. When he dragged himself out from under his deceased horse the scenery was undisturbed save for a small cloud of dust hovering over a distant rise to the north of him. After delivering a short and bitter monologue he struck out for the ranch and arrived in a very hot and wrathful condition. It was contagious, that condition, and before long the entire outfit was in the saddle and pounding north, Pete overjoyed because his wound was so slight as not to bar him from the chase. The shock was on the way, and as events proved, was to be one long to linger in the minds of the inhabitants of Perry's Bend and the surrounding range.

The patrons of the Oasis liked their tobacco strong. The pungent smoke drifted in sluggish clouds along the low, black ceiling, following its upward slant toward the east wall and away from the high bar at the other end. This bar, rough and strong, ran from the north wall to within a scant two feet of the south wall, the opening bridged by a hinged board which served as an extension to the counter. Behind the bar was a rear door, low and double, the upper part barred securely—the lower part was used most. In front of and near the bar was a large round table, at which four men played cards silently, while two smaller tables were located along the north wall. Besides dilapidated chairs there were half a dozen low wooden boxes partly filled with sand, and attention was directed to the existence and purpose of these by a roughly lettered sign on the wall, reading: "Gents will look for a box first," which the "gents" sometimes did. The majority of the "gents" preferred to aim at various knotholes in the floor and bet on the result, chancing the outpouring of the proprietor's wrath if they missed.

On the wall behind the bar was a smaller and neater request: "Leave your guns with the bartender.—Edwards." This, although a month old, still called forth caustic and profane remarks from the regular frequenters of the saloon, for hitherto restraint in the matter of carrying weapons had been unknown. They forthwith evaded the order in a manner consistent with their characteristics—by carrying smaller guns where they could not be seen. The majority had simply sawed off a generous part of the long barrels of their Colts and Remingtons, which did not improve their accuracy.

Edwards, the new marshal of Perry's Bend, had come direct from Kansas and his reputation as a fighter had preceded him. When he took up his first day's work he was kept busy proving that he was the rightful owner of it and that it had not been exaggerated in any manner or degree. With the exception of one instance the proof had been bloodless, for he reasoned that gun-play should give way, whenever possible, to a crushing "right" or "left" to the point of the jaw or the pit of the stomach. His proficiency in the manly art was polished and thorough and bespoke earnest application. The last doubting Thomas to be convinced came to five minutes after his diaphragm had been rudely and suddenly raised several inches by a low right hook, and as he groped for his bearings and got his wind back again he asked, very feebly, where "Kansas" was; and the name stuck.

When Harlan heard the nickname for the first time he stopped pulling the cork out of a whiskey bottle long enough to remark, casually, "I allus reckoned Kansas was purty close to hell," and said no more about it. Harlan was the proprietor and bartender of the Oasis and catered to the excessive and uncritical thirsts of the ruck of range society, and he had objected vigorously to the placing of the second sign in his place of business; but at the close of an incisive if inelegant reply from the marshal, the sign went up, and stayed up. Edwards' language and delivery were as convincing as his fists.

The marshal did not like the Oasis; indeed, he went further and cordially hated it. Harlan's saloon was a thorn in his side and he was only waiting for a good excuse to wipe it off the local map. He was the Law, and behind him were the range riders, who would be only too glad to have the nest of rustlers wiped out and its gang of ne'er-do-wells scattered to the four winds. Indeed, he had been given to understand in a most polite and diplomatic way that if this were not done lawfully they would try to do it themselves, and they had great faith in their ability to handle the situation in a thorough and workmanlike manner. This would not do in a law-abiding community, as he called the town, and so he had replied that the work was his, and that it would be performed as soon as he believed himself justified to act. Harlan and his friends were fully conversant with the feeling against them and had become a little more cautious, alertly watching out for trouble.

On the evening of the day which saw Pete Wilson's discomfiture most of the *habitués* had assembled in the Oasis where, besides the card-players already mentioned, eight men lounged against the bar. There was some laughter, much subdued talking, and a little whispering. More whispering went on under that roof than in all the other places in town put together; for here rustling was planned, wayfaring strangers were "trimmed" in "frame-ups" at cards, and a hunted man was certain to find assistance. Harlan had once boasted that no fugitive had ever been taken from his saloon, and he was behind the bar and standing on the trap door which led to the six-by-six cellar when he made the assertion. It was true, for only those in his confidence knew of the place of refuge under the floor: it had been dug at night and the dirt carefully disposed of.

It had not been dark very long before talking ceased and card-playing was suspended while all looked up as the front door crashed open and two punchers entered, looking the crowd over with critical care.

"Stay here, Johnny," Hopalong told his youthful companion, and then walked forward, scrutinizing each scowling face in turn, while Johnny stood with his back to the door, keenly alert, his right hand resting lightly on his belt not far from the holster.

Harlan's thick neck grew crimson and his eyes hard. "Lookin' fer something?" he asked with bitter sarcasm, his hands under the bar. Johnny grinned hopefully and a sudden tenseness took possession of him as he watched for the first hostile move.

"Yes," Hopalong replied coolly, appraising Harlan's attitude and look in one swift glance, "but it ain't here, now. Johnny, get out," he ordered, backing after his companion, and safely outside, the two walked towards Jackson's store, Johnny complaining about the little time spent in the Oasis.

As they entered the store they saw Edwards, whose eyes asked a question.

"No; he ain't in there yet," Hopalong replied.

"Did you look all over? Behind th' bar?" Edwards asked, slowly. "He can't get out of town through that cordon you've got strung around it, an' he ain't nowhere else. Leastwise, I couldn't find him."

"Come on back!" excitedly exclaimed Johnny, turning

towards the door. "You didn't look behind th' bar! Come on—bet you ten dollars that's where he is!"

"Mebby yo're right, Kid," replied Hopalong, and the marshal's nodding head decided it.

In the saloon there was strong language, and Jack Quinn, expert skinner of other men's cows, looked inquiringly at the proprietor. "What's up now, Harlan?"

The proprietor laughed harshly but said nothing—taciturnity was his one redeeming trait. "Did you say cigars?" he asked, pushing a box across the bar to an impatient customer. Another beckoned to him and he leaned over to hear the whispered request, a frown struggling to show itself on his face. "Nix; you know my rule. No trust in here."

But the man at the far end of the line was unlike the proprietor and he prefaced his remarks with a curse. "*I* know what's up! They want Jerry Brown, that's what! An' I hopes they don't get him, th' bullies!"

"What did he do? Why do they want him?" asked the man who had wanted trust.

"Skinning. He was careless or crazy, working so close to their ranch houses. Nobody that has any sense would take a chance like that," replied Boston, adept at sleight-of-hand with cards and very much in demand when a frame-up was to be rung in on some unsuspecting stranger. His one great fault in the eyes of his partners was that he hated to divvy his winnings and at times had to be coerced into sharing equally.

"Aw, them big ranches make me mad," announced the first speaker. "Ten years ago there was a lot of little ranchers, an' every one of 'em had his own herd, an' plenty of free grass an' water fer it. Where are th' little herds now? Where are th' cows that *we* used to own?" he cried, hotly. "What happens to a maverick-hunter now-a-days? By God, if a man helps hisself to a pore, sick dogie he's hunted down! It can't go on much longer, an' that's shore."

Cries of approbation arose on all sides, for his auditors ignored the fact that their kind, by avarice and thievery, had forever killed the occupation of maverick-hunting. That belonged to the old days, before the demand for cows and their easy and cheap transportation had boosted the prices and made them valuable.

Slivers Lowe leaped up from his chair. "Yo're right, Harper! Dead right! *I* was a little cattle owner once, so was you, an' Jerry, an' most of us!" Slivers found it convenient to forget that fully half of his small herd had perished in the bitter and long winter of five years before, and that the remainder had either flowed down his parched throat or been lost across the big round table near the bar. Not a few of his cows were banked in the East under Harlan's name.

The rear door opened slightly and one of the loungers looked up and nodded. "It's all right, Jerry. But get a move on!"

"Here, *you!*" called Harlan, quickly bending over the trap door, *"Lively!"*

Jerry was half way to the proprietor when the front door swung open and Hopalong, closely followed by the marshal, leaped into the room, and immediately thereafter the back door banged open and admitted Johnny. Jerry's right hand was in his side coat pocket and Johnny, young and self-confident, and with a lot to learn, was certain that he could beat the fugitive on the draw.

"I reckon you won't blot no more brands!" he cried, triumphantly, watching both Jerry and Harlan.

The card-players had leaped to their feet and at a signal from Harlan they surged forward to the bar and formed a barrier between Johnny and his friends; and as they did so that puncher jerked at his gun, twisting to half face the crowd. At that instant fire and smoke spurted from Jerry's side coat pocket and the odor of burning cloth arose. As Johnny fell, the rustler ducked low and sprang for the door. A gun roared twice in the front of the room and Jerry staggered a little and cursed as he gained the opening, but he plunged into the darkness and threw himself into the saddle on the first horse he found in the small corral.

When the crowd massed, Hopalong leaped at it and strove to tear his way to the opening at the end of the bar, while the marshal covered Harlan and the others. Finding that he could not get through, Hopalong sprang on the shoulder of the nearest man and succeeded in winging the fugitive at the first shot, the other going wild. Then, frantic with rage and anxiety, he beat his way through the crowd, hammering mercilessly at heads with the butt of his Colt, and knelt at his friend's side.

Edwards, angered almost to the point of killing, ordered the crowd to stand against the wall, and laughed viciously when he saw two men senseless on the floor. "Hope he beat in yore heads!" he gritted, savagely. "Harlan, put yore paws up in sight or I'll drill you clean! Now climb over an' get in line—quick!"

Johnny moaned and opened his eyes. "Did—did I—get him?"

"No; but he gimleted you, all right," Hopalong replied. "You'll come 'round if you keep quiet." He arose, his face hard with the desire to kill. "I'm coming back for *you*, Harlan, after I get yore friend! An' all th' rest of you pups, too!"

"Get me out of here," whispered Johnny.

"Shore enough, Kid; but keep quiet," replied Hopalong, picking him up in his arms and moving carefully towards the door. "We'll get him, Johnny; an' all th' rest, too, when—" the voice died out in the direction of Jackson's and the marshal, backing to the front door, slipped out and to one side, running backward, his eyes on the saloon.

"Yore day's about over, Harlan," he muttered. "There's going to be some few funerals around here before many hours pass."

When he reached the store he found the owner and two Double-Arrow punchers taking care of Johnny. "Where's Hopalong?" he asked.

"Gone to tell his foreman," replied Jackson. "Hey, youngster, you let them bandages alone! Hear me?"

"Hullo, Kansas," remarked John Bartlett, foreman of the Double-Arrow. "I come nigh getting yore man; somebody rode past me like a streak in th' dark, so I just ups an' lets drive for luck, an' so did he. I heard him cuss an' I emptied my gun after him."

"Th' rest was a-passing th' word along to ride in when I left th' line," remarked one of the other punchers. "How you feeling now, Johnny?"

XVI

♦

The End of the Trail

The rain slanted down in sheets and the broken plain, thoroughly saturated, held the water in pools or sent it down the steep sides of the arroyo, to feed the turbulent flood which swept along the bottom, foam-flecked and covered with swiftly moving driftwood. Around a bend in the arroyo, where the angry water flung itself against the ragged bulwark of rock and flashed away in a gleaming line of foam, a horseman appeared, bending low in the saddle for better protection against the storm. He rode along the edge of the stream on the farther bank, opposite the steep bluff on the northern side, forcing his wounded and jaded horse to keep fetlock deep in the water which swirled and sucked about its legs. He was trying his hardest to hide his trail. Lower down the hard, rocky ground extended to the water's edge, and if he could delay his pursuers for an hour or so, he felt that, even with his tired horse, he would have more than an even chance.

But they had gained more than he knew. Suddenly above him on the top of the steep bluff across the torrent a man loomed up against the clouds, peered intently into the arroyo, and then waved his sombrero to an unseen companion. A puff of smoke flashed from his shoulder and streaked away, the report of the shot lost in the gale. The fugitive's horse reared and plunged into the deep water and with its rider was swept rapidly towards the bend, the way they had come.

"That makes th' fourth time I've missed that coyote!" angrily exclaimed Hopalong as Red Connors joined him.

The other quickly raised his rifle and fired; and the horse, spilling its rider out of the saddle, floated away tail first. The fugitive, gripping his rifle, bobbed and whirled at the whim of the greedy water as shots struck near him. Making a desperate effort, he staggered up the bank and fell exhausted behind a boulder.

"Well, th' coyote is afoot, anyhow," said Red, with great satisfaction.

"Yes; but how are we going to get to him?" asked Hopalong. "We can't get th' cayuses down here, an' we can't swim *that* water without them. And if we could, he'd pot us easy."

"There's a way out of it somewhere," Red replied, disappearing over the edge of the bluff to gamble with Fate.

"Hey! Come back here, you chump!" cried Hopalong, running forward. "He'll get you, shore!"

"That's a chance I've got to take if I get him," was the reply.

A puff of smoke sailed from behind the boulder on the other bank and Hopalong, kneeling for steadier aim, fired and then followed his friend. Red was downstream casting at a rock across the torrent but the wind toyed with the heavy, water-soaked *reata* as though it were a string. As Hopalong reached his side a piece of driftwood ducked under the water and an angry humming sound died away downstream. As the report reached their ears a jet of water spurted up into Red's face and he stepped back involuntarily.

"He's some shaky," Hopalong remarked, looking back at the wreath of smoke above the boulder. "I reckon I must have hit him harder than I thought in Harlan's. Gee! he's wild as blazes!" he explained as a bullet hummed high above his head and struck sharply against the rock wall.

"Yes," Red replied, coiling the rope. "I was trying to rope that rock over there. If I could anchor to that, th' current would push us over quick. But it's too far with this wind blowing."

"We can't do nothing here 'cept get plugged. He'll be getting steadier as he rests from his fight with th' water," Hopalong remarked, and added quickly, "Say, remember that meadow back there a ways? We can make her from there, all right."

"Yo're right; that's what we've got to do. He's sending 'em nearer every shot—Gee! I could 'most feel th' wind of that one. An' blamed if it ain't stopped raining. Come on."

They clambered up the slippery, muddy bank to where they had left their horses, and cantered back over their trail. Minute after minute passed before the cautious skulker among the rocks across the stream could believe in his good fortune. When he at last decided that he was alone again he left his shelter and started away, with slowly weakening stride, over cleanly washed rock where he left no trail.

It was late in the afternoon before the two irate punchers appeared upon the scene, and their comments, as they hunted slowly over the hard ground, were numerous and bitter. Deciding that it was hopeless in that vicinity, they began casting in great circles on the chance of crossing the trail further back from the river. But they had little faith in their success. As Red remarked, snorting like a horse in his disgust, "I'll bet four dollars an' a match he's swum down th' river clean to hell just to have th' laugh on us." Red had long since given it up as a bad job, though continuing to search, when a shout from the distant Hopalong sent him forward on a run.

"Hey, Red!" cried Hopalong, pointing ahead of them. "Look there! Ain't that a house?"

"Naw; course not! It's a—it's a ship!" Red snorted sarcastically. "What did you think it might be?"

"G'wan!" retorted his companion. "It's a mission."

"Ah, g'wan yorself! What's a mission doing up here?" Red snapped.

"What do you think they do? What do they do anywhere?" hotly rejoined Hopalong, thinking about Johnny. "There! See th' cross?"

"Shore enough!"

"An' there's tracks at last—mighty wobbly, but tracks just th' same. Them rocks couldn't go on forever. Red, I'll bet he's cashed in by this time."

"Cashed nothing! Them fellers don't."

"Well, if he's in that joint we might as well go back home. We won't get him, not nohow," declared Hopalong.

"Huh! You wait an' see!" replied Red, pugnaciously.

"Reckon you never run up agin' a mission real hard," Hopalong responded, his memory harking back to the time he had disagreed with a convent, and they both meant about the same to him as far as winning out was concerned.

"Think I'm a fool kid?" snapped Red, aggressively.

"Well, you ain't no *kid*."

"You let *me* do th' talking; *I'll* get him."

"All right; an' I'll do th' laughing," snickered Hopalong, at the door. "Sic 'em, Red!"

The other boldly stepped into a small vestibule, Hopalong close at his heels. Red hitched his holster and walked heavily into a room at his left. With the exception of a bench, a table, and a small altar, the room was devoid of furnishings, and the effect of these was lost in the dim light from the narrow windows. The peculiar, not unpleasant odor of burning incense and the dim light awakened a latent reverence and awe in Hopalong, and he sneaked off his sombrero, an inexplicable feeling of guilt stealing over him. There were three doors in the walls, deeply shrouded in the dusk of the room, and it was very hard to watch all three at once.

Red was peering into the dark corners, his hand on the butt of his Colt, and hardly knew what he was looking for. "This joint must 'a' looked plumb good to that coyote, all right. He had a hell of a lot of luck, but he won't keep it for long, damn him!" he remarked.

"Quit cussing!" tersely ordered Hopalong. "An' for God's sake, throw out that damned cigarette! Ain't you got no manners?"

Red listened intently and then grinned. "Hear that? They're playing dominoes in there—come on!"

"Aw', you chump! 'Dominee' means 'mother' in Latin, which is what they speaks."

"How do you know?"

"Hanged if I can tell—I've heard it somewhere, that's all."

"Well, I don't care what it means. This is a frame-up so that coyote can get away. I'll bet they gave him a cayuse an' started him off while we've been losing time in here. I'm going inside an' ask some questions."

Before he could put his plan into execution, Hopalong nudged him and he turned to see his friend staring at one of the doors. There had been no sound, but he would swear that a monk stood gravely regarding them, and he rubbed his eyes. He stepped back suspiciously and then started forward again.

"Look here, stranger," he remarked, with quiet emphasis, "we're after that cow-lifter, an' we mean to get him. Savvy?"

The monk did not appear to hear him, so he tried another tack. *"Habla Española?"* he asked, experimentally.

"You have ridden far?" replied the monk in perfect English.

"All th' way from th' Bend," Red replied, relieved. "We're after Jerry Brown. He tried to kill Johnny, an' near made good. An' I reckon we've treed him, judgin' from th' tracks."

"And if you capture him?"

"He won't have no more use for no side pocket shooting."

"I see; you will kill him."

"Shore's it's wet outside."

"I'm afraid you are doomed to disappointment."

"Ya-as?" asked Red with a rising inflection.

"You will not want him now," replied the monk.

Red laughed sarcastically and Hopalong smiled.

"There ain't a-going to be no argument about it. Trot him out," ordered Red, grimly.

The monk turned to Hopalong. "Do you, too, want him?"

Hopalong nodded.

"My friends, he is safe from your punishment."

Red wheeled instantly and ran outside, returning in a few moments, smiling triumphantly. "There are tracks coming in, but there ain't none going away. He's here. If you don't lead us to him we'll shore have to rummage around an' poke him out for ourselves: which is it?"

"You are right—he is here, and he is not here."

"We're waiting," Red replied, grinning.

"When I tell you that you will not want him, do you still insist on seeing him?"

"We'll see him, an' we'll want him, too."

As the rain poured down again the sound of approaching horses was heard, and Hopalong ran to the door in time to see Buck Peters swing off his mount and step forward to enter the building. Hopalong stopped him and briefly outlined the situation, begging him to keep the men outside. The monk met his return with a grateful smile and, stepping forward, opened the chapel door, saying, "Follow me."

The unpretentious chapel was small and nearly dark, for the usual dimness was increased by the lowering clouds outside. The deep, narrow window openings, fitted with stained glass, ran almost to the rough-hewn rafters supporting the steep-pitched roof, upon which the heavy rain beat again with a sound like that of distant drums. Gusts of rain and the water from the roof beat against the south windows, while the wailing wind played its mournful cadences about the eaves, and the stanch timbers added their creaking notes to swell the dirge-like chorus.

At the farther end of the room two figures knelt and moved before the white altar, the soft light of flickering candles playing fitfully upon them and glinting from the altar ornaments, while before a rough coffin, which rested upon two pedestals, stood a third, whose rich, sonorous Latin filled the chapel with impressive sadness. "Give eternal rest to them, O Lord,"—the words seeming to become a part of the room. The ineffably sad, haunting melody of the mass whispered back from the roof between the assaults of the enraged wind, while from the altar came the responses in a low, Gregorian chant, and through it all the clinking of the censer chains added intermittent notes. Aloft streamed the vapor of the incense, wavering with the air currents, now lost in the deep twilight of the sanctuary, and now faintly revealed by the glow of the candles, perfuming the air with its aromatic odor.

As the last deep-toned words died away the celebrant moved slowly around the coffin, swinging the censer over it and then, sprinkling the body and making the sign of the cross above its head, solemnly withdrew.

From the shadows along the side walls other figures silently emerged and grouped around the coffin. Raising it they turned it slowly around and carried it down the dim aisle in measured tread, moving silently as ghosts.

"He is with God, Who will punish according to his sins," said a low voice, and Hopalong started, for he had forgotten the presence of the guide. "God be with you, and may you die as he died—repentant and in peace."

Buck chafed impatiently before the chapel door leading to a small, well-kept graveyard, wondering what it was that kept quiet for so long a time his two most assertive men, when he had momentarily expected to hear more or less turmoil and confusion.

C-r-e-a-k! He glanced up, gun in hand and raised as the door swung slowly open. His hand dropped suddenly and he took a short step forward; six black-robed figures shouldering a long box stepped slowly past him, and his nostrils were assailed by the pungent odor of the incense. Behind them came his fighting punchers, humble, awed, reverent, their sombreros in their hands, and their heads bowed.

"What in blazes!" exclaimed Buck, wonder and surprise struggling for the mastery as the others cantered up.

"He's cashed," Red replied, putting on his sombrero and nodding toward the procession.

Buck turned like a flash and spoke sharply: "Skinny! Lanky! Follow that glory-outfit, an' see what's in that box!"

Billy Williams grinned at Red. "Yo're shore pious, Red."

"Shut up!" snapped Red, anger glinting in his eyes, and Billy subsided.

Lanky and Skinny soon returned from accompanying the procession.

"I had to look twice to be shore it was him. His face was plumb happy, like a baby. But he's gone, all right," Lanky reported.

"Deader'n hell," remarked Skinny, looking around curiously. "This here is some shack, ain't it?" he finished.

"All right—he knowed how he'd finish when he began. Now for that dear Mr. Harlan," Buck replied, vaulting into the saddle. He turned and looked at Hopalong, and his wonder grew. "Hey, *you!* Yes, *you!* Come out of that an' put on yore lid! Straddle leather—we can't stay here all night."

Hopalong started, looked at his sombrero and silently obeyed. As they rode down the trail and around a corner he turned in his saddle and looked back; and then rode on, buried in thought.

Billy, grinning, turned and playfully punched him in the ribs. "Gettin' glory, Hoppy?"

Hopalong raised his head and looked him steadily in the eyes; and Billy, losing his curiosity and the grin at the same instant, looked ahead, whistling softly.

XVII

♦

Edwards' Ultimatum

Edwards slid off the counter in Jackson's store and glowered at the pelting rain outside, perturbed and grouchy. The wounded man in the corner stirred and looked at him without interest and forthwith renewed his profane monologue, while the proprietor, finishing his task, leaned back against the shelves and swore softly. It was a lovely atmosphere.

"Seems to me they've been gone a long time," grumbled the wounded man. "Reckon he led on a long chase—had six hours' start, th' toad." He paused and then as an afterthought said with conviction: "But they'll get him—they allus do when they make up their minds to it."

Edwards nodded moodily and Jackson replied with a monosyllable.

"Wish I could 'a' gone with 'em," Johnny growled. "I like to square my own accounts. It's allus that way. I get plugged an' my friends clean th' slate. There was that time Bye-an'-Bye went an' ambushed me—ah, th' devil! But I tell you one thing: when I get well I'm going down to Harlan's an' clean house proper."

"Yo're in hard luck again: that'll be done as soon as yore friends get back," Jackson replied, carefully selecting a dried apricot from a box on the counter and glancing at the marshal to see how he took the remark.

"That'll be done before then," Edwards said crisply, with the air of a man who has just settled a doubt. "They won't be back much before tomorrow if he headed for the country I think he did. I'm going down to th' Oasis an' tell that gang to clear out of this town. They've been here too long now. I never had 'em dead to rights before, but I've got it on 'em this time. I'd 'a' sent 'em packing yesterday only I sort of hated to take a man's business away from him an' make him lose his belongings. But I've wrastled it all out an' they've got to go." He buttoned his coat about him and pulled his sombrero more firmly on his head, starting for the door. "I'll be back soon," he said over his shoulder as he grasped the handle.

"You better wait till you get help—there's too many down there for one man to watch an' handle," Jackson hastily remarked. "Here, I'll go with you," he offered, looking for his hat.

Edwards laughed shortly. "You stay here. I do my own work by myself when I can—that's what I'm here for, an' I can do this, all right. If I took any help they'd reckon I was scared," and the door slammed shut behind him.

"He's got sand a plenty," Jackson remarked. "He'd try to push back a stampede by main strength if he reckoned it was his duty. It's his good luck that he wasn't killed long ago—I'd 'a' been."

"They're a bunch of cowards," replied Johnny. "As long as you ain't afraid of 'em, none of 'em wants to start anything. Bunch of sheep!" he snorted. "Didn't Jerry shoot me through his pocket?"

"Yes; an' yo're another lucky dog," Jackson responded, having in mind that at first Johnny had been thought to be desperately wounded. "Why, yore friends have got th' worst of this game; they're worse off than you are—out all day an' night in this cussed storm."

While they talked Edwards made his way through the cold downpour to Harlan's saloon, alone and unafraid, and greatly pleased by the order he would give. At last he had proof enough to work on, to satisfy his conscience, for the inevitable had come as the culmination of continued and clever defiance of law and order.

He deliberately approached the front door of the Oasis and, opening it, stepped inside, his hands resting on his guns—he had packed two Colts for the last twenty-four hours. His appearance caused a ripple of excitement to run around the room. After what had taken place, a visit from him could mean only one thing—trouble. And it was entirely possible that he had others within call to help him out if necessary.

Harlan knew that he would be the one held responsible and he ceased wiping a glass and held the cloth suspended in one hand and the glass in the other. "Well?" he snapped, angrily, his eyes smouldering with fixed hatred.

"Mebby you think it's well, but it's going to be a blamed sight better before sundown tomorrow night," evenly replied the marshal. "I just dropped in sort of free-like to tell you to pack up an' get out of town before dark—load yore wagon an' vamoose; an' take yore friends with you, too. If you don't—" he did not finish in words, for his tightening lips made them unnecessary.

"*What!*" yelled Harlan, red with anger. He placed his hands on the bar and leaned over it as if to give emphasis to his words. "*Me* pack up an' git! *Me* leave this shack! Who's going to pay me for it, hey? *Me* leave town! You drop out again an' go back to Kansas where you come from—they're easier back there!"

"Well, so far I ain't found nothing very craggy 'round here," retorted Edwards, closely watching the muttering crowd by the bar. "Takes more than a loud voice an' a pack of sneaking coyotes to send me looking for something easier. An' let me tell you this: *You* stay away from Kansas—they hangs people like you back there. That's whatever. You pack up an' git out of this town or I'll start a burying plot with you on yore own land."

The low, angry buzz of Harlan's friends and their savage, scowling faces would have deterred a less determined man; but Edwards knew they were afraid of him, and the men on whom he could call to back him up. And he knew that there must always be a start, there must be one man to show the way; and each of the men he faced was waiting for some one else to lead.

"You all slip over th' horizon before dark tonight, an' it's dark early these days," he continued. *"Don't get restless with yore hands!"* he snapped ominously at the crowd. "I means what I say—you shake th' mud from this town off yore boots before dark—before that Bar-20 outfit gets back," he finished meaningly.

Questions, imprecations, and threats filled the room, and the crowd began to spread out slowly. His guns came out like a flash and he laughed with the elation that comes with impending battle. "Th' first man to start it'll drop," he said, evenly. "Who's going to be th' martyr?"

"I *won't* leave town!" shouted Harlan. "I'll stay here if I'm killed for it!"

"I admire yore loyalty to principle, but you've got damned little sense," retorted the marshal. "You ain't no practical man. *Keep yore hands where they are!"*—his vibrant voice turned the shifting crowd to stone-like rigidity and he backed slowly toward the door, the poor light gleaming dully from the polished blue steel of his Colts. Rugged, lion-like, charged to the finger tips with reckless courage and dare-devil self-confidence, his personality overflowed and dominated the room, almost hypnotic in its effect. He was but one against many, but he was the master, and they knew it; they had known it

long enough to accept it without question, and the training now stood him in good stead.

For a moment he stood in the open doorway, keenly
scrutinizing them for signs of danger, his unwavering
guns charged with certain death and his strong face made
stronger by the shadows in its hollows. "Before dark!"—
and he was gone.

He left behind him deep silence, which endured for
several moments.

"By th' Lord, I *won't!*" cried Harlan, still staring at
the door.

The spell was broken and a babel of voices filled the
room, threats mingling with excuses, hot, vibrant, profane. These men were not cowards all the way through,
but only when face to face with the master. They had
flourished in a way by their wits alone on the same
range with the outfits of the C-80 and the Double-Arrow,
for individually they were "bad," and collectively they
made a force of no mean strength. Edwards had landed
among them like a thunderbolt and had proved his prowess, and they still held him in awesome respect. His
reckless audacity and grim singleness of purpose had
saved him on more than one occasion, for had he wavered once he would have been shot down without mercy.
But gradually his enforcement of hampering laws became more and more intolerable, and their subordi-
nated spirits were nearly on the point of revolt. When
he faced them they resumed their former positions in
relation to him—but once out of his sight they plotted
to destroy him. Here was the crisis: it was now or never.
They could not evade his ultimatum—it was obey or
fight.

Submission was not to be thought of, for to flee would
be to lose caste, and the story of such an act would follow
them wherever they went, and brand them as cowards.

Here they had lived, and here they would stay if possible, and to this end they discussed ways and means.

"Harlan's right!" emphatically announced Laramie Joe. "We can't pull out and have this foller us."

"We should have started it with a rush when he was in here," remarked Boston, regretfully.

Harlan stopped his pacing and faced them, shoving out a bottle of whiskey as an aid to his logic.

"That chance is past, an' I don't know but what it is a good thing," he began. "He was primed an' looking fer trouble, an' he'd shore got a few of us afore he went under. What we want is strategy—that's th' game. You fellers have got as much brains as him, an' if we thrash this thing out we can find a way to call his play—an' get him! No use of any of us getting plugged 'less we have to. But whatever we do we've got to start it right quick an' have it over before that Bar-20 gang comes back. Harper, you an' Quinn go scouting—an' don't take no guns with you, neither. Act like you was hitting th' long trail out, an' work back here on a circle. See how many of his friends are in town. While you are gone th' rest of us will hold a pow-wow an' take th' kinks out of this game. Chase along, an' don't lose no time."

"Good!" cried Slivers Lowe emphatically. "There's blamed few fellers in town now that have any use for him, for most of them are off on th' ranges. Bet we won't have more than six to fight, an' there's that many of us here."

The scouts departed at once and the remaining four drew close in consultation.

"One more drink around and then no more till this trouble is over," Harlan said, passing the bottle. The drinks, in view of the coming drouth and the thirsty work ahead, were long and deep, and new courage and vindictiveness crept through their veins.

"Now here's th' way it looks to me," Harlan continued,

placing the bottle, untasted by himself, on the floor behind him. "We've got to work a surprise an' take Edwards an' his friends off their guard. That'll be easy if we're careful, because they think we ain't looking for fight. When we get them out of the way we can take Jackson's store an' use one of th' other shacks an' wait for th' Bar-20 to ride in. They'll canter right in, like they allus do, an' when they get close enough we'll open th' game with a volley an' make every shot tell. 'T won't last long, 'cause every one of us will have his man named before they get here. Then th' few straddlers in town, seeing how easy we've gone an' handled it, 'll join us. We've got four men to come in yet, an' by th' time th' C-80 an' Double-Arrow hears about it we'll be fixed to drive 'em back home. We ought to be over a dozen strong by dark."

"That sounds good, all right," remarked Slivers, thoughtfully, "but can we do it that easy?"

"Course we can! We ain't fools, an' we all can shoot as well as them," snapped Laramie Joe, the most courageous of the lot. Laramie had taken only one drink, and that a small one, for he was wise enough to realize that he needed his wits as keen as he could have them.

"We can do it easy, if Edwards goes under first," hastily replied Harlan. "An' me an' Laramie will see to that part of it. If we don't get him, you-all can hit th' trail an' we won't be sore about it. That is, unless you are made of th' stuff that stands up an' fights 'stead of running away. I reckon I ain't none mistaken in any of you. You'll all be there when things get hot."

"You can bet th' shack *I* won't do no trail-hitting," growled Boston, glancing at Slivers, who squirmed a little under the hint.

"Well, I'm glued to th' crowd; you can't lose me, fellers," Slivers remarked, recrossing his legs uneasily. "Are we going to begin it from here?"

"We ought to spread out cautious and surround Jackson's, or wherever Edwards is," Laramie Joe suggested. "That's my—"

"Yo're right! Now you've hit it plumb on th' head!" interrupted Harlan, slapping Laramie heartily across the back. "What did I tell you about our brains?" he cried, enthusiastically. He had been on the point of suggesting that plan of operations when Laramie took the words out of his mouth. "I'd never thought of that, Laramie," he lied, his face beaming. "Why, we've got 'em licked to a finish right now!"

"That *is* a hummer of a game," laughed Slivers. "But how about th' Bar-20 crowd?"

"I've told you that already," replied the proprietor.

"You bet it's a hummer," cried Boston, reaching for the whiskey bottle under cover of the excitement and enthusiasm.

Harlan pushed it away with his foot and raised his clenched fist. "Do you wonder I didn't think of that plan?" he demanded. "Ain't I been too mad to think at all? Hain't I seen my friends treated like dogs, an' made to swaller insults when I couldn't raise my hand to stop it? Didn't I see Jerry Brown chased out of my place like a wild beast? If we are what we've been called, then we'll sneak out of town with our tails atween our laigs; but if we're men we'll stay right here an' cram th' insults down th' throats of them that made 'em! If we're *men* let's prove it an' make them liars swaller our lead."

"My sentiments an' allus was!" roared Slivers, slapping Harlan's shoulder.

"We're men, all right, an' we'll show 'em it, too!"

At that instant the door opened and four guns covered it before it had swung a foot.

"Put 'em down—it's Quinn!" exclaimed the man in the doorway, flinching a bit. "All right, Jed," he called

over his shoulder to the man who crowded him. After
Quinn came Big Jed and Harper brought up the rear.
They had no more than shaken the water from their sombreros when the back door let in Charley Rich and his
two companions, Frank and Tom Nolan. While greetings
were being exchanged and the existing conditions explained to the newcomers, Harper and Quinn led Harlan
to one side and reported, the proprietor smiling and nodding his head wisely. And while he listened, Slivers sur-
reptitiously corralled the whiskey bottle and when the
last man finished with it there was nothing in it but air.

"Well, boys," exclaimed Harlan, "things are our way.
Quinn, here, met Joe Barr, of th' C-80, who said Converse
an' four other fellers, all friends of Edwards, stopped at
th' ranch an' won't be back home till th' storm stops.
Harper saw Fred Neal going back to his ranch, so all
we've got to figger on is th' marshal, Barr, an' Jackson,
an' they're all in Jackson's store. Lacey might cut in,
since he'd sell more liquor if I went under, but he can't do
very much if he does take a hand. Now we'll get right at
it." The whole thing was gone over thoroughly and in
detail, positions assigned and a signal agreed upon. Seeing that weapons were in good condition after their long
storage in the cellar, and that cartridge belts were full,
the ten men left the room one at a time or in pairs, Harlan and Laramie Joe being the last. And both Harlan and
Laramie delayed long enough to take the precaution of
placing horses where they would be handy in case of
need.

XVIII

♦

Harlan Strikes

Joe Barr laughingly replied to Johnny Nelson's growled remarks about the condition of things in general and tried to soothe him, but Johnny was unsoothable.

"An' I've been telling him right along that he's got th' best of it," complained Jackson in a weary voice. "Got a measly hole through his shoulder—good Lord! if it had gone a little lower!" he finished with a show of exasperation.

"An' ain't I been telling you all along that it ain't th' measly hole in my shoulder that's got me on th' prod?" retorted Johnny, with more earnestness than politeness. "But why couldn't I go with my friends after Jerry an' get shot later if I had to get it at all? Look what I'm missing, roped an' throwed in this cussed ten-by-ten shack while they're having a little excitement."

"Yo're missing some blamed nasty weather, Kid," replied the marshal. "You ain't got no kick coming at all. Why, I got soaked clean through just going down to th' Oasis."

"Well, I'm kicking, just th' same," snapped Johnny. "An' furthermore, I don't see nobody big enough to stop me, neither—did you all get that?"

The rear door opened and Fred Neal looked in. "Hey, Barr; come out an' gimme a hand in th' corral. Busted my cinch all to pieces half a mile out—an' how th' devil it ever busted like that is—" the door slammed shut and softened his monologue.

"Would you listen to that!" snorted Barr in an injured

tone. "Didn't I go an' tell him near a month ago that his cussed cinch wouldn't hold no better'n a piece of wet paper?" His complaint added materially to the atmosphere of sullen discontent pervading the room. "An' now I gotter go out in this rain an'—" the slam of the door surpassed anything yet attempted in that line of endeavor. Jackson grabbed a can of corn as it jarred off the shelf behind him and directed a pleasing phrase after the peevish Barr.

"Say, won't somebody please smile?" gravely asked Edwards. "I never saw such a happy, cheerful bunch before."

"I might smile if I wasn't so blamed hungry," retorted Johnny. "Doesn't anybody ever eat in this town?" he asked in great sarcasm. "Mebby a good feed won't do me no good, but I'm going to fill myself regardless. An' after that, if th' grub don't shock me to death, I'm shore going to trim somebody at Ol' Sledge—for two bits a hand."

"If I could play you enough hands at that price I could sell out an' live high without working," grinned Jackson, preparing to give the reckless invalid all he could eat. "That's purty high, Kid; but I just feel real devilish, an' I'm coming in."

"An' I'll go over to my shack, get some money, an' bust th' pair of you," laughed Edwards, again buttoning his coat and going towards the door. "Holy Cats! A log must 'a' got jammed in th' sluice-gate up there," he muttered, scowling at the black sky. "It's coming down harder'n ever, but here goes," and he stepped quickly into the storm.

Jackson paused with a frying pan in his hands and looked through the window after the departing marshal, and saw him stagger, stumble forward, then jerk out his guns and begin firing. Hard firing now burst out in front and Jackson, cursing angrily, dropped the pan and reached for his rifle—to drop it also and sink down, struck by the bullet which drilled through the window. Johnny let out a yell of rage, grabbed his Colt, and ran to the door in time to see Edwards slowly raise up on one elbow, fire his last shot, and fall back riddled by bullets.

Jackson crawled to his rifle and then to the side window, where he propped his back against a box and prepared to do his best. "It was shore a surprise," he swore. "An' they went an' got Edwards before he could do anything."

"They did not!" retorted Johnny. "He—" the glass in the door vibrated sharply and the speaker, stepping to one side out of sight, with a new and superficial wound, opened fire on the building down the street. Two men were lying on the ground across the street—these Edwards had shot—and another was trying to drag himself to the shelter of a building. A man sprinted from an old corral close by in a brave and foolhardy attempt to save his friend, and Johnny swore because he had to fire twice at the same mark.

The rear door crashed open and shut as Barr, closely followed by Neal, ran in. They had been caught in the corral but, thanks to Harlan's whiskey, had managed to hold their own until they had a chance to make a rush for the store.

"Where's th' marshal?" cried Barr, catching sight of Jackson. "Are you plugged bad?" he asked, anxiously.

"Well, I ain't plugged a whole lot *good!*" snapped Jackson. "An' Edwards is dead. They shot him down without warning. We're going to get ours, too—these walls don't stop them bullets. How many out there?"

"Must be a dozen," hastily replied Neal, who had not remained idle. Both he and Barr were working like mad men moving boxes and barrels against the walls to make a breastwork capable of stopping the bullets which came through the boards.

"I reckon—I'm bleeding inside," Jackson muttered, wearily and without hope. "Wonder how—long we—can hold out?"

"We'll hold out till we're good an' dead!" replied Johnny, hotly. "They ain't got us yet an' they'll pay for it before they do. If we can hold 'em off till Buck an' th' rest come back we'll have th' pleasure of seein' 'em buried."

"Oh, I'll get you next time!" assured Barr to an enemy, slipping a fresh cartridge into the Sharps and peering intently at a slight rise on the muddy plain. "You shoot like yo're drunk," he mumbled.

"But what is it all about, anyhow?" asked Neal, finding time for an immaterial question. "Who are they?—can't see nothing but blurs through this rain."

"Yes; what's th' game?" asked Barr, mildly surprised that he had not thought of it before.

"It's that Oasis gang," Johnny responded. He fired, and growled with disappointment. "Harlan's at th' head of it," he added.

"Edwards—told Harlan to—get out of—town," Jackson began.

"An' to take his gang with him," Johnny interposed quickly to save Jackson from the strain. "They had till dark. Guess th' rest. Oh, you *coyote!*" he shouted, staggering back. There was a report farther down the barricade and Neal called out, "I got him, Nelson; he's done. How are you?"

"Mad! Mad!" yelled Johnny, touching his twice-wounded shoulder and dancing with rage and pain. "Right in th' same place! Oh, wait! *Wait!* Hey, gimme a rifle—I can't do nothing with a Colt at this range; my name ain't Hopalong," and he went slamming around the room in hot search of what he wanted.

"There ain't—no more—Johnny," feebly called Jackson, raising slightly to ease himself. "You can have—my gun purty—soon. I won't be able—to use it—much longer."

"Why don't Buck an' Hoppy hurry up!" snarled Johnny.

"Be a long time—mebby," mumbled Jackson, his trembling hands trying to steady the rifle. "They're all—around us. *Ah*, missed!" he intoned hoarsely, trying to pump the lever with unobeying hands: "I can't last—much—" the words ceased abruptly and the clatter of the rifle on the floor told the story.

Johnny stumbled over to him and dragged him aside, covering the upturned face with his own sombrero, and picked up the rifle. Rolling a barrel of flour against the wall below the window he fixed himself as comfortably as possible and threw a shell into the chamber.

"Now, you coyotes; you pay *me* for *that!*" he gritted, resting the gun on the window sill and holding it so he could work it with one hand and shoulder.

"Wonder how them pups ever pumped up enough courage to cut loose like this?" queried Neal from behind his flour barrel.

"Whiskey," hazarded Barr. "Harlan must 'a' got 'em drunk. An' that's three times I've missed that snake. Wish it would stop raining so I could see better."

"Why don't you wish they'd all drop dead? Wish good when you wish at all: got as much chance of having it come true," responded Neal, sarcastically. He smothered a curse and looked curiously at his left arm, and from it to the new, yellow-splintered hole in the wall, which was already turning dark from the water soaking into it. "Hey, Joe; we need some more boxes!" he exclaimed, again looking at his arm.

"Yes," came Johnny's voice. "Three of 'em—five of 'em, an' about six feet long an' a foot deep. But if my outfit gets here in time we'll want more'n a dozen."

"Say! Lacey's firing now!" suddenly cried Barr. "He's shooting out of his windy. That'll stop 'em from rushing us! Good boy, Lacey!" he shouted, but Lacey did not hear him in the uproar.

"An' he's worse off than we are, being alone," commented Neal. "Hey! One of us better make a break for help—my ranch's th' nearest. What d'ye say?"

"It's suicide; they'll get you before you get ten feet," Barr replied with conviction.

"No; they won't—th' corral hides th' back door, an' all th' firing is on this side. I can sneak along th' back wall an' by keeping th' buildings atween me an' them, get a long ways off before they know anything about it. Then it's a dash—an' they can't catch me. But can you fellers hold out if I do?"

"Two can hold out as good as three—go ahead," Johnny replied. "Leave me some of yore Colt cartridges, though. You can't use 'em all before you get home."

"Don't stop fer that; there's a shelfful of all kinds behind th' counter," Barr interposed.

"Well, so long an' good luck," and the rear door closed, and softly this time.

"Two hours is some wait under th' present circumstances," Barr muttered, shifting his position behind his barricade. "He can't do it in less, nohow."

Johnny ducked and looked foolish. "Missed me by a foot," he explained. "He can't do it in two—not there an' back," he replied. "Th' trail is mud over th' fetlocks. Give him three at th' least."

"They ain't shooting as much as they was before."

"Waiting till they gets sober, I reckon," Johnny replied.

"If we don't hear no ruction in a few minutes we'll know he got away all right," Barr soliloquized. "An' he's got a fine cayuse for mud, too."

"Hey, why can't you do th' same thing if he makes it?" Johnny suddenly asked. "I can hold her alone, all right."

"Yo're a cheerful liar, you are," laughed Barr. "But can *you* ride?"

"Reckon so, but I ain't a-going to."

"Why, we *both* can go—it's a cinch!" Barr cried. "Come on!"

"Lord!—an' I never even thought of that! Reckon I was too mad," Johnny replied. "But I sort of hates to leave Jackson an' Edwards," he added, sullenly.

"But they're gone! You can't do them no good by staying."

"Yes; I know. An' how about Lacey chipping in on our fight?" demanded Johnny. "I ain't a-going to leave him to take it all. You go, Barr; it wasn't yore fight, nohow. You didn't even know what you was fighting for!"

"Huh! When anybody shoots at me it's my fight, all right," replied Barr, seating himself on the floor behind the breastwork. "I forgot all about Lacey," he apologized. At that instant a tomato can went *spang!* and fell off the shelf. "An' it's too late, anyhow; they ain't a-going to let nobody else get away on that side."

"An' they're tuning up again, too," Johnny replied, preparing for trouble. "Look out for a rush, Barr."

XIX

♦

The Bar-20 Returns

Hopalong Cassidy stopped swearing at the weather and looked up and along the trail in front of him, seeing a hard-riding man approach. He turned his head and spoke to Buck Peters, who rode close behind him. "Somebody's shore in a hurry—why, it's Fred Neal."

It was. Mr. Neal was making his arms move and was also shouting something at the top of his voice. The noise of the rain and of the horses' hoofs splashing in the mud and water at first made his words unintelligible, but it was not long before Hopalong heard something which made him sit up even straighter. In a moment Neal was near enough to be heard distinctly and the outfit shook itself out of its weariness and physical misery and followed its leader at reckless speed. As they rode, bunched close together, Neal briefly and graphically outlined the relative positions of the combatants, and while Buck's more cautious mind was debating the best way to proceed against the enemy, Hopalong cried out the plan to be followed. There would be no strategy—Johnny, wounded and desperate, was fighting for his life. The simplest way was the best—a dash regardless of consequences to those making it, for time was a big factor to the two men in Jackson's store.

"Ride right at 'em!" Hopalong cried. "I know that bunch. They'll be too scared to shoot straight. Paralyze 'em! Three or four are gone now—an' th' whole crowd wasn't worth one of th' men they went out to get. Th' quicker it's over th' better."

"Right you are," came from the rear.

"Ride up th' arroyo as close as we can get, an' then over th' edge an' straight at 'em," Buck ordered. "Their shooting an' th' rain will cover what noise we make on th' soft ground. An' boys, *no quarter!*"

"Reckon *not!*" gritted Red, savagely. "Not with Edwards an' Jackson dead, an' th' Kid fighting for his life!"

"They're still at it!" cried Lanky Smith, as the faint and intermittent sound of firing was heard; the driving wind was blowing from the town, and this, also, would deaden the noise of their approach.

"Thank th' Lord! That means that there's somebody

left to fight 'em," exclaimed Red. "Hope it's th' Kid," he muttered.

"They can't rush th' store till they get Lacey, an' they can't rush him till they get th' store," shouted Neal over his shoulder. "They'd be in a cross fire if they tried either—an' that's what licks 'em."

"They'll be in a cross fire purty soon," promised Pete, grimly.

Hopalong and Red reached the edge of the arroyo first and plunged over the bank into the yellow storm-water swirling along the bottom like a miniature flood. After them came Buck, Neal, and the others, the water shooting up in sheets as each successive horse plunged in. Out again on the farther side they strung out into single file along the narrow foot-hold between water and bank and raced towards the sharp bend some hundreds of yards ahead, the point in the arroyo's course nearest the town. The dripping horses scrambled up the slippery incline and then, under the goading of spurs and quirts, leaped forward as fast as they could go across the level, soggy plain.

A quarter of a mile ahead of them lay the scattered shacks of the town, and as they drew nearer to it the riders could see the flashes of guns and the smoke-fog lying close to the ground. Fire spat from Jackson's store and a cloud of smoke still lingered around a window in Lacey's saloon. Then a yell reached their ears, a yell of rage, consternation, and warning. Figures scurried to seek cover and the firing from Jackson's and Lacey's grew more rapid.

A mounted man emerged from a corral and tore away, others following his example, and the outfit separated to take up the chase individually. Harlan, wounded hard, was trying to run to where he had left his horse, and after him fled Slivers Lowe. Hopalong was gaining on them when he saw Slivers raise his arm and fire deliberately into the back of the proprietor of the Oasis, leap over the falling body, vault into the saddle of Harlan's horse and gallop for safety. Hopalong's shots went wide and the last view any one had of Slivers in that part of the country was when he dropped into an arroyo to follow it for safety. Laramie Joe fled before Red Connors and Red's rage was so great that it spoiled his accuracy, and he had the sorrow of seeing the pursued grow faint in the mist and fog. Pursuit was tried until the pursuers realized that their mounts were too worn out to stand a show against the fresh animals ridden by the survivors of the Oasis crowd.

Red circled and joined Hopalong. "Blasted coyotes," he growled. "Killed Jackson an' Edwards, an' wanted th' Kid! He's shore showed 'em what fighting is, all right. But I wonder what got into 'em all at once to give 'em nerve enough to start things?"

"Edwards paid his way, all right," replied Hopalong. "If I do as well when my time comes I won't do no kicking."

"Yore time ain't coming that way," responded Red, grinning. "You'll die a natural death in bed, unless you gets to cussing me."

"Shore there ain't no more, Buck?" Hopalong called.

"Yes. There was only five, I reckon, an' they was purty well shot up when we took a hand. You know, Johnny was in it all th' time," replied the foreman, smiling. "This town's had th' cleaning up it's needed for some time," he added.

They were at Jackson's store now, and hurriedly dismounted and ran in to see Johnny. They found him lying across some boxes, which brought him almost to the level of a window sill. He was too weak to stand, while near him in similar condition lay Barr, too weak from loss of blood to do more than look his welcome.

"How are you, Kid?" cried Buck anxiously, bending over him, while others looked to Barr's injuries.

"Tired, Buck, awful tired; an' all shot up," Johnny slowly replied. "When I saw you fellers—streak past this windy—I sort of went flat—something seemed to break inside me," he said, faintly and with an effort, and the foreman ordered him not to talk. Deft fingers, schooled by practice in rough and ready surgery, were busy over him and in half an hour he lay on Jackson's cot, covered with bandages.

"Why, hullo, Lacey!" exclaimed Hopalong, leaping forward to shake hands with the man Red and Billy had gone to help. "Purty well scratched up, but lively yet, hey?"

"I'm able to hobble over here an' shake han's with these scrappers—they're shore wonders," Lacey replied. "Fought like a whole regiment! Hullo, Johnny!" and his hand-clasp told much.

"Yore cross fire did it, Lacey; that was th' whole thing," Johnny smiled. "Yo're all right!"

Red turned and looked out of the window toward the Oasis and then glanced at Buck. "Reckon we better burn Harlan's place—it's all that's left of that gang now," he suggested.

"Why, yes; I reckon so," replied the foreman. "That's as—"

"No, we won't!" Hopalong interposed quickly. "That stands till Johnny sets it off. It's th' Kid's celebration—he was shot in it."

Johnny smiled.

XX

◆

Barb Wire

After the flurry at Perry's Bend the Bar-20 settled down to the calm of routine work and sent several drive herds to their destination without any unusual incidents. Buck thought that the last herd had been driven when, late in the summer, he received an order that he made haste to fill. The outfit was told to get busy and soon rounded up the necessary number of three-year-olds. Then came the road branding, the final step except inspection, and this was done not far from the ranch house, where the facilities were best for speedy work.

Entirely recovered from all ill effects of his afternoon in Jackson's store up in Perry's Bend, Johnny Nelson waited with Red Connors on the platform of the branding chute and growled petulantly at the sun, the dust, but most of all at the choking, smarting odor of burned hair which filled their throats and caused them to rub the backs of grimy hands across their eyes. Chute-branding robbed them of the excitement, the leaven of fun and frolic, which they always took from open or corral branding—and the work of a day in the corral or open was condensed into an hour or two by the chute. This was one cow wide, narrow at the bottom and flared out as it went up, so the animal could not turn, and when filled was, to use Johnny's graphic phrase, "like a chain of cows in a ditch." Eight of the wondering and crowded animals, guided into the pen by men who knew their work to the smallest detail and lost no time in its performance, filed into the pen after those branded had filed out. As the first to enter reached the farther end a stout bar dropped into place, just missing the animal's nose; and as the last cow discovered that it could go no farther and made up its mind to back out, it was stopped by another bar, which fell behind it. The iron heaters tossed a hot iron each to Red and Johnny and the eight were marked in short order, making about two hundred and fifty they had branded in three hours. This number compared very favorably with that of the second chute where Lanky Smith and Frenchy McAllister waved cold irons and sarcastically asked their iron men if the sun was supposed to provide the heat; whereat the down-trodden heaters provided heat with great generosity in their caustic retorts.

"Oh, Susanna, don't you cry for me," sang Billy Williams, one of the feeders. "But why in Jericho don't you fellers get a move on you? You ain't no good on th' platform—you ought to be mixin' biscuits for cookie. Frenchy an' Lanky are th' boys to turn 'em out," he offered, gratis.

Red's weary air bespoke a vast and settled contempt for such inanities and his iron descended with exaggerated slowness and exactitude against the side of the victim below him—he would not deign to reply. Not so with Johnny, who could not refrain from hot retort.

"Don't be a fool *all* th' time," snapped Johnny. "Mind yore own business, you shorthorn. Big-mouthed old woman, that's what—" his tone dropped and the words sank into vague mutterings which a strangling cough cut short. "Blasted idiot," he whispered, tears coming into his eyes at the effort. Burning hair is bad for throat and temper alike.

Red deftly knocked his companion's iron up and spoke sharply. "You mind yourn better—that makes th' third you've tried to brand twice. Why don't you look what yo're doin'? Hot iron! Hot iron! What're you fellers doin'?" he shouted down at the heaters. "This ain't no time to go to sleep. How d' y' expect us to do any work when you ain't doin' any yoreselves!" Red's temper was also on the ragged edge.

"You've got one in yore other hand, you sheep!" snorted one of the iron heaters with restless pugnacity. "Go tearin' into us when you—" he growled the rest and kicked viciously at the fire.

"Lovely bunch," grinned Billy who, followed by Pete Wilson, mounted the platform to relieve the branders. "Chase yoreselves—me an' Pete are shore going to show you cranky bugs how to do a hundred an hour. Ain't we, Pete? An' look here, you," he remarked to the heaters, "don't you fellers keep *us* waitin' for hot irons!"

"That's right! Make a fool out of yoreself first thing!" snapped one of the pair on the ground.

"Billy, I never loved you as much as I do this minute," grinned Johnny wearily. "Wish you'd 'a' come along to show us how to do it an hour ago."

"I would, only—"

"Quit chinning an' get busy," remarked Red, climbing down. "Th' chute's full; an' it's all yourn."

Billy caught the iron, gave it a preliminary flourish, and started to work with a speed that would not endure for long. He branded five out of the eight and jeered at his companion for being so slow.

"Have yore fun now, Billy," Pete replied with placid good nature. "Before we're through with this job you'll be lucky if you can do two of th' string, if you keep up that pace."

"He'll be missing every other one," growled his heater with overflowing malice. "That iron ain't cold, you Chinaman!"

"Too cold for me—don't miss none," chuckled Billy sweetly. "Fill th' chute! Fill th' chute! Don't keep us waitin'!" he cried to the guiders, hopping around with feigned eagerness and impatience.

Hopalong Cassidy rode up and stopped as Red returned to take the place of one of the iron heaters. "How they coming, Red?" he inquired.

"Fast. You can sic that inspector on 'em th' first thing to-morrow mornin', if he gets here on time. But he's off som'ers gettin' full of redeye. Who're goin' with you on this drive?"

"Th' inspector is all right—he's here now an' is going to spend th' night with us so as to be on hand th' first thing to-morrow," replied Hopalong, grinning at the hardworking pair on the platform. "Why, I reckon I'll take you, Johnny, Lanky, Billy, Pete, an' Skinny, an' we'll have two hoss-wranglers an' a cook, of course. We'll drive up th' right-hand trail through West Valley this time. It's longer, but there'll be more water that way at this time of th' year. Besides, I don't want no more foot-sore cattle to nurse along. Even th' West Valley trail will be dry enough before we strike Bennett's Creek."

"Yes; we'll have to drive 'em purty hard till we reach th' creek," replied Red, thoughtfully. "Say; we're going to have three thousand of th' finest three-year-old steers ever sent north out of these parts. An' we ought to do it in a month an' deliver 'em fat an' frisky. We can feed 'em good for th' last week."

"I just sent some of th' boys out to drive in th' cayuses," Hopalong remarked, "an' when they get here you fellers match for choice an' pick yore remuda. No use takin' too few. About eight a piece'll do us nice. I shore like a good cavvieyeh."

"Hullo, Hoppy!" came from the platform as Billy grinned his welcome through the dust on his face. "Want a job?"

"Hullo yoreself," growled Pete. "Stick yore iron on that fourth steer before he gets out, an' talk less with yore mouth."

"Pete's still rabid," called Billy, performing the duty Pete suggested.

"That may be th' polite name for it," snorted one of the iron heaters, testing an iron, "but that ain't what I'd say. Might as well cover th' subject thoroughly while yo're on it."

"Yea, verily," endorsed his companion.

"Here comes th' last of 'em," smiled Pete, watching several cattle being driven towards the chute. "We'll have to brand 'em on th' move, Billy; there ain't enough to fill th' chute."

"All right; hot iron, you!"

Early the next morning the inspector looked them over and made his count, the herd was started north and at nightfall had covered twelve miles. For the next week everything went smoothly, but after that, water began to be scarce and the herd was pushed harder, and became harder to handle.

On the night of the twelfth day out four men sat around the fire in West Valley at a point a dozen miles south of Bennett's Creek, and ate heartily. The night was black— not a star could be seen and the south wind hardly stirred the trampled and burned grass. They were thoroughly tired out and their tempers were not in the sweetest state imaginable, for the heat during the last four days had been almost unbearable even to them and they had had their hands full with the cranky herd. They ate silently, hungrily—there would be time enough for the few words they had to say when the pipes were going for a short smoke before turning in.

"I feel like hell," growled Red, reaching for another cup of coffee, but there was no reply; he had voiced the feelings of all.

Hopalong listened intently and looked up, staring into the darkness, and soon a horseman was seen approaching the fire. Hopalong nodded welcome and waved his hand towards the food, and the stranger, dismounting, picketed his horse and joined the circle. When the pipes were lighted he sighed with satisfaction and looked around the group. "Drivin' north, I see."

"Yes; an' blamed glad to get off this dry range," Hopalong replied. "Th' herd's gettin' cranky an' hard to hold—but when we pass th' creek everything'll be all right again. An' ain't it hot! When you hear us kick about th' heat it means something."

"I'm going yore way," remarked the stranger. "I came down this trail about two weeks ago. Reckon I was th' last to ride through before th' fence went up. Damned outrage, says I, an' I told 'em so, too. They couldn't see it that way an' we had a little disagreement about it. They said as how they was going to patrol it."

"Fence! What fence?" exclaimed Red.

"Where's there any fence?" demanded Hopalong sharply.

"Twenty mile north of th' creek," replied the stranger, carefully packing his pipe.

"What? Twenty miles north of th' creek?" cried Hopalong. "What creek?"

"Bennett's. Th' 4X has strung three strands of barb wire from Coyote Pass to th' North Arm. Thirty mile long, without a gate, so they says."

"But it don't close this trail!" cried Hopalong in blank astonishment.

"It shore does. They say they owns that range an' can fence it in all they wants. I told 'em different, but naturally they didn't listen to me. An' they'll fight about it, too."

"But they *can't* shut off this trail!" Billy said, with angry emphasis. "They don't own it no more'n we do!"

"I know all about that—you heard me tell you what they said."

"But how can we get past it?" demanded Hopalong.

"Around it, over th' hills. You'll lose about three days doin' it, too."

"I can't take no sand-range herd over them rocks, an' I ain't going to drive 'round no North Arm or Coyote Pass if I could," Hopalong replied with quiet emphasis. "There's poison springs on th' east an' nothing but rocks on th' west. We go straight through."

"I'm afraid that you'll have to fight if you do," remarked the stranger.

"Then we'll fight!" cried Johnny, leaning forward. "Blasted coyotes! What right have they got to block a drive trail that's as old as cattle-raising in these parts! That trail was here before I was born, it's allus been open, an' it's going to stay open! You watch us go through!"

"Yo're dead right, Kid; we'll cut that fence an' stick to this trail, an' fight if we has to," endorsed Red. "Th' Bar-20 ain't crawlin' out of no hole that it can walk out of. They're bluffing; that's all."

"I don't think they are; an' there's twelve men in that outfit," suggested the stranger, offhand.

"We ain't got time to count odds; we never do down our way when we know we're right. An' we're right enough in this game," retorted Hopalong, quickly. "For th' last twelve days we've had good luck, barrin' th' few on this dry range; an' now we're in for th' other kind. By th' Lord, I wish we was here without th' cows to take care of—we'd show 'em something about blockin' drive trails that ain't in their little book!"

"Blast it all! Wire fences coming down this way now," mused Johnny, sullenly. He hated them by training as much as he hated horsethieves and sheep; and his companions had been brought up in the same school. Barb wire, the death-knell to the old-time punching, the bar to riding at will, a steel insult to fire the blood—it had come at last.

"We've shore got to cut it, Red,—" began Hopalong, but the cook had to rid himself of some of his indignation and interrupted with heat.

"Shore we have!" came explosively from the tail board of the chuck wagon. "Got to lay it agin my li'l axe an' swat it with my big ol' monkey wrench! An' won't them posts save me a lot of trouble huntin' chips an' firewood!"

"We've shore got to cut it, Red," Hopalong repeated slowly. "You an' Johnny an' me'll ride ahead after we cross th' creek to-morrow an' do it. I don't hanker after no fight with all these cows on my han's, but we've got to risk one."

"Shore!" cried Johnny, hotly. "I can't get over th' gall of them fellers closing up th' West Valley drive trail. Why, I never heard tell of such a thing afore!"

"We're short-handed; we ought to have more'n we have to guard th' herd if there's a fight. If it stampedes—oh, well, that'll work out to-morrow. Th' creek's only about twelve miles away an' we'll start at daylight, so tumble in," Hopalong said as he arose. "Red, I'm going out to take my shift—I'll send Pete in. Stranger," he added, turning, "I'm much obliged to you for th' warning. They might 'a' caught us with our hands tied."

"Oh, that's all right," hastily replied the stranger, who was in hearty accord with the plans, such as they were. "My name's Hawkins, an' I don't like range fences no more'n you do. I used to hunt buffalo all over this part of th' country before they was all killed off, an' I allus rode where I pleased. I'm purty old, but I c'n still see an' shoot; an' I'm going to stick right along with you fellers an' see it through. Every man counts in this game."

"Well, that's blamed proper of you," Hopalong replied, greatly pleased by the other's offer. "But I can't let you do it. I don't want to drag you into no trouble, an'—"

"You ain't draggin' me none; I'm doing it myself. I'm

about as mad as you are over it. I ain't good for much no more, an' if I shuffles off fightin' barb wire I'll be doing my duty. First it was nesters, then railroads an' more nesters, then sheep, an' now it's wire—won't it never stop? By th' Lord, it's got to stop, or this country will go to th' devil an' won't be fit to live in. Besides, I've heard of your fellers before—I'll tie to th' Bar-20 any day."

"Well, I reckon you must if you must; yo're welcome enough," laughed Hopalong, and he strode off to his picketed horse, leaving the others to discuss the fence, with the assistance of the cook, until Pete rode in.

XXI

♦

The Fence

When Hopalong rode in at midnight to arouse the others and send them out to relieve Skinny and his two companions, the cattle were quieter than he had expected to leave them, and he could see no change of weather threatening. He was asleep when the others turned in, or he would have been further assured in that direction.

Out on the plain where the herd was being held, Red and the three other guards had been optimistic until half of their shift was over and it was only then that they began to worry. The knowledge that running water was only twelve miles away had the opposite effect than the one expected, for instead of making them cheerful, it caused them to be beset with worry and fear. Water was all right, and they could not have got along without it for another day; but it was, in this case, filled with the possibility of grave danger.

Johnny was thinking hard about it as he rode around the now restless herd, and then pulled up suddenly, peered into the darkness and went on again. "Damn that disreputable li'l rounder! Why th' devil can't he behave, 'stead of stirring things up when they're ticklish?" he muttered, but he had to grin despite himself. A lumbering form had blundered past him from the direction of the camp and was swallowed up by the night as it sought the herd, annoying and arousing the thirsty and irritable cattle along its trail, throwing challenges right and left and stirring up trouble as it passed. The fact that the challenges were bluffs made no difference to the pawing steers, for they were anxious to have things out with the rounder.

This frisky disturber of bovine peace was a yearling that had slipped into the herd before it left the ranch and had kept quiet and respectable and out of sight in the middle of the mass for the first few days and nights. But keeping quiet and respectable had been an awful strain, and his mischievous deviltry grew constantly harder to hold in check. Finally he could stand the repression no longer, and when he gave way to his accumulated energy it had the snap and ginger of a tightly stretched rubber band recoiling on itself. On the fourth night out he had thrown off his mask and announced his presence in his true light by butting a sleepy steer out of its bed, which bed he straightway proceeded to appropriate for himself. This was folly, for the ground was not cold and he had no excuse for stealing a body-warmed place to lie down; it was pure cussedness, and retribution followed hard upon the act. In about half a minute he had discovered the great difference between bullying poor, miserable, defenceless dogies and trying to bully a healthy, fully developed, and pugnacious steer. After assimilating the preliminary punishment of what promised to be the most thorough and workmanlike thrashing he had ever known,

the indignant and frightened bummer wheeled and fled
incontinently with the aroused steer in angry pursuit.
The best way out was the one most puzzling to the venge-
ful steer, so the bummer cavorted recklessly through the
herd, turning and twisting and doubling, stepping on any
steer that happened to be lying down in his path, butting
others, and leavening things with great success. Under
other conditions he would have relished the effect of his
efforts, for the herd had arisen as one animal and seemed
to be debating the advisability of stampeding; but he was
in no mood to relish anything and thought only of getting away. Finally escaping from his pursuer, that had
paused to fight with a belligerent brother, he rambled off
into the darkness to figure it all out and to maintain a
sullen and chastened demeanor for the rest of the night.
This was the first time a brick had been under the hat.

But the spirits of youth recover quickly—his recovered so quickly that he was banished from the herd the
very next night, which banishment, not being at all to his
liking, was enforced only by rigid watchfulness and hard
riding; and he was roundly cursed from dark to dawn by
the worried men, most of whom disliked the bumming
youngster less than they pretended. He was only a cub, a
wild youth having his fling, and there was something irresistibly likable and comical in his awkward antics and
eternal persistence, even though he was a pest. Johnny
saw more in him than his companions could find, and
had quite a little sport with him: he made fine practice
for roping, for he was about as elusive as a grasshopper
and uncertain as a flea. Johnny was in the same general
class and he could sympathize with the irrepressible nuisance in its efforts to stir up a little life and excitement in
so dull a crowd; Johnny hoped to be as successful in his
mischievous deviltry when he reached the town at the
end of the drive.

But to-night it was dark, and the bummer gained his

coveted goal with ridiculous ease, after which he started right in to work off the high pressure of the energy he had accumulated during the last two nights. He had desisted in his efforts to gain the herd early in the evening and had rambled off and rested during the first part of the night, and the herders breathed softly lest they should stir him to renewed trials. But now he had succeeded, and although only Johnny had seen him lumber past, the other three guards were aware of it immediately by the results and swore in their throats, for the cattle were now on their feet, snorting and moving about restlessly, and the rattling of horns grew slowly louder.

"Ain't he having a devil of a good time!" grinned Johnny. But it was not long before he realized the possibilities of the bummer's efforts and he lost his grin. "If we get through th' night without trouble I'll see that you are picketed if it takes me all day to get you," he muttered. "Fun is fun, but it's getting a little too serious for comfort."

Sometime after the middle of the second shift the herd, already irritable, nervous, and cranky because of the thirst they were enduring, and worked up to the fever pitch by the devilish manœuvres of the exuberant and hard-working bummer, wanted only the flimsiest kind of an excuse to stampede, and they might go without an excuse. A flash of lightning, a crash of thunder, a wind-blown paper, a flapping wagon cover, the sudden and unheralded approach of a careless rider, the cracking and flare of a match, or the scent of a wolf or coyote—or water, would send an avalanche of three thousand crazed steers crashing its irresistible way over a pitch-black plain.

Red had warned Pete and Billy, and now he rode to find Johnny and send him to camp for the others. As he got halfway around the circuit he heard Johnny singing a mournful lay, and soon a black bulk loomed up in the dark ahead of him. "That you, Kid?" he asked. "That you, Johnny?" he repeated, a little louder.

The song stopped abruptly. "Shore," replied Johnny. "We're going to have trouble aplenty tonight. Glad daylight ain't so very far off. That cussed li'l rake of a bummer got by me an' into th' herd. He's shore raising Ned to-night, th' li'l monkey: it's getting serious, Red."

"I'll shoot that yearling at daylight, damn him!" retorted Red. "I should 'a' done it a week ago. He's picked th' worst time for his cussed devilment! You ride right in an' get th' boys, an' get 'em out here quick. Th' whole herd's on its toes waitin' for th' signal; an' th' wink of an eye'll send 'em off. God only knows what'll happen between now and daylight! If th' wind should change an' blow down from th' north, they'll be off as shore as shootin'. One whiff of Bennett's Creek is all that's needed, Kid; an'—"

"Oh, pshaw!" interposed Johnny. "There ain't no wind at all now. It's been quiet for an hour."

"Yes; an' that's one of th' things that's worrying me. It means a change, shore."

"Not always; we'll come out of this all right," assured Johnny, but he spoke without his usual confidence. "There ain't no use—" he paused as he felt the air stir, and he was conscious of Red's heavy breathing. There was a peculiar hush in the air that he did not like, a closeness that sent his heart up in his throat, and as he was about to continue a sudden gust snapped his neck-kerchief out straight. He felt that refreshing coolness which so often precedes a storm and as he weighed it in his mind a low rumble of thunder rolled in the north and sent a chill down his back.

"Good God! Get th' boys!" cried Red, wheeling. "It's *changed!* An' Pete an' Billy out there in front of—*there they go!*" he shouted as a sudden tremor shook the earth and a roaring sound filled the air. He was instantly lost to ear and eye, swallowed by the oppressive darkness as he spurred and quirted into a great, choking cloud of dust which swept down from the north, unseen in the night. The deep thunder of hoofs and the faint and occasional flash of a six-shooter told him the direction, and he hurled his mount after the uproar with no thought of the death which lurked in every hole and rock and gully on the uneven and unseen plain beneath him. His mouth and nose were lined with dust, his throat choked with it, and he opened his burning eyes only at intervals, and then only to a slit, to catch a fleeting glance of—nothing. He realized vaguely that he was riding north, because the cattle would head for water, but that was all, save that he was animated by a desperate eagerness to gain the firing line, to join Pete and Billy, the two men who rode before that crazed mass of horns and hoofs and who were pleading and swearing and yelling in vain only a few feet ahead of annihilation—if they were still alive. A stumble, a moment's indecision, and the avalanche would roll over them as if they were straws and trample them flat beneath the pounding hoofs, a modern Juggernaut. If he, or they, managed to escape with life, it would make a good tale for the bunk house some night; if they were killed it was in doing their duty—it was all in a day's work.

Johnny shouted after him and then wheeled and raced towards the camp, emptying his Colt in the air as a warning. He saw figures scurrying across the lighted place, and before he had gained it his friends raced past him and gave him hard work catching up to them. And just behind him rode the stranger, to do what he could for his new friends, and as reckless of consequences as they.

It seemed an age before they caught up to the stragglers, and when they realized how true they had ridden in the dark they believed that at last their luck was turning for the better, and pushed on with renewed hope. Hopalong shouted to those nearest him that Bennett's Creek could not be far away and hazarded the belief that the steers would slow up and stop when they found the water they craved; but his words were lost to all but himself.

Suddenly the punchers were almost trapped and their escape made miraculous, for without warning the herd swerved and turned sharply to the right, crossing the path of the riders and forcing them to the east, showing Hopalong their silhouettes against the streak of pale gray low down in the eastern sky. When free from the sudden press of cattle they slowed perceptibly, and Hopalong did likewise to avoid running them down. At that instant the uproar took on a new note and increased threefold. He could hear the shock of impact, whip-like reports, the bellowing of cattle in pain, and he arose in his stirrups to peer ahead for the reason, seeing, as he did so, the silhouettes of his friends arise and then drop from his sight. Without additional warning his horse pitched forward and crashed to the earth, sending him over its head. Slight as was the warning it served to ease his fall, for instinct freed his feet from the stirrups, and when he struck the ground it was feet first, and although he fell flat at the next instant, the shock had been broken. Even as it was, he was partly stunned, and groped as he arose on his hands and knees. Arising painfully he took a short step forward, tripped and fell again; and felt a sharp pain shoot through his hand as it went first to break the fall. Perhaps it was ten seconds before he knew what it was that had thrown him, and when he learned that he also learned the reason for the whole calamity—in his torn and bleeding hand he held a piece of barb wire.

"Barb wire!" he muttered, amazed. "Barb wire! Why, what th'— *Damn that ranch!*" he shouted, sudden rage sweeping over him as the situation flashed through his mind and banished all the mental effects of the fall. "They've gone an' strung it south of th' creek as well! Red! Johnny! Lanky!" he shouted at the top of his voice, hoping to be heard over the groaning of injured cattle and the general confusion. "Good Lord! *are they killed*?"

They were not, thanks to the forced slowing up, and to the pool of water and mud which formed an arm of the creek, a back-water away from the pull of the current. They had pitched into the mud and water up to their waists, some head first, some feet first, and others as they would go into a chair. Those who had been fortunate enough to strike feet first pulled out the divers, and the others gained their feet as best they might and with varying degrees of haste, but all mixed profanity and thankfulness equally well; and were equally and effectually disguised.

Hopalong, expecting the silence of death or at best the groaning of injured and dying, was taken aback by the fluent stream of profanity which greeted his ears. But all efforts in that line were eclipsed when the drive foreman tersely explained about the wire, and the providential mud bath was forgotten in the new idea. They forthwith clamored for war, and the sooner it came the better they would like it.

"Not now, boys; we've got work to do first," replied Hopalong, who, nevertheless, was troubled grievously by the same itching trigger finger. They subsided—as a steel spring subsides when held down by a weight—and went off in search of their mounts. Daylight had won the skirmish in the east and was now attacking in force, and revealed a sight which, stilling the profanity for the moment, caused it to flow again with renewed energy. The plain was a shambles near the creek, and dead and dying steers showed where the fence had stood. The rest of the herd had passed over these. The wounded cattle and three horses were put out of their misery as the first duty. The horse that Hopalong had ridden had a broken back; the other two, broken legs. When this work was out of the way the bruised and shaken men gave their attention to the scattered cattle on the other side of the creek, and when Hawkins rode up after wasting time in hunting for the trail in the dark, he saw four men with the herd, which was still scattered; four others near the creek, of whom only Johnny was mounted, and a group of six strangers riding towards them from the west and along the fence, or what was left of that portion of it.

"That's awful!" he cried, stopping his limping horse near Hopalong. "An' here come th' fools that done it."

"Yes," replied Johnny, his voice breaking from rage, "but they won't go back again! I don't care if I'm killed if I can get one or two of that crowd—"

"Shut up, Kid!" snapped Hopalong as the 4X outfit drew near. "I know just how you feel about it; feel that way myself. But there ain't a-goin' to be no fightin' while I've got these cows on my han's. That gang'll be here when we come back, all right."

"Mebby one or two of 'em won't," remarked Hawkins, as he looked again over the carnage along the fence. "I never did much pot-shootin', 'cept agin Injuns; but I dunno—" He did not finish, for the strangers were almost at his elbow.

Cranky Joe led the 4X contingent and he did the talking for it without waste of time. "Who th' hell busted that fence?" he demanded, belligerently, looking around savagely. Johnny's hand twitched at the words and the way they were spoken.

"I did; did you think somebody leaned agin it?" replied Hopalong, very calmly,—so calmly that it was about one step short of an explosion.

"Well, why didn't you go around?"

"Three thousand stampedin' cattle don't go 'round wire fences in th' dark."

"Well, that's not our fault. Reckon you better dig down an' settle up for th' damages, an' half a cent a head for water; an' then go 'round. You can't stampede through th' other fence."

"That so?" asked Hopalong.

"Reckon it is."

"Yo're real shore it is?"

"Well, there's only six of us here, but there's six more that we can get blamed quick if we need 'em. It's so, all right."

"Well, comin' down to figures, there's eight here, with two hoss-wranglers an' a cook to come," retorted Hopalong, kicking the belligerent Johnny on the shins. "We're just about mad enough to tackle anything: ever feel that way?"

"Oh, no use gettin' all het up," rejoined Cranky Joe. "We ain't a-goin' to fight 'less we has to. Better pay up."

"Send yore bills to th' ranch—if they're O. K., Buck'll pay 'em."

"Nix; I take it when I can get it."

"I ain't got no money with me that I can spare."

"Then you can leave enough cows to buy back again."

"I'm not going around th' fence, neither."

"Oh, yes; you are. An' yo're goin' to pay," snapped Cranky Joe.

"Take it out of th' price of two hundred dead cows an' gimme what's left," Hopalong retorted. "It'll cost you nine of them twelve men to pry it out'n me."

"You won't pay?" demanded the other, coldly.

"Not a plugged *peso*."

"Well, as I said before, I don't want to fight nobody 'less I has to," replied Cranky Joe. "I'll give you a chance to change yore mind. We'll be out here after it t'-morrow, cash or cows. That'll give you twenty-four hours to rest yore herd an' get ready to drive. Then you pay, an' go back, 'round th' fence."

"All right; to-morrow suits me," responded Hopalong, who was boiling with rage and felt constrained to hold it back. If it wasn't for the cows—!

Red and three companions swept up and stopped in a swirl of dust and asked questions until Hopalong shut them up. Their arrival and the manner of their speech riled Cranky Joe, who turned around and loosed one more remark; and he never knew how near to death he was at that moment.

"You fellers must own th' earth, th' way you act," he said to Red and his three companions.

"We ain't fencin' it in to prove it," rejoined Hopalong, his hand on Red's arm.

Cranky Joe wheeled to rejoin his friends. "T'-morrow," he said, significantly.

Hopalong and his men watched the six ride away, too enraged to speak for a moment. Then the drive foreman mastered himself and turned to Hawkins. "Where's their ranch house?" he demanded, sharply. "There must be some way out of this, an' we've got to find it; an' before tomorrow."

"West; three hours' ride along th' fence. I could find 'em th' darkest night what ever happened; I was out there once," Hawkins replied.

"Describe 'em as exact as you can," demanded Hopalong, and when Hawkins had done so the Bar-20 drive foreman slapped his thigh and laughed nastily. "One house with one door an' only two windows—are you shore? Good! Where's th' corrals? Good again! So they'll take pay for their blasted fence, eh? Cash or cows, hey! Don't want no fight 'less it's necessary, but they're going to make us pay for th' fence that killed two hundred head, an' blamed nigh got us, too. An' half a cent a head for drinkin' water! I've paid that more'n once—some of th' poor devils squattin' on th' range ain't got nothin' to sell but water, but I don't buy none out of Bennett's Creek! Pete, you mounted fellers round up a little—bunch th' herd a little closer, an' drive straight along th' trail towards that other fence. We'll all help you as soon as th' wranglers bring us up somethin' to ride. Push 'em hard, limp or no limp, till dark. They'll be too tired to go crow-hopping 'round any in th' dark to-night. An' say! When you see that bummer, if he wasn't got by th' fence, drop him clean. So they've got twelve men, hey? Huh!"

"What you goin' to do?" asked Red, beginning to cool down, and very curious.

"Yes; tell us," urged Johnny.

"Why, I'm going to cut that fence, an' cut it all to hell. Then I'm going to push th' herd through it an' as far out of danger as I can. When they're all right cookie an' th' hoss-wranglers will have to hold 'em during th' night while we do th' rest."

"What's th' rest?" demanded Johnny.

"Oh, I'll tell you that later; it can wait," replied Hopalong. "Meanwhile, you get out there with Pete an' help get th' herd in shape. We'll be with you soon—here comes th' wranglers an' th' cavvieyeh. 'Bout time, too."

XXII

♦

Mr. Boggs Is Disgusted

The herd gained twelve miles by dark and would pass through the northern fence by noon of the next day, for Cook's axe and monkey wrench had been put to good use. For quite a distance there was no fence: about a mile of barb wire had been pulled loose and was tangled up into several large piles, while rings of burned grass and ashes surrounded what was left of the posts. The cook had embraced this opportunity to lay in a good supply of firewood and was the happiest man in the outfit.

At ten o'clock that night eight figures loped westward along the southern fence and three hours later dismounted near the first corral of the 4X ranch. They put their horses in a depression on the plain and then hastened to seek cover, being careful to make no noise.

At dawn the door of the bunk house opened quickly and as quickly slammed shut again, three bullets in it being the reason. An uproar ensued and guns spat from the two windows in the general direction of the unseen besiegers, who did not bother about replying; they had given notification of their presence and until it was necessary to shoot there was no earthly use of wasting ammunition. Besides, the drive outfit had cooled down rapidly when it found that its herd was in no immediate danger and was not anxious to kill any one unless there was need. The situation was conducive to humor rather than anger. But every time the door moved it collected more lead, and it finally remained shut.

The noise in the bunk house continued and finally a sombrero was waved frantically at the south window and a moment later Nat Boggs, foreman of the incarcerated 4X outfit, stuck his head out very cautiously and yelled questions which bore directly on the situation and were to the point. He appeared to be excited and unduly heated, if one might judge from his words and voice. There was no reply, which still further added to his heat and excitement. Becoming bolder and a little angrier he allowed his impetuous nature to get the upper hand and forthwith attempted the feat of getting through that same window; but a sharp *pat!* sounded on a board not a foot from him, and he reconsidered hastily. His sombrero again waved to insist on a truce, and collected two holes, causing him much mental anguish and threatening the loss of his worthy soul. He danced up and down with great agility and no grace and made remarks, thereby leading a full-voiced chorus.

"Ain't that a hell of a note?" he demanded plaintively as he paused for breath. "Stick *yore* hat out, Cranky, an' see what *you* can do," he suggested, irritably.

Cranky Joe regarded him with pity and reproach, and moved back towards the other end of the room, muttering softly to himself. "I know it ain't much of a bonnet, but he needn't rub it in," he growled, peevishly.

"Try again; mebby they didn't see you," suggested Jim Larkin, who had a reputation for never making a joke. He escaped with his life and checked himself at the side of Cranky Joe, with whom he conferred on the harshness of the world towards unfortunates.

The rest of the morning was spent in snipe-shooting at random, trusting to luck to hit some one, and trusting in vain. At noon Cranky Joe could stand the strain no longer and opened the door just a little to relieve the monotony. He succeeded, being blessed with a smashed shoulder, and immediately became a general nuisance, adding greatly to the prevailing atmosphere. Boggs called him a few kinds of fools and hastened to nail the door shut; he hit his thumb and his heart became filled with venom.

"*Now* look at what they went an' done!" he yelled, running around in a circle. "Damned outrage!"

"Huh!" snorted Cranky Joe with maddening superiority. "That ain't nothing—just look at me!"

Boggs looked, very fixedly, and showed signs of apoplexy, and Cranky Joe returned to his end of the room to resume his soliloquy.

"Why don't you come out an' take them cows?" inquired an unkind voice from without. "Ain't changed yore mind, have you?"

"We'll give you a drink for half a cent a head—that's th' regular price for waterin' cows," called another.

The faint ripple of mirth which ran around the plain was lost in opinions loudly expressed within the room; and Boggs, tears of rage in his eyes, flung himself down on a chair and invested new terms for describing human beings.

John Terry was observing. He had been fluttering around the north window, constantly getting bolder, and had not been disturbed. When he withdrew his sombrero and found that it was intact he smiled to himself and leaned his elbows on the sill, looking carefully around the plain. The discovery that there was no cover on the north side cheered him greatly and he called to Boggs, outlining a plan of action.

Boggs listened intently and then smiled for the first time since dawn. "Bully for you, Terry!" he enthused. "Wait till dark—we'll fool 'em."

A bullet chipped the 'dobe at Terry's side and he ducked as he leaped back. "From an angle—what did I tell you?" he laughed. "We'll drop out here an' sneak behind th' house after dark. They'll be watching th' door—an' they won't be able to see us, anyhow."

Boggs sucked his thumb tenderly and grinned. "After which—," he elated.

"After which—," gravely repeated Terry, the others echoing it with unrestrained joy.

"Then, mebby, I can get a drink," chuckled Larkin, brightening under the thought.

"Th' moon comes up at ten," warned a voice. "It'll be full to-night—an' there ain't many clouds in sight."

"Ol' King Cole was a merry ol' soul," hummed McQuade, lightly.

"An' —a—merry—ol'—soul—was—he! was—he!" thundered the chorus, deep-toned and strong. *"He had a wife for ev-ery toe, an' some toes coun-ted three!"*

"Listen!" cried Meade, holding up his hand.

"An' ev-ery wife had sixteen dogs, an' ev-ery dog a flea!" shouted a voice from the besiegers, followed by a roar of laughter.

The hilarity continued until dark, only stopping when John Terry slipped out of the window, dropped to all-fours and stuck his head around the corner of the rear wall. He saw many stars and was silently handed to Pete Wilson.

"What was that noise?" exclaimed Boggs in a low voice. "Are you all right, Terry?" he asked, anxiously.

Three knocks on the wall replied to his question and then McQuade went out, and three more knocks were heard.

"Wonder why they make that funny noise," muttered Boggs.

"Bumped inter somethin', I reckon," replied Jim Larkin. "Get out of my way—I'm next."

Boggs listened intently and then pushed Duke Lane back. "Don't like that—sounds like a crack on th' head. Hey, Jim! *Say* something!" he called softly. The three knocks were repeated, but Boggs was suspicious and he shook his head decisively. "T'ell with th' knockin'—*say* something!"

"Still got them twelve men?" asked a strange voice, pleasantly.

"An' ev-ery dog a flea," hummed another around the corner.

"Hell!" shouted Boggs. "To th' door, fellers! To th' door—quick!"

A whistle shrilled from behind the house and a leaden tattoo began on the door. "Other window!" whispered O'Neill. The foreman got there before him and, shoving his Colt out first to clear the way, yelled with rage and pain as a pole hit his wrist and knocked the weapon out of his hand. He was still commenting when Duke Lane pried open the door and, dropping quickly on his stomach, wriggled out, followed closely by Charley Beal and Tim. At that instant the tattoo drummed with greater vigor and such a hail of lead poured in through the opening that the door was promptly closed, leaving the three men outside to shift for themselves with the darkness their only cover.

Duke and his companions whispered together as they lay flat and agreed upon a plan of action. Going around the ends of the house was suicide and no better than waiting for the rising moon to show them to the enemy; but there was no reason why the roof could not be utilized. Tim and Charley boosted Duke up, then Tim followed, and the pair on the roof pulled Charley to their side. Flat roofs were great institutions they decided as they crawled cautiously towards the other side. This roof was of hard, sunbaked adobe, over two feet thick, and they did not care if their friends shot up on a gamble.

"Fine place, all right," thought Charley, grinning broadly. Then he turned an agonized face to Tim, his chest rising. *"Hitch! Hitch!"* he choked, fighting with all his will to master it. *"Hitch-chew! Hitch-chew! Hitch-chew!"* he sneezed, loudly. There was a scramble below and a ripple of mirth floated up to them.

"Hitch-chew?" jeered a voice. "What do we want to hit you for?"

"Look us over, children," invited another.

"Wait until th' moon comes up," chuckled the third. "Be like knockin' a baby down for Red an' th' others. Ladies an' gents: We'll now have a little sketch entitled 'Shootin' snipe by moonlight.' "

"Jack-snipe, too," laughed Pete. "Will somebody please hold th' bag?"

The silence on the roof was profound and the three on the ground tried again.

"Let me call yore attention to th' trained coyotes, ladies an' gents," remarked Johnny in a deep, solemn voice. "Coyotes are not birds; they do not roost on roofs as a general thing: but they are some intelligent an' can be trained to do lots of foolish tricks. These ani-mules were—"

"Step this way, people; on-ly ten cents, two nickels," interrupted Pete. "They bark like dogs, an' howl like hell."

"Shut up!" snapped Tim, angrily.

"After th' moon comes up," said Hopalong, "when you fellers get tired dodgin', you can chuck us yore guns an' come down. An' don't forget that this side of th' house is much th' safest," he warned.

"Go to hell!" snarled Duke, bitterly.

"Won't; they're laying for me down there."

Johnny crawled to the north end of the wall and, looking cautiously around the corner, funnelled his hands: "On th' roof, Red! On th' roof!"

"Yes, dear," was the reply, followed by gunshots.

"Hey! Move over!" snapped Tim, working towards the

edge farthest from the cheerful Red, whose bullets were not as accurate in the dark as they promised to become in a few minutes when the moon should come up.

"Want to shove me off!" snarled Charley, angrily. "For heaven's sake, Duke, do you want th' whole earth?" he demanded of his second companion.

"You just bet yore shirt I do! An' I want a hole in it, too!"

"Ain't you got no sense?"

"Would I be up here if I had?"

"It's going to be hot as blazes up here when th' sun gets high," cheerfully prophesied Tim: "an' dry, too," he added for a finishing touch.

"We'll be lucky if we're live enough to worry about th' sun's heat—*say*, that was a *close* one!" exclaimed Duke, frantically trying to flatten a little more. "Ah, thought so—there's that blamed moon!"

"Wish I'd gone out th' window instead," growled Charley, worming behind Duke, to the latter's prompt displeasure.

"You fellers better come down, one at a time," came from below. "Send yore guns down first, too. Red's a blamed good shot."

"Hope he croaks," muttered Duke. "*That's* closer yet!"

Tim's hand raised and a flash of fire singed Charley's hair. "Got to do somethin', anyhow," he explained, lowering the Colt and peering across the plain.

"You damned near succeeded!" shouted Charley, grabbing at his head. "Why, they're three hundred, an' you trying for 'em with a—*oh!*" he moaned, writhing.

"Locoed fool!" swore Duke, "showin' 'em where we are! They're doing good enough as it is! You ought—got *you*, too!"

"*I'm* going down—that blamed fool out there ain't caring what he hits," mumbled Charley, clenching his hands from pain. He slid over the edge and Pete grabbed him.

"Next," suggested Pete, expectantly.

Tim tossed his Colt over the edge. "Here's another," he swore, following the weapon. He was grabbed and bound in a trice.

"When may we expect you, Mr. Duke?" asked Johnny, looking up.

"Presently, friend, presently. I want to—*wow!*" he finished, and lost no time in his descent, which was meteoric. "That feller'll *kill* somebody if he ain't careful!" he complained as Pete tied his hands behind his back.

"You wait till daylight an' see," cheerily replied Pete as the three were led off to join their friends in the corral.

There was no further action until the sun arose and then Hopalong hailed the house and demanded a parley, and soon he and Boggs met midway between the shack and the line.

"What d' you want?" asked Boggs, sullenly.

"Want you to stop this farce so I can go on with my drive."

"Well, I ain't holding you!" exploded the 4X foreman.

"Oh, yes; but you are. I can't let you an' yore men out to hang on our flanks an' worry us; an' I don't want to hold you in that shack till you all die of thirst, or come out to be all shot up. Besides, I can't fool around here for a week; I got business to look after."

"Don't you worry about us dying with thirst; that ain't worrying us none."

"I heard different," replied Hopalong, smiling. "Them fellers in th' corral drank a quart apiece. See here, Boggs: you can't win, an' you know it. Yo're not buckin' me, but th' whole range, th' whole country. It's a fight between conditions—th' fence idea agin' th' open range idea, an' open trails. Th' fence will lose. You closed a drive trail that's 'most as old as cow-raising. Will th' punchers of this part of th' country stand for it? Suppose you lick us,—which you won't—can you lick all th' rest of us, th' JD, Wallace's, Double-Arrow, C-80, Cross-O-Cross, an' th' others? That's just what it amounts to, an' you better stop right now, before somebody gets killed. You know what that means in this section. Yo're six to our eight, you ain't got a drink in that shack, an' you dasn't try to get one. You can't do a thing agin' us, an' you know it."

Boggs rested his hands on his hips and considered, Hopalong waiting for him to reply. He knew that the Bar-20 man was right but he hated to admit it, he hated to say he was whipped.

"Are any of them six hurt?" he finally asked.

"Only scratches an' sore heads," responded Hopalong, smiling. "We ain't tried to kill anybody, yet. I'm putting that up to you."

Boggs made no reply and Hopalong continued: "I got six of yore twelve men prisoners, an' all yore cayuses are in my han's. I'll shoot every animal before I'll leave 'em for you to use against me, an' I'll take enough of yore cows to make up for what I lost by that fence. You've got to pay for them dead cows, anyhow. If I do let you out you'll have to road-brand me two hundred, or pay cash. My herd ain't worrying me—it's moving all th' time. It's through that other fence by now. An' if I have to keep my outfit here to pen you in or shoot you off I can send to th' JD for a gang to push th' herd. Don't make no mistake: yo're getting off easy. Suppose one of my men had been killed at th' fence—what then?"

"Well, what do you want me to do?"

"Stop this foolishness an' take down them fences for a mile each side of th' trail. If Buck has to come here th' whole thing 'll go down. Road-brand me two hundred of yore three-year-olds. Now as soon as you agree, an' say that th' fight's over, it will be. You can't win out; an' what's th' use of having yore men killed off?"

"I hate to quit," replied the other, gloomily.

"I know how that is; but yo're wrong on this question, dead wrong. You don't own this range or th' trail. You ain't got no right to close that old drive trail. Honest, now; have you?"

"You say them six ain't hurt?"

"No more'n I said."

"An' if I give in will you treat my men right?"

"Shore."

"When will you leave?"

"Just as soon as I get them two hundred three-year-olds."

"Well, I hate a quitter; but I can't do nothing, nohow," mused the 4X foreman. He cleared his throat and turned to look at the house. "All right; when you get them cows you get out of here, an' don't never come back!"

Hopalong flung up his arm with a shout to his men and the other kicked savagely at an inoffensive stick and slouched back to his bunk house, a beaten man.

XXIII

◆

Tex Ewalt Hunts Trouble

Not more than a few weeks after the Bar-20 drive outfit returned to the ranch a solitary horseman pushed on towards the trail they had followed, bound for Buckskin and the Bar-20 range. His name was Tex Ewalt and he cordially hated all of the Bar-20 outfit and Hopalong in particular. He had nursed a grudge for several years and now, as he rode south to rid himself of it and to pay a long-standing debt, it grew constantly stronger until he thrilled with anticipation and the sauce of danger. This grudge had been acquired when he and Slim Travennes had enjoyed a duel with Hopalong Cassidy up in Santa Fé, and had been worsted; it had increased when he learned of Slim's death at Cactus Springs at the hands of Hopalong; and, some time later, hearing that two friends of his, "Slippery" Trendley and "Deacon" Rankin, with their gang, had "gone out" in the Panhandle with the same man and his friends responsible for it, Tex hastened to Muddy Wells to even the score and clean his slate. Even now his face burned when he remembered his experiences on that never-to-be-forgotten occasion. He had been played with, ridiculed, and shamed, until he fled from the town as a place accursed, hating everything and everybody. It galled him to think that he had allowed Buck Peters' momentary sympathy to turn him from his purpose, even though he was convinced that the foreman's action had saved his life. And now Tex was returning, not to Muddy Wells, but to the range where the Bar-20 outfit held sway.

Several years of clean living had improved Tex, morally and physically. The liquor he had once been in the habit of consuming had been reduced to a negligible quantity; he spent the money on cartridges instead, and his pistol work showed the results of careful and dogged practice, particularly in the quickness of the draw. Punching cows on a remote northern range had repaid him in health far more than his old game of living on his wits and other people's lack of them, as proved by his clear eye and the pink showing through the tan above his beard; while his somber, steady gaze, due to long-held fixity of purpose, indicated the resourcefulness of a perfectly reliable set of nerves. His low-hung holster tied securely to his trousers leg to assure smoothness in drawing, the restrained swing of his right hand, never far from the well-worn scabbard which sheathed a trigger-less Colt's "Frontier"—these showed the confident and ready gun-man, the man who seldom missed. "Frontiers" left the factory with triggers attached, but the absence of that part did not always incapacitate a weapon. Some men found that the regular method was too slow, and painstakingly cultivated the art of thumbing the hammer. "Thumbing" was believed to save the split second so valuable to a man in argument with his peers. Tex was riding with the set purpose of picking a fair fight with the best six-shooter expert it had ever been his misfortune to meet, and he needed that split second. He knew that he needed it and the knowledge thrilled him with a peculiar elation; he had changed greatly in the past year and now he wanted an "even break" where once he would have called all his wits into play to avoid it. He had found himself and now he acknowledged no superior in anything.

On his way south he met and talked with men who had known him, the old Tex, in the days when he had made his living precariously. They did not recognize him behind his beard, and he was content to let the oversight pass. But from these few he learned what he wished to know, and he was glad that Hopalong Cassidy was where he had always been, and that his gun-work had improved rather than depreciated with the passing of time. He wished to prove himself master of The Master, and to be hailed as such by those who had jeered and laughed at his ignominy several years before. So he rode on day after day, smiling and content, neither underrating nor over-rating his enemy's ability with one weapon, but trying to think of him as he really was. He knew that if there was any difference between Hopalong Cassidy and himself that it must be very slight—perhaps so slight as to result fatally to both; but if that were so then it would have to work out as it saw fit—he at least would have accomplished what many, many others had failed in.

In the little town of Buckskin, known hardly more than locally, and never thought of by outsiders except as the place where the Bar-20 spent their spare time and money, and neutral ground for the surrounding ranches, was Cowan's saloon, in the dozen years of its existence the scene of good stories, boisterous fun, and quick deaths. Put together roughly, of crude materials, sticking up in inartistic prominence on the dusty edge of a dustier street; warped, bleached by the sun, and patched with boards ripped from packing cases and with the flattened sides of tin cans; low of ceiling, the floor one huge brown discoloration of springy, creaking boards, knotted and split and worn into hollows, the unpretentious building offered its hospitality to all who might be tempted by the scrawled, sprawled letter of its sign. The walls were smoke-blackened, pitted with numerous small and clean-cut holes, and decorated with initials carelessly cut by men who had come and gone.

Such was Cowan's, the best patronized place in many hot and dusty miles and the Mecca of the cowboys from the surrounding ranches. Often at night these riders of the range gathered in the humble building and told tales of exceeding interest; and on these occasions one might see a row of ponies standing before the building, heads down and quiet. It is strange how alike cow-ponies look in the dim light of the stars. On the south side of the saloon, weak, yellow lamp light filtered through the dirt on the window panes and fell in distorted patches on the plain, blotched in places by the shadows of the wooden substitutes for glass.

It was a moonlit night late in the fall, after the last

beef round-up was over and the last drive outfit home again, that two cow-ponies stood in front of Cowan's while their owners lolled against the bar and talked over the latest sensation—the fencing in of the West Valley range, and the way Hopalong Cassidy and his trail outfit had opened up the old drive trail across it. The news was a month old, but it was the last event of any importance and was still good to laugh over.

"Boys," remarked the proprietor, "I want you to meet Mr. Elkins. He came down that trail last week, an' he didn't see no fence across it." The man at the table arose slowly. "Mr. Elkins, this is Sandy Lucas, an' Wood Wright, of th' C-80. Mr. Elkins here has been a-lookin' over th' country, sizin' up what th' beef prospects will be for next year; an' he knows all about wire fences. Here's how," he smiled, treating on the house.

Mr. Elkins touched the glass to his bearded lips and set it down untasted while he joked over the sharp rebuff so lately administered to wire fences in that part of the country. While he was an ex-cow-puncher he believed that he was above allowing prejudice to sway his judgment, and it was his opinion, after careful thought, that barb wire was harmful to the best interests of the range. He had ridden over a great part of the cattle country in the last few years, and after reviewing the existing conditions as he understood them, his verdict must go as stated, and emphatically. He launched gracefully into a slowly delivered and lengthy discourse upon the subject, which proved to be so entertaining that his companions were content to listen and nod with comprehension. They had never met any one who was so well qualified to discuss the pros and cons of the barb-wire fence question, and they learned many things which they had never heard before. This was very gratifying to Mr. Elkins, who drew largely upon hearsay, his own vivid imagination, and a healthy logic. He was very glad to talk to men who had the welfare of the range at heart, and he hoped soon to meet the man who had taken the initiative in giving barb wire its first serious setback on that rich and magnificent southern range.

"You shore ought to meet Cassidy—he's a fine man," remarked Lucas with enthusiasm. "You'll not find any better, no matter where you look. But you ain't touched yore liquor," he finished with surprise.

"You'll have to excuse me, gentlemen," replied Mr. Elkins, smiling deprecatingly. "When a man likes it as much as I do it ain't very easy to foller instructions an' let it alone. Sometimes I almost break loose an' indulge, regardless of whether it kills me or not. I reckon it'll get me yet." He struck the bar a resounding blow with his clenched hand. "But I ain't going to cave in till I has to!"

"That's purty tough," sympathized Wood Wright, reflectively. "I ain't so very much taken with it, but I know I would be if I knowed I couldn't have any."

"Yes; that's human nature, all right," laughed Lucas. "That reminds me of a little thing that happened to me once—"

"Listen!" exclaimed Cowan, holding up his hand for silence. "I reckon that's th' Bar-20 now, or some of it— sounds like them when they're feelin' frisky. There's allus something happening when them fellers are around."

The proprietor was right, as proved a moment later when Johnny Nelson, continuing his argument, pushed open the door and entered the room. "I didn't neither; an' you know it!" he flung over his shoulder.

"Then who did?" demanded Hopalong, chuckling. "Why, hullo, boys," he said, nodding to his friends at the bar. "Nobody else would do a fool thing like that; nobody but you, Kid," he added, turning to Johnny.

"I don't care a hang what you think; I say I didn't an'—"

"He shore did, all right; I seen him just afterward," laughed Billy Williams, pressing close upon Hopalong's heels. "Howdy, Lucas; an' there's that ol' coyote, Wood Wright. How's everybody feeling?"

"Where's th' rest of you fellers?" inquired Cowan.

"Stayed home to-night," replied Hopalong.

"Got any loose money, you two?" asked Billy, grinning at Lucas and Wright.

"I reckon we have—an' our credit's good if we ain't. We're good for a dollar or two, ain't we, Cowan?" replied Lucas.

"Two dollars an' four bits," corrected Cowan. "I'll raise it to three dollars even when you pay me that 'leven cents you owe me."

"'Leven cents? What 'leven cents?"

"Postage stamps an' envelope for that love letter you writ."

"Go to blazes: that wasn't no love letter!" snorted Lucas, indignantly. "That was my quarterly report. I never did write no love letters, no-how."

"We'll trim you fellers to-night, if you've got th' nerve to play us," grinned Johnny, expectantly.

"Yes; an' we've got that, too. Give us th' cards, Cowan," requested Wood Wright, turning. "They won't give us no peace till we take all their money away from 'em."

"Open game," prompted Cowan, glancing meaningly at Elkins, who stood by idly looking on, and without showing much interest in the scene.

"Shore! Everybody can come in that wants to," replied Lucas, heartily, leading the others to the table. "I allus did like a six-handed game best—all th' cards are out an' there's some excitement in it"

When the deal began Elkins was seated across the table from Hopalong, facing him for the first time since that day over in Muddy Wells, and studying him closely. He found no change, for the few years had left no trace of their passing on the Bar-20 puncher. The sensation of facing the man he had come south expressly to kill did not interfere with Elkins' card-playing ability for he played a good game; and as if the Fates were with him it was Hopalong's night off as far as poker was concerned, for his customary good luck was not in evidence. That instinctive feeling which singles out two duellists in a card game was soon experienced by the others, who were careful, as became good players, to avoid being caught between them; in consequence, when the game broke up, Elkins had most of Hopalong's money. At one period of his life Elkins had lived on poker for five years, and lived well. But he gained more than money in this game, for he had made friends with the players and placed the first wire of his trap. Of those in the room Hopalong alone treated him with reserve, and this was cleverly swung so that it appeared to be caused by a temporary grouch due to the sting of defeat. As the Bar-20 man was known to be given to moods at times this was accepted as the true explanation and gave promise of hotly contested games for revenge later on. The banter which the defeated puncher had to endure stirred him and strengthened the reserve, although he was careful not to show it.

When the last man rode off, Elkins and the proprietor sought their bunks without delay, the former to lie awake a long time, thinking deeply. He was vexed at himself for failing to work out an acceptable plan of action, one that would show him to be in the right. He would gain nothing more than glory, and pay too dearly for it, if he killed Hopalong and was in turn killed by the dead man's friends—and he believed that he had become acquainted with the quality of the friendship which bound the units of the Bar-20 outfit into a smooth, firm whole. They were like brothers, like one man. Cassidy must do the forcing as far as appearances went, and be clearly in the wrong before the matter would be settled.

The next week was a busy one for Elkins, every day
finding him in the saddle and riding over some one of the
surrounding ranches with one or more of its punchers for
company. In this way he became acquainted with the men
who might be called on to act as his jury when the show-
down came, and he proceeded to make friends of them in
a manner that promised success. And some of his suggestions for the improvement of certain conditions on the
range, while they might not work out right in the long run,
compelled thought and showed his interest. His remarks
on the condition and numbers of cattle were the same in
substance in all cases and showed that he knew what he
was talking about, for the punchers were all very optimistic about the next year's showing in cattle.

"If you fellers don't break all records for drive herds
of quality next year I don't know nothing about cows; an'
I shore don't know nothing else," he told the foreman of
the Bar-20, as they rode homeward after an inspection of
that ranch. "There'll be more dust hangin' over th' drive
trails leading from this section next year when spring
drops th' barriers than ever before. You needn't fear for
th' market, neither—prices will stand. Th' north an' central ranges ain't doing what they ought to this year—it'll
be up to you fellers down south, here, to make that up;
an' you can do it." This was not a guess, but the result
of thought and study based on the observations he had
made on his ride south, and from what he had learned
from others along the way. It paralleled Buck's own private
opinion, especially in regard to the southern range; and
the vague suspicions in the foreman's mind disappeared
for good and all.

Needless to say Elkins was a welcome visitor at the
ranch houses and was regarded as a good fellow. At
the Bar-20 he found only two men who would not thaw to
him, and he was possessed of too much tact to try any

persuasive measures. One was Hopalong, whose original cold reserve seemed to be growing steadily, the Bar-20 puncher finding in Elkins a personality that charged the atmosphere with hostility and quietly rubbed him the wrong way. Whenever he was in the presence of the newcomer he felt the tugging of an irritating and insistent antagonism and he did not always fully conceal it. John Bartlett, Lucas, and one or two of the more observing had noticed it and they began to prophesy future trouble between the two. The other man who disliked Elkins was Red Connors; but what was more natural? Red, being Hopalong's closest companion, would be very apt to share his friend's antipathy. On the other hand, as if to prove Hopalong's dislike to be unwarranted, Johnny Nelson swung far to the other extreme and was frankly enthusiastic in his liking for the cattle scout. And Johnny did not pour oil on the waters when he laughingly twitted Hopalong for allowing "a lickin' at cards to make him sore." This was the idea that Elkins was quietly striving to have generally accepted.

The affair thus hung fire, Elkins chafing at the delay and cautiously working for an opening, which at last presented itself, to be promptly seized. By a sort of mutual, unspoken agreement, the men in Cowan's that night passed up the cards and sat swapping stories. Cowan, swearing at a smoking lamp, looked up with a grin and burned his fingers as a roar of laughter marked the point of a droll reminiscence told by Bartlett.

"That's a good story, Bartlett," Elkins remarked, slowly refilling his pipe. "Reminds me of th' lame Mexican, Hippy Joe, an' th' canned oysters. They was both bad, an' neither of 'em knew it till they came together. It was like this. . . ." The malicious side glance went unseen by all but Hopalong, who stiffened with the raging suspicion of being twitted on his own deformity. The humor of the tale failed to appeal to him, and when his full senses returned Lucas was in the midst of the story of the deadly game of tag played in a ten-acre lot of dense underbrush by two of his old-time friends. It was a tale of gripping interest and his auditors were leaning forward in their eagerness not to miss a word. "An' Pierce won," finished Lucas, "some shot up, but able to get about. He was all right in a couple of weeks. But he was bound to win: he could shoot all around Sam Hopkins."

"But th' best shot won't allus win in that game," commented Elkins. "That's one of th' minor factors."

"Yes, sir! It's *luck* that counts there," endorsed Bartlett, quickly. "Luck, nine times out of ten."

"Best shot ought to win," declared Skinny Thompson. "It ain't all luck, nohow. Where'd I be against Hoppy, there?"

"Won't neither!" cried Johnny, excitedly. "Th' man who sees th' other first wins out. That's wood-craft, an' brains."

"Aw! What do you know about it, anyhow?" demanded Lucas. "If he can't shoot so good what chance has he got—if he misses th' first try, what then?"

"What chance has he got! First chance, miss or no miss. If he can't see th' other first, where th' devil does his good shootin' come in?"

"Huh!" snorted Wood Wright, belligerently. "Any fool can *see*, but he can't *shoot!* An' it's as much luck as wood-craft, too, an' don't you forget it!"

"Th' first shot don't win, Johnny; not in a game like that, with all th' dodgin' an' duckin'," remarked Red. "You can't put one where you want it when a feller's slippin' around in th' brush. It's th' most that counts, an' th' best shot gets in th' most. I wouldn't want to have to stand up against Hoppy an' a short gun, not in that game; no, sir!" and Red shook his head with decision.

The argument waxed hot. With the exception of Hopalong, who sat silently watchful, every one spoke his opinion and repeated it without regard to the others. It appeared that in this game, the man with the strongest lungs would eventually win out, and each man tried to show his superiority in that line. Finally, above the uproar, Cowan's bellow was heard, and he kept it up until some notice was taken of it. "Shut up! *Shut up!* For God's sake, *quit!* What does it all matter? Who gives a hang? Never saw such a bunch of tinder—let somebody drop a cold, burned-out match in this gang, an' hell's to pay. Here, *all* of you, play cards an' forget about cross-tag in th' scrub. You'll be arguyin' about playin' marbles in th' dark purty soon!"

"All right," muttered Johnny, "but just th' same, th' man who—"

"Never mind about th' man who! Did you hear *me*?" yelled Cowan, swiftly reaching for a bucket of water. "*This* is a game where *I* gets th' most in, an' don't forget it!"

"Come on; play cards," growled Lucas, who did not relish having his decision questioned on his own story. Undoubtedly somewhere in the wide, wide world there was such a thing as common courtesy, but none of it had ever strayed onto that range.

The chairs scraped on the rough floor as the men pulled up to a table. "I don't care a hang," came Elkins' final comment as he shuffled the cards with careful attention. "I'm not any fancy Colt expert, but I'm damned if I won't take a chance in that game with any man as totes a gun. Leastawise, of *course*, I wouldn't take no such advantage of a lame man."

The effect would have been ludicrous but for its deadly significance. Cowan, stooping to go under the bar, remained in that hunched-up attitude, his every faculty concentrated in his ears; the match on its way to the cigarette between Red's lips was held until it burned his fingers, when it was dropped from mere reflex action, the hand still stiffly aloft; Lucas, half in and half out of his chair, seemed to have got just where he intended, making no effort to seat himself. Skinny Thompson, his hand on his gun, seemed paralyzed; his mouth was open to frame a reply that never was uttered and he stared through narrowed eyelids at the blunderer. The sole movement in the room was the slow rising of Hopalong and the markedly innocent shuffling of the cards by Elkins, who appeared to be entirely ignorant of the weight and effect of his words. He dropped the pack for the cut and then looked up and around as if surprised by the silence and the expressions he saw.

Hopalong stood facing him, leaning over with both hands on the table. His voice, when he spoke, rumbled up from his chest in a low growl. "You won't *have* no advantage, Elkins. Take it from me, you've had yore last fling. I'm glad you made it plain, this time, so it's something I can take hold of." He straightened slowly and walked to the door, and an audible sigh sounded through the room as it was realized that trouble was not immediately imminent. At the door he paused and turned half around, looking back over his shoulder. "At noon tomorrow I'm going to hoof it north through th' brush between th' river an' th' river trail, startin' at th' old ford a mile down th' river." He waited expectantly.

"Me too—only th' other way," was the instant rejoinder. "Have it yore own way."

Hopalong nodded and the closing door shut him out into the night. Without a word the Bar-20 men arose and followed him, the only hesitant being Johnny, who was torn between loyalty and new-found friendship; but with a sorrowful shake of the head, he turned away and passed out, not far behind the others.

"Clannish, ain't they?" remarked Elkins, gravely.

Those remaining were regarding him sternly, questioningly, Cowan with a deep frown darkening his face. "You hadn't ought to 'a' said that, Elkins." The reproof was almost an accusation.

Elkins looked steadily at the speaker. "You hadn't ought to 'a' let me say it," he replied. "How did I know he was so touchy?" His gaze left Cowan and lingered in turn on each of the others. "Some of you ought to 'a' told me. I wouldn't 'a' said it only for what I said just before, an' I didn't want him to think I was challenging him to no duel in th' brush. So I says so, an' then he goes an' takes it up that I *am* challenging him. I ain't got no call to fight with nobody. Ain't I tried to keep out of trouble with him ever since I've been here? Ain't I kept out of th' poker games on his account? Ain't I?" The grave, even tones were dispassionate, without a trace of animus and serenely sure of justice.

The faces around him cleared gradually and heads began to nod in comprehending consent.

"Yes, I reckon you have," agreed Cowan, slowly, but the frown was not entirely gone. "Yes, I reckon—mebby—you have."

XXIV

♦

The Master

It was noon by the sun when Hopalong and Red shook hands south of the old ford and the former turned to enter the brush. Hopalong was cool and ominously calm while his companion was the opposite. Red was frankly suspicious of the whole affair and nursed the private opinion that Mr. Elkins would lay in ambush and shoot his enemy down like a dog. And Red had promised himself a dozen times that he would study the signs around the scene of action if Hopalong should not come back, and take a keen delight, if warranted, in shooting Mr. Elkins full of holes with no regard for an even break. He was thinking the matter over as his friend breasted the first line of brush and could not refrain from giving slight warning. "Get him, Hoppy," he called, earnestly; "get him good. Let *him* do some of th' moving about. I'll be here waiting for you."

Hopalong smiled in reply and sprang forward, the leaves and branches quickly shutting him from Red's sight. He had worked out his plan of action the night before when he was alone and the world was still, and as soon as he had it to his satisfaction he had dropped off to sleep as easily as a child—it took more than gun-play to disturb his nerves. He glanced about him to make sure of his bearings and then struck on a curving line for the river. The first hundred yards were covered with speed and then he began to move more slowly and with greater regard for caution, keeping close to the earth and showing a marked preference for low ground. Sky-lines were all right in times of peace, but under the present conditions they promised to become unhealthy. His eyes and ears told him nothing for a quarter of an hour, and then he suddenly stopped short and crouched as he saw the plain trail of a man crossing his own direction at a right angle. From the bottom of one of the heel prints a crushed leaf was slowly rising back towards its original position, telling him how new the trail was; and as if this were not enough for his trained mind he heard a twig snap sharply as he glanced along the line of prints. It sounded very close, and he dropped instantly to one knee and thought quickly. Why had the other left so plain a trail, why had he reached up and broken twigs that projected above his head as he passed? Why had he kicked aside a small stone, leaving a patch of moist, bleached grass to tell where it had lain? Elkins had stumbled here, but there were no toe marks to tell of it. Hopalong would not track, for he was no assassin; but he knew what he would do if he were, and careless. The answer leaped to his suspicious mind like a flash, and he did not care to waste any time in trying to determine whether or not Elkins was capable of such a trick. He acted on the presumption that the trail had been made plain for a good reason, and that not far ahead at some suitable place,—and there were any number of such within a hundred yards,—the maker of the plain trail lay in wait. Smiling savagely he worked backward and turning, struck off in a circle. He had no compunctions whatever now about shooting the other player of the game. It was not long before he came upon the same trail again and he started another circle. A bullet *zipped* past his ear and cut a twig not two inches from his head. He fired at the smoke as he dropped, and then wriggled rapidly backward, keeping as flat to the earth as he could. Elkins had taken up his position in a thicket which stood in the centre of a level patch of sand in the old bed of the river,—the bed it had used five years before and forsaken at the time of the big flood when it cut itself a new channel and made the U-bend which now surrounded this piece of land on three sides. Even now, during the rainy season, the thicket which sheltered Mr. Elkins was frequently an island in a sluggish, shallow overflow.

"Hole up, blast you!" jeered Hopalong, hugging the ground. The second bullet from Mr. Elkins' gun cut another twig, this one just over his head, and he laughed insolently. "I ain't ascared to do th' movin', even if you are. Judging from th' way you keep out o' sight th' canned oysters are in th' can again. *I* never did no ambushin', you coyote."

"You can't make remarks like that an' get away with

'em—I've knowed you too long," retorted Elkins, shift-ing quickly, and none too soon. "You went an' got Slim afore he was wide awake. I know *you*, all right."

Hopalong's surprise was but momentary, and his mind raced back over the years. Who was this man Elkins, that he knew Slim Travennes? "Yo're a liar, Elkins; an' so was th' man who told you that!"

"Call me Ewalt," jeered the other, nastily. "Nobody'll hear it, an' you'll not live to tell it. Ewalt, Tex Ewalt; call me that."

"So you've come back after all this time to make me get you, have you? Well, I ain't a-goin' to shoot no but-tons off you *this* time. I allus reckoned you learned something at Muddy Wells—but you'll learn it here," Hopalong rejoined, sliding into a depression, and work-ing with great caution towards the dry river bed, where fallen trees and hillocks of sand provided good cover in plenty. Everything was clear now and despite the seri-ousness of the situation he could not repress a smile as he remembered vividly that day at the carnival when Tex Ewalt came to town with the determination to kill him and show him up as an imitation. His grievance against Elkins was petty when compared to that against Ewalt, and he began to force the issue. As he peered over a stranded log he caught sight of his enemy disappearing into another part of the thicket, and two of his three shots went home. Elkins groaned with pain and fear as he real-ized that his right kneecap was broken and would make him slow in his movements. He was lamed for life, even if he did come out of the duel alive; lamed in the same way that Hopalong was—the affliction he had made cruel sport of had come to him. But he had plenty of courage and he returned the fire with remarkable quickness, his two shots sounding almost as one.

Hopalong wiped the blood from his cheek and wormed

his way to a new place; when half way there he called out again, "How's your health—Tex?" in mock sympathy.

Elkins lied manfully and when he looked to get in another shot his enemy was on the farther bank, moving up to get behind him. He did not know Hopalong's new position until he raised his head to glance down the dried river bed, and was informed by a bullet that nicked his ear. As he ducked, another grazed his head, the third going wild. He hazarded a return shot, and heard Hopalong's laugh ring out again.

"Like th' story Lucas told, th' best shot is going to win out this time, too," the Bar-20 man remarked, grimly. "You thought a game like this would give you some chance against a better shot, didn't you? You are a fool."

"It ain't over yet, not by a damned sight!" came the retort.

"An' you thought you had a little th' best of it if you stayed still an' let me do th' movin', didn't you? You'll learn something before I get through with you: but it'll be too late to do you any good," Hopalong called, crouched below a hillock of sand so the other could not take advantage of the words and single him out for a shot.

"You can't learn me nothing, you assassin; I've got my eyes open, this time." He knew that he had had them open before, and that Hopalong was in no way an assassin; but if he could enrage his enemy and sting him into some reflex carelessness he might have the last laugh.

Elkins' retort was wasted, for a sudden and unusual, although a familiar sound, had caught Hopalong's ear and he was giving all his attention to it. While he weighed it, his incredulity holding back the decision his common sense was striving to give him, the noise grew louder rapidly and common sense won out in a cry of warning an instant before a five-foot wall of brown water burst upon his sight, sweeping swiftly down the old, dry river bed; and behind it towered another and greater wall. Tree trunks were dancing end over end in it as if they were straws.

"Cloud-burst!" he yelled. "Run, Tex! Run for yore life! Cloud-burst up th' valley! Run, you fool; *Run!*"

Tex's sarcastic retort was cut short as he instinctively glanced north, and his agonized curse lashed Hopalong forward. "Can't run—knee cap's busted! Can't swim, can't do—ah, hell—!"

Hopalong saw him torn from his shelter and whisked down the raging torrent like an arrow from a bow. The Bar-20 puncher leaped from the bank, shot under the yellow flood and arose, gasping and choking, many yards downstream, fighting madly to get the muddy water out of his throat and eyes. As he struck out with all his strength down the current, he caught sight of Tex being torn from a jutting tree limb, and he shouted encouragement and swam all the harder, if such a thing were possible. Tex's course was checked for a moment by a boiling back-current and as he again felt the pull of the rushing stream Hopalong's hand gripped his collar and the fight for safety began. Whirled against logs and stumps, drawn down by the weight of his clothes and the frantic efforts of Tex to grasp him—fighting the water and the man he was trying to save at the same time, his head under water as often as it was out of it, and Tex's vice-like fingers threatening him—he headed for the west shore against powerful cross-currents that made his efforts seem useless. He seemed to get the worst of every break. Once, when caught by a friendly current, they were swung under an overhanging branch, but as Hopalong's hand shot up to grasp it a submerged bush caught his feet and pulled him under, and Tex's steel-like arms around his throat almost suffocated him before he managed to beat the other into insensibility and break the hold.

"I'll let you go!" he threatened; but his hand grasped the other's collar all the tighter and his fighting jaw was set with greater determination than ever.

They shot out into the main stream, where the U-bend channel joined the short-cut, and it looked miles wide to the exhausted puncher. He was fighting only on his will now. He would not give up, though he scarce could lift an arm and his lungs seemed on fire. He did not know whether Tex was dead or alive, but he would get the body ashore with him, or go down trying. He bumped into a log and instinctively grasped it. It turned, and when he came up again it was bobbing five feet ahead of him. Ages seemed to pass before he flung his numb arm over it and floated with it. He was not alone in the flood; a coyote was pushing steadily across his path towards the nearer bank, and on a gliding tree trunk crouched a frightened cougar, its ears flattened and its sharp claws dug solidly through the bark. Here and there were cattle, and a snake wriggled smoothly past him, apparently as much at home in the water as out of it. The log turned again and he just managed to catch hold of it as he came up for the second time.

Things were growing black before his eyes and strange, weird ideas and images floated through his brain. When he regained some part of his senses he saw ahead of him a long, curling crest of yellow water and foam, and he knew, vaguely, that it was pouring over a bar. The next instant his feet struck bottom and he fought his way blindly and slowly, with the stubborn determination of his kind, towards thc brush-covered point twenty feet away.

When he opened his eyes and looked around he became conscious of excruciating pains and he closed them again to rest. His outflung hand struck something that made him look around again, and he saw Tex Ewalt, face down at his side. He released his grasp on the other's collar and slowly the whole thing came to him, and then the necessity for action, unless he wished to lose what he had fought so hard to save.

Anything short of the iron man Tex had become would have been dead before this or have been finished by the mauling he now got from Hopalong. But Tex groaned, gurgled a curse, and finally opened his eyes upon his rescuer, who sank back with a grunt of satisfaction. Slowly his intelligence returned as he looked steadily into Hopalong's eyes, and with it came the realization of a strange truth: he did not hate this man at all. Months of right living, days and nights of honest labor shoulder to shoulder with men who respected him for his ability and accepted him as one of themselves, had made a new man of him, although the legacy of hatred from the old Tex had disguised him from himself until now; but the new Tex, battered, shot-up, nearly drowned, looked at his old enemy and saw him for the man he really was. He smiled faintly and reached out his hand.

"Cassidy, yo're th' boss," he said. "Shake."

They shook.